THE FIRST MISADVENTURE OF FRAGGER SPARKS

A Ranger Leads the Way

A Novel

By

Steven D. Fisher

THE FIRST MISADVENTURE OF FRAGGER SPARKS

ISBN 1-59113-395-5

Published by Steven D. Fisher.

PRINTED IN THE UNITED STATES OF AMERICA

Booklocker.com, Inc.

2003

For Alfred Bester and wild imaginations everywhere.

Books by Steven Fisher

The Relentless Pursuit of Everett Pick

ISBN: 0-7388-0435-5

THE FIRST MISADVENTURE OF FRAGGER SPARKS

A Ranger Leads the Way

CHAPTER 1

The chittering voice of an angry squirrel interrupted Fragger's recurrent dream. Annoyed, he ordered the rodent to shut the fuck up. The animal didn't belong in his sleeping mind, and, above all, Fragger wanted to finish the dream because he was *never* able to complete it, and that fact pissed him off beyond all reason. He was a soldier-- a U. S. Army Ranger, by God!--and a Ranger always accomplished any task set to him, even a creation of his own rebellious brain. To his frustration, the squirrel ignored the order and rambled on in a bizarre fashion.

--"specifics, they always want the ripping specifics. As if anyone cared about a Rerun, for Corporation's sake, even another so-called 'special' one! As if anyone was present to hear me talking to myself. 'Oh, get on with it, Leery.' That's what Supervisor Wetz would say, if he were here, the fat coward. To take a man of my capabilities and stick him all alone in the middle of the Khanwati Desert—as if there were anything but desert on this dirtball planet--with the enemy in orbit ready to up-and-off me. As if I had anything to defend myself with except a pistol. As if...all right, all right, Leery, calm yourself down. Just record the specifics. It'll take your mind off the situation and maybe, just maybe, a little attention will come your way."

There was a faint click, and the squirrel continued, "Recording. Revival Technician Lakwirth Leery is the RT of record. Date..."

Leery's voice paused at series of faint thumps. Fragger scowled at the familiar sound--explosions. He frowned a second time when he couldn't figure out how his mind had come up with something so strange as a squirrel, especially a squirrel who could talk and also be a Revival Technician, whatever that was.

"Oh, rip the date!" Leery resumed nervously. "The recorder will note it, anyway. Damned protocol. And if I survive and you hear this, Wetz, I don't care about protocol. Bird you, you officious, incompetent prick! Okay, here's the basic information while I wait for the HSP results. HSP. Don't know what that term means, do you, Wetz, you idiot? Well, I'm not going to tell you what the acronym stands for. No more stealing of my ideas! Let's see you explain HSP to the Regional Planetary Manager and try to take credit for something you haven't got a prayer of understanding! You're such an imbecile, such an incompet…oh hell, what's the use? I haven't got enough words in my vocabulary to adequately describe your stupidity. Back to the task at hand. Uhhmm…let's see…I implanted the translator as required although the module isn't exactly OEM, that's for sure. So, the subject may experience slowness in understanding a few subtle language concepts, but then I had to re-configure somewhere. Anyway, Reruns are dense by nature, aren't they? In this case, our subject is Sergeant First Class Jonathan Sparks. Nickname 'Fragger', according to records. He's typical mongrel Earth Stock, nearly two meters tall with a weight of close to 80 kilograms. Hair, black. Eyes, blue. He'd be handsome if he weren't a Rerun. Just your type, Wetz, you faggot. The subject hasn't spoken yet, but I gave him the standard voice marker so he'll have the typical Rerun rasp. Skin—light brown as a result of miscegenation, apparently a mixture of Irish-European, Mexican, and American Indian bloodlines as defined in 20th Century terms. Obviously, Old Americans were more than a little careless about purity of race."

Fragger started at the mention of purity of race. *Shit, what the hell is my mind doing dredging up such crap? As if Amanda and I haven't faced enough racism in our lives! And coming from a squirrel! Stop such thoughts, damn it!*

The contemptuous monologue continued, anyway.

"Well, this Rerun might be a mutt, but OldNet military personnel files as well as those nuisance family sites that clutter ancient electronic records indicate he has strong potential. For one thing, he served in a highly elite military force geared to dangerous missions and still survived two wars in radically different Terran environments—one tropical and one desert. In addition, the words 'luck' and 'lucky' occur repeatedly, not only on the family site but also in his personnel file. To put it mildly, "luck" is not a usual military term so that indicates definite promise. Then, there's the unspecified 'detachment' to DARPA—the Defense Advanced

Research Projects Agency—an agency with an affinity for grandly stupid projects like sleepless soldiers...Okay, here come the HSP results, finally. Bloody computer is damned slow. You know, Wetz, if we're going to do up-to-date research, you might invest in some new equipment instead of skimming the money to feed your fat face. Okay, the HSP results read...can that be right? Let me verify."

Another click sounded. Apparently, Leery had turning his recording device off. Fragger marveled at the ability of his mind to generate such realistic details in a dream even if it--

"Sparks! Wake up, Rerun!" Leery's squirrel voice shouted at him,

"Fuck off!" Fragger muttered. He didn't care how realistic his dreams got; he wasn't about to obey a command from a squirrel, especially an order interfering with his ability to get back to the persistent dream. It was maddening that it never changed and exasperating because it was always so vivid, painted in the too-bright hues of an old Fifties Technicolor movie. In it, Amanda Whitefeather Sparks, his second wife, stood outside base housing which, in the absurd logic of dreams, was painted in camouflage colors against an orange sky and chartreuse grass. The dream made Amanda beautiful, and she was chuckling about it because she knew she was not attractive—not on the outside anyway. She was short, 20 pounds overweight, and still bore the scars of untreated acne, courtesy of life on the rez. Sparks chuckled with her because Amanda was a great believer in the power of dreams and would appreciate starring in his, especially one that made her gorgeous. He'd never been able to convince her that that was how she always looked to him—beautiful. God, how he missed that woman and the smell of her lilac perfume! How he missed his family!

"Sergeant First Class Jonathan Sparks! Stop laughing!"

"Screw you, man!" he swore at the squirrel as he concentrated on the images generated by his mind.

Libby, their 15-year-old with the same silken black hair as her mother, stood next to Amanda and was busy complaining that her Dad was the dumbest father to come down the pike in history of parenting while simultaneously wondering why he never came home any more. On the other side of his wife, his son, John, nodded his head in vigorous agreement. Sparks swallowed the anger he always felt at the changes in his boy since he'd gone off to Berkeley—Berkeley, for Christ's sake, a yuppie liberal haven! John had shaved his head, grown a goatee uglier than a camel's ass, and become a pacifist during his freshman year. Fragger knew it was all part of the separation crap psychologists talked about, but it still pissed him off. It was no way for a soldier's son to act. He brushed aside the thought as he tried to figure out why his family all of sudden cried out, "Come home!", then burst into tears that began washing away the camouflage colors and--

"Sergeant First Class Jonathan Sparks! Fragger!"

"Shove it where the sun don't shine!" Fragger snarled at the squirrel, turning his attention back to the dream. Why the hell was his family telling him to come home? He hadn't been deployed since Desert Storm and had been at DARPA when....when what? Fragger groaned in frustration as he tried to remember. The effort was giving him a terrible headache. He needed more bunk time to get rid of it, and this puke creation of his brain kept nagging him worse than Emily, his first wife!

"Fragger Sparks! I've implanted a translator in your head, so I know you can understand Standard. On your feet, soldier!"

Now Fragger was mad enough to wake up even if it was into a dream. This maggot of a squirrel, Leery, was using his nickname and hadn't earned the right to do that. His Nam team had rewarded him with "Fragger" in Cu Chi. The Rangers had stepped into an NVA ambush, and machine guns in well-hidden bunkers chewed them up until 20-year-old Jonathan Sparks gathered fragmentation grenades and limbered up his All State high school pitching arm. He'd thrown strikes into the bunker ports and then led a flanking maneuver to rout the attackers. It'd been the most embarrassing and yet proudest moment of his life when after the fire fight, Colonel Tennison had called him the "fastest and luckiest fucking maniac I've ever seen" in front of the surviving Rangers and tagged him with the nickname he'd carried up through Desert Storm and DARPA and...

Fragger shook his head, trying to remember what had happened next, but nothing specific came, only a vague recollection of some "special" project. The inability to recall any details made him angry so he snapped, "Stop calling me 'Fragger'! My correct name is Jonathan."

Fragger forced his eyes open as he made the demand. His voice sounded harsh and grating as if his vocal cords were vibrating in gravel not air. It also seemed detached from his body as if it were floating around the bright lights on the ceiling. He squinted through gummy lids trying to get a better look at Leery and laughed at what he saw. The Revival Technician wasn't a squirrel. He was a man—a sweaty little pile of crap who looked squirrel-like—but a man nonetheless and wearing a strange uniform.

"On your feet, soldier!" the order came again.

Fragger attempted to get up to brace the little fucker right up against the wall, but either he didn't have any feet or he couldn't feel them. Dream terror surged.

"A mine?" he asked, forcing his body upright and discovering he was naked. He hated being naked, even in dreams. "Did I step on a mine?"

"What? No," Leery answered. The Revival Technician couldn't seem to decide where to place his focus. He alternated between gawking at Fragger as if he were some exotic beast and glancing anxiously at a resumption of the distant explosions while wiping perspiration from a sallow forehead. In the odd logic of the dream, the detonations appeared to come from a wall-sized painting of a bizarre chilly landscape dotted with rust-streaked rocks under a dusty pink sky. "You have all your extremities."

Fragger checked his body just to be sure. His feet were still there and all ten toes, but with limited sensation. "What the hell's wrong?" he demanded. "I can't feel much of anything. Am I paralyzed?"

"No, no, it's a side effect," Leery reassured him. "It goes away within a few minutes."

"Within a few minutes of what?"

"Revival, Sergeant."

"What on earth are you talking about?" Fragger asked, annoyed by the little man's anxious rubbing at pale skin beneath a twitching eye, apparently a reaction to whatever the hell was going on outside the building. As he waited for an answer, the Ranger decided that while Leery was definitely not an actual squirrel, he was as close to one as a human being could possibly get. The man had puffy cheeks and a slight lower lip which he sucked at with two long front teeth. His black eyes were buttons of fear. Fragger guessed the technician was no taller than five-six. An oversized gray uniform trimmed with red epaulets did little to hide the slumped shoulders and paunchy gut. A big red "EC" insignia was stitched above the left pocket of the shirt. Leery's name was below it in white letters. A holstered pistol the likes of which Fragger had seen only on episodes of *Star Trek* hung from a wide black belt. Ankle high black boots completed the picture—a picture that made Fragger think of his son when he was a young boy trying on his father's uniform. Leery was obviously a civilian playing military dress-up or, more likely, had been pressed into service and was not happy about it.

Scientist, Fragger guessed. *Squirrel-face has got the look of another kind of rodent—a lab rat. Definitely a rear echelon motherfucker. Damn, can't get away from REMFs, even when I'm asleep!*

"Well?" Fragger barked impatiently when Leery couldn't seem to drag his attention away from the noise.

Leery twitched and jerked his gaze from the painting back to the Ranger. "Like I said, man. Revival. You know. Reborn, rebirthed, revived, cloned, good karma in a previous life, cool, that kind of thing, far out. Rock n' roll, booyah, mess up the Mohammeds."

Fragger glared at the jittery technician and snapped, "Are you trying to be funny, you damned squirrel?"

A startled expression crossed Leery's face. "No, why? What's a squirrel?"

"A little rodent, just like you. You're talking like I'm some damned moron. You're aping my speech. Making fun of me."

The *crrump!* of explosions grew louder. Leery winced at the noise and explained quickly, "I haven't got time to make fun of you, Sergeant, believe me. I just used the speech pattern indicated for your particular part of the Terran Twentieth Century, that's all. Revival Technicians are trained to do such things."

Fragger studied the man's face to see if Leery was playing out a practical joke that wasn't particularly funny, but the squirrel eyes showed no humor. They had the look of prey certain that a predator was about to strike.

"My particular part of the Twentieth Century?" the Ranger asked.

Leery flashed an insincere grin. "Happy Day of Second Birth, Sparks. As of today, you're about six centuries old. I hope you live to celebrate it."

Confusion swirled in Fragger's head. "What? What's going on?"

"Never mind," the technician replied, his hand hovering over the oddly shaped pistol. "I'll get you some clothes because we need to move *right now!*"

Fragger followed the man's eyes toward the wall painting, wondering what Leery found so fascinating about it. As far as the Ranger was concerned, it was a terrible work of art, all pink sky and red dirt. It looked like a terribly boring part of the Painted Desert.

Then lightning-quick motion streaked into the middle of the painting.

It's not a painting at all! Fragger realized. *It's a window. A very thick window onto a very strange world.*

Outside the window, the blur stopped and transformed itself into a solid object.

This is rich! It's a robot, a damned robot, armed with a sword and a shield of all things! And it looks like a samurai! I spent way too much time studying military history and obviously far too many hours on the Japanese military. My mind is mixing the past with the future!

As best Fragger could judge, the robot was close to seven feet tall and unmistakably Japanese in origin. The sword the machine wielded glittered with unnatural brightness and shimmered with some internal source of light. Flared like a tori gateway, a helmeted head swiveled toward the window. In a motion so swift Fragger wasn't sure at first it had really happened, the robot charged the window and laid the blade into it. Although the glass looked to be at least a foot thick, a single stroke shattered it. Warm air blew out of the room, replaced by the in-rush of a cold, bitter wind. Fragger shivered under its impact and gasped for breath as the robot shouldered its way inside the building, sword raised high. The Ranger turned toward Leery to see what kind of defense the technician could offer. He had no confidence in Squirrel-face, but as long as a man had a weapon, there was a chance.

Fragger's heart stuttered at what he saw

Leery had the pistol trained on him, not the robot.

Shit! Fragger swore as the technician took shaky aim. *What a dream! Everybody's trying to kill me! Man, I must have eaten too much pizza to generate this kind of nightmare!*

As if to confirm bad digestion, the dream twisted in a new direction. In an instant, the robot blurred into action and put its bulk between Fragger and Leery. A bright light pulsed and splashed against the samurai's armor, lighting the room up in a garish green hiss.

My God, that pistol Leery has is a laser! Fragger realized. *And a helluva powerful one. Can the robot handle the impact?*

Sizzling like a downed power line, the sword hummed through the air, and Fragger's question was answered nearly before he'd asked it. Leery's head, sliced from his body, thumped onto the floor and rolled toward the window. The stroke had been so swift and surgical the technician's expression hadn't had time to change. Leery still squinted his squirrel eyes as if aiming his weapon at Fragger. Before the body hit the floor, the robot spun around with the tip of the curved sword pointed directly at the Ranger. The technician's laser hadn't even left a mark on the armor.

Damn! Fragger thought with grim amusement. *Out of the frying pan, into the fire. I might have survived Leery's attack, but my dream sure as hell isn't going to let me escape this monster.*

"Finish me off, robot," Fragger said, determined at least to keep his dignity even if the situation wasn't real. He was a Ranger, after all, and Rangers kept their cool under any circumstances. "I don't have a weapon, and I want out of this dream."

To Fragger's astonishment, the robot paused and then lowered his sword.

Trying to catch his breath in the increasingly thin and freezing air, Fragger waited as the machine stood still, seeming to ponder the situation. Impatient, the Ranger urged, "If you're going to kill me, do it now! Damn, this is a really aggravating!"

The robot ignored his plea. But, a second later, it spoke in a harsh, but clear amplified voice, "I am not a robot. I am a powered armor soldier of the Royal and Imperial Commonwealth of Nipponese Empires. And this is no dream."

Fragger ignored the intense reality of his sleeping mind and said with a shrug, "Who cares? Real or dream, either way, you're going to kill me. End it, so I can wake up."

"Watanabe does not kill unarmed men. Even if they are Reruns," the samurai said in a heavy, breathy voice that indicated damage had been done to his respiratory system.

"Rerun? What the hell is a Rerun? Why does everyone keep calling me that?" Fragger asked. This part of the dream was bewildering. The only time the Ranger had heard that term used was in referring to the repeat showings of television programs. "And what's a 'Whataknobby'?"

"You are a Rerun! And Watanabe is my name. Isoruku Watanabe. The correct way to pronounce it is, 'Whaat-a-*nob*-bay'."

"Whatever you say," Fragger said, resigned to letting the goofball dream run its course while at the same time trying to force more air into his lungs. "Well, WhattaNobHead...samurais are supposed to hold honor as their highest standard. So, prove it. Instead of just letting me let me die from...cold and lack of...oxygen, why not make it quick? Kill me with that sword of yours. Or are you a coward? Remember…" Fragger searched his head for a quote from ancient Japanese military history that was rattling around in his head just beyond reach.

"Remember what, Rerun?" the samurai asked with the infinite patience of an executioner who had all the time in the world that his victim did not.

"Oh, I forgot…no, wait a minute…'he…he who advances is sure of heaven, but he who retreats will suffer eternal damnation.' So, advance damn it; otherwise, you're a coward!"

At this remark, the samurai bent toward the Ranger and held the sword close to his throat. Its power buzzed in Fragger's ears.

"Rerun, insults from experiments are usually rewarded with instant death, but this time you are lucky. Unlikely as it may be, you may have worth to us, so I'll spare your life for now and take you to a place of safety."

Fragger had had enough of this nonsense and decided to talk to himself rather than a creation of his imagination. "Experiment? Now I'm a freaking experiment? Okay, Sergeant Sparks, let's cut this crap short. You're a soldier who's got duties to perform. Wake up and wake up now!"

His mind wouldn't obey! Watanabe uttered a noise of annoyance before grabbing several items from a table and tucking them into a belt. Then, he seized Fragger. The Ranger squawked as the samurai tucked him under an arm as if he weighed no more than a bag of feathers, raced out of the room and then lifted up into the pink sky to hover above a building that reminded Fragger of a giant, plastic Quonset hut. Watanabe twisted in the air, pulled an object from his side, and dropped it straight down. A few seconds later, the building blew itself into debris, followed by an oddly thin and thunderous concussion. For a moment, Fragger was afraid they'd be caught in the cloud of ashes and sand boiling upward, but the samurai simply jetted away from the detonation.

What a wild dream! Fragger thought as the icy wind generated by the samurai's acceleration numbed his mind into unconsciousness. *Damn, Rangers lead the way! We even do dreams better than anyone else!*

CHAPTER 2

Fragger started awake, relieved to be out of the dream, but the room he was in was as black as a drill sergeant's heart. Annoyed, the Ranger groped for a light. Instead, his fingers jammed against a hard surface close above his face. Fragger cursed at the pain. He tried again to locate a switch and hurt his hand again. Feeling around more carefully, he soon discovered he wasn't in a room at all.

He was trapped in a casket.

Gasping, he bucked up in the dark trying to force the lid open until logic beat down the claustrophobia clawing at his sanity.

I'm still in the damned dream! That must be it. Or maybe I'm wounded, and I've got morphine in my system. Drugs cause this kind of shit in your head. But, man, it sure is real!

Fragger took a deep breath. When his mind calmed, he continued the exploration of his surroundings. It didn't take long to determine the coffin was made of extremely hard plastic or something very similar to it. When he knocked on the material, it gave back a dull thunk that said it wasn't metal. He sniffed at the smell stirred up by the motion of his arm. An odor of stale, recirculated air and rank sweat—his own—rose about his body which caused the entry of a disturbing thought into his head.

I've had some vivid dreams before, but never one equipped with recirculated air.

Fragger lay back, trying to come up with a rational explanation for his situation. Gradually, he became aware he wasn't in the total blackness of a grave as he'd originally thought. There was a faint light above his face.

My eyes are adjusting to the dark. There's something outside this box which is not a coffin. I'm in some sort of capsule.

The Ranger watched in relief as the dim light separated into distinct stars outside a small window. Then, a vibration ran though the capsule, and the stars whirled. Fragger fought vertigo until a shape edged into the periphery of his vision and took his astonished mind off the nausea.

"Sonuvabitch! It's an honest-to-God space ship!"

His awe increased as the vessel slid fully into view like a weightless mountain.

It's more than a space ship! It's a war ship of some kind. I know military lines when I see them. What's it designed fort?

Fragger couldn't decide its purpose because the configuration confused him. The odd vessel looked like a submarine with a sharp-edged keel crossed with a missile cruiser crossed with an aircraft carrier. Turrets dotted the scarred exterior. The designation on the hull was not in Japanese characters as he'd expected from his encounter with the samurai, but in English. The letters read *HELOT 204.* With few reference points in the blackness of space, Fragger had no idea of the HELOT's size, other than that it was huge. Much smaller vehicles buzzed about the warship like hornets. He tried comparing the HELOT's size against that of the small ships and still came up blank. Then, among blinding flares of light, he saw tiny, space-suited figures crawling over the HELOT's gun-metal gray surface and had his reference points. He estimated the warship to be somewhere in the vicinity of 500 to a 1000 feet long. As he watched, a silent explosion knocked one of the figures into a spin away from the vessel, and Fragger knew two things with certainty.

One, he was seeing a fire fight.

Two, he was *not* in a dream. There was none of the nonsense of a mind dreaming. The experience had a cold, objective logic to it. But his brain didn't want to accept the reality. It kept babbling thoughts right out of his mouth, "Oh shit, oh man, oh fuck me, oh shit, oh...Leery was real! The samurai was real. I'm in the frigging future!"

Fragger couldn't shut himself up, so he was grateful for the distraction when something kicked the capsule forward until all that could be seen was the dull gray of the warship's surface hurtling in his direction. Twisted beams and girder ribbing flowered from scorch marks along the hull as soldiers battled each other. Improbably, the sight cheered the Ranger.

"A fire fight!" he babbled, anchoring his sanity in the sound of his voice. "I know fire fights! Maybe the samurais attacked the ship, or the other way around, but the battle is still going on. Leery said I was six centuries into the future, but it looks to me as if war is still around. And that samurai showed me the weapons have changed, yet he was still basically a grunt. And isn't that what it always come down to--the individual soldier? I'll bet courage, a cool head, and a fair amount of luck will work here as well as back in my time. And information! That's what I need most of all. Who and what am I going to be dealing with? And why the hell does everyone seem to have a low opinion of Reruns?"

Fragger had several other questions he wanted answered, but he put them aside as the warship swallowed his capsule like a whale swallowing krill.

As the stars disappeared, a wave of homesickness rolled through the Ranger's body. *I'm several centuries away from the Army, from Amanda, John and Libby, from anything familiar. What the hell am I going do without my family and my buddies?*

Tears started. Fragger shook off the urge to cry and pulled himself together. *I'm a Ranger, by God! And a Ranger can survive anything! I haven't got a clue why they woke me up, but I've been given a chance to see the future. Make the most of it, Sergeant Sparks.*

As the capsule rushed forward into darkness, he defiantly shouted his outfit's slogan, "Rangers lead the way!"

CHAPTER 3

Inside the ship, two samurai guards pulled Fragger roughly from the capsule. They set him on his feet and pushed him down a smoke-filled passageway through blown hatches. The air smelled of ozone, burnt plastic, and the torn intestines of the soldiers over which they stepped. Most of the downed troopers were dead. A few still screamed and clawed at their wounds with armored fingers. The guards kicked the enemy soldiers aside. Downed comrades, they checked quickly. Right away, it was obvious to the Ranger who could be saved and who was dog meat. The lucky ones got tagged with bright orange patches to help medics locate them.

After a few minutes of this tour of combat hell, the guards shoved Fragger up against a cold bulkhead next to an open hatch and told him to wait. One of them disappeared through the door while the other amused himself by poking a dagger at the vulnerable parts of the Ranger's body. Fragger didn't let it bother him. He knew the guard wouldn't damage him badly, at least not until after an officer had a chance to conduct an interrogation. What disturbed him more at the moment was the fact that he was still naked and his bare feet were covered with the blood and flesh of the downed soldiers they'd passed in the corridors. The odor of death stuck with him as well. He stank of bile and shit and cooked flesh. He forced his mind away from nausea by listening to a dry voice that emerged through the room's open door. Its impersonal, yet pompous tone told Fragger the man was another rear echelon motherfucker like Leery. The owner of the voice was reading a document and trying to score points with somebody.

Probably combat troops since REMFs always feel inferior in the presence of real soldiers, Fragger guessed.

"...distinguishing features are listed, of course, so that in case of rogue behavior, he can easily be picked up as a fugitive. These features are important in this case because, apparently, the technician, Leery, didn't have time for a forehead brand. These features include a broken nose, a typical voice marker—"

Me! It's me they're talking about! Fragger realized.

An impatient female voice broke in, "Why are you telling me this dogsquat, Truthseeker? It's a mere Rerun we're discussing, correct?"

"Yes, Major Shimazu. But, you're aware of the special circumstances concerning this particular—"

"--piece of trash? Yes, damn it, I'm aware of the situation, Harada, you idiot interrogator! Just speed it up, will you? We've got control of the Corpse ship for now, but as the optimists always say, the situation is fluid."

Snorts of derision erupted from the room, making Fragger realize he'd been right about the audience being front-line troops. They obviously had as little time for REMFs as he did.

"As you wish, Major," the interrogator responded, acceding to a superior's order with a bow in his voice.

"Background," she demanded.

Harada recited facts again. "Earth-period, late decades of 20th century. His nation was the United States of America. Apparently, this Rerun was –"

"Not historical background. Just the Rerun's background, Harada!"

Fragger jumped and swore when the guard, disappointed that his prisoner was showing no fear at the dagger-poking efforts, took to flicking an armored finger against the Ranger's flesh. The taps stung hard because of the suit's power. Fragger tuned out the pain by listening to the REMF continue on in a dry tone.

"Gleaning of the OldNet military personnel records Watanabe brought back indicates remarkably complete files for that particular period of time. The Rerun belonged to the Old American Rangers, a force roughly equivalent to our Marauder classification. Approximately 41 Earth years of age, Sergeant First Class Sparks was a career soldier. Assigned duties in both the Asian and Middle Eastern wars: Operate behind enemy lines to gather intelligence and to undertake special missions as required. Rangers were regarded as a highly elite light combat force. They--"

"Harada, get to the point!" Shimazu ordered. "Or do I have to hook you up to your own interrogation machine?"

There was a stiffness in Harada's reply that Fragger couldn't miss, even standing out in the corridor with the guard turning patches of his skin red with each snap of an armored finger.

"Yes, sir. I was about to point out that the words 'luck' and 'lucky' keep popping up in the files to describe this particular Rerun. As Leery, the Corpse technician indicated, military records are usually very terse and do not mention matters of luck. The records also seem to indicate early attempts at identifying soldiers who possessed what were called "special" abilities. Early efforts were strictly military and dismissed as, to use the Terran term, "boondoggles". Later, they appear to become joint military-corporation ventures. My best guess is that the EarthCorp personnel did an extensive sweep of ancient records to isolate probables from these ventures. They then most likely used records to locate genetic banks. After that, it was a simple numbers game. In other words, revive Reruns in the hope of discovering an individual capable of mind abilities, teleportation and the like. So, the EarthCorp forces seek what they're always seeking to overcome their deficiencies in armored suit mobility--"

"A soldier who can be mentally enhanced. A Rerun with innate abilities no one's been able to isolate," Shimazu interrupted again, then added with an exasperated sigh, "What I don't understand is why EarthCorp is always looking for these abilities in less intelligent products of the past. You'd think they'd realize we've evolved since that time. Well, it's not likely that a simple RT would have come up with anything new, but we have to be sure. Did the RT mention anything specific in his recorded log?"

"He talked about something called 'HSP', Major," Harada answered.

"Which is?"

"I don't know."

"Does anyone else know what HSP is?" Shimazu asked the room.

When no one answered, she said, "All right. If he knows it, will you be able to dig the meaning of this term out of the Rerun,

Truthseeker? Or confirm or deny the existence of any special abilities?"

"Perhaps, Major. My equipment is set up in the next room. As you know, a proper interrogation takes time, and we don't--"

"Then, do it, Harada. Conduct a short, initial probe. Then, analyze the translator module for any modifications. RTs are always trying to get cute with those things," the major ordered and quickly added a warning, "Make sure the probe doesn't do any damage, Harada! What little mind this Rerun has, it might be important to keep it whole until we can determine exactly what kind of opportunity—or threat—he represents."

Keep my mind whole? Keep my mind whole? Fragger shrieked in his head. Panic drove him to duck under the guard's arm and burst into the room to shout, "Who the fuck do you people think you are? You're not touching my damned mind! You're talking to a U.S. Army Ranger, just remember that. I'm not an experiment. I'm not a Rerun or whatever your term for 'nigger' is in this time. And you people must have shit for brains because you sure don't have any common sense. Why don't you just ask me why they woke me up? Maybe I have the answer. Did you ever think of that?"

Good bluff, Fragger! the Ranger thought as astonished faces greeted his intrusion. *I don't have any more idea of why I've been revived than I have about the workings of a nuclear reactor, but I need any edge I can dig up.*

While the guard sputtered an inadequate explanation for his carelessness, Fragger surveyed the room and its occupants. The room was damaged with soot streaks and impact craters on the bulkheads. Soldiers, most in armor with helmets tucked beneath arms, stood around a battered grey table which leaned crazily due to a buckled leg. Behind the table, someone had hung a blood-stained battle flag on the wall. It was made of a white fabric decorated with several red suns radiating from a lemon-yellow chrysanthemum placed in the center of the banner. Sudden concussions shook the walls and prompted a mental jab from Fragger at his enemy about the banner, *The flag is a nice touch, people, but a trifle overconfident since the battle doesn't seem to be over yet.*

He shifted his attention away from that thought to quickly assess the occupants of the room. Only one person was sitting and had to be Major Shimazu, the woman he'd heard from the corridor. She was the lone female in the room.

For a moment, disdain rose in Fragger's mind. Despite all the efforts of officers to eliminate his aversion to females in the military, it still went against his grain to see a woman in the army--especially one in battle. It was a sexist notion, the Ranger knew that, but one he'd never rid himself of. His old-fashioned idea was that men were for death. That was their lot. But, women? Women were for life, not war.

Until I met this woman, Fragger amended as he studied the officer more intently. For a moment, the Ranger thought he was looking at a Picasso painting come to life. Framed by close-cropped black hair, Shimazu's face was all fragmented planes coming together at wrong angles. Cheek bones sharp as razors formed ridges under tightly stretched and puckered skin. A livid scar furrowed its way down from a once-delicate nostril across the left side of her mouth. Whatever weapon had hit the officer had burned a gash across the small, pointed chin and down onto her neck.

A power sword did that, Fragger guessed. *I've seen burns and slashes from knives, but never both in the same wound. Jesus, look at her! I'll bet she was as good as dead by the time the medics got to her. Somehow, they were able to piece her back together.*

The ruined face wasn't what frightened Fragger, though. It was her eyes. They seized his attention and made the dog of his fear tuck its tail between its legs and run yipping in circles around the inside of his head seeking a place to hide. They were like concrete in January—cold, grey, and brittle.

I've seen the thousand-yard stare on Rangers who've spent too much time in the jungle, too much time killing. But these eyes are beyond even that. Combat killed something in this woman, and something new and nasty was born in its place.

What further unnerved Fragger was the major's body. Although he couldn't see it beneath the uniform, it was obvious damage had been done there as well as to her face. A normal woman had curves and soft angles. Shimazu's torso had no curves. Instead, it was a sharp-cornered block. A gun-metal grey uniform hung badly on the edges of the shoulders, and Fragger found himself imagining that the uniform had been surprised to find itself dressing a wedge of metal or plastic instead of a human body. He shuddered as the hardened eyes studied him from a far-off mental land whose occupants he didn't care to meet. Finally, an amused, superior smile cracked a corner of the seared mouth, and the major spoke in the patient tone of voice reserved for explaining things to children or idiots, "My appearance scares you…Sparks, is it? It scares most Reruns. And it should scare you. I don't like Reruns. And let me tell you why. This composite body"—the major thumped at her chest and two dull *thunks* sounded from the action of her fist—"is courtesy of an honest engagement with EarthCorp infantry."

The major raised a hand to gesture at her ruined face, "But this…souvenir…was the result of an uprising on my estate by Reruns like yourself, ungrateful for revival. They killed my brother and two cousins before we brought them under control. The ring leaders we roasted over a slow fire, cooking them like the animals they were."

Oh, fuck! Fragger groaned inwardly. *Deep shit time!*

Shimazu continued, "So, now you know where you stand with me—lower than garbage. As for asking you what the RT did, it's pointless. A technician wouldn't bother to explain research to an experiment. And, if for some unknown reason, he'd taken the time to tell you, you wouldn't understand because you're too dim to comprehend abstract concepts. As for your so-called mind, it doesn't belong to you. It belongs to us. That means we'll do with it whatever we please."

She dismissed his presence by turning toward the soldier on her right. The major seemed to regard her own man with only slightly less contempt than she'd regarded Fragger.

And obviously interested in asserting her authority over him, Fragger realized as she continued to stare at the man without speaking. *I'm not the only one on her shit list.*

In the silence, the burly soldier's breathing rasped from a small pug nose planted above an underslung jaw that looked like it chewed boulders for breakfast. Sporting crew-cut black hair and a heavy brow with the overhang of a rocky cliff, the soldier gave every indication of a bulldog imitating a man. Fragger noticed that the brown eyes, clearly unhappy with some aspect of the situation, showed the tenacity of that venerable canine. And, although the soldier stood perfectly at attention, the Ranger got the impression he wished he were anywhere else but in the room.

"Sergeant Watanabe," the major said.

So this is the guy who dragged me off the planet! Fragger thought as he sized the sergeant up. *Jesus, with that jaw, he probably didn't really need that sword to kill Leery. He could have simply bit the technician's head off.*

Watanabe bowed slightly and acknowledged the officer in a non-com's gruff bark, "Major Shimazu."

"Where did you find this Rerun, Sergeant?"

"About 20 klicks to the east of the main EarthCorp lab, Major."

"This was your assigned sector?"

"No, sir."

"What were you doing there, then?"

"I eliminated the activity within my area. I thought I would be of more use—"

"You thought?" the officer interrupted. "The *Burakumin* are not noted for thought. It must be the first time that has occurred."

Watanabe flushed as suppressed snickers escaped from other soldiers. Anger tightened the massive chin, temporarily making it look more like a dragline bucket than a dog's jaw. Fragger's translator implant struggled for a moment with the term "Burakumin" before popping two definitions into his head regarding an inferior caste of ancient Japan-- *Eta* (extreme filth) and *Hinin* (non-human) classes.

Fragger studied Watanabe to see how the sergeant would handle the insult while simultaneously calculating, *Okay, we've got prejudice in the future as well as in the past. That means some level of dissension in the ranks. Is this something I can exploit? Pay close attention, Fragger. Your life may depend upon it.*

Watanabe plowed on in spite of the humiliation. "The lab was camouflaged to look like a maintenance building but it had too many defenders for such an unimportant facility. I eliminated the guards and--"

The sergeant fell silent as he saw the major was ignoring the information. A moment later, Shimazu asked a question that appeared to come out of left field to Fragger. "What happened to your brother, Sergeant Watanabe?"

Stiffly, the sergeant replied, "Sir, you know very well what happened to my brother. What has that got to do with what's occurred on this--"

"Watanabe, explain again. Everyone in the room may not know the story and the lesson it taught. A lesson you appear to have forgotten."

Watanabe's nostrils flared and his furious eyes swept the room before he said, "They all know the story, major. You've repeated it many times for their benefit."

Under the impact of the sergeant's glare, the soldiers kept silence, casting embarrassed glances toward the deck and clanking their armored boots as they shifted their feet. Fragger was pretty sure he knew the reason they kept their mouths shut. In combat, caste didn't matter, and from the look of the man, Watanabe could probably tear them several new assholes without breaking a sweat.

The tone of the sergeant's reply carried an insubordination that caused the major's burned face to ice itself into further rigidity. "You're right, Sergeant. I have repeated it many times. For a purpose. To make sure you've learned the lesson it teaches. But, the Rerun has never heard it. Repeat it for him."

"Explain something for a Rerun? Never, sir!"

"And I repeat the order, Sergeant. Tell the Rerun about your brother."

"I respectfully decline, Major! Besides, this is no time for past history. May I remind you that we do not have complete control of the HELOT?"

Major Shimazu emitted a theatrical sigh and drummed her fingers on the tabletop.

Bitch! Fragger cursed, even though he was pissed with Watanabe's own prejudiced attitude toward him as being lower than pond scum. *A good officer never humiliates a soldier, not unless she's looking for trouble in the future.*

"The sooner you tell the story, the sooner we'll be out of here, Watanabe," the major said. "Plus, if you don't tell the story, then you'll be out of your armor and boiling rice in the *Hiroshima's* mess for the rest of your military career. You belong in a kitchen, anyway."

Watanabe recoiled as if the officer had actually hit him. "I am a front-line combat soldier with honors!"

"In my eyes, you are a fool *Buraku* who kills many enemies, yes, but whose rashness gets more of his men killed than is necessary!" Shimazu snapped. "Tell the tale or prepare for transfer. An apron suits you."

For a moment, Fragger was afraid a stroke would drop Watanabe on the spot. The veins in the sergeant's temples convulsed under the skin, and the eyes filled with a lethal rage while a hand quivered over the sword hilt. Around the room, soldiers sucked breath in. In the stillness, Watanabe and Shimazu locked gazes until the sergeant gave a slight nod of acquiescence to his superior officer.

But I've never seen such a small action more full of contempt, Fragger noted with approval as Watanabe swung around to face in his direction. *He gave in—no true soldier would miss a chance for combat—but, by God, he didn't give up.*

"Rerun, according to official reports from the planet *Lehgun*, my brother, Yukio Watanabe, was responsible for the deaths of three men, including his commanding officer because of an overeagerness for honor. He attacked the enemy too early, alerting the Corpses—to you, EarthCorp soldiers--to their ambush position.

Yukio's lack of discipline revealed their position, and the Corpses killed Lieutenant Nintoku."

"Who was?" Shimazu prompted.

Watanabe answered formally, "First Son of Kogen, Emperor of the Royal and Imperial Commonwealth of Nipponese Empires and Achiever of Complete Peace in the Heavens."

Fragger suppressed a snort at the title. *Achiever of Complete Peace in the Heavens? Yeah, that's what we have right here on this ship—complete peace! It sounds to me like Kogen is just another bloodthirsty bastard, and Watanabe's brother had the misfortune of being in the wrong place at the wrong time. From Watanabe's reaction, I'd be willing to bet that the emperor's son was royal all right—a royal fuck-up who got himself and the others killed. Most likely, Kogen needed a scapegoat, and Watanabe is paying the price.*

"Fortunately for you, Watanabe, your brother had the grace to get himself killed in a later battle," Shimazu said. "Possibly the only time your family has done something right. And now you know why I assigned you to a sector by yourself. I did not wish for more good soldiers to die needlessly."

Whew, this lady has a death wish real bad! Fragger whistled in his mind. *You can't treat people like that without it coming back to you sooner or later.*

Apparently satisfied with the humiliation she'd dealt out to Watanabe, the major slapped a palm on the table. "Enough of this subject. You said the Corpse building was disguised as a maintenance facility, Sergeant. How did you know it was not such a building?"

"It struck me as unusual to have a structure like that in the middle of the Khanwati Desert with no apparent equipment to be repaired," Watanabe answered, clearly relieved the conversation had moved on to less sensitive matters. "So, I investigated."

"But why did you see fit to bring this particular Rerun back with you?" the major asked. "EarthCorp continually runs such tests, even, it seems, within contested territory."

"The Revival Technician tried to kill it before he engaged me in combat."

Shimazu's brow rose. "Really? Now, why would a simple RT risk certain death to keep a Rerun out of our hands?"

"I don't know," Watanabe replied. "But I thought it was worth short-hopping to an Emergency Pod and re-configuring it so the Rerun could be returned safely for questioning. I seized as many data files as time allowed before blowing the building to deny further use to the enemy."

"For once, you've earned honor for the Jump Infantry," Shimazu said sarcastically as she turned her attention back to Fragger. The Ranger shivered under the impact of her speculative gaze. He felt like he was being measured for a very small coffin, one just large enough to contain all the pieces left after she got through with him.

Watanabe continued, "Major, as we've heard, we have the basic information on this Rerun, but many of the files I retrieved are heavily encrypted. Intelligence says it may take some time to decode."

The officer nodded, then stood and limped heavily around the table toward the Ranger. To Fragger, the artificially square build of the woman's body made it look as if a cement block had donned a grey uniform and black boots and decided to go for a walk. When she stopped in front of him, he was not surprised to find she was nearly as tall as he was.

"Well, what do we have?" the major asked the room as her eyes bored into Fragger's. "EarthCorp has revived soldiers before. So have we. So, the question remains. Why try to revive this particular Rerun stuck on a planet in the Outer Wastes and then deem it so important that the RT had orders to kill it before it fell into our hands? And why have we provoked such a hornet's nest on a simple raid? Thoughts?"

"Beyond the attempt to kill the Rerun and the mention of HSP, I didn't see anything out of the ordinary, Major," Watanabe answered. "But, then I'm not a technician or a truthseeker."

Fragger noticed the sergeant spat the word "Truthseeker" out of his mouth as if it had been soaked in vinegar. He guessed the source of disgust when a thin, severe man planted himself next to Major Shimazu, and the soldiers behind them exchanged quick glances of loathing.

Harada, the REMF I heard when I was out in the hall, Fragger realized. In a room full of dirty, sweaty, fully-alive soldiers, the truthseeker was a spotless, barely animated cadaver with a bald head, a nose as sharp as the creases in his pants, and narrowed dark eyes flirting coolly with madness in the name of military necessity. Fragger felt his testicles shrivel to the size of peas under the impact of Harada's calculating gaze.

"Quite right," the man said over his shoulder to Watanabe, "you're not a technician. You're a simple *Buruku.* This is my area of expertise now."

"Get on with it, Harada. Is your interrogation device ready?" Major Shimazu asked.

"Of course, Major. I'll scan for unusual implants in addition to the usual mental extraction."

The words slithered out of the truthseeker's mouth like snakes seeking prey. Fragger panicked at the thought of Harada messing with his head so to buy time, he blurted out, "Hey, why not use some common sense like I said before and just ask me? You said yourself these Corpses think I'm something special. Maybe I *can* help you, in spite of what you think. I haven't got any choice but cooperation, have I?"

"None," Shimazu agreed. "That fact is irrelevant to us, however, Rerun. With his interrogation machinery, Harada can get the information we need much faster."

The woman's sub-zero attitude unnerved Fragger. He ransacked his brain for options to escape from an intolerable situation.

From Watanabe's reactions on the planet and in this room, honor is an important concept to these people and especially important to the sergeant.

That thought caused contemptuous words to erupt from his mouth. "Real soldiers—soldiers with *honor*—don't use torture."

The spasm of a smile jerked across Shimazu's seared lips again. "Our methods are not so crude as those in your era, Rerun. Harada can extract the information painlessly. Although," she added bluntly, "if he does not get what he wants, he's not above inflicting physical pain. As long as the job gets done."

Fragger regarded Harada as coldly as the other soldiers had. "That means pain is guaranteed then, isn't it? I'll bet Harada lives for that shit because he doesn't have the balls for combat. Scum like him always seem to form on the surface when war comes around."

The truthseeker's backhand laid him on the floor. Fragger got up immediately. He spat in front of Harada and said with as much disgust as he could muster, "A man without a trace of honor."

Harada decked him a second time. Through the stars orbiting his eyes in crazy circles, Fragger saw approval in the watching soldiers' faces. He stood up again.

"If I'm going to die, I demand the honor Harada does not possess. Let me die in battle."

Laughter erupted in the room.

"You would not stand a chance against the sword and armor," Watanabe said.

"I'm not talking about a coward's protection," Fragger pressed on, hoping against hope his tactic of insults would pay further dividends. "Real soldiers don't need armor."

Watanabe's bulldog jaw tensed as he colored with rage. Mutters replaced the laughter around the table.

Fragger pushed harder, saying, "Hand to hand combat. *Real* hand to hand combat. That's what I'm talking about, where you taste your enemy's blood and do him the honor of looking him in the eyes."

Major Shimazu waved a hand for silence amidst the growls of anger. "You don't know anything about our form of war, Rerun. The suits are necessary now. Biological and chemical agents have been engineered into extremely deadly forms. A warrior without a powered suit will die an agonizing death. Whether it's a fast or slow death, depends upon the agent."

"Yeah, well, the people in this room have their helmets off and you're not wearing any protection so you don't have any of those things in this part of the ship, do you?" Fragger pointed out. "There's nothing to prevent man to man combat."

"This section of the HELOT is decontaminated," Shimazu acknowledged. She considered his request for a moment, then nodded. "All right, Sparks. You'll have your fight. Watanabe, when the vessel is secured, you will fight him. B*urakumin* should kill its like."

To Fragger's surprise, the sergeant absorbed the insult without reaction. "There is no honor in killing a Rerun," Watanabe said. "But I saved his life. I should end it."

"Then, you *will* fight Watanabe, Rerun," the major said. "But not today. You are in no shape for combat after revival, and we still need the information from your mind. So, I will promise you this. Harada will extract it without pain, then we will allow you time to recover your strength, and Watanabe will see to it your second death is quick and easy."

"What happens when I kill him?" Fragger asked.

Laughter filled the room again. He waited until it died down, then insisted, "What happens?"

A genuine perplexity crossed Major Shimazu's scarred face. "None of the few Reruns who've made that request have ever survived. I have no answer for you."

"Probably because you made the choice of weapons and laid the odds in your favor."

The soldiers stirred at Fragger's insult, but the major kept her composure. "What choice of weapons would you have, Rerun?

"One of those silly swords you people use."

"I don't think you found what I did to that dirtside technician with a sword so funny," Watanabe growled.

"Your ancestors had a bad habit of cutting off my unarmed ancestor's heads when they were prisoners in the Second World War," Fragger responded as he figured, *I'm on a roll so I might as well continue the provocation.* "Apparently, the strain of cowardice still runs deep."

Watanabe charged half way around the table before the major barked the command to halt. She pinned the soldier to the spot with a scornful, "The Rerun shows more cunning in several hours of unexpected life than you've shown in 20 years of soldiering, Watanabe. Already, he's under your skin, irritating you into *Burakumin* stupidity. He may well kill you if you persist in such irrational behavior. A soldier who is not cool in battle is a dead soldier. Or would you like to tell the story of your brother to the Rerun one more time?"

A slow snarl of frustration escaped Watanabe's mouth before he stepped back.

Fragger let his breath out slowly, keeping his eyes on the major. *She reads me well. Too damned well. Every meeting with her—assuming there is another one—will be a contest, and I'll have to win all of them if I hope to stay alive.*

"Harada," Shimazu said to the truthseeker. "The prisoner is yours. Remember what I said—no harm. Watanabe would not be happy fighting an idiot Rerun. More important, *I* will be extremely unhappy. Do you understand what that means?"

"I do, Major."

"Do you?" she demanded. "I don't want another 'mistake' like the one you made earlier with the valuable EarthCorp prisoner. As far as I'm concerned, you've cost me ten good soldiers in this battle because you damaged him before we could obtain full schematics on this vessel. And we have yet to discover what an EarthCorp heavy-lift orbital transport vessel is doing in orbit around such a contested planet. All thanks to your... recklessness."

Harada bowed submission to the major while, at the same time, offering the Ranger a fleeting, sadistic smile that promised a painful interrogation in spite of the officer's order. Fragger broke into a sweat and yelped, "You're not going to put me in the hands of this pervert, are you? You know damned well he's not going to do what you say!"

"He's overzealous at times, Rerun," Shimazu conceded. "He's lost family to EarthCorp forces, as have I. But he'll obey my orders."

"Then, you're a fool to believe that, major. If he damages me and I really am of value, then what? I'm of no use to you. You can't get information from a mental vegetable. Make sure you have something left to work with by sending somebody along to ensure Harada does it all by the book!" Fragger pleaded.

"Who?" she asked.

"Him," Fragger said, pointing at Watanabe. "If the sergeant wants to kill me so badly, let him make sure he's got a whole opponent to fight."

Chuckles sounded around the table from everyone but Harada. Shimazu's scarred lips cracked into the semblance of a smile. "You have a sense of humor, Rerun."

"Let's make it even funnier," Fragger suggested. "Watanabe brings his sword along. If I end up mentally damaged, he gets Harada's head instead of mine."

This time, hands slapped over mouths to contain the laughter.

"Done," the major said with obvious pleasure at the interrogator's discomfort. "Harada, if I were you, I would proceed very carefully. Watanabe, escort the Rerun to interrogation."

Fragger maintained a sneer as Harada glared at him. Watanabe gestured for the truthseeker to exit first, then took the Ranger by the arm and whispered into his ear as they followed Harada out the door, "Rerun, it's going to be much less of a pleasure to kill you now."

"Thanks a whole helluva lot," Fragger answered while he thought ruefully, *I know damned well Watanabe isn't going to do a thing to the security man, but I feel better for having thrown sand into Harada's gears before he breaks my mind into pieces.*

CHAPTER 4

"Could I at least get some clothes?" Fragger complained as Watanabe pushed him into the chair Harada indicated. The Ranger scanned the makeshift interrogation room nervously as Watanabe mulled over the request. Piles of debris from the battle littered the floor. The sharp smell of ozone filled the air.

"Clothes? For what?" Watanabe asked, genuinely puzzled by the request.

"I'm cold, that's why." Fragger answered. He actually felt fine, even a little warm, but his dignity was definitely suffering.

"The temperature is normal."

"I don't care," Fragger said. "I'm cold. I come--came--from a warm climate on Earth. I need something to wear."

"Stop talking and lean back in the chair," Harada ordered, "We're wasting time."

Fragger stiffened, but leaned back and waited while the truthseeker set up and adjusted an oval shaped device over the chair and over the Ranger's head.

"How's it work?" the Ranger asked to allay his nervousness.

"Shut up," Harada ordered.

"At least tell me what to expect!"

Harada came around from behind the chair and said, "What you can expect is this, Rerun," then pressed a button on the side of the interrogation device.

Fragger tensed, but nothing horrible happened. Instead, he felt good, very good as a wonderful warmth spread from his mind throughout his body. It was a mixture of orgasm and forgiveness and eternal motherly love invading every cell of his being. He gasped at the pleasure and when a gentle female voice inside his head asked, "Do you want more?", he could barely get the word "Yes" out of his mouth.

"You'll have more," the voice promised. "Just answer this question as best you can--what makes you so special? Why does EarthCorp want you alive?"

"I don't know," he answered. "More."

The pleasure dropped. Fragger moaned. "No, bring it back, please!"

"Why are you so special?" the voice insisted.

"Oh, God, I wish I knew!" he answered. "More, please!"

Suddenly, he felt as if he were at the peak of never-ending sexual joy.

"Ahhhhhhhh...!" he groaned in pleasure.

"What does EarthCorp want from you?" the voice asked again.

Fragger searched his mind frantically and came up with nothing. "I'm--sorry, I don't know, but please don't stop."

"Of course not," the voice said, and the joy increased.

"Oh, yes!" the Ranger said and let the bliss envelop him. He'd never known such ecstasy.

And yet it increased again. Fragger's heart jumped with anticipation of still more.

When the pleasure came, it was so intense it was tinged with a hint of pain, but in spite of the hurt, he urged another jump.

"What do the Corpses want?" the question came again. This time it was his mother asking.

I can't refuse her, Fragger thought, *but I don't know what the answer is! Oh, what is it? I want to give it so badly!*

Pleasure leaped again, this time straight into pain. The Ranger fought for breath and for an answer--anything to make it stop--

A voice cut short in mid-scream sliced through the pleasure-pain. Fragger reached out for his mother, and she shattered into shards of glass that drove into his mind. He shuddered and opened his eyes to Watanabe's glowing sword cleaving Harada's head from his body.

"Jesus, Watanabe, another head?" Fragger asked, staring down at Harada's still open eyes. "Do you have a daily quota or something?"

Watanabe answered, "I don't know what you mean, but I have saved your life once more."

The Ranger looked around in confusion. "What are you talking about?"

"Harada heard the enemy coming close and wanted to push you beyond the addiction level so he could either get the answer or deny you to EarthCorp through destruction of your mind. However, you now have a worse fate in store as an addict doomed to a lifetime of craving for the interrogation machine. Once it stimulates the brain's pleasure receptors beyond a certain point, permanent addiction occurs. You crave it already. The eyes tell all."

Fragger knew Watanabe was right. A hunger, amorous as cancer, fed upon his body at that very moment. It felt as if it were working its way down from his head, cell by cell. Somehow he knew it would make his skin an eternal torch of desire that could never be extinguished. It would be an agony that would drive him to any means to either hook himself up eternally to the machine or end it all before he went mad with synthetic passion. He looked directly into Watanabe's eyes and the pity he saw there made him plead, "Use that sword on me. Now."

Watanabe raised the sword, and then faltered. "We don't know your value yet. Whatever knowledge you possess could be vital."

"You would treat a fellow soldier like this?" Fragger demanded. "You saved my life twice only to dishonor me in this fashion--to see me turned into a pathetic addict?"

When Watanabe hesitated again, Fragger pressed home his advantage. "Kill me now if you have any respect for me or for yourself! Hell, this way you deny me to the enemy, anyway, and nobody gets Leery's research. So, what's to lose?"

The warrior nodded in sudden decision. Raising the sword above his shoulder, he said, "Die then, Rerun."

Pleased, Fragger closed his eyes, and waited for the death stroke. He re-opened them instantly when the door clanged open. A round object the size of a large apple clunked on the deck and rolled across the room as the door swung shut. The high tech lights blinking on the object didn't fool Fragger for a moment.

Grenade! his mind screamed. Instinct threw his body out of the chair and away from the bomb. As he rolled into a ball and covered his head, Watanabe placed his armored body between him and the explosive.

The concussion drove Fragger against a bulkhead. Deafened, he watched the Imperial Commonwealth trooper drop the sword, stagger backward and crash to the deck.

Without his helmet, he's almost as vulnerable as I am, the objective soldier's part of Fragger's brain analyzed as he wiped blood from his mouth and marveled, *Three times! Three times the man has saved my life! It must be some kind of record.*

He forced himself to crawl over to Watanabe to see if the sergeant was dead or merely unconscious. He was almost there when the door burst open again. Out of instinct, he grabbed Watanabe's sword and whirled to meet two armored figures charging into the room.

Watanabe's EarthCorp enemies! he knew immediately.

Blunt and utterly functional, the black suits lacked the grace of the Commonwealth's Japanese-influenced armor. The first soldier wielded a power sword as straight and practical as the armor. The other struck the sword from Fragger's stinging hands with a weapon the Ranger could only stare at in astonishment.

It was a mace with a studded head and pulsing from whatever power source energized the weapon. His skull vibrated from the weapon's energy output. Fragger guessed it could be used either to disrupt armor somehow or simply to mash an unprotected head as if it were no more than a marshmallow.

Oh well, he decided as the soldier swung the mace high again, *after I'm dead, I won't give a shit how I died.*

He closed his eyes again and waited for the killing blow.

Instead, he found himself lifted into the air, slung over the shoulder of the first soldier, and hauled out into the corridor as the mace-wielder ran ahead and cleared Imperial Commonwealth soldiers from the path with great sweeps of his weapon. Bouncing up and down hard on the armored shoulder, Fragger found himself nauseated. Rounds from pursuing Imperial Commonwealth troopers struck all around them, pinging off the bulkheads as the Ranger desperately wished someone would hook him back up to the interrogation machine.

The two EarthCorp soldiers skidded to a halt before a hatch. As one of them worked to open it, the other jerked Fragger's head around so the Ranger was looking directly into the dark helmet. The soldier pointed at a spot on the helmet where the ears would be, then grabbed one of Fragger's ears, indicating he should listen. Fragger shouted, "I can't hear!" His own words sounded like a faint whisper to his stunned hearing. The soldier nodded, paused for moment, and then his amplified words cut through Fragger's deafness. "If you want to live, expel all the air in your lungs!"

The command didn't make any sense, but Fragger carried it out. In the next second, the hatch was opened, and, along with the two soldiers, he was sucked out into open space.

CHAPTER 5

For a moment, Fragger thought he was back in the embrace of Emily, his first wife. She'd frozen him solid as a block of ice as a way of telling him she'd had an affair with Lieutenant Dantly in revenge for all his whoring. Oddly, the thought cheered him as the stars revolved around his head with dizzying speed.

Damn, this isn't so bad. Space isn't half so cold as a pissed-off wife. If I die, what a way to go! My buddies would get a yuk out of this! Fragger Sparks butt naked in outer space!

The Ranger wanted to laugh. A gloved hand clamped over his mouth and prevented that deadly urge. At the same time, the spinning stopped. A quick burst of acceleration thrust them toward the open hatch of a small, dark vessel shaped like a bayonet with a serrated blade. In a few seconds, they were inside the ship. One of the soldiers pressed an orange button, causing the air lock door to slide shut with such speed the Ranger was glad he hadn't been in its way--it would have sliced him in two. Just as quickly, the inner hatch opened, and the soldier threw him in onto the deck. Fragger rolled onto his back, gratefully drawing in deep and ragged breaths until his lungs no longer felt like they were ready to burst. The two soldiers removed their helmets and stood impatiently over him while he recovered.

Both men had the tough look of combat soldiers. One was black. He had a bald head, a square jaw and a flared nose separating belligerent brown eyes that seemed to regard the Ranger as a bug to be squashed. The other was white with blue eyes, a brush of red hair atop a bullet-shaped skull, and a hawk nose beaten out of shape by combat or brawling. His gaze said he considered Fragger to be several levels below the opinion of his comrade. The attitudes pissed the Ranger off to the point where he gave them the finger and said, "Fuck you and the horse you rode in on!"

The soldiers obviously didn't understand the exact, obscene reference he'd made, but they recognized an insult when they heard one. They jerked Fragger to his feet, frog-marched him through several corridors, then tossed him roughly into a brig. The bald one pointed at a bunk.

"Lie down," he ordered.

"What for?" Fragger asked, unable to stop shivering from his exposure to space.

"Just lie down and strap in."

"For more torture? Screw you!"

“We don’t have time for this,” the soldier said and nodded at his companion. “Grab him, Red.”

The two men gripped Fragger with the vise-like hands of their suits and slammed him down into the bunk, securing his body with straps. Red poked a finger up at a blinking orange sign on the wall.

"Jump in two minutes."

"Jump?" Fragger asked. "Jump where?"

"Hyperspace jump, stupid!" Red replied.

"What's that?"

"Never mind, Rerun," the bald soldier said. "We're just going somewhere real fast using the Drive. You'll handle it better with this."

The soldier produced a needle from somewhere and stuck it in the Ranger's arm. Then both men walked out of the room, and the door slid shut behind them.

Fragger tested the restraints and realized he wouldn’t be going anywhere--not that he had anyplace to escape to. He tried to calm his mind, but couldn't help wonder about the “jump” the soldiers were talking about. In a moment, he didn't really care. Whatever drug he'd been given, it was fast. Fragger felt wonderfully relaxed until, like an overly fussy snake, the universe swallowed him up and vomited him back out again.

CHAPTER 6

Fragger felt like a piece of shit.

Ten shivering tons of it, the Ranger amended as he opened his eyes in sockets that had been lubricated with sand while he was unconscious. Every bone in his body was dialing up pain central.

Did these guys thrash the hell out of me while I wasn't looking? he wondered.

It felt just like a beating—nausea, weakness, dizziness, pain and the desire to go someplace far, far away where there was peace and contentment.

An itch on his shoulder maddened him, and Fragger attempted to scratch it. A strap brought his effort up short. He swore as he craned his neck up from the bunk to check the condition of his body.

Jesus, still naked, and my skin is red as a beet! Now, where the hell did that come from? Maybe I reacted with that drug.

Fragger woke again to an ashen-faced Red staggering through the door with a cup in hand. Out of his space suit, the trooper appeared to be auditioning for the role of Incredible Hulk. The massive shoulders straining the khaki uniform gave his head the look of a SABOT round that had shot through his body and lodged atop his body without exploding. The crooked raptor nose and cauliflower ears made it appear as if three of the stabilizing vanes of the projectile had deformed upon impact. A jaw hard as a shell casing chewed at something foul smelling as the trooper stooped to undo the straps holding Fragger down.

"Damn, man!" Fragger complained as the odor rolled over him. "What are you eating?"

"What's it to you?" Red shot back in a voice that sounded like a stump grinder. "Sit up."

"It smells like garlic and onions with swamp gas mixed in."

"It's just *gark*, Rerun."

"What's that?"

"You didn't have *gark* in your time? No, of course not. Well, I guess the closest thing in your time would have been coca leaves. It grows on my home planet, Rockpile. Keeps you from getting hungry when there's no food around—which happens a lot at home—and keeps you mellow. Here, drink this. It'll help overcome the effects."

Fragger sniffed at the cup Red handed to him and wrinkled his nose. "Damn, this smells worth than your breath."

"Drink it, or I'll stuff it up your ass, and you can drink it backwards. For a Rerun, you got an uppity attitude."

"What effects am I trying to get rid of by swallowing?" the Ranger asked as he took a sip of the liquid. He grimaced at the flavor. The liquid tasted and looked like someone had cut tar with a paint thinner, but he drank it all. A few seconds later, colored lights illuminated the inside of his head as if an evil carnival had set up camp on his brain.

"I told you before!" Red said in irritable tones. "The effects. Of the jump. Hyperspace."

"What's that?"

"What's hyperspace? Faster than light travel, moron. You know, jumping between planets and systems."

"No, I don't know," Fragger responded in equally irritable tones, handing the cup back. The vile-smelling liquid worked fast and well—only half the bones in his body ached now-- but left his tongue feeling as it had just been paved with fresh asphalt.

"You're as dumb as the day is long, ain't you?" Red said.

"Smart enough to admit I don't know everything."

"You Reruns, man, you're ignorant, that's for sure."

Fragger let Red run on about the stupidity of revived soldiers while his body continued its recovery. It seemed to be a common, if aggravating, way for the trooper to pass the time. When Red's monologue got too tedious, Fragger broke in by asking, "You feel like this after every one of these hyperspace jumps?"

Red was visibly miffed at the interruption, but answered, "It don't get any easier, that's for sure."

"Where are we now?"

"Damned if I can tell, Rerun. When they want us to know, they'll give us a briefing. Away from the fight, that's for sure. Them Ricer troopers can't find us now."

"'Ricers'? Why do you call them that?"

"Because that's all those vacuum-heads eat—rice. And because it fits the oh-so-grand name of their miserable nation--the Royal and Imperial Commonwealth of something or other."

"Why won't they find us?" Fragger asked.

"Because we're a standard minimum of two light years away, that's why. They ain't got a clue which way we went."

Tired of sitting on the edge of the bunk, Fragger shifted his body to lean back against the bulkhead. The action brought a yelp out of his mouth.

"Damn, my skin is on fire all over. What happened?"

Red laughed. "Ain't nothing more than a bad sunburn from radiation in open space. You're going to peel, Rerun, leave skin all over this place. And you're lucky skin is all you lost. Not many troops could pull that stunt off, but Hakeem and me did. We brought you across in one piece. Good thing you were so easy to handle. I swear you just about hyperspaced yourself across the vacuum into the hatch. That scared, hunh?"

"Wouldn't you be?" Fragger grumbled.

Red ignored Fragger's response, pursuing a line of thought that obviously pleased him more than thinking about the question just posed. "May be a stripe in this for Hakeem and me. Might make sergeant at last."

Fragger decided to bolster the hope for a promotion. Although there seemed to be a steely tenacity to the man, Red didn't strike him as the brightest of EarthCorp's soldiers. A little flattery might provide a lot of information. Red was a motormouth already. It was simply a matter of directing the conversation in the right direction.

"Hey, I hope you get that stripe, man."

"Thanks," Red said, beaming with pride that was interrupted with sudden suspicion. "Wait a minute. What do you care? You're nothing but a Rerun."

"I may be a Rerun, but I was a soldier in my day—a Sergeant First Class —so I know what it takes to earn a stripe. A lot of hard work, that's what it takes. Plus, you saved me from that bastard Ricer interrogator, didn't you? You're a real professional. I would have been proud to have you in my unit because you're obviously a soldier who can be counted on when the enemy wants to put your balls in a vise."

Red grinned. "Ain't no higher praise than that."

"You earned it. Of course, you might have had a tougher time of it back on Earth in my day."

"What are you talking about?"

Fragger feigned a reluctance to deliver bad news. "I don't know if I should tell you. You might not like the answer."

Red snorted. "Do I look like I can't handle the truth?"

"You sure?"

"Yes, damn it!"

Fragger sighed. 'Well, Red, it was *real* fighting back then."

Red arched an eyebrow at this information. "What do you mean—*real* fighting?"

"Without those pussy suits you guys wear."

"'Pussy?'"

"Yeah. You know, protection that *real* soldiers don't need. We fought hand to hand, took it to the enemy personally."

For a moment, Fragger was afraid his implied insult would detonate Red's shell-shaped head. "Suits ain't pussy, Rerun!" Red said with heat. "You ever faced the blade or a spear? They run you right through if you ain't good."

"Kiddy shit!"

"What?"

"You heard me," the Ranger said. "Games for kids to play. Last Iraqi—last enemy—I took out, I killed eyeball-to-eyeball with my bare hands—no weapons."

Inwardly, Fragger shuddered. It was no lie. The Iraqi had come out of the trench and damned near cut his throat. Only the sixth sense developed from many years of combat had saved his life.

He'd flipped the man over his head, taken the knife away, and plunged it deep into his enemy's heart.

"So what?" Red said. "All of us fight man to man, too. We got to wear suits. Bugs or chemicals get us otherwise."

Fragger gave a contemptuous snort. "Kiddy shit," he repeated. "We were the real soldiers back then."

He leaned toward Red and asked, "Do you know how I know that?"

"I know you don't know shit, Rerun, that's what I know."

Fragger spread his hands wide and shrugged. "Okay, if you don't want to know...."

"All right, all right! What makes you think you were better soldiers than we are?"

"Because everybody keeps trying to save my hairy hide, that's why. That must mean I'm something special, right?"

"I don't know. Maybe," Red admitted.

"And there isn't but one reason for your superiors to raise me from the dead, is there? They want the toughest soldiers around. That's me."

"You don't look so tough, now," Red said. "You look like a ripping lobster."

"Hey, you ever been naked in space?"

"No."

"You ever take out a Ricer armored trooper with your bare hands?"

Red's eyes opened wide at this remark before narrowing back into slits. "You're really full of it, aren't you, Rerun?"

"How about two?"

"What!"

"I did," Fragger lied. "Took them right out."

"Oh yeah, how?"

The Ranger tapped his head meaningfully. "Brains and speed, that's how. Took a power sword away from one and cut the other one's head off."

The lie sounded appropriately gory to Fragger. In reality, he couldn't imagine any way to defeat a single soldier in powered armor, let alone two.

For a moment, admiration crept into Red's eyes. It was swept away by a sudden realization.

"Hey, Rerun, you almost had me for a moment! But you're jacking me bad now. If you just got revived, how the hell could you have fought one Ricer trooper, let alone two?"

Oops! Think fast! Fragger cursed, then he remembered the HELOT, Harada, and Watanabe and the interrogation Red and his companion had interrupted.

"You saw my Ricer victims. Don't you believe your own eyes?"

"What are you talking about?"

"You saw me back on the HELOT, remember?"

"Yeah, sure, but the grenade I threw in the room--"

"Didn't do a thing, except stun me. Lucky for you, by the way. If you'd killed me, you'd probably be cleaning latrines from here to…wherever. Now, think a little harder about that situation. Do grenades cut heads off cleanly?"

"No."

"Was there a head on the floor when you burst in?"

"Yeah."

"Where was the power sword?"

"In your hand."

"There was another man in that room, too, wasn't there? And where was he?"

"But I thought the gren--."

"Like I said, your grenade didn't do squat. I'd put both men down before you even got into the room."

"Aw, rip you, man. You're full of shit," Red protested, but the Ranger saw confusion creep into his eyes, so he pressed his advantage.

"If I'm so full of crap, Red, how come everybody's going to so much trouble for me?" He gestured around the cell. "How many people get their own personal escort out of trouble? A ship like this—it must be for special people."

His face showing obvious relief at being able to move on to a subject that didn't give him so much difficulty, Red nodded enthusiastically, "The *Lethal.* A Dagger class corvette. It's all speed and minimal armament. First time I been on one. Better than any HELOT, that's for sure. Don't stink like troop quarters do."

"Must usually be for brass," Fragger suggested in a sympathetic tone. "Brass can afford not to stink. They're not on the front lines getting their hands dirty."

"Ain't it the truth?" the soldier agreed. "This is good duty. You can even eat the food."

The more things change, the more they stay the same, the Ranger thought in amusement. *Even six centuries into the future, all you have to do is give a grunt good food and a clean bunk, and he's happy.*

"You didn't answer my question," he reminded Red.

"What? About you being special? Well, you're just a Rerun, so you ain't nothing special."

"In other words, you don't know a thing."

"Hey, I know as much as the next trooper!"

Well, that answers my question for sure, Fragger thought in frustration. *The only thing the average soldier knows is scuttlebutt—and half of it he's made up himself.*

"I heard something from big Stack Wembly, though," Red said as if prompted by Fragger's thoughts.

"Who's Wembly?"

"First Sergeant. He's the Top. In on all the latest scuzz."

Feigning disbelief, Fragger said, "Yeah, sure."

"He is," Red insisted.

Fragger kept his mouth shut. Sometimes silence was the best way to get the answers you needed.

"Stack says we jumped to near 70 Virginis and are headed to Goldilocks."

Startled by a familiar name, the Ranger asked, "Goldilocks?"

"Yeah, big planet."

"How big?"

"Huge."

Fragger could think of only one planet for comparison and asked, "Bigger than Jupiter?"

Red laughed at his ignorance. "Only about eight times more mass."

"You're bullshitting me."

"I'm doing what?"

"You're just making this stuff up, Red. You don't really know," Fragger explained.

"Damned if I don't! I got it straight from Stack Wembly," Red said with the massive indignation only a grunt could muster when challenged. "He has to know his stuff. If we drop onto a planet and he doesn't know his stuff, we buy quick graves."

"Okay, okay, sorry I doubted you," Fragger said to placate Salinsky.

"Stack says average surface temp is around 45 degrees."

"Sounds like a pretty decent place."

Red stared at him. "You're kidding, right?"

"Why would I do that? Back on Earth, that was comfortable."

"You're nuts, Rerun. Ain't a human being who can stand that temperature long unsuited."

Fragger stared back at the soldier, then realized his mistake and asked, "Are we talking Celsius here?"

"Of course. What else would we be talking?"

Fahrenheit, Fragger thought. He did a quick conversion and came up with an approximate number. *Jesus, we're talking around 120 degrees!*

"How in the world did such a hellhole get a name like Goldilocks?" he asked.

"Old Terran terminology, Stack tells me. Something about it's not too close to its sun and yet not too far."

Fragger's head whirled at the idea of a planet eight times the size of Jupiter with ungodly high temperatures. To stop the confusion threatening to overwhelm his thoughts, he concentrated on the here-and-now. "Stack? What kind of name is that?"

A low, wicked chuckle answered his question. "It's a name he earned, you better believe. When Wembly goes into battle, the bodies stack up in front of him."

"That good, huh?"

"Good? Good don't half cover it. Over 40 drops..."

"And not a scratch on my armor," a voice said from behind them. It was so deep it made Fragger think of the freight train rumble of heavy artillery shells passing overhead. He looked up at the door. At the sight of the man, the words involuntarily escaped his lips.

"My God!"

CHAPTER 7

"Top!" Red said as he snapped to attention.

Fragger tried to get his eyes around Stack Wembly. The only thought his mind could hold was, *He's bigger than a soldier's boast. All muscle, all hard purpose.*

Dressed in the dark EarthCorp uniform, the man was a planet unto himself. Crew-cut black hair, piggy eyes, broken nose, and battering-ram jaw --Wembly was a poster boy for a First Sergeant.

"You been flapping your gums again, haven't you, Salinsky?" Wembly accused.

"Just talking, that's all, Top."

"To a Rerun? Wasting your breath, that's all you're doing! They don't last long enough to be worth the time."

"But I like hearing about the ancient days," Red protested weakly.

"You know what you're going to hear about? You're going to hear about your suit not being up to spec, that's what you're going to hear about!" Wembly snarled. "Last drop we made, you lost weapons power way too fast. That tells me you didn't check your fusion cells. You're gonna get your armored ass kicked past orbit if you don't follow procedures. Now snap back to the armory."

Salinsky hurried out of the room. The First Sergeant turned his attention to Fragger. "Here," he said, offering clothes and boots. "Put these fatigues on. Then follow me"

Fragger grabbed the black uniform and put it on with relief--for a moment.

"Shit!" he swore.

"What's the problem Rerun?"

"Sunburn. This uniform scrapes like mad. What's it made out of?"

"Garbage, like you," the First Sergeant and pointed at the door.

"Hey, up yours, you ugly sonuvabitch!" the Ranger shot back.

The itching was maddening, but in the next moment, he forgot all about the irritation caused by the fatigues. Wembly bellied him hard him up into a bulkhead and squashed his snout straight against Fragger's nose. Then, the First Sergeant farted, a giant ripping noise the Ranger was sure would have torn the pants off an ordinary man.

"You smell that, Rerun? My farts are bigger than you are and smell better too. You mouth off to me again, and I'll see to it that your short, new life is so miserable you'll be sorry you were reborn. Do you understand me?"

It's nice to see some of the old tricks are still in use, Fragger thought as Wembly's bulk crushed him. *Getting your face into somebody's personal space always worked for me. Oh, well, give as good as you get. I can do the unexpected too.*

Shrugging off the disgust, he planted a kiss on the reddened face of the non-com.

Wembly jerked back, spitting and wiping his mouth in revulsion.

"You son of three whores!" the First Sergeant swore and raised his fist.

"Sorry, but I had to kiss you, Top."

"What? Why?"

"You don't have any balls. That means you must be a woman, and every woman deserves a kiss."

Wembly drive a fist straight into Fragger's belly. The Ranger gagged and doubled over. Only the satisfaction that he'd cracked the First Sergeant's hardass control cut through the pain. A meaty hand jerked Fragger erect. Wembly marched him by the collar out of the room and down the corridor. Troopers flattened themselves against the sides as the two passed, and Fragger didn't have to guess it was the look on the non-com's face that was doing the flattening.

It sure isn't me, he thought, fighting the nausea caused by Wembly's blow. *I must be one pathetic sight.*

Wembly stopped outside a door marked "INTEL" and spoke a command. When the door slid open, the First Sergeant shoved Fragger through and followed him inside.

"Captain Bryne, the Rerun!" Wembly announced, then ordered Fragger, "Come to attention."

The Ranger obeyed, not because he wanted to but because he was going to show the sonuvabitch who the tough one in the room was. Then, a voice, chillingly quiet, cut through his façade.

"What did you tell the Ricers, Rerun?"

An officer, with a beefy face and balding head, sat behind a desk in a tailored uniform. He had the look all interrogators had--one of infinite patience and the false mask of finding the whole process more painful than the prisoner.

Fragger answered, "I didn't tell them anything because I don't know anything. You know that as well as I do."

Wembly poked a finger hard into Fragger's kidney area and prompted, "Say 'Sir' when you're talking to an officer."

"Sir."

"I'll ask you again. What did they find out?" the captain demanded.

"What they found out is that you wanted me back real bad," Fragger answered. "They were using some kind of interrogation machine on me when Salinsky and the other guy rolled a concussion grenade into the room and interrupted the whole process."

Captain Bryne looked at Wembly. "Does that track, First Sergeant?"

"It does, Captain."

"Very well, then. Rerun, we have our machines too. On Goldilocks, we'll find out what we need to know."

Hell, these guys don't know what makes me special, either! Fragger realized. *Probably the project was so secret that few people knew about it. Trust the military to not let the right hand know what the left one is doing.*

The Ranger shivered at the thought of another interrogation by machine. *There's no withstanding the damned things, and you can't fight the addiction. You can't--"*

"Wait a minute!" he said out loud in spite of himself.

"For what?" the officer asked.

"You can't do this to me!" Fragger said to cover his realization. *I don't feel any addiction! Watanabe said it was permanent. Is that what Leery was trying to accomplish—make people resistant to their machines?*

"I'm afraid we can," Captain Bryne said.

"The Geneva Conventions--"

"The what?"

"The Geneva Conventions state that a prisoner of war should be treated with respect and—"

"Shut up!" Wembly commanded, jabbing him in the side again.

Captain Bryne said, "I don't know what the Geneva Conventions are, but you're a Rerun, not a prisoner of war. Now, you were about to complete a thought. What-"

To keep the interrogator away that thought, Fragger blurted out, "Did you know, sir, that First Sergeant Wembly is a very good kisser?"

Bryne raised an eyebrow toward the First Sergeant. Wembly rewarded Fragger's joke by delivering a single powerful blow to the temple. The Ranger dropped to the deck, feeling like somebody had put his head under a pile driver.

Before he lost consciousness, a single thought about his action floated through his head and out the hole Wembly had apparently punched into his skull.

It was a smart move, Jon-boy, but you've never had one that hurt worse.

CHAPTER 8

Wembly shook Fragger awake with a rough hand. The Ranger didn't appreciate it in the least.

"You want another kiss, you sonuvabitch?" he warned the First Sergeant, not caring whether the big non-com hit him again or not. His head couldn't hurt any worse than it already did.

Wembly shook him again, and this time Fragger was really hacked off. He opened his eyes, ready to cuss the First Sergeant up one side and down the other.

Nobody was there.

He was strapped down again in the brig, the only person in the room. Wembly wasn't doing any shaking. It was the ship itself, violently yawing about. Noise shrieked outside the hull while the Ranger fought to keep the contents of his stomach where they belonged.

Secured to the bunk, there was nothing Fragger could do about whatever was going on but ride it out. Soon after the flight smoothed, the cell door banged open and a green-faced Salinsky staggered into the room.

"Damn, but I hate re-entries like that," Red complained. "I'd rather suit-drop, anytime. At least, you have your own control then and don't have to rely on some idiot pilot who thinks it's fun to fly through a storm."

"We're landing on Goldilocks?" Fragger asked.

The trooper nodded and seemed to regret the motion. He steadied himself against the wall with one hand and covered his mouth with the other before answering.

"Clear of the storm for now, anyway," Red finally explained. "This bloody planet is nothing but one big hurricane, that's what I hear. We should touch down in about 30 minutes."

"What's it look like?"

Red shrugged. "Never been here. Not much to see, I guess. It's like a big steam bath. According to Stack, visibility is close to zero most of the time."

"Goldilocks sounds like a hellhole. Why put a facility here?" Fragger asked.

"You just answered your own question, Rerun. A hellhole is perfect for prisoners, isn't it? You want to escape, go ahead. You'll end up a boiled potato. Plus, the enemy couldn't find this place in a million years. That always means the brass is doing something they don't want the Ricers--or anybody else--to know about."

Great, Fragger grumbled. *The future seems to be a great place for sadists and intel spooks.*

Red undid the straps and helped Fragger to his feet although he was nearly as unsteady as the Ranger himself. They wobbled toward the door.

"We make a fine pair," Fragger said.

"Not for long. There's two interrogators waiting for you out in the corridor," the trooper informed him with the relieved cheerfulness of a man who was glad he was not about to undergo what Fragger would experience.

Gestapo! was Fragger's first thought when Salinsky released his arm outside the door and he saw the two waiting officers. *In every picture I've seen from World War II, they all have the same dead faces and eyes and the mouths pursed in everlasting smug superiority. All they need is a Death's Head emblem, and they'd be the same as the kraut creeps. These guys have never seen a minute of combat in their lives. They probably wash their hands 50 times a day and still don't get the blood off. Well, I might as well get my licks in now and prove they're not the supermen they think they are.*

Fragger kicked the taller one straight in the knee and put a fist deep into gut of the other one, dropping both men. He waited for Red Salinsky to return the favor and put him down hard. Instead, the trooper grabbed him roughly around the neck and hauled him back. Fragger swore he heard a snicker under the man's breath and thought with some satisfaction, *When you're a torturer, nobody's your friend!*

Fragger braced against the retribution he knew was coming. The taller man--*Meitz* was the name stitched onto his uniform--rose first, rubbing hard at his knee. Meitz looked down at his gagging companion, then glared at Fragger and drew a baton from a loop in his wide belt.

"Corporal Salinsky, release the prisoner unless you wish to share in the charge I'll put through this Rerun's body." Meitz had a voice wet with anticipation.

"Get up, Meissner, and charge your goad," Meitz ordered his partner.

Panic paddled around in the Ranger's stomach, splashing acid into his throat.

A man who looked like he'd been born with a smirk, Meissner obeyed, and both men pushed studs in the handles of their weapons. A shrill hum filled the corridor as the goads shimmered in a rapid vibratory pattern.

Some variation on the powered weapons I've seen, Fragger guessed, striving to keep his mind focused on anything but the pain to come.

Salinsky released him, and the two interrogators backed the Ranger up against the bulkhead. Meitz dropped his baton low, leaving no doubt about where he intended to strike first.

"You don't even know what this is, do you, Rerun?" the interrogator asked. His voice had the hiss of steam escaping under pressure.

"I know what it isn't," Fragger answered.

"Tell me," Meitz said.

"It isn't your dick. It's way too big. In fact, I don't think you have a dick at all, that's why you're in the business you're in."

"Funny," the interrogator responded. "But not funny enough to prevent an application of juice to your sense of humor."

Fragger tensed again, but managed to say, "A little electricity, I can handle that."

A smirk lit up Meitz's dismal face. "No electricity. Fusion power, fusion power applied in microbursts--or macrobursts if you don't cooperate and tell us what you know. The power of the sun, just for you and your sensitive nerve endings."

"I can't tell you what I don't know," Fragger said. "I'm a Rerun, remember? How can I tell you anything? The Ricers didn't get squat from me with their machine, and you won't, either."

The interrogator regarded this news with sudden interest. "They hooked you up?"

Fragger nodded.

"And you claim they didn't come up with a single bit of information?"

"They were interrupted by Red and his buddy."

"Do you know what level they applied to him?" Meitz asked Salinsky.

The trooper shook his head and answered, "It was all too quick. We had to grab him and run."

"Any signs of addiction?" the interrogator asked.

"Not a one," Salinsky answered.

Meitz gave Fragger an appraising look. "Then, Sergeant, either you interrupted the process early on, or this man is lying to us and is resistant to cortical addiction. Which is it, Rerun?"

"How the hell should I know?" Fragger lied.

Meissner spoke for the first time. "It's not likely he'd be resistant. It's a rare occurrence."

"Yes," Meitz agreed, "but possible. It could be one reason why the Ricers kept a Rerun beyond the usual time before assignment or termination."

The interrogator dropped his baton. "No damage for now, Rerun. We're going to treat you as gently as the Ricers did until we determine your value to EarthCorp."

Fragger sagged against the wall in relief, then straightened convulsively as Meitz drove the goad into his groin area and triggered a burst. The Ranger tried to scream, but the pain froze the sound deep in his throat. It felt as if the interrogator had triggered a claymore between his legs--ball bearings of agony burst in every direction throughout his body. He clutched at his scrotum and tried to squeeze the burn away.

"Just a taste," Meitz said. "You'll cooperate now, won't you?"

Fragger fought to say no, but shook his head in the affirmative.

"And no more smart remarks, either?"
Fragger whimpered. It was all he could do.

CHAPTER 9

Salinsky supported Fragger as they followed the two interrogators down a long corridor. Attempting to take his mind off the pain seeking exit through every nerve in his body, the Ranger stole glances at the windows lining the passageway like portholes in a ship. There was nothing to see but a swirling white mist and drops of moisture on the glass

Just like Red described it, Fragger realized. *A big steam bath. No escape in that direction.*

Meitz and Meissner interrupted his thoughts on the subject by banging open a door and motioning the men in. Salinsky dragged Fragger across the room and plunked him down in a plain plastic chair. Meitz wasted no time.

"Are you resistant to the Ricers' interrogator program, Rerun?"

"Yes," Fragger said, thinking, *And that half-truth is all you'll ever get out of me, you descendant of a Gestapo whore!*

"How?"

"Hell, I don't know! I wake up six centuries into the future to find barbarians cutting each other's heads off and screwing with minds, and I don't even know where I am or why I'm here! I haven't got a clue, and you know it!"

Meitz offered a smile as brittle as rotten ice. "Finished? Feel better? Now, try again--how are you resistant?"

"I don't know, damn it!"

"Think about it," Meitz prompted.

"What do you mean?"

"When the program was running in your head, what was it about?"

"Sex. It was all mixed up, but it was about sex and my mother and--it was sick."

"Standard pain-pleasure program," Meissner said.

"And you loved it, didn't you, Rerun?" Meitz asked.

"Yes," Fragger answered as faint thrills of joy and disgust shivered through his body.

Meitz persisted. "They must have talked to you before the standard interrogation procedure. What did they say?"

"They thought I might have some special abilities, but didn't seem convinced of it. They sent me to interrogation to find out what they are."

Fragger watched puzzled glances pass between the two interrogators and realized, *These guys don't know any more about what Leery was up to on Khanwat than I do.*

"Okay," Meitz said, "I think you're telling the truth, but there's one way to make sure."

Fragger glanced involuntarily at the baton hanging by the interrogator's side.

Meitz laughed. "No goad this time. We have our own programs. Better than the Ricers. You'll see." He turned to his partner and ordered, "Set up the equipment." Then, he turned back to Fragger.

"We're going to take you up to the addiction level, Rerun. We'll see just how resistant you are. But we won't addict you to sex or love or your mother."

Meitz paused. A nasty chuckle escaped his lips.

"Okay, I'll bite. What's so funny? What will I be addicted to?" Fragger asked nervously.

"To me, Rerun, to me," Meitz answered.

CHAPTER 10

Twenty dreams ago, that was when Fragger knew he'd fallen in love with Interrogator Meitz. Oh, it wasn't really love in the carnal sense. He was no more gay than the interrogator was a bad man. It was just the kind of love a son has for his father, manly, good love, the kind of love that made you willing to walk into battle or hell itself with such a man by your side, the type of man who deserved total loyalty, the kind of man you would die for.

"You're doing well, Fragger," Interrogator Meitz said.

The Ranger beamed with pride at the praise as he lovingly studied every chiseled feature of Meitz's face. He was a man who had looks any movie star would envy.

"Are you willing to help me get to the bottom of this mystery?" the interrogator asked.

"Of course, anything I can do!"

"Good. Now, think back from the time you were awakened on the planet. Do you remember anything unusual?"

"Oh, everything was unusual, very unusual."

"I know," Meitz said sympathetically. "It must have all been strange, but I'm here for you. I'm here to guide you safely through all those memories."

"Thank you, thank you!"

"When you woke up, who was there?"

"A Revival Technician. His name was Leery."

"What did he say to you?"

Fragger concentrated hard on the memory. He very much wanted to please Interrogator Meitz. "He talked to me, trying to use the slang of my day. It sounded silly."

"I'll bet it did," the interrogator's smooth voice encouraged him.

"Leery was very nervous. With good reason, too. This samurai came blasting through a window and had us dead to rights."

"The RT tried to protect you?" Meitz asked.

"No, he tried to kill me! It was the Imperial Commonwealth warrior who protected me. He sliced Leery's head off with one of those Japanese style swords they used to call *katanas*."

"What?" the interrogator said.

Fragger felt an instant anxiety. "Did I do something wrong?"

"No, no," Interrogator Meitz assured him. "What was the trooper's name?"

"One of those odd Japanese ones--Watanabe."

"What was his rank?"

"Sergeant."

"What happened then?"

"I guess Watanabe stuffed me in a capsule and shot me up into space to the..Hel...that ship."

"HELOT," Meitz kindly spelled out the designation to ease Fragger's frustration. "It's a heavy-lift orbital troop carrier. The Spartan System specializes in building them for the great fleets of the galaxy."

"Some carrier," the Ranger said with admiration. "It's huge."

"What happened when you got into the ship?" the interrogator urged.

"They took me to an officer. A woman."

"What was her name and rank?"

"She's a Major...a Major...Shim....Shimazu, that was her name. Mean as a pissed-off cobra."

"How do you know this?" Meitz asked. "Did she do something to you?"

"No, I can just tell, that's all. It was those eyes. I've seen that look before."

"What look is that?"

Fragger searched for exactly the right words, eager to please the Interrogator. "Nothing behind them, you know what I mean? Somebody who's been in combat too long."

"What did she ask?"

"Same kind of questions you're asking. Mainly, she was curious, just like you, about why Leery would want to kill a Rerun before enemy soldiers got their hands on him."

"Good, good! Now, let's go back to that very question, Fragger. Think hard on it because I'd really, really like an answer to it, and I know you'll do your best to give me what I need."

"Oh, yes!"

"What made you so important that the tech would try to liquidate you so a Ricer samurai couldn't make a capture?"

Fragger strained for an answer, frantically ransacking his memory for a clue--anything--to provide the interrogator the information he needed. There was nothing. He groaned in frustration, feeling the veins in his temples bulge into an avalanche of pain that threatened to slide down from his head and bury his worthless heart in the rubble of his inability to satisfy Meitz's reasonable request. It was agony. It was--

"Easy, easy," the interrogator said, instantly erasing the hurt with the soothing voice of a father who cared deeply about his son. "You don't have the answer right now. I understand. I understand. But you will keep trying to find that information for me, won't you, Fragger?"

"Yes, definitely!"

"You won't forget, will you?" Meitz asked in a gently chiding tone.

"Never!"

"I believe you. You've done well. Now, it's time for some rest. You've earned it. I'm proud of you."

Relief and pride swirled in Fragger's mind as he watched Meitz and Meissner walk out of the room together, gesturing at each other. The Ranger didn't know what they were talking about, but he did know one thing for sure.

He loved Interrogator Meitz.

CHAPTER 11

Red Salinsky woke the Ranger. Fragger didn't have to open his eyes to know who it was. The smell of *gark* mugged the air in the room. Fragger had no idea why Red bothered to key in the entry code because the Ranger was convinced Salinsky's breath alone would pry open the cell door.

"Get your ass up, Rerun. Breakfast," Red barked.

Fragger winced at the irritable tone before squinting at the tray the frowning corporal held. It was the usual. Gray Rerun gruel and a glass of water.

Fragger groaned, swung his feet off the bunk and sat up. Immediately, he regretted the action. His head throbbed like a fibrillating heart. "Damn, that hurts," he complained.

"Tough."

"What's your problem today, Red?"

"You. You're always the problem."

"Hell, I'm your problem everyday, and I haven't heard you complain before, so the trouble's not coming from my direction."

Red let the scowl on his face relax and admitted, "Yeah, you're right. Captain Hilger is on my ass again. "

"Officers!" Fragger commiserated.

"Bastards," Red agreed. "Can't ever do shit details themselves. Got new troops coming in and they need space we ain't got, maintenance is behind, my desk has disappeared beneath rosters and….oh, hell, I don't know what else."

""Sorry," Fragger said, trying hard to muster up sympathy for the complaining corporal and failing miserably at the task. "Do you think you could manage to answer a question for me in spite of all your trouble today?"

"You want to know why your head hurts?"

"Yeah."

"Soft interrogation."

"What are you talking about?"

Red sighed with exaggerated forbearance. "You don't remember, do you? They never do."

"Remember what, damn it?"

"Meitz's signature treatment. The interrogator put you under and asked you lots of questions."

"Oh, shit! Am I addicted to something now?"

"Love, probably, if Meitz employed his favorite tactic," Red answered, putting the tray on the bare plastic table next to the bunk.

"What?"

"Never mind. You'll find out. Eat your chow. We have to be out of here by 0630."

Fragger tried futilely to rub the ache out of his head. "More interrogation?"

"Nope. I told you I'm behind today. Captain Hilger said to get some work out of you while they decide on how to handle your situation. Hey, that's good news for you on two counts. First of all, it means they're keeping you alive."

"Big of them. What's the second count?"

"You're going with me to the armory."

"What's good about that, Red?"

"You are ignorant, aren't you, Rerun?"

"So you keep telling me."

"Most of your kind, they automatically assign to a labor squad."

"That's bad?"

"Damned straight. That means you do jobs outside the dome."

"But you said it averages 120 degrees on this planet!"

"Nope, I said about 45 degrees."

Fragger cursed inwardly at his inability to think in Celsius. "Okay, 45 degrees then. Nobody could stand that kind of temperature for long."

"Too true," Red agreed, "but they condition you first and work you in short shifts, kind of like they were supposed to have done in the diamond mines back on Terra. That means Reruns, convicts and the like last longer."

"How long?"

Red shrugged. "Don't know the figures. The longest I've seen is six months. If the heat and humidity don't get you, then the winds will. Blow you away in a heartbeat. Pick you up and never put you down."

"You've seen this?" Fragger asked.

"Me, no! That's strictly Rerun duty for guards. But I hear the scuzz. Reruns like to complain a lot."

I can't imagine why, the Ranger thought sourly as he spooned down the bland cereal and drank the tepid water.

"So, the armory is good duty, then, relatively speaking?" he asked.

"Yeah, as long as you keep your mouth shut and do your job and do it well. Troopers are real particular about the condition of their power suits."

"I'll be doing maintenance?"

Red nodded.

"What's involved in taking care of the suits?"

"It's easier to show you than explain it," the corporal answered. "Come on."

Fragger followed Red out and down a long corridor. After five minutes of walking, they cycled through a lock into the biggest room the Ranger had seen in the installation. It had a transparent dome, apparently made of the same material that Watanabe had sliced through in the Khanwati installation when he'd killed Leery and taken Fragger.

But much thicker from the looks of it, Fragger decided, hurriedly examining the 100-foot high structure as he followed in Salinsky's quick footsteps. Outside, thick mist rolled and boiled at the peak of the structure while allowing a shaft of weak sunlight to penetrate now and again as gusts of wind tore holes in the gloom. It gave Fragger the shivers to think about working outside in such conditions, so he turned his attention to the inside of the dome.

Around them, men and women in black EarthCorp uniforms talked together or headed purposefully toward duties Fragger could only guess at. Ranks were still a confusion to him, but he had no trouble recognizing a Rerun labor squad when it entered the dome led by a noisy little guard who sported a toothbrush mustache and a contemptuous attitude. Each laborer bore the brand “R” that had been lasered onto his forehead. Exhaustion had written its signature on their sweaty faces, and they staggered under the weight of their tools. Reddened skin showed through the thin cloth of the gray uniforms plastered against emaciated bodies. The lucky men wore tattered boots. The others limped on scalded bare feet, wincing with each step.

"Dress that line," the guard shouted at them. "We were not going anywhere until you people show a little discipline."

Wearily, the Reruns shuffled into line, doing their best to stay upright. It wasn't enough for the small guard who tapped his goad against a thigh with impatience.

The sight angered Fragger, and he couldn’t resist a verbal jab as they passed by. “Fucking little Hitler pervert!”

The guard whirled around to glare at the Ranger and demand, “What did you say?”

“I said your dick is so small you should be pissing all over yourself instead of other people.”

Fragger watched as the guard’s translator implant struggled to cope with the slang. When it managed to define the terms, Little Hitler's lips worked hard to get words of rage past contorted lips.

"Rerun scum!" the guard shouted and charged his goad.

Red stepped in front of Fragger. "Power that thing down, Wolk."

"What’s the matter with you, Red? Didn’t you hear what he said?” the guard demanded.

“I did. He's got a big mouth.”

“Well, then, step aside, and I'll shut it for him!”

“Orders, Wolk, I got orders. Nobody touches this Rerun in any way until orders to the contrary come down.”

“Orders? Who issued such stupid orders?”

“Interrogator Meitz.”

Fragger watched Wolk go limp faster than a man told by a woman he's no good in bed. Bluster replaced the bravado.

“Well, get him out here, then, before I lose my discipline and stick this goad in his ear!”

Salinsky looked scornfully down at the little man and said, "Yeah, sure, Wolk."

As they headed toward a lock labeled *Armory*, Red said under his breath something that translated to Fragger as "dipshit." Then, he glanced slyly back at the Ranger. “First, Meitz and Meissner and now Wolk! You got a thing for pissing off dickheads, Rerun? Don't try that with a real trooper. He'll lop your head off in a microsecond.”

“Who is that creep?”

“Wolk? Trooper reject. He likes to take it out on Reruns.”

“No shit!”

The corporal shrugged as he punched a code into another door. “Can't blame him in a way. Around here, if you're not an officer or one of the EarthCorp management aristocracy, you might as well hang it up for any respect.”

Fragger’s ears picked up at this hint of dissatisfaction. He decided to exploit the opportunity to gather more information with a little flattery.

“Why aren't you an officer, Red?” he asked. “Hell, you've got the makings, man.”

It was an outright lie. Fragger suspected the bullet-headed corporal was lethal on the battlefield, but the man wasn’t close to office material. Even a corporal, though, could tell him a lot about the structure of EarthCorp military.

"Damned right I got the makings!" Salinsky answered bitterly. "But I ain't rich and I ain't royalty, so I'm stuck right where I am."

"A shame, a real shame, Red. You mean to tell me that ability doesn't count?"

After checking around to make sure no one was close enough to overhear his answer, the corporal replied in a low voice, "Money and breeding, that's all that counts."

“So what you’re saying is that someone of your skills doesn't have the opportunity for advancement?”

"Not a chance, Rerun, not unless you find yourself a rich corporate patron—a CEO or somebody like that. The upper corporate crust *will* sponsor a trooper but only if it amuses them or if you're that one in a million soldier, a man who's a natural-born leader and killer. Patrons find somebody like that, they sell their contracts to the merc worlds or, if they're really ambitious and smart, post them within the EarthCorp military. Whatever makes the most money."

"'Mercs'? You mean, mercenaries? They've got their own worlds?"

"Yeah," Red confirmed. "A lot of them in the Ursus Combine, especially. It's a wild area out there, especially in the Gulag sector. Nobody really owns that part of space, not EarthCorp or the Ricers. That's where the old Terran aristocracy ended up after the Second Expansion. You know nobility. They were always pining for the good old days when life was perfect under a king and all that monarchy bullshit. Well, when the Exploration Service opened up Ursus, most of the aristocrats took off for that sector. At the time, EarthCorp didn't much care what their governments would be as long as they gave Terrans a share of any profits. It was a good arrangement for a hundred years or so. Then the nobles decided Terra was getting greedy and formed a combine. Now there's a laugh—the greedy complaining other people are too greedy. Anyway, the nobility started courting the Ricers and other star nations and have been playing the systems against each other ever since. The resource-rich Urus planets, they sell grain, fruit and goods. The resource-poor worlds, they sell the services of their soldiers to the highest bidder. Mercs are *jits* just like me, only independent."

"That's the first time I've heard that term," Fragger said. "What's a *jit*?"

"A just-in-time trooper."

"What? You mean like just-in-time inventory?"

"Yeah, same concept. Most of us *jits* come from Rockpile. It's an Outsource World. Slum planet, basically. That's why Terrans call us 'slummers' sometimes, but I don't ever want to hear you use that term, you understand me, Rerun? If you do, I'll slap a hull charge up along side your head and blow you back to the 20th Century!"

"I'll remember not to use it," Fragger promised. "Explain this to me, though: Are you under contract to EarthCorp like the mercs are?"

"I wish! But it don't work that way. Once a merc finishes his contract, he's free to move on to another employer. Us Rockpilers, basically we're tied to EarthCorp for life."

"What do you mean?"

Red shrugged. "EarthCorp owns everything on Rockpile. Gotta buy the armor from EarthCorp. Gotta buy EarthCorp uniforms. Gotta buy everything from EarthCorp! It all gets deducted from your pay. That leaves you in a financial hole, most of the time. Me, I'm in deeper than most."

"Why's that? Gambling, drugs?"

"Naw, nothing like that. A funeral for my wife and kids."

"Jesus, I'm sorry! What happened?"

"Largepox spread from Ricer orbitals. Lots of Rockpilers died in the attack before we drove the enemy off. Most bodies got cremated. It's cheaper that way. But Tria—my wife—always wanted a nice Terran-style Christian burial with a casket and flowers and a service and a real preacher. She was a good woman, and I always honored her wishes so…six caskets and one service later, I was nose-deep in debt."

"Six caskets! You had five kids?"

"Yeah."

"In a way, I lost my wife and two kids as well, but, man, nothing like what you've been through. I really am sorry, Red."

"Life on Rockpile, that's all."

"Well, damn, why don't you just take off and become a mercenary? Screw EarthCorp. Sounds to me like you don't own them a bloody thing. If fact, they owe you!"

"A Rerun's telling me to commit treason? That's rich. I got a choice between three squares a day and getting deep-spaced. Guess you know the answer to that one, don't you?"

"Yeah, I hear you, Red. Still, you might consider the merc option. Because when you think hard about it—really hard—there's not that much difference between being a *jit* and being a Rerun, is there?"

"Hey, don't try saying you're equal to a trooper! There's one big difference between me and a Rerun like you, Sparks. I'll live a lot longer."

"You sure about that?"

"Yeah, I'm sure!" Red answered in a curt tone as he stepped through the door, then ordered, "Quit talking and get on in here. You've got work to do."

As he followed Salinsky into the armory, the smells struck the Ranger's nose. They were oddly familiar and strange at the same time. Cosmoline, or something very much like it, was in use to grease and protect weapons, but it was overlaid with the odor of lubricants and an ozone-like smell that signaled a considerable power source.

"Combat Armor is on the left," Red explained. "Mostly CBA-10 and 12mi Power Armor. Army pukes use the 10s. Marines use the 12s."

"Damn!" Fragger said at the sight.

The suits were impressive. So impressive, he wasn't really sure how to describe them. Massive armored shoulders dwarfed the small helmets, presumably to provide protection to the vulnerable head area, giving them the appearance of body builders who'd lifted way too much weight.

On the other hand, with their arms held out by their sides like that, they look like tall mutant cowboys, minus the hats, ready to draw down on an enemy with six guns or whatever the future's equivalent of a Colt Peacemaker is.

Less subtle than the Ricer armor he'd seen, everything about the design said one thing--blunt, massive force.

"What are these things made out of?" Fragger asked.

'You don't need to know anything about them, Rerun. Except how to clean them."

"In other words, you don't have a clue."

Red bristled at the insult as Fragger had hoped.

"You don't get to be an EarthCorp trooper without knowing your stuff, Rerun."

"Yeah, right," Fragger said in a dismissive tone.

Red took the bait and launched into an explanation. "Composite armor combined with an internal powered skeleton. Controlled by direct input from the SYA suit."

"The what?"

"SaveYourAss suit, dummy. That's what we call it because it'll save your ass when you're in combat. It has three layers. First layer is permeable SecondSkin covered with sensors/transmitters. The next layer is like our version of the chainmail of ancient times. It acts as the nerve center, sending signals from the first layer out to the armor. Third layer is the armor itself. It's made up of composite and ablative materials. Very strong. Stands up well in combat."

Red's voice showed a combination of pride in the units and the lecturing tone of a soldier who'd been through all this before with raw recruits, but he cut the lecture short when a heavy walking noise echoed in the chamber. "You don't need to know any more than that, Rerun. Captain Hilger finds us loafing, I'll cop extra duty I don't need. Come on."

Fragger followed Red around the corner and came to a sudden stop. "Jeeezus!" he swore. "Is that the Captain?"

It was another powered suit, only in motion this time and much taller and wider than the armor Salinsky had just shown him. Atop a 12-foot body, the head looked like a skull. The shoulders were huge, covered with two protective and overlapping plates. Its arms reached past articulated knees. At the end of the arms were hands with two curved and nastily pointed fingers opposed by equally lethal thumbs. The armored feet reminded Fragger of hooves combined with talons.

Red's laugh cut off the Ranger's wonderment. "No, that's not the captain. It's not even human. That's a light RAM unit. In the low tonnage range."

"It rams things, you mean?" Fragger asked in confusion.

"No. RAM is just an acronym. It stands for Robot, Assault, Mobile. This guy's a Destroyer class. No human inside, just an artificial intelligence. Limited smarts. It goes where we tell it to."

Fragger shrank aside as the monster strode by. Only the noise of the hooves clopping on the floor and a faint whirring sound came from the machine. "It looks damned dangerous to me," he said.

"To the Ricers, it is," Red replied. "It can be armed with everything from a particle accelerator cannon to an ion disrupter, but, most important, it has MAC capability."

"I don't know any of those weapons," Fragger said. "What's MAC capability?"

"A Magnetic Accelerator Cannon, a big anti-armor weapon. It's real heavy so only the RAMs carry them. It fires large SABOT rounds with solid core penetrator rods by using alternating rings of positive and negative charged magnetic energy."

At least SABOT is a term I can understand, Fragger thought with some relief. *Otherwise, I don't know what the hell he's talking about.*

"Powerful?" he asked to keep the corporal talking.

Red laughed again. "SABOTs? They'll penetrate just about anything you want to name, short of fixed defenses."

"It looks to me like a single trooper wouldn't stand a chance against a machine like that," Fragger suggested.

"He wouldn't, but most of the RAMS are programmed for larger weapons like Primary Battle Tanks, anyway. A MAC isn't a real accurate weapon, and going after a trooper would be like trying to swat a fly with a fusion blast."

"Fusion? Is that how you power the units?"

"That's how we power everything, Rerun--all the RAMS and all the assault or defensive armor."

"Nuclear fuel is a virtually inexhaustible power source, or at least it was seen that way in my day," Fragger said. "You must be able to fight forever."

"Not a chance. See that pack on the back of the RAM unit?"

Fragger checked out the retreating monster. A vented rectangular pack rode its massive back.

The corporal explained, “That's an extended-range standard fuel pack. It powers the RAM unit and its armament. It does the same for a trooper's armor and his weapons as well, but it usually needs to be recharged after every combat. Combat these days requires massive amounts of energy.”

Fragger's head was whirling from so much information he couldn't think of another question to ask so he settled for following Red deeper into the armory. They went down an aisle flanked by immobile RAM units on one side and empty power suits on the other until Red stopped in front of a different kind of suit. It was ugly and functional, the kind of suit, the Ranger suspected, intended for dirty work. It reminded him of the suits worn by deep sea divers, thick and clumsy-looking. Salinsky immediately confirmed his suspicions.

"Your first job, Rerun, is to refuel the packs. That's your gear right here--a maintenance suit. Get into a SecondSkin, then I'll show you how to get the armored suit on."

As Fragger struggled into the odd-feeling suit, Red touched a button, and the armor rotated on a rack until the back faced them. Then, he pulled the top half of the armor away from the legs and said to Fragger, “Get in.”

“Not until you tell me what it’s for.”

“It’s just a rad suit. Fuel transfer don't always go the way it should, so you need protection from the radiation.”

“I thought I was too important to be put at risk.”

Red grinned. “You ain't that important, at least not as far as I'm concerned. Get in.”

When Fragger hesitated, Red shoved him toward the suit, saying, “I did done time in there myself when I was a youngblood. You'll survive. Hell, you’re the one who says he killed two Ricer troopers barehanded. Or maybe you ain't as tough as you say you are.”

The Ranger gave Salinsky the finger, a gesture which puzzled the trooper.

"What's that mean?" Red asked.

"Never mind."

"I'll find out," Red promised.

Apparently, the middle finger is no longer a universal symbol for "Up yours!," Fragger realized as he stepped inside the legs of the mechanism.

"What do I do now?" he asked.

"I'll help you with the rest," Red said, sliding the main body of the suit toward Fragger and maneuvering it close enough for the Ranger to stick his hands through the arm holes. The suit startled the Ranger by magnetically slapping the arm and leg joints together. Red maneuvered the helmet over Fragger's head, and the Ranger was closed in.

"What do I do now?" he asked Red.

"Seal the suit."

"How do I do that?" Fragger asked, looking around inside the helmet for a button or a switch.

"I just told you, damn it! Talk to the system. Tell it to seal the suit."

"Seal suit," the Ranger said, feeling foolish about talking to an inanimate object. The suit obeyed immediately in a series of smooth clicks. Uncomfortable comparisons with an iron maiden ran through his mind as a prickling sensation raced over his scalp.

"Now what?" Fragger asked.

"Tell it to 'Activate Normal Mode'," Salinsky said in a voice muffled by the thickness of the suit.

The Ranger repeated the words and felt the maintenance suit come alive.

"It *is* like a second skin!" he said, marveling at the fact that he no longer felt heavy and immobile. Instead, it was like wearing a summer weight uniform. "How does it do that?"

"Direct input, like I told you before," Red answered with impatience. Now that the communication mode was active, the corporal's voice was as clear as if he were in the suit with Fragger. "SecondSkin translates your actions to the suit as fast as you can think. Come down from there, and you'll see what I mean."

"Do I have to command it to walk or something?"

"No, just relax and walk like you normally do. The suit won't let you fall."

Fragger obeyed, and the maintenance suit moved smoothly down from the storage spot and onto the floor. He lifted one arm and then another, astonished at the human-like flexibility of the hands, fingers and joints.

"Do the combat suits work like this too?" he asked.

"Same principle, Rerun, much more sophisticated though. Kind of like the difference between walking speed and hyperspace travel. Now, shut up so you can get some work done. See that hatch over there?"

Fragger followed the trooper's pointing finger and saw a thick hatch marked with the still-familiar yellow and black radiation sign.

"That's the refueling station. Get your butt in there, Rerun. Once you're inside, I'll tell you what to do."

"Where will you be?" Fragger asked.

"Out here, removing the cells from the power packs so you can refuel them."

Fragger had no wish to be near a radiation source, but couldn't see any way out of it. When Red cycled the thick hatch open, he stepped into a chamber and waited until the inner hatch opened into the station. As the door closed behind him, Fragger entered the room and studied the layout. To his left, six self-locking nozzles protruded from the wall. Above each nozzle, a painted sign read "Fusion Connector Output." He looked across to the right and saw six sockets, labeled "Fuel Cell Input."

"Rerun?" Red's voice entered Fragger's suit.

"Yeah?"

"I'm setting up six cells. Your job is simple. Take the fusion connectors from the reactor side of the room and pull them across and shove them into the input slots until you hear a click. That means they're secure."

Fragger pulled the first connector from the wall. It was heavier than he thought, yet it came smoothly from the socket and went into the input slot with ease. As he went back for the next one, he asked,

"I don't understand, Red. With all the automation and electronics you've got, why do you need people to do this job?"

"Money? What else? Some bureaucrat decided it was too expensive to ship modern hard- and software to a small installation when you could get grunts and Reruns to do the job. He probably pocketed the difference."

Fragger continued talking as he dragged the connectors across the room. "Things never change, do they?"

"What do you mean?" Red asked.

"The foot soldier is still at the bottom of the rung. We had a term for it--cannon fodder."

"What's that mean?"

"It means soldiers like you and me have only one purpose. We're food for weapons."

"Yeah, Rerun, ain't it the truth? Then, the civilians are the first to scream bloody murder when the shit hits the cooling vents."

Fragger chuckled. The translator had done the best it could with the old terminology, substituting "vents" for "fan", but had nailed the essence of the phrase.

"Last connector hooked up," he announced a few minutes later.

"Yeah, I see that," Salinsky confirmed. "Got a green on all connections over here."

"What do I do now?" Fragger asked.

"Sit tight. Even these old refuelers are pretty effective. Takes about half an hour tops, not worth the trouble of coming out and getting your suit off and back on again."

Fragger wasn't too sure about that. "What about the radiation?"

"No problem. Your suit's rated for maximum exposure."

"Yeah, but how do I know that? Radiation's invisible. If this suit has a weak link, I wouldn't know if I was getting a dose or not."

"Ask your suit."

"What do I ask it?"

Red sighed. "Ask it for current suit integrity in regard to radiation."

Fragger asked the question, and the suit responded, “Suit integrity is uncompromised. Occupant is safe from current radiation and heat levels.”

The answer didn't make the Ranger feel any better. His silence prompted Salinsky to say, “It's a fusion plant. That means heat and radiation. What'd you expect?”

“I don't know,” Fragger responded. “With all this advanced technology, I thought it'd be a lot more efficient, that's all.”

A snort greeted this thought. “Ain't nothing military that ain't nasty in some way. Just sit tight, and you'll be okay. The only danger is if you didn't get the connections tight, and, like I said, my board shows green all the way across.”

Nervous, Fragger didn't sit tight. Instead, he practiced manipulating the suit to keep his mind off the hazard surrounding him. He walked around the room until he felt comfortable, lifting and lowering his arms as he went. Then, he attempted a run and immediately banged hard into a wall. Amazingly, he barely felt the impact. Red’s voice sounded in his helmet.

“Cut that shit out, Rerun.”

“Just trying to get used to this suit, that's all.”

“Well, don't. Maintenance suits are expensive, and any damage comes out of my pay.”

“These things look indestructible,” Fragger said.

“Nothing's indestructible except for the military's ability to mess up a trooper. Besides, it's time to disconnect the lines. Turn the connectors a half-turn to the left. That'll disengage them. Then, return the lines to where you got them. When you're finished, go into the entry chamber and decontaminate.’

Fragger stowed the connectors and moved into the entry chamber. As the hatch closed automatically behind him, he asked, “What do I do now?”

“Nothing. It's all programmed.”

A rush of steam and water hissed into the chamber, beating a tattoo of noise while scrubbers worked the length of the suit. In a couple of minutes, the cramped room went silent, and the outer hatch cycled open. Fragger stepped out and stood still at Salinsky's command. The trooper pointed a device at him, then checked the readings.

"You're clean," Salinsky said. "Get out of the suit."

"How?"

"Get back up where it was stored, plant your feet in the slots, then tell the suit to open."

The Ranger obeyed. The suit opened, and he was glad to back out and breathe the air, even if it was recycled. When he turned around, Red had been joined by two officers.

"Captain Hilger," the corporal said as he saluted crisply. "Interrogator Meitz."

"Finished recharging the cells, Salinsky?" the captain asked.

"Yes, sir."

"Good. Now, get over to the Repo Depot. We've got some virgins reporting in. Orient them and assign them quarters."

"How many are there, sir?"

"Twelve."

"We don't have that many bunks, sir."

Hilger scowled. "Figure out a solution, then, Sergeant. Use some initiative. Get moving."

Red saluted and disappeared down the corridor. Fragger stood waiting for the two officers to say something. Instead, Meitz was staring at him, and Hilger was frowning at the interrogator.

"Something wrong, Meitz?" the captain asked.

"I'll say."

"What?"

Meitz ignored the question, instead asking one of his own. "Rerun, tell me something. How do you feel about me?"

Fragger didn't hesitate with his answer. "You're a puke, just like all of your kind--a sadistic mind fucker who's happy for war because you're such a loser in civilian life. Women avoid you like the plague, and real soldiers spit on you."

The captain had his goad out and powered in an instant, but, to Fragger's amazement, Meitz held him back.

"I don't believe it," the interrogator said.

"I've never seen such stupidity in a Rerun," the captain agreed.

"That's not what I'm talking about, Hilger."

"What do you mean, then?"

"I conditioned him thoroughly. He should think I'm his father-equivalent right now. He should be ready to do anything for a father's love. In his mind, he should think I can do no wrong."

The captain's eyes widened. "You mean, he resisted the treatment?"

"Better than resisted, apparently. It doesn't seem to have taken at all."

Meitz, a father-figure? Fragger thought. Nausea churned his stomach, and the Ranger made the only answer he could to the sickening thought.

He vomited all over the interrogator's boots.

CHAPTER 12

Red Salinsky woke Fragger again, this time in the middle of the night.

At least, I think that's what time it is, the Ranger guessed, trying to get groggy thoughts in order while he pulled on clothes.

"What kind of shit duty have you got for me this time?" he grumbled at Red. The last few weeks, the corporal had worked him hard in the armory while they waited for word from the interrogator on what was to happen next.

"No questions, Rerun."

Fragger came alert at the impersonal tone. Red was on his best behavior which meant there was an officer somewhere in the area, and an officer meant something besides powering fuel cells, polishing armor, oiling joints, and repairing damaged exoskeleton components. Red had even let him try out power suits and swords and dry-fire the weapons so he could get familiar with the maintenance requirements.

"Come on, Red, tell me what's going on. Don't play stiffneck with me."

"I said, no questions. Get dressed and come with me."

Fragger obeyed and followed Salinsky down the now familiar corridors, through the dome and a hatch. They came out into an area he'd never seen before but there was no doubt of its purpose.

It's a hangar, or whatever the equivalent term for it is this far into the future, he realized.

They stood on a walkway that overlooked several spacecraft and what appeared to be giant, armored Hummer-like vehicles equipped with tank treads and automatic weapons. The now-familiar ozone smell pervaded the air, a byproduct, he'd learned, of the fusion engines powering all EarthCorp vehicles. Above the vehicles, hooks hung down from the ceiling from mobile block and tackle apparatus. A maintenance crew was busy using one of the hooks to pull an engine from a floater. Fragger had seen the vehicles occasionally flit by at high speed outside the dome, usually filled with grim EarthCorp troopers sent to quell riots in the Rerun barracks. Without its engine, this floater had no speed at all. It sat grounded with air skirts flounced around it as if, instead of a nasty weapons platform, it was an exhausted woman who'd collapsed on the deck.

Next to the floater was a familiar sight, the *Lethal*, the Dagger-class ship that had brought him to the planet. The large cables connected to it and the number of technicians running about indicated it was being readied for launch. When he saw Interrogator Meitz appear in the ship's hatch and signal impatiently at Salinsky, Fragger was certain he was leaving Goldilocks. He followed Red down the steps, feeling oddly sentimental about the corporal. After thinking about the feeling for a moment, he decided, *I feel that way because although he's not a friend, he's the closest thing I have to one. He's a hardass, but fair. Damn, I'm actually going to miss him. Too bad, he doesn't feel the same.*

They made their way across and around a jumble of power cables and maintenance and repair equipment. Just before they rounded the fender of a floater, Red signaled for Fragger to stop out of sight of the *Lethal*. The corporal moved close to speak to him in a low voice. As usual, the smell of *gark* rolled out of his mouth along with the words.

"Sparks, you're nothing but a Rerun and will never be anything but a Rerun."

"And your breath stinks worse than a buzzard on a bait wagon. Tell me something new, Red."

"Shut up and listen. I ain't got time for Reruns of any kind, but fair's fair so I wanted to let you know you're the best worker I ever had. Damned fast too. Kept Captain Hilger off my back about maintenance, and since we ain't never going to meet again, I thought I'd tell you I appreciate the effort."

"Thanks. But we are going to meet again, Red. You know why?"

"Why?"

"I'm going to stay alive so I can kick your corporal's ass all the way across three galaxies and back."

Red snorted. "I'll kick your ass first."

The corporal gave the Ranger an unexpected rap on the head with his knuckles.

Fragger flinched and rubbed at the stinging spot on his scalp as he complained, "What the hell did you do that for?"

"Rerun, I just wanted to let you know that you're a good soldier, even if you're the biggest bullshitter around."

"Takes one to know one, Red."

"Ain't it the truth? Now, come on."

Fragger followed Red toward the *Lethal*, touched to realize that the trooper actually did care about him. When they came to the side of the *Lethal*, Salinsky's concern ended. He booted the Ranger up the mobile steps and through the hatch onto the ship's deck. As Fragger turned around to cuss the trooper out, Red grinned, raised his middle finger and waggled it at the Ranger.

"Told you I'd kick your ass first, didn't I, Rerun? Also told you I'd find out what this gesture meant. Goodbye, Sparks, and fuck you!"

The Ranger laughed in spite of his aching butt.

CHAPTER 13

This time they didn't put him in Lethal's brig. It was worse. They put him on mess duty. Elbow deep in greasy suds and dirty dishes and ten long hours into his latest shift, Fragger longed for the solitude of a cell. Chief Mess Cook Bagwell, a man lumpier than the sacks of potatoes the Ranger had peeled earlier in the day, delighted in his absolute power over the kitchen. He ran Fragger ragged.

The only saving grace is, he runs everyone ragged, the Ranger consoled himself. *That and the fact the man can actually cook.*

The trouble was, after their latest hyperspace jump, Fragger wasn't hungry at all. In fact, the smell of roast lamb, mint jelly and brussel sprouts drifting into his confined work space was making him sick. Not as sick as the first couple of jumps, but it still wasn't pleasant. He sought comfort in the fact that experienced hyperspacers didn't seem to get so violently ill.

Maybe it just takes repeated exposure to hyperspace to adjust, he thought. *God, I hope that's true! It's like being seasick and turned inside out all at once.*

To keep the gorge from rising any further in his throat, Fragger turned his thoughts away from the touchy state of his stomach and marveled at the immense power the EarthCorp vessel possessed to be able to carry fresh food in such quantities. The *Lethal's* chow was a far cry from the Tang and food tubes of early space exploration. Fragger had covered every shift and guessed the *Lethal's* complement to be around 50 well-fed men and women.

From time to time, he caught curious glances from the crew coming his way. He hadn't caught a single slap or blow since coming on board the ship so it was clear the word was out that he wasn't to be touched.

And that order has set off the scuttlebutt. Grapevining hasn't changed any in the future. I suppose it relieves the tedium of a long voyage.

That thought touched off another.

With the ability to go anywhere in a virtual instant, why is it taking so long to get to Earth? Hell, we got to Goldilocks in a heartbeat.

The hyperspace transitions warped his sense of time, but Fragger knew he'd done a minimum of seven shifts in the mess hall so the *Lethal* had been underway for at least a week. He'd tried asking everyone from other Reruns to Bagwell to tell him why the voyage was so long. They either didn't know, or in the Chief Cook's case, had told him to shut his Rerun mouth and get back to work.

Speaking of mouths, here comes the big one, Fragger sighed as he heard the noisy blusterings of Chief Cook Bagwell headed in his direction. A second later, the veteran cook appeared in the doorway to the dishwashing room, chewing noisily at a lamb bone. The Ranger glanced warily at Bagwell. He'd learned quickly that the big, blond Chief Cook held considerable strength beneath the suety body. Bagwell had arms as thick as his manner. Fragger had seen those arms swat aside unsuspecting Reruns with the casual ease of a pile driver and learned to stay well clear of their reach. He kept silent until the usual taunting words came out of the grease-stained mouth.

"Rerun, you hungry after the jump? I saved some mutton for you. The best part--the drippings."

Fragger fought down the nausea, unwilling to give the cook the satisfaction of seeing him vomit. Instead, he said, "Jeez, Bagwell, that's kind of you. It's the only edible part, right?"

The Chief Cook grinned, continuing to chew at the meat. "Tomorrow, Rerun, I'll cook some liver and onions--a special dish just for you."

"Don't do me any favors."

Bagwell swallowed the last of the lamb and wiped his lips with a hairy arm. "Funny you should mention favors. I'm about to do you one, right now."

Fragger shot a suspicious look in the cook's direction. "What is it? Tacking another shift on top of this one?"

Bagwell snickered. “Even better, Rerun. Report to Interrogator Meitz. Now. After him, you'll be glad to come back to work for me.”

“I wouldn't count on it,” Fragger said, removing the soaked apron and drying his hands on a towel.

“Me, neither,” Bagwell agreed. “In fact, you might not count on coming back at all.”

“I've survived so far,” the Ranger pointed out as he slipped quickly past the cook’s bulk and out into the main mess hall.

“You’ve been lucky so far, Rerun. There's a lot more of them than there is of you. Whatever you got that interests the interrogators, they don't take failure easy.”

“That's not true," Fragger said, making sure he was a safe distance from Bagwell. "They eat your failures every day.”

Bagwell reddened at the insult, as the Ranger knew he would. There was only subject the man was sensitive about—his cooking. Fragger ducked as the lamb bone splatted against the bulkhead next to his head. Then he ran out the door and was well out of sight of the mess hall before he slowed down.

He'd once toured a submarine with a Navy buddy and couldn't help but feel he was in one now as he navigated narrow corridors toward the interrogation room. Like a submarine, the design clearly indicated a fighting vessel. Every inch of cramped space was designed for engagement--damage control stations, fire-fighting equipment, weapons centers--and all critical positions were guarded by EarthCorp marines in mobile light-armor suits. They held their short-range pulse laser pieces at the ready and eyed him as little better than potential target practice. Outside the interrogation room, the last guard patted him down for weapons before motioning him through the door.

Interrogators Meitz and Meissner sat side by side behind a table, greeting his entrance with sour faces. Fragger surveyed the entire room quickly and was surprised to see no interrogation equipment in place.

“Rerun,” Interrogator Meitz said, “You're a black hole in my life, did you know that?”

"I try," Fragger responded.

"Because of you, we're stuck on this ship for an additional two weeks instead of being home in the usual time."

"What have I got to do with it?"

"You've become a very popular man."

"The Imperial Commonwealth is after me, is that what you mean?"

"The Ricers? They're the most serious threat, but now they're not the only one, Rerun. These days, spies appear to be unusually efficient at discovering secrets and equally good at spreading the word about those secrets. Several empires know about your existence now. The Spartans, the Rollers, the Ursus Combine…Gulag pirates…hell, never mind, *everybody* knows about you. We've had to maneuver our way willy-nilly back to Earth to throw them off the track."

"Glad to be of service!"

"Smart-ass answers aren't going to do you any good, Rerun," Meissner threatened, pulling his goad from his belt and laying it on the table.

"Maybe not, but is there a point in telling me all of this?"

"There is," Meitz responded. "Your resistance to interrogation techniques can be a valuable weapon for EarthCorp if we can isolate that ability. It would be a valuable weapon for any empire. But that ability alone doesn't explain the hot pursuit. Either you're hiding something from us or you possess another talent that not even you are aware of. Once we're back on Earth, I plan on pulling that information out of you. Is that clear?"

"Perfectly," Fragger responded.

"Good. Until we get to Earth then, I'm bunking you on the mess deck instead of the brig because it's one of the safest places on the *Lethal*, smack in the middle of the ship."

"To keep me out of enemy hands?"

The interrogator rubbed at his face, and Fragger noticed the man's eyes. They looked tired and red. Something was putting a strain on Meitz.

About damned time! the Ranger rejoiced silently.

"The answer to your question is yes, Sparks. There's a remote possibility we may be intercepted by enemy vessels. In anticipation of that minor possibility, my orders are to protect you at all costs. This means we have to instruct you in the use of evvies and space suits."

"What are evvies?"

"Escape Vehicles. In case we end up eating space, you'll have a chance for survival. However, my orders also state that you are not to be captured by the enemy. If we feel we won't make it, you die with us."

Fragger stood wordless. There was nothing to say.

"However, as you know, nothing is certain in combat," Meitz continued. "It's possible we could die and you survive. In that case, EarthCorp wants you breathing and out of enemy hands. We've configured several evvies on the mess deck area to home in on a particular location once it's ejected from the *Lethal*. If we're damaged or boarded, your job is to find the right evvie and launch."

"What's to prevent me from simply going over to one of your enemies?" Fragger asked.

"Nothing," Meitz admitted. "But they might just kill you on the spot, Rerun. If you launch an evvie, you at least have a chance of staying alive until we can pick you up. I can promise you I'll do my best to make sure you remain upright and breathing because that's what EarthCorp wants."

Lying through his teeth, I'll bet, Fragger thought as he asked, "You mentioned a particular location for me to land. Where is it?"

"It's not in our interests for you to know that at this point. Starting right now, you're confined to the mess deck. Study this schematic readout and locate where the designated Evvie Tubes are, then physically find them so you have no doubt of your ability to get to the right place in the fastest time possible."

Fragger took the readout and studied it with an interest beyond its potential in ensuring his survival. It wasn't paper. It was an electronic screen of some kind and was almost as light as the tree product. On it, the deck layout glowed in bright green letters, blinking white dots indicating the evac tubes.

"What do I have to know to operate these escape pods?" he asked.

"Nothing," the Interrogator responded. "It's automatic, but you do need to know how to get into a space suit. Meissner will show you how to do it, and you will practice until you can get into one at a moment's notice."

"Do I get off mess duty to do this?" Fragger asked.

"Not a chance. You'll practice on your hours off."

"I haven't had any hours off!"

"The expression from your day was, I believe, tough titty?" the interrogator said.

Fragger fumed inwardly. The interrogators and others, despite their disdain for his "ancient" ways, seemed to delight in using the computer to dredge up 20th century slang to torment him.

"One more change," Meitz said. "You're bunking with Meissner now. In fact, you two are going to be inseparable."

Meissner's natural smirk broadened until the Ranger wanted to take several of his teeth out.

"He'll be your bodyguard," Meitz added.

Right, Fragger thought. *He's been assigned to eliminate me if things go wrong, and he'll enjoy the hell out of it, too.*

"How about leveling with me, Meitz?" the Ranger said.

"What do you mean?"

"You wouldn't be going to all this trouble if you weren't expecting an imminent attack, would you?"

"No," Meitz admitted after a pause, "we wouldn't. Enemy vessels have been detected closing on us in a standard search pattern. That's why it's important you learn your assignment quickly. After all, you want to live as much as the rest of us, don't you?"

Fragger responded, "I wouldn't be too sure about that. Everybody wants me so bad they're willing to kill me to make sure the other guy doesn't get hold of whatever secret it is I'm carrying around."

Meitz came up with another 20th Century expression. "Life is a bitch."

The increasing reference to sayings from his day pissed the Ranger off, not only because they were doing it to aggravate him, but also because they seemed to enjoy mouthing the words as if they were a particularly new and enjoyable flavor of candy. It was as if they didn't have the imagination to think their own phrases up. He wanted to tell the interrogators that. Instead, he concentrated on the task at hand--staying alive.

"So, where do we begin?" he asked.

"Meissner, show him," Meitz ordered.

Meissner crooked an imperious finger at Fragger and set off down the corridor at a quick pace. The Ranger resisted the temptation to break the man's beckoning finger and stick it up his nose and followed the interrogator.

Meissner was efficient. He showed Fragger the location of every Evvie Tube, then put the Ranger through several run-throughs to make sure that he knew where to go if an attack occurred. Then, he demonstrated how to get into a space suit quickly and repeated the run-throughs. When the interrogator was satisfied, he punctuated a comment with his usual smirk, saying, "Okay, Rerun, you've got the idea. Now, back to the kitchen. Bagwell is probably already bitching he's short of help."

Fragger went back to the mess, discouraged by the thought that now he not only had to deal with the Chief Mess Cook and clean up, but had to suffer Meissner's presence as well. Bagwell greeted him with a snarl and pointed toward a sink full of dirty dishes while the interrogator grabbed a cup of stimjuice and sat in a corner close to the clean-up area, propping his booted feet up on a chair.

Two days and hundreds of dishes later, Fragger had devised a multitude of ways to kill the cook, yet had decided Meissner would be the first to go if ever he got a chance to take the man out. The interrogator had taken full advantage of his easy duty, spending hours drinking stimjuice, sipping like an old lady to avoid spotting his uniform, and reading news-scans full of obviously censored news regarding the Imperial Commonwealth and the other dominions making up the political scene throughout human-occupied space. Meissner was in the middle of another one of his explanations as to the strategic and tactical stupidities of the Ricers when a shrill whine pierced through the steamy noise of the dishwasher and rose into a racket that grabbed Fragger's skull and vibrated it into a reflexive spasms. The Ranger held tightly onto the pan of hot gravy he was carrying, afraid the sound was going to separate his head from its shoulders. His only consolation was that the smirk had vanished from the interrogator's face. Meissner's face had gone pale and his mouth shouted the nonsense word, "Loop! Loop!" Amidst all the chaos, Fragger realized that everybody had gone nuts. They were all shouting, "Loop!" and bolting from the mess.

"What is it?" he shouted at the interrogator.

"Someone is looping us!"

"What the hell is that?"

"They've targeted the hyperspace drive and introduced a random phasing program!" Meissner yelled.

"What does that mean?"

"It means we'll phase in and out of hyperspace uncontrolled until we're all bloody spots on the deck."

After his bouts with hyperspace entries and exits, Fragger knew it would be a particularly unpleasant form of death and asked, "What do we do?"

"Unless countermeasures work, we evacuate the ship," the interrogator answered, then drew his goad from its sheath and pressed the button to charge the weapon. "But, first, I do my duty."

Fragger didn't hesitate. He dumped the scalding gravy on Meissner, grabbed the goad from the interrogator's hand, then stuck it in the man's screaming mouth at full charge.

"Chew on that, you sonuvabitch!' the Ranger yelled. Meissner's head shook itself apart as Fragger ran out of the mess toward the designated Evvie Tube. He rounded the corner to find several men fighting over entrance to the escape vehicle. He worked his way past the panicked crowd and sprinted toward his secondary option. There was only one man there--Bagwell.

Fragger charged without further thought and threw his body against the Chief Mess Cook, driving him up against the bulkhead.

Both men thumped to the deck, but Bagwell was quicker than any big man had a right to be. He heaved the Ranger off his legs, scrambled up, and laid a kick into Fragger's kidneys. Fragger screamed and rolled away as the cook launched another kick. The Ranger got to his feet and charged again. This time, Bagwell met him in the middle of the corridor and, with his superior weight, slammed Fragger's head hard against the wall. Fragger fought against the explosion of lights and nausea, but the Chief Cook was too strong. Bagwell jerked his knee hard into the Ranger's groin, and Fragger dropped hard. As the Ranger fought to get air into his lungs, he watched the cook key open the tube hatch and disappear into the escape vehicle. A few seconds later, a "thoop" sounded as if a heavy-duty cork had been popped from a bottle.

Fragger cursed the ache in his testicles as he got up. He forced his body into a standing position and limped down the corridor to find another Evvie Tube. He checked every one Meissner had designated. All were gone. Fragger checked the bulkhead outside the last tube. A space suit still hung in its receptacle.

But what damned good will it do? he thought. *It don't mean shit in this situation as far as I know.*

The Ranger laughed at his predicament. *They worked so hard to make sure I had a way to get off the Lethal, but they didn't plan on me remaining behind all by myself.*

There was nothing to do, so he went back to the mess and drank stimjuice, as the phasing assault spun his brain around the inside of his skull like a crazed yo-yo.

While he waited for the future to splatter him back into death, the Ranger raised the cup and saluted the interrogator's pulped head.

"You never looked better, Meissner."

Fragger thought that was pretty funny until the phasing attack laced on spiked boots and began stomping his own brain into gelatin.

CHAPTER 14

The headache woke Fragger.

It's more than a headache, he groaned, refusing to open his eyes for fear the pain would increase if light hit them. *Somebody's stuck a street gang inside my skull, armed them with iron bars, and they're beating my brain down into my spine.*

It hurt to think. It hurt to breathe. It hurt to move, and Fragger vowed he'd stay motionless until the pain stopped or he died. He didn't care which. The hand jerking him to his feet broke that vow in an instant. He forced his eyelids open to the sight of a blurry, tall armored preying mantis who had many friends backing him up.

"You the Rerun?" the lead insect asked, shaking Fragger when the Ranger found words too difficult to form. "I asked you a question. Answer it."

Fragger moaned at the jarring impact of the insect's actions on his head. "Oh, God! Don't!"

"Then answer the question."

"Yes, Jesus, yes, I'm Sparks! Leave me alone!"

"Fat opportunity of that," the mantis said.

"Fat chance, you mean," Fragger corrected. "Damned translator doesn't always work the way it should."

The Ranger's eyes swam into focus, and he saw his tormentor was not a preying mantis, but a man in a space suit with an insect-shaped helmet. From what little he could discern through the reflections on the visor, the wearer of the suit was 90% beard and 10% eyes hard as a whore's heart. A stylized chest insignia in the form of a bear decorated the chest of the suit. Above it was the name "Lesto".

"Thanks for the grammar lesson, Rerun."

The other mantises snickered at the joke, but the laughter had a nervous tinge to it as helmets continuously swiveled to check the security of the deck.

"I'm Lesto," the mantis said. "You're coming with us."

"I don't want to!"

"As if you've got a choice."

"Shit, man, my head hurts like there's no tomorrow."

"You're my prisoner now, so there *is* no tomorrow unless you do what I say."

"Oh, hell, who cares about tomorrow, anyway?"

"Not me, Rerun, but you're coming with me, one way or the other. You're a piece of trash, but you're money in the bank."

"What?"

Lesto didn't bother to answer. He jerked his helmet toward the interrogator's body where the goad remained protruding from Meissner's pulped head. "You do that, Rerun?"

"Yeah."

"Creative."

Fragger couldn't tell if the man's tone was one of sarcasm or admiration. He didn't get a chance to decide because Lesto immediately issued a command to his team. "You know the drill. Take point, clear the way for me, and get off the ship."

The soldiers obeyed without answering. In a second, Fragger was alone with Lesto who ordered, "Come on. Get moving."

Lesto shoved the Ranger out the mess door and down the corridor. They climbed outward toward the hull through three decks and the noise of several skirmishes as Lesto's men eliminated opposition in their path. When they came to an open air lock, Lesto motioned him through, and the Ranger stepped out of the military cleanliness of the *Lethal* into Lesto's ship.

Fragger's nose wrinkled at smell in the air. *This isn't really a ship. It's a garbage dump!*

The atmosphere in the ship was a heady brew of sweat, tea, and, worst of all, the sour smell of *kim chee*, the Korean fermented cabbage. Plastic containers littered the deck, and Fragger couldn't walk without crunching something beneath his feet. He turned from the food-stained bulkheads to stare at Lesto.

"You got a problem with the mess, Rerun? The ship flies, that's all that counts," Lesto said as he punched a button to close the hatch.

As the man unsealed his helmet and removed it, Fragger got his first good look at his "rescuer." His first thought was that Lesto had been recruited from a platoon of Viking berserker warriors born of Korean mothers. Big, black-haired, and bearded with a face led by an axe of a nose, Lesto grew dark fur from high on his cheeks to down inside the neck of his armor. Epicanthic lids did little to hide the ice-hard blue eyes of a predator. Fragger guessed his age to be in the mid-forties.

When Lesto spoke, it was an accusation. "It's your fault, Rerun!"

Without the filter of the commlink, the man's voice had a brusque, dismissive quality embedded in every syllable. Beyond the usual military brusqueness, the tone hinted at an aristocratic background.

"What's my fault?" Fragger asked.

"All this clutter. This smell. I took a near-hit before we slipped through. The concussion shook the provisions loose."

"Slipped through?"

"The *Lethal* had an escort. Several corvette-class Harriers. Nasty little bastards. All particle accelerator cannons and minimal armament."

"Wait a minute," the Ranger said as a realization struck him. "They told me that some sort of random phasing program had attacked the hyperspace drive and—"

"And you're supposed to be dead," Lesto finished the sentence for him.

"Yeah."

"Well, if it'd been an actual phasing program, you *would* be dead, Rerun."

"It was false?"

"You're still here, aren't you?"

While Fragger tried to digest this information, he sized up Lesto's vessel. At the fore end, he could see stars out the windows. Aft, about ten feet away, was the hatch to the engine compartment. He estimated the vessel could be no more than 40 or 50 feet long. That fact made him realize Lesto couldn't have taken the *Lethal* with such a small ship, and he said so.

“You're smart for a Rerun,” Lesto responded. “The ship *doesn’t* have the power or sophistication to accomplish such a mission, but a planetary loop system works just fine when the enemy's in range. A tight-beam transmission can raise hell, provided you've got the energy.”

“The *Lethal* was attacked from a planet?”

“Our people on Mars. Now, shut up. Take the co-pilot’s seat and hang on.”

Fragger obeyed while Lesto ran through a systems check, then issued a command to his team, “All units disperse. Repeat--disperse!”

Without warning, Lesto powered his craft away from the *Lethal.* Fragger's stomach tied itself in more than knots than a sailor could manage. He wanted to puke, but suppressed the reflex by asking, “Is there anything I can do to help?”

Busy with the controls, Lesto glanced at him and asked, “Like what?”

“Shit, I don't know. I gotta do something. Man some weapons?”

Lesto found this very funny. "First off, you’re a Rerun so you’re not smart enough to handle a broom much less a particle accelerator cannon."

Fragger bristled at the laughter. "Try me!" he challenged.

"Second of all, we're not armed."

"What?"

"Oh, we've got light armament, about enough to knock a flea off a dog but we're not going to use it."

"Why not?"

"Because this is an *Evader*-class ship. It’s 99% engine and 1% hull. It's designed for escaping, not fighting. My troopers will do all the combat on this mission while we slip you through."

"But what if we're hit?" Fragger asked.

"Then you and I are truly fucked."

Great, the Ranger grumbled. *For once, the translator gets exactly the right word.*

"Relax," Lesto said. "We'll be hard to find."

Fragger watched as Lesto keyed in a code, said "Prepare Evasion Pattern 1", then leaned back into his chair.

"That's it?" the Ranger asked. "Don't you have to fly this thing?"

"Rerun, at the speeds we'll be running, there isn't a human being alive who could handle the controls. If something goes wrong, I'll take over. Then, it's time for you to really start worrying."

"But nothing's happening," Fragger said.

"Initiate safety protocol," Lesto ordered the ship.

Fragger nearly panicked when a human-shaped mold hissed into place, coming down from overhead to seal him and the smell of the spilled *kim chee* securely in the seat. A small visor allowed him limited vision. The whole mechanism was claustrophobic and reminded him of the pod Watanabe had sealed him in to send him up to the HELOT. He wanted to break out in a sweat but there didn't seem to be room for even that.

"Execute Evasion Pattern 1," Lesto commanded.

Fragger's stomach panicked at the instant acceleration and clawed its way up into his mouth where it fought a pitched battle with a scream trying to escape his lips.

The scream won.

CHAPTER 15

Space combat unnerved Fragger.

There was no roar of 155s, the crack of a sniper's rifle, or the death-rattle of an M60 spraying rounds into the enemy.

In a vacuum, war was silent.

The only thing he could hear was the sound of his own breathing, a noise that was not reassuring since his lungs seemed capable only of erratic gasps as they tried to cope with the enormous acceleration applied to his chest in spite of the protective cocoon.

An irrational thought ran around inside the Ranger's head. *In my book, war should be noisy! There should be explosions and whizz of bullets. Something, anything. Instead, it's like being in a silent heavy sea, yawing around until you want to retch your guts out. Lesto wasn't kidding when he said this ship was all engine.*

The ceaseless maneuvering of the vessel was bad enough, but Fragger's mind had a hard time translating the light show outside the cockpit into the hard reality of combat. He searched for a comparison from his time that would make sense of it all, and there was only one that came close.

Spooky, the C-47 armed with a gatling gun. It could spew out thousands of rounds per minute in a show that lit up the night sky like a crazed fireworks show. This fight is most like that, but old Spook made a noise like a chainsaw ripping through sheet metal. A space engagement is nothing but cold, nasty silence.

Fragger shivered. *You can die here and not even have the satisfaction of having your screams heard.*

To keep his mind from panic, the Ranger concentrated on the light show. Like Spooky's gatling gun, it had an awful beauty--stabs of green, red, and yellow interspersed with the intensely white flowering of explosions he assumed were hits.

A high-pitched whistling sound drilled into the Ranger's ears, followed by Lesto's warning, "Hang on, Rerun! Proximity spread on its way. They're throwing nukes out like confetti. They really don't want to lose you."

An actinic glare seared Fragger's eyes for an instant before the visor went black. A second later, he knew how a mouse feels when the cat decides to play with its food. Paws of concussion batted the vessel around in teeth-jarring impacts and sent it whirling bow over stern.

"Integrity breach!" Lesto shouted over the commlink. "We've lost atmosphere, but the pods will keep us safe. Stay calm!"

Fragger chuckled at the command.

"What are you laughing at, Rerun?"

"Shit, there's nothing left to do but remain calm, is there?"

It was Lesto's turn to laugh. "You got that right. We're not dead yet, though. Let me see if I can get our rate of spin slowed down."

"And then what?"

"And then, we eject."

"To where? There's nowhere to go."

"Hold on," Lesto ordered.

The Ranger waited while Lesto worked the console again. A few seconds later, Fragger felt the spin lessen slightly.

"We still have some attitudinal control," the pilot informed him, "so I can get the spin down to a manageable level. When it's the right time to eject, I'll let you know."

"Like I said, eject to where?"

"Look out the window, Rerun."

For a moment, Fragger saw nothing. Then, the bloody eye of Mars winked at him as it flew past the ship. With each spin, it blinked at him again.

"How the hell do we get down there?" he asked.

"You're in a standard Escape Module, Rerun. It's a self-contained unit, air for you and propulsion for a limited distance--more than enough, in this case. I'm punching in the landing coordinates right now. All you have to do is hang on for the ride. The scenery on the way down is great."

"Wonderful! Assuming I survive the landing, what do I do then?"

"Stay put. The module computer will put out an encrypted position indicator. We'll pick you up."

"Well, what do I do if this module is hit and or cracks up on the ground?"

"First of all, Rerun, you won't be able to breathe. The lack of air will kill you. If that doesn't kill you, then the cold temperatures will. On top of that, breathing and freezing to death may be the least of your problems if you're unlucky. There are still spots of war bug contamination on Mars, you know."

"Bugs?"

Lesto nodded. "Biological agents. Lots of bad choices if that happens. Hemorrhage your lungs out....fry your brain like an egg...get quick-fever--"

The Ranger interrupted, "Just get on with it, okay?"

Lesto turned his attention back to the console, fingers moving expertly over the panel controls until the ship's rotation slowed to a gentle spin. Then, Lesto punched hard one final time, and Fragger heard small explosions overhead. He followed Lesto's gaze and saw the stars appear above as the blown hull panels floated away from the vessel.

"Okay, Rerun, here we go. See you on the surface."

Compressed gas hissed under Fragger's seat. The module lifted gently and floated out of the ship. It rotated enough so that the Ranger could see Lesto's module follow, then the pilot was out of sight as the propulsion system kicked in, correcting pitch until the red glare of Mars struck the Ranger full in the face.

"Wow!" Fragger said, impressed by the sight. Below, dust swirled in the atmosphere as the module accelerated downward.

At least, I assume it's dust. What I know about Mars you could put in a thimble and still have room left over.

When an area of the atmosphere cleared briefly to reveal grids of light, Fragger knew it was definitely dust.

"Cities on Mars!" he marveled.

I've traveled through hyperspace to worlds much farther away from Earth, but somehow this is more personal, more real. Mars is something I'm familiar with. In this future, it counts as close to home.

Involuntarily, the Ranger craned his neck around to catch a glimpse of Earth, then cursed his sudden and foolish homesickness. He wasn't sure he could see it from this distance and didn't know where to look, anyway.

Besides, Mars is coming up fast!

The steadily increasing acceleration of the module pushed the planet into Fragger's face until the stars disappeared. All he could see was friendly lights winking at him as a light shriek built up around the craft. Seconds later, the module decided to make the smooth ride into a gut-dropping, twisting trajectory. Fragger swore at the craft's manic maneuvers, wishing he had some control over the emergency vehicle. Then, several concussions shook him hard.

Those lights aren't so friendly after all, the Ranger realized. *Somebody's trying to shoot me down!*

Fragger switched from cursing the module's gyrations to urging it to go faster. It answered his unspoken wish by dropping like a flaming rock toward the Martian surface. All the Ranger could see in the twisting and turning was alternating glimpses of horizon and red dirt that grew rapidly into a rock-strewn desert and then even faster into a jagged range of hills. As the surface filled his field of vision, Fragger hoped the module's guidance system was still in one piece.

If not, I'm going to be as flat as a French pancake!

The hiss of attitudinal jets, then the blast of the engine knocked that fear from his head. Swinging to a landing position, the module lowered swiftly to touch down hard on a slope overlooking a shallow valley.

When the module swayed precariously back and forth, Fragger held his breath until the craft settled into immobility with a jarring lurch.

A display flashed on the visor in green letters, "Monitoring atmospheric conditions....please wait."

"What else can I do but wait, you idiot machine!" the Ranger cursed. "You better have not put a crack in the hull with that rough landing. I don't want to die from any of the war bugs Lesto talked about."

Fragger cussed again. The view was limited not only by the dust kicked up by the engine exhaust but also by the visor's constricted range. That made him nervous. He needed to know what he was facing when the dust settled down. Then he remembered the new technology and commanded, "Widen the field of vision."

Another message flashed on the visor—"To what degree?"

Fragger had expected the computer to answer him in a voice.

Maybe it's a combat security feature, he decided. *Or maybe it's just a simple unit not designed for speech.*

"Hell, I don't know. Maximum, try that."

The upper half of the module cleared.

When I can see through this dust, I'll have a 360 degree view, Fragger realized. *That is, I would if I could turn around in this thing.*

The computer finally displayed its atmospheric analysis. "Atmosphere is insufficient for human life if exposure prolonged. Chemical and biological agents are not detected at present location."

Another message came up, "Enemy forces detected."

"Which enemy?"

The module told him more than he wanted to know. "EarthCorp combat pursuit team. Ten personnel--eight PBUs and two RAM Kay-Nine units."

"Now give that to me in English, will you?" Fragger asked.

"Unable to process that command," the computer printed on the visor.

"Explain function of enemy units designated PBU and MARS--canine?--units."

"Designation PBU indicates Powered Body Armor units, human occupants. Armament, fusion Power Blade weapons. RAM Kay-Nines are small, reconnaissance units of the Robot, Assault, Mobile classification. Armament, light Gauss multi-barrel rifles. Primary purpose of Kay-Nine units is detection. Colloquial term is 'snoop-sniffers'."

What the hell are those things? Robotic dogs? Fragger wondered. Then, he asked the computer the important question. "Have they found us--me?"

"They know you are in the general area," the display answered. "Deployment of camouflage only partly effective."

"Advise action."

"None to be taken. This system is not armed."

"Oh, that's just great."

"Lesto forces are near," the message added.

"How near?"

The computer ignored his question. Instead, it presented new information.

"Targeting detected. Enemy weapons attempting to lock on."

The Ranger laid down a string of profanities he hoped would fry the useless computer's innards, then relaxed. There was nothing to be done as he thought with resignation, *Look at me. All dressed up and nowhere to go.*

CHAPTER 16

The EarthCorp pursuit units raced toward Fragger across the floor of the valley. Their speed kicked up wide rooster tails of red against the pink, dusty sky and blurred their shapes so he couldn't make out exactly what they looked like. The cold, combat part of his mind analyzed the situation, even though he was helpless to affect the outcome.

Ten of them, just like the suit said.

The rocks around Fragger began re-arranging themselves into smaller pieces at a frantic pace. A thin, stuttering rip of sound penetrated the module.

Here comes the attack!

Light winked from one of the attackers, and the Ranger didn't recognize the specific type of weapon firing at him, but he knew when one was on full automatic. It chewed up the landscape in a searching pattern around the module. Whoever was firing was attempting to panic him out into the open for a clean shot.

"Sorry," the Ranger muttered. "No room for panic in here."

Fragger estimated he was 200 feet above the floor of the valley, and the valley itself looked to be about two kilometers wide. When they were a klick from his position, the attackers deployed into a skirmish line and slowed to advance toward the module in a deliberate search pattern.

A precise distance between them, the Ranger noted. *Whatever the equivalent of artillery in this future, they have to account for blast radius just as we did. The only difference is the two units out in front--Kay Nine models, I assume, but they sure as hell don't look anything like dogs. At the rate they're going, they'll take a while to get here. Time enough to study their tactics--for all the good it'll do if they kill me.*

"Hey!" Fragger let out a sudden shout of surprise.

One of the advance Kay-Nine units had disappeared.

Then reappeared a hundred feet closer.

The other unit did the same, leapfrogging ahead of the first.

Damn, how the hell did they do that? the Ranger swore. He had no time to come up with answers to the question because both units disappeared again, then re-materialized.

Fifty feet away.

"Snoop-sniffers have locked gauss weapons on" the module's computer informed him.

"Tell me something I don't know," Fragger snapped.

The display responded with a large question mark.

The two EarthCorp RAM units did have the K-9 designation stamped into their frames in bright red letters. As he'd suspected, they didn't look anything like dogs. What they did look like was two small flying armored tanks with very bad attitudes.

Fragger waited for them to blow him and the module into oblivion. Instead, the two snoop-sniffers hovered a foot above the rocky ground, apparently communicating with the rest of the squad. The hum of immense power sent vibrations through the module's hull, jarring the Ranger's teeth until his gums ached.

A blinding blue-white flash shook his mind free of the pain in his mouth. For a moment, he was sure he was dead because everything was black. Then, the module visor gradually lightened, and the Ranger stared out at two burning Kay-Nine hulks smashed into the ground. When he lifted his eyes to the floor of the valley, he saw the enemy caught in a rain of death. From a position above his head, withering fire poured down the slope. It was over in seconds with the EarthCorp unit reduced to smoldering black heaps on the pink soil.

If it's Lesto, the man knows what he's doing, Fragger thought with admiration. *The attack had the nasty efficiency of a seasoned combat soldier. The EarthCorp forces were hit so fast and so effectively they didn't have time to do anything.*

Minutes later, several mantis-like powered armor suits planted themselves in front of the Ranger. The lead suit's darkened outer visor slid up, and Lesto's hairy face appeared.

"Welcome to Mars, Rerun," he said. "Sorry, you won't see much of it right away. Time to go hide."

"Why hide? You smoked the pursuit."

"Smoked?"

"Wasted them. Killed the enemy.'

"Oh. Well, Rerun, let's put it this way. There's more of them than there is of us. Many more."

Fragger realized the confusion on his face must have been obvious when Lesto quickly continued, "Mars doesn't belong to us. It's enemy territory. An EarthCorp planet."

The Ranger felt doubly confused. "Then who are you with, the Imperial Commonwealth?"

Laughter crackled over the communications link.

"No, we're not Ricer troops," Lesto answered.

"You're mercs?"

"That's us," Lesto said.

It was a quick answer, too quick for Fragger's taste. The Ranger was suspicious and said so. "I don't believe you. In my day, no mercenary force could have mounted an operation of that complexity and sophistication."

Lesto's voice came like a shrug over the commlink. "Okay, we're not mercenaries."

"Then, who are you?"

"Troopers carrying out orders. That's all you need to know for now."

"That's not a good answ---."

"Rerun, you know by now that whatever information is in your head can be pulled out with little trouble. So you can understand I'm not going to put my men and the mission in danger by giving you anything of value. There's only one thing you need to understand. Shut up and follow my orders."

"Which are?" Fragger asked.

"Get out of the module."

"Are you crazy? I'll freeze to death!"

Lesto uttered a command over the commlink. Without warning, the top half of the module popped open in a hiss of actuated mechanism, and the pod enclosing him followed suit. The thin Martian air bit at Fragger's skin with icy teeth. Lesto pointed at two of his men holding a black suit between them.

I don't need to be told twice! Fragger thought as he jumped free of the module. Stumbling in a deep pool of rust-colored dirt, he fell to his hands and knees as the cold hit him like a solid block of ice. With amazing speed, powerful armored hands caught him, jerked him up and pushed him toward the suit. Its back seemed to melt into an opening as the Ranger's arms were thrust into the sleeves. Fragger thought the suit wasn't much protection until the garment crawled up over his body and head like a thousand busy spiders and sealed him away from the bitter cold. Warmth shot through his body, gradually subduing the spasmodic shivering of his muscles. Over the chattering of his teeth, he heard Lesto's laugh on the commlink.

"Rerun, damn, you're fast as lightning when you're scared! That's a Martian survival suit you just scooted into," he explained. "It'll keep your balls from falling off until we reach our objective."

"How'd it do that?" Fragger asked as he examined the suit and the wrist instrumentation that told him the temperature and other weather conditions. The fabric seemed to be some kind of metal or plastic or a combination of the two, but it felt like a soft, fine wool against his skin.

"Do what?"

"I don't know. The damned thing just seemed to put itself--whoa, shit!"

"What's the matter?" Lesto asked.

"Something's pulling at my dick and going up my ass!" Fragger wiggled wildly at the invasion of his body.

A snort of laughter greeted this remark. "Nanotechs," Lesto explained.

"What's that?"

"Think of it as millions of very tiny robots who can knit themselves into whatever shape you want. They provide you with oxygen and recycle your body wastes at the same time. As long as you provide energy, you're in good shape."

"These nanotechs are intelligent, you mean?" Fragger asked.

"They have limited intelligence. Kind of like Earth ants. Geared to the purpose of the group which, in this case, is to protect you. Unfortunately, they're not protecting me from your questions, Rerun. Come on, get moving."

"How am I supposed to keep up with you people in your armored suits? I've seen how fast you can move."

"No problem," Lesto answered.

Scooping Fragger up into his arms, the leader accelerated to a speed that transformed the harsh landscape into a pink blur. Dizzied by the suddenness of the action, the Ranger kept his eyes on the horizon which resolved itself into an endless series of low, eroded hills as if the Great Plains of the Midwest had decided to rust itself into a harsh, nearly airless desert.

Fragger had no idea how long Lesto forced a quick pace, but the entire time he felt foolish as if he were a helpless woman who needed to be carried to safety. He was glad when Lesto finally ordered a stop and put him down next to one of the interminably identical ridges they'd crossed during their journey.

"What now?" Fragger asked.

"Shut up," Lesto ordered.

The Ranger waited while some silent communication passed among Lesto and his unit. Finally, Lesto issued a command. "All right, DEEPs on the prowl. Locate an underground spot."

His team spread out. After a brief search, a signal from one of the members caused Lesto to point a finger toward a black opening at the far end of a shallow depression. "In there, Rerun."

Fragger obeyed and found the opening led to a small cave in the side of a ridge. He slipped through the entrance easily and waited in darkness as Lesto's soldiers forced their bulky suits through and joined him. Even in the thin atmosphere, he could hear the creaking of suit joints that had sand worked into them. In a moment, everyone was still. The darkness made Fragger nervous.

"Isn't there a light in here somewhere?" he asked.

"It's a cave," Lesto said. "They don't come equipped with lights, you ass."

"I thought it might be, well...."

"Well, what?"

"I don't know--the entrance to an underground base or something?" Fragger suggested.

"Where do you get these ideas, Rerun?"

"It's the future for me, remember? I was expecting something more...high tech."

A short laugh came from Lesto. "Sorry to disappoint you. This is the only future I can offer, and it's going to be a mighty short one if you say another word because if the Deep Peepers find us, either they'll kill you or I will."

Fragger had no idea what Deep Peepers were, but like everything else he'd run into in the future, he was sure it had an extravagant means of ending his life.

"Everybody power down to minimum sustainability," Lesto ordered. "That includes you, Rerun. Sit down and tell your suit to execute minimum occupant status. It's going to get cold, then it's going to get real uncomfortable but no matter what happens inside your head or out--don't move."

Fragger wondered what the devil Lesto was talking about, but obeyed and was surprised to find that the frigid air of Mars didn't immediately penetrate the suit.

Its insulation factor must be extremely high, he reasoned as he sat down and tried to squirm into a comfortable position.

"No movement, either," Lesto ordered. "Absolute stillness."

Ranger training let Fragger obey the command without much thought.

Ambush tactics called for stillness, both to surprise the enemy and to prevent him from surprising you. What he couldn't figure out was how EarthCorp units could possibly detect them underground in the midst of a Martian desert.

Sleepiness crept in as nothing happened and a chill gradually seeped through the suit. Fragger was tired. A lot had happened since Lesto had stolen him off the *Lethal.*

That's the trouble with the future. There's always something happening, and I never get a chance to catch up with it. Oh well, sooner or later, the odds say that I'll get a breather.

Chattering teeth brought him out of a drowsy numbness.

Damn, he thought. *Is it that cold?*

Then he realized that his teeth were responding to a sound, not the freezing temperature. A distant buzz grew, shaking dirt and pebbles down onto his helmet.

Like the hum of high tension wires, the Ranger decided.

The sound increased, not in volume, but in bone-shaking intensity. It penetrated his suit and tried to vibrate his skeleton right out of his body.

Some sort of subsonics, Fragger realized.

He wanted to cry out at the pain as the noise swept closer, but hearing no sound from the other men in the cave, he vowed he wasn't going to let them beat him at the endurance game. That promise was nearly broken when a light flashed outside the cave, and a heat-burst shot through the entrance. Fragger suppressed a gasp, feeling like he was being fried alive inside his suit. A second later the heat was gone.

Godamnit, they're throwing everything at us. What's next? he wondered.

Fragger braced for another blast of heat or sound. Instead, he was startled when a sweet female voice began whispering seductively in his ear, "Fragger Sparks, Fragger Sparks, I'm waiting for you. I'm so close to you now that all you have to do is reach out and touch me. Tell me where you are so I can come to you. Do it now."

Oh, no, not again! Fragger cursed, remembering the irresistible lure of the women in his first interrogation by the Ricer, Harada, in the HELOT. *This time I know I can resist! I know I can! It's only a false voice inside my head. It's not real.*

To his relief, his resistance was working. He felt only a slight urge to get up and run out of the cave to seek the source of the voice.

Then, a second woman's voice spoke softly into his other ear. "I want you too, Fragger Sparks! You're mine, all mine. She can't have you. You're mine, mine, mine! Come out so you can have me!"

Fragger swallowed at the force of the seductive assault. *Counter the voices by concentrating on the ugliest sights you can think of, Sparks!* he ordered himself. *Major Shimazu, Interrogator Meitz, Chief Mess Cook Bagwell-*

"Come to us, come...come...come to us!" the voices urged. "We can't live without you, Fragger Sparks! We'll die if you don't love us!"

The ugly images of Shimazu and the others faded away under the impact of the sheer amount of love the women felt for him. Fragger made a sudden decision that felt so, so right. *By God, I've never had women want me so badly. I'll be damned if I'll pass up an opportunity like this!*

He scrambled to get up and run out to meet the women. Strong hands threw him back to the ground. He struggled wildly to get free until he felt a tap against the side of his helmet and his visor slid open. The razor's edge of the Martian cold slashed his face into numbness. The shock knocked his mind free of the hypnotic insistence of the false summons. He relaxed back into the grip of the troopers, letting them know he was okay. They made sure he stayed still by keeping a tight grip until the seductive voices faded into silence amidst the diminishing hum of the probe.

Fragger had no idea how long Lesto and his squad waited to make sure the area was clear. He only knew he couldn't feel his nose anymore and was grateful when the visor slid shut and warmth returned to the suit. A light flicked on inside Lesto's helmet, and a hairy face grinned at Fragger as he asked, "Enjoy the Loreleis, Rerun?"

The only response the Ranger could make was, "Damn!"

"You're pretty good," Lesto said. "You held out longer than most."

"I only resisted them for a minute or two," he pointed out. For some reason, he felt thoroughly ashamed at such weakness.

"That's twice as long as most people," Lesto reassured him. "You're tougher than you look."

"How come you and the others didn't fall prey to it?"

"Several reasons. They keyed it primarily to your brain signature, not ours. Plus, we have resistance training as well as passive blocking programs built into our suits. And, of course, we're superior."

For an unguarded moment, Fragger thought Lesto had told a small joke in his last remark to relax everyone from the tension of their encounter with the Deep Peepers. When there was no laughter from anyone and an arrogant certainty on Lesto's face, Fragger returned to earth from the brief moment of comradeship. Lesto *did* believe he and his fellow soldiers were better men than a Rerun.

Fuck 'em all, Fragger swore and placed the Ranger motto squarely in the front of his thoughts. *By the end of all this shit, Lesto will know who the better man is. And he'll know that Rangers lead the way!!*

"What now?" he asked Lesto in an even tone to keep his anger hidden. "One of your spacecraft comes down and picks us up? Or we do vanish from one spot and show up at another like I saw those Kay-Nines do?"

A round of snickers passed through the troopers.

"We do it the hard way, Rerun," Lesto answered. "We walk."

CHAPTER 17

"Walk?" Fragger said, his anger doubled because of the laughter of Lesto's men. "Some future this is. All this technological shit, and you can't do any better than we did back in the Twentieth Century. A raw Ranger recruit could do better than you people."

"We bring down a ship now, it'll get blown out of the sky," Lesto explained. "As for the 'disappearing act', as you put it, we don't have the equipment. Tapping into hyperspace takes energy. It's not for a quick strike force."

"Sounds like excuses to me," Fragger said with contempt to cover his surprise that Lesto had finally revealed some information about himself and his command. *Lesto probably wouldn't refer to his team as a 'quick strike force' if they were mercs. That remark implies they're part of a real standing army. Lesto is more than what he seems.*

Inside his helmet, Lesto raised an eyebrow at the implied insult. "Excuses, Rerun?"

"Yeah, I think you're just a bunch of pussies."

"Pussies? The translator doesn't seem to have a definition for that term. What does it mean?" Lesto asked.

"Pussies. You know, women. It's a way of saying a woman could do better than you people."

Lesto started to chuckle, then broke into outright laughter.

Fragger waited until Lesto got control of himself before asking, "What's so damned funny?"

Lesto explained, "Rerun, you may want to take that remark back. Half the troopers around you *are* women."

Silently, Fragger cursed his stupidity and tried to rescue the situation by saying, "Well, not women then, but children…children could do better. They could…"

The Ranger shut up because he knew his ridicule had lost all its steam, and from the rustling of armor, he knew he was in the midst of some very unhappy women. That was proved when one of them shoved him out the cave and into the open. He landed on his back, kicking up a cloud of dust that failed to obscure the soldier looming over him.

"Okay, okay, I'm sorry," the Ranger said.

The apology had no effect. The trooper leaned down and grabbed his leg. In a second, Fragger hung upsidedown in the air.

"Sooz, put him down," Lesto ordered as he emerged from the cave.

The Ranger fell as fast as he'd been picked up, thumping his helmet against a rock.

"Damn!" he swore as he tried to rub the sore spot through the suit and failed to accomplish any relief. He decided sitting still for a while was the safest course. While he waited, Lesto commanded silence from his team so he could scan the area. After long moments, he said, "We're clear for now. Do the lizard thing, then let's move."

As Fragger watched, each of the soldiers turned into a blur, barely distinguishable against the landscape. He strained his eyes trying to focus on the nearly invisible forms.

I'm impressed, the Ranger admitted. *Almost total camouflage. Like chameleons.*

One of the blurs moved toward him and abruptly snapped into focus. It was Lesto.

"Get up, Rerun. We've got a good distance to cover."

"Do you mind telling me where we're going?" Fragger asked as he got up out of the dust.

"Valles Marineris?"

"What's that?"

"You can't be that ignorant, Rerun. Even in your time, you must have known about the great canyon of Mars."

"Oh, yeah, sure," Fragger said, unwilling to acknowledge he knew nothing about the canyon.

"Pick him up," Lesto ordered one of his troopers.

"Wait a minute!" the Ranger protested. "Can't I ride on somebody's back this time?"

"Why?" Lesto asked. "What's the difference?"

"It's uncomfortable," Fragger lied. It wasn't really uncomfortable but he wasn't about to admit to Lesto that he found it embarrassing to be carried like a child across the sand.

"Suit yourself," Lesto said. "Climb aboard Sooz's armor."

Fragger leapt on the soldier's back and wrapped his arms around her neck. She leaped up the slope by the cave and out onto a plain strewn with rocks. As Lesto's team raced across the terrain, Fragger studied the terrain and found it boring. It looked to him as if the planet had decided to rust itself to death over the centuries. It was a bleak reddish-brown landscape, whose mind-numbing sameness was relieved only by a sky that was dark blue when not obscured by the pinkish dust.

God, what a dreary place! he complained. *Colder than hell and tedious to boot.*

The monotony made him drowsy. He tried to stay awake, but the steady pace of the troopers and the sameness of the landscape overpowered his tired body and sent him off to sleep.

When Fragger woke, he was still hanging onto Sooz's back as she ran at the rear of the team. As he shook the sleep from his system, he realized he was hungry and thirsty. He discovered quickly that two plastic nipples--one on each side of the helmet--gave him water, but there didn't seem to be any provision for food in the suit. His stomach growled.

But I'll be damned if I'll admit hunger to Lesto and his troopers, he vowed, remembering his promise to show Lesto who was the better soldier.

Fragger forgot about his rumbling stomach when Lesto topped a rise and called a halt.

"Sooz," he ordered. "Bring the Rerun up here and put him down so he can see the Valles Marineris."

Sooz obeyed and unceremoniously dumped Fragger hard into the dust on his tailbone. He was about to cuss her out when he followed the line of Lesto's pointing finger.

"Damn, double damn, and triple damn!" he swore in astonishment at the sight that lay before him. "'Canyon' is not a big enough word, Lesto!"

The walls stretched so deeply into Mars that Fragger wasn't sure whether he was seeing the bottom of the canyon or not. Dust hung in the air, obscuring details. The Ranger was puzzled by the patches of pinkish white dotting the rubble-strewn slopes. It looked like ice, but Mars didn't have any surface water so far as he knew. He tried to recall information from his science classes in high school before sheepishly remembering, *Unfortunately, I slept through most of those lectures. I was too eager to enlist to pay attention to school.*

When he couldn't come up with an answer as to the composition of the patches, the Ranger asked, "What is that stuff?"

"What stuff?" Lesto responded.

"The white ice, or whatever it is, on the sides of the canyon."

"Carbon dioxide."

"Oh. Well, I can see why you chose this place to hide, Lesto. Nobody could find us. It'd be like trying to locate a bunch of ants in the Grand Canyon."

"Where?"

"The Grand Canyon. You know, on Earth. I hiked it many times."

"Oh, yeah," Lesto replied absently as if he were distracted by other matters.

The response annoyed Fragger. He wasn't used to people being indifferent to the Grand Canyon. It had always been one of the glories of America, and Lesto gave it no more thought than he would a rut in the road.

Still, the Ranger admitted, *this place does make the Grand Canyon seem kind of like a rut in the road. My God, it's huge!*

"Okay, people," Lesto announced abruptly. "Let's get down into Marineris. I'm detecting heavy surveillance activity again. Time to disappear."

"Sir, fuel cell check shows I'm running low," Sooz said.

"How low?"

"Barely 30% capacity."

"That'll just get you to the rendezvous point. Rerun, you walk from here. The rest of you, we need to slow down to conserve fuel and to avoid leaving a dust trail in the air. The DEEPS will be on us like starving dogs if we leave that kind of sign behind us. Take the lizard off to reduce fuel consumption. They'll be looking for blur signatures, and we'll stand out like sore thumbs against the canyon walls."

Fragger fell into step behind the troopers as they complied with Lesto's orders, then filed down the trail at a normal speed. The pace made him feel better, more like he was on an equal footing with them.

Don't get too complacent, he warned himself. *Just one of those armored suits could crush me like a bug.*

And I certainly feel no bigger than a bug, he added, adjusting his stride to match the skipping march of the troopers in the light gravity. The sheer cliffs of Marineris rose steadily around them until the sky seemed to Fragger as if it had placed itself at the wrong end of a telescope, and yet they kept descending, flattening against the rocks when ordered to do so by Lesto. Several times, Fragger saw dark objects soar slowly across the rim of the canyon, running methodical search patterns. Some loosed bolts of energy down into the rock, apparently hoping Lesto's troops would lose their discipline and reveal their location. It was a fruitless endeavor. The soldiers marched down without a word. The only noise picked up by Fragger's external audio was the thin sound of their footsteps and an odd, faint creaking from the team's armor that grew louder the longer they walked. It puzzled Fragger until he realized, *It's the dust. I'll bet it works itself into everything here.* He listened closely to his survival suit and was mystified to hear nothing. After a few seconds of thought, he had the difference between his suit and the armor figured out. *It must be the nano-whatevers. They must be able to, in effect, weave so tightly that dust and dirt can't penetrate the surface. Helluva design!*

Fragger's marvel at the sophistication of the suit occupied only a small portion of his thoughts for the next ten hours. Thoughts about steaks, chops, hamburgers—any kind of meat—occupied the rest. Lesto finally called a halt under an overhang of rock that provided cover from aerial reconnaissance. Hunger didn't seem to provide any distraction to Lesto, but the noise of the suits obviously did as he swore, “Damned dust! We might as well be banging drums to announce our position.”

"Well, it's just about to get worse, sir," one of the troopers said, pointing ahead of them.

Fragger looked and saw nothing but more canyon layered in shadows.

Then, the shadows moved and shifted toward them.

“What is that?” the Ranger asked.

“Dust storm,” Lesto answered in a worried tone. “Everybody stay put so we don't get separated.”

Picking up on Lesto's tone, Fragger asked, “What's the big deal? I should think you'd be happy. Your enemy can't find you in a storm, can they?”

“No, they can't, but the winds on Mars can blow for a long time, Rerun. A very long time. Long enough for us to run out of air.”

“Oh,” Fragger said. “So, what do we do?”

“Sit tight. There's nothing else to do. We'll just hope it doesn't last long, and we have enough air to make it to the nearest OEP.”

“What's an OEP?”

“Oxygen extraction plant. Mars has plenty of O^2 in its rocks. It's just a matter of money and the right equipment to get it out. There's a ring of OEPs around the planet.”

“How far is the nearest---?” Fragger began to ask, but dust swept past his helmet and he suddenly felt like he was swimming in a pink sea. A thin, high-pitched wind keened into his ears as if a Martian banshee were announcing a death.

Not mine, the Ranger hoped as he tried to shut the sound out of his head.

He sat down, turning his back to the storm out of instinct even though the storm couldn’t penetrate his suit. There was nothing to see, just dust. It reminded him of the black and white photos of the Dirty Thirties his parents had shown him. One had featured a light pole at high noon barely visible through a black haze of soil blown off dry fields.

This is far worse, Fragger grumbled. *At least, on earth they didn't have worry about running out of air.*

"Shit!" he yelled just to make himself feel better.

"Rerun," Lesto ordered. "Shut up."

"Oh, fuck you! If I'm going to asphyxiate out here, I'm damned well not going to go quietly."

"What makes you think you won't be able to breathe?"

"You said we might run out of air, that's what."

"My team and I might run out of air but not you, so you can stop hollering."

"What do you mean?"

"You're wearing a Martian survival suit, Rerun. It operates like a miniature OEP. It extracts what little oxygen there is from the air, plus the nanotechs in your feet, hand, knee, and butt areas are designed like miniature ore processors. Every time you touch a rock, you're getting oxygen."

"Your suits can't do that?" Fragger asked.

"No."

"Why not?"

"Powered armor is designed for combat in space and on planetary surfaces of all kinds. Usually, there's no need for OEP equipment. The fusion cells power the oxygen functions."

"Oh," Fragger said. "Then I might--."

"Survive, and we won't? Won't happen, Rerun. I don't know exactly what your special abilities are, but I'll kill you before I let any of our enemies exploit them."

"Don't feel special," Fragger shot back. "Everyone wants to kill me rather than let the other side get hold of me. It seems to be some sort of standing order."

A wheedling tone came into Lesto's voice, "Well, if you give me the information about those abilities right now so I can transmit it to my extraction team, I promise you that I won't kill you or harm you in any way."

Fragger gave a scornful response to the suggestion. "What a liar you are, Lesto! If I gave you the information, you'd kill me on the spot. And here's the kicker—I can't give you any details about my abilities because I don't know what those abilities are."

"I think you're lying, Rerun."

"Then that makes two of--"

A gust of wind cut the exchange short by nearly knocking the men over. The Ranger squatted down to escape its force. Unconsciously, he wrapped his arms around his body to preserve heat then felt instantly stupid when he remembered it was a useless gesture on Mars. He was perfectly warm. The clash of his Earth weather instincts with the reality of the Mars environment sent a wave of frustration through him. To take his mind off the irritation, he asked Lesto, "So, what do we do now? Wait the storm out?"

"Sure, if it's a short one. Real short."

"It can't last very long, can it?"

"Sometimes, they go on for a year, Rerun."

"Jeezus! What if that does happen?"

"Then we're screwed," came the blunt answer.

"Well, hell, shouldn't we be doing something about our situation?"

"Instrumentation is no good in all this dust," Lesto answered. "If we try walking blind, we could end up stepping off a cliff. In the Valles Marineris, that can be a very, very long way down."

"We don't weigh that much in this atmosphere, do we?" Fragger asked. "A fall shouldn't hurt that much."

"The atmosphere may be 98% carbon dioxide with light gravity but there's still your body mass, Rerun. That'll kill you just as dead."

Frustrated by Lesto's answer, Fragger complained, "You'd think that with all your advanced technology, some one would thought to give Mars a breathable atmosphere."

"Not much point in it," Lesto said. "Takes a long time to terraform, and there's money--lots of it--to be made on Mars right now."

"Doing what?"

"Minerals and oxygen."

"I thought there wasn't any oxygen here!"

"Rerun, you don't listen well, do you? I already told you about the OEPs. Mars is red because it's one big rusty ball. You need oxygen to make rust. That means there's a lot of it trapped in the planet's surface. Human beings don't go anywhere without oxygen. Mars is a major supplier to commercial and military fleets. That's why there are so many OEPs. You own a piece of Mars, you're a very rich man."

"That sounds funny--selling oxygen like it was soap or something," Fragger said.

"Makes you appreciate your home planet, doesn't it, Sparks?"

"You'll never know. It's been six hundred years for me. What's Earth like now?"

"Don't know. Haven't been there for about 10 years myself," Lesto replied.

"Well, what was it like the last time you were there?"

Fragger heard a shrug in the man's voice as he answered, "Big, messy, sprawling, people everywhere you look. Like a bunch of ants, but wealthy ones."

"You mean all the people are wealthy?" the Ranger asked.

"Compared to us, they are," Lesto said, a tinge of bitterness in his voice. "They've got the good things in life. Don't have to worry about paying for oxygen or fuel or shipping weights. Shit, they're so rich a single Terran can own a personal nanoforge. You can build yourself anything you want, provided you've got the raw materials."

A resentful tone came over the commlink as Lesto added, "And guess who supplies those at prices damned near below cost?"

"People like you?" Fragger prompted.

"Yeah."

Disgust and despair filled that one word.

"Are you miners or something?" the Ranger asked.

"Maybe," Lesto said curtly as if he'd realized he'd given away more information than he'd intended to. "You don't need to know."

Uncomfortable in the squat, Fragger stood to move into a different position and found his feet were slow to move. For a moment, he panicked, thinking that the suit's integrity had been breached and his feet were freezing, but after a brief, frantic shuffle of his boots, realized it was simply that he was now ankle-deep in dust.

"If this wind keeps up, we're going to be buried under all this sand and dust," he told Lesto.

Squeaks and scrapes of movement accompanied Lesto's voice. "Saves us having to dig our own graves, doesn't it?"

Fragger disapproved of Lesto's response. *That's no way for a combat leader to talk. A bad attitude like that can infect his entire team. Next thing you know, unit cohesion will be gone, and everyone will be giving in to the storm. He should be pumping them up not--*

A suspicion froze the Ranger in mid-thought. Through the keening of the wind, he heard Lesto maneuvering closer. The sound of grit in his armor's joints gave him away.

He knows I have an opportunity for escape now! Fragger realized. *He's either trying to make sure I don't get away, or he wants to kill me so I don't fall into anybody else's hands. I'll be damned if I'll give him the chance!*

The Ranger lowered himself to his knees, then lay down on the ground and began low crawling in the opposite direction from the sound of Lesto's creaking armor.

It took only a few moments for Lesto to ask, "Rerun? Where are you? I can't see a thing in all this dust. Start talking so I can find you. We need to stick together for everybody's safety."

Everybody's safety but mine, you sonuvabitch! Fragger swore as he kept up the low crawl in silence.

Lesto's voice rose over the commlink. "Rerun, I didn't mean to scare you with all that negative talk. My extraction team is on the way. They'll find us. Rerun? Don't panic and run out there blindly. You'll get yourself killed."

Right, Fragger thought. *What a liar you are, Lesto! Nobody can find us in this storm. I hope you get everything you deserve! I hope you end up breathing Martian air!*

After a second's silence, Lesto's tone changed abruptly as he transmitted a command to his team. "The Rerun's trying to escape! Key on my suit signature and form up around me so we don't end up shooting each other."

Fragger crawled as fast as he could, trying to put as much distance as possible between him and Lesto's team before they could open up with their weapons. He hadn't gone far before he heard Lesto's "Fire!" command, and explosions shook the ground. The Ranger sped up the crawl until he rammed his head hard into a rock. Shaking off the impact, he felt around with his hands and discovered that it was a boulder he'd hit and big enough to provide cover. He scrambled around behind it and made himself as small as possible while the fire from Lesto's men probed the dust storm in dark, dirty flashes of light. Fragger wasn't worried they'd hit him directly, but rock shrapnel from the blasts was another story. He was sure the protection level of the survival suit didn't reach that of the powered armor worn by Lesto and his troopers. Shivering with fear, the Ranger hugged the boulder closely until he heard Lesto give the command to cease fire.

"Rerun? You don't really want to be out there all by yourself, do you? It's dangerous. You haven't got any food. You'll starve to death. Come on back to us, and you stand a better chance of living. I'll do my best to make sure you stay alive. That's a promise--one soldier to another."

Fragger couldn't resist a reply. "Lesto, you must be desperate. All of a sudden I'm promoted from a Rerun to an actual soldier."

"That's right, you are a real soldier. And a real soldier uses common sense. You've only got two choices—die in the storm or come on back here and take a chance with me."

"Helluva choice!" Fragger said. "I'll take the storm just to deny you the satisfaction of killing me."

The guns fired again on Lesto's command, but the fusillade came nowhere near the Ranger's position.

They can't find me, Fragger exulted. Emboldened, he taunted Lesto again, "You're not going anywhere, are you, Lesto? All this dust has screwed up your suit joints, hasn't it? You can't move well. Otherwise, you'd be coming after me. I'm talking to dead men. You're stuck here."

Weapons fire searched for him again.

Fragger's spirits soared. He couldn't help it. *I might be dead myself in the end, but, by God, Lesto and his people are dying with me. It's the first time in this screwed-up future that I'm on top!*

"Lesto!" he shouted. "You and your team can kiss your asses goodbye!"

Lesto responded in a quiet voice, "You'd leave us here, Sparks?"

"Just like you'd leave me."

"No true soldier would abandon his comrades," Lesto said.

"Comrades? All of a sudden, you're buddies with a Rerun? Come on, Lesto, cut the crap! You're pathetic. In my day, soldiers acted like men. They didn't whine."

"I'm not whining, Sparks. It's my team I'm concerned about, that's all. I'm responsible for their lives."

"Right now, their lives aren't worth dick because of you, Lesto. You said I had a choice. Well, you've got one too. Die slowly from lack of oxygen or use your weapons on yourselves and die quick. To show you the same concern you showed me, I hope it's the first choice!"

This time, the troopers cut loose with everything they had in a furious response. Fragger's body bounced off the ground at the force of the explosions, but he felt only small pieces of gravel ping off his suit without any apparent damage. He waited until the firing died down, then turned around and maintained a steady crawl away from the trapped soldiers. He had no idea of where he was or where he was going. He knew one thing, however. With the survival suit, he had a chance of survival that Lesto and his men didn't have.

The hatred warmed his heart but heat from the emotion didn't last long. Through the increasingly degraded signal, Lesto said, "Rerun, we'll die, but so will you. You haven't got any food. Your body's only got so much water the suit can extract. I'll be there to greet you at the gates of Hell."

"Sorry," Fragger replied. "I plan on living. You'll be in Hell all by yourself, remembering forever that you failed in your mission, outclassed by a mere Rerun. Enjoy a lonely eternity, Lesto."

The Ranger had the satisfaction of receiving no reply, but when he stared out into the pinkish dust obscuring any detail of the landscape, his words to Lesto sounded a lot braver than he felt.

To buck up his courage, Fragger shouted, "Rangers lead the way!"

His mind cut that effort short with the obvious thought, *But they were never intended to do it on Mars!*

CHAPTER 18

Fragger hadn't low-crawled so much since basic training, but he couldn't figure out any other safe way to put distance between himself and Lesto. All the time, the question kept nagging at him.

How the hell do you survive on a planet where you can't eat? Rangers are taught to eat bugs for protein and lick water from leaves, but those items are in damned short supply on Mars.

Fragger both hated and welcomed the question of how to survive. He hated it because there didn't seem to be any answer to it. He welcomed it because it took his attention away from the hunger taking bigger and bigger bites out of his stomach. But consideration of the survival question still didn't allow him to ignore his biggest problem.

I'm lost in all this dust. What's worse, even if the stuff clears from the sky, I still have no idea of which direction to head. In fact, I'm not even certain what the directions are on Mars. There's only thing I am sure of. I'm learning to detest any shade of the color red.

"It's like living inside some woman's damned cosmetic case," Fragger complained out loud to give himself some company, not worrying about radio silence because he was sure the dust was limiting any communications. Then he quit the useless activity and continued clambering across Mars, blinded by the dust, until his arms gave out. Rolling onto his back, the Ranger let a brief moment of despair break through.

I wonder if I'll ever be able to see where I'm going? Lesto said these storms could last up to a year.

The Ranger shoved that depressing thought aside with the self-admonition, *If a storm lasts a year, I'm dead anyway so just worry about the present. Take a rest, then find one of those oxygen-extraction plants Lesto talked about. That's your hope, Fragger Sparks.*

The Ranger heaved himself up and crawled around until he found a rock big enough to offer shelter from the wind and all the dirt and gravel it was flinging through the pink air. Fragger didn't know much about physics. With lighter gravity, he'd assumed that the wind wouldn't have much force to it, but the breeze threatened to blow him around just as much as any Earthly wind.

Maybe it's because I'm lighter too, he decided. *It's probably all relative.*

Hunkering back against the boulder, he forced his body to relax and tried to sleep.

It was less difficult to grab some shuteye than I thought, Fragger realized as he woke with a start. Smacking the helmet with his hand to rub an eye he couldn't reach, he swore then realized something was different in his surroundings. Ghosts of rocky rubble showed now and then through the dust as if he were having a dream bent on tantalizing him with fragments of images that didn't quite make sense. Then the reality hit him.

The wind is slacking off! I can see something. Not much, but something.

Fragger let out a deep, relieved breath, realizing how much he'd dreaded being lost in the fog of Martian dust. The only earthly equivalent he could think of was the one white-out he'd experienced in a South Dakota spring blizzard. The snow had wiped out all reference points, preventing him from telling up from down and giving him the feeling he was lost forever in a formless limbo of weather.

Hunger sucked at Fragger's gut and broke off the comparison with Earth. His stomach was dialing up his brain with constant demands for food, but the Ranger forced himself to sit up and wait patiently for the wind to die down.

As if someone had spilled dirty orange soup in the air, dust remained suspended above the ground but the haze no longer had the opaque quality of the storm. Gradually, it settled toward the Martian surface and revealed the landscape Fragger had to cross. For a moment, he wished the dust would return and obliterate the view, then settled for some healthy cursing of his luck.

He was still at the bottom of the canyon, there was no doubt about that. The walls soared like the sides of steep mountains up toward the Martian heavens. Ahead, the canyon showed several klicks of dust-covered rock leading toward--hell, he didn't know what it was leading toward. He couldn't see that far. He checked the opposite direction. It was more of the same. The only good thing about his position was that he didn't see anybody in pursuit.

Fragger laid out another long string of profanities, remembering every foul phrase that Drill Sergeant Wompner had taught him in basic, then invented a few new ones that applied more directly to the Red Planet. The cursing made him feel better for a moment, but when he was done he still had to face the fundamental question.

How the devil do I get out of here?

The Ranger considered climbing the steep canyon walls, then remembered what Lesto had said. If you fall, mass will kill you just as dead as weight.

Well, at least it makes the choice easy, Fragger decided as he stood up and avoided the temptation to brush the dust off his suit as if it were an ordinary pair of fatigues. *Straight ahead is the ticket while I look for an easier way out of here. At least, I think it is. For all I know, I'm headed back the way I came. It's not a comforting thought; however, some action is better than none.*

The Ranger set off, experimenting with a stride until he found a ground-eating pace that didn't exhaust his strength. The gait felt foolish to him at first, like he was doing a weird variation on some kid's hopscotch game. But it worked and that was all that mattered. Loping past boulders the size of small buildings, Fragger searched the canyon walls for any sign of climbable terrain. He had no idea of the ideal location for an oxygen-extraction plant but assumed it wouldn't be at the bottom of the incredibly deep canyon. Presumably, Mars had updrafts, downdrafts and other obstacles to transportation that would make a bottomless canyon site less than desirable so his first goal was to find flat ground above the valley's walls. Before he starved to death.

God, I'm hungry! his stomach whined at him.

Shut up! Fragger told it. *I'm looking for food.*

As soon as the thought popped into his head, the Ranger cussed himself for being foolish. There was no food. This was Mars.

How the hell do you survive in a place where there's nothing to eat?

The unspoken answer to his question came far too quickly. *You don't.*

A shudder ran through Fragger's body that had nothing to do with the Martian cold. Starving to death was bad enough, but there was also no dignity to it. He'd always thought he'd die in battle, not trudging through inches of red dust in an environment that was, for all practical purposes, airless.

"Shit!" he said out loud and was royally pissed, not because he'd sworn but because there was nobody there to hear his anger.

Dying alone isn't so great, either, he complained and kicked at the dust just to kick something.

"Rangers lead the way!" Fragger shouted, not caring if someone was monitoring his communications. Enemy or "friend", if they caught him, they'd either feed him or they'd shoot him and it'd all be over with.

"This Ranger is leading the way but there's no one to follow!" he yelled again.

"Stop it!" he reprimanded himself immediately. "There's always a way to survive. A real soldier finds that way, so be a real soldier and keep moving."

Fragger trudged on, resisting the urge to dig at the maddening itch in his ass. The damned survival suit was too efficient in its recycling of his body wastes.

I'm the heroic Ranger all right, the morose thought came to him. *The heroic Ranger with hemorrhoids. They never write about that stuff in the books, do they?*

As he strode onward, Fragger decided to keep the condition of the hemorrhoids to himself if he survived. If some damned writer ever got hold of his story, he had no doubt what the title would be:

Fragger Sparks, Hemorrhoid Hero.

He shook the negative thinking off by concentrating on the awesome beauty of the Martian canyon. It reminded him of a Grand Canyon excavated even deeper by some diligent giant who'd been unhappy with previous digging efforts. Gazing upward, he noticed there were even clouds in the sky although the sky was a dark blue and not the wonderful lighter blue of the Arizona desert.

Fragger fought the sense he'd wandered into one of Van Gogh's unknown paintings. Every detail seemed distorted on this planet. There was not enough of the right colors and too much of the wrong ones, plus Mars couldn't seem to make up its mind about the weather it preferred. Every time he checked the suit's instrumentation it seemed to have changed--clouds and cold one minute, dust and "heat" the next minute. With reckless abandon, temperatures rose and plunged 40 degrees within the same day.

The thought of the extreme range of temperatures made the suit's effectiveness all the more astonishing to Fragger. As far as his skin was determined, he was walking about in a 70 degree day. Thinking back on his patrol days, the Ranger wished he'd had one of survival suits in Nam or Iraq on the missions where you boiled to death during the day or froze during the night. Besides being more comfortable, it would have meant that he and his fellow Rangers could have sought out the enemy almost indefinitely. The only limit would have been food and ammunition.

The wishful thinking disappeared as he came over a short rise and looked down a sharp incline into a valley that ran into deep shadows.

"Shit and double shit!" the Ranger swore. "I want out of this canyon, and it just keeps going down into the planet."

Sitting on a rock to preserve his strength, Fragger studied the walls of the canyon more carefully as he remembered one of the lessons he'd learned early in his Grand Canyon hikes. There could be a trail right in front of your eyes and you might not see it. At a distance, the colors and contours tended to obscure the obvious. The same could be true on Mars, he realized, and he sought out signs of ridge backs that led up to small plateaus. Fragger wasn't sure whether water or lava had flowed on Mars, but there had to be a point where some kind of fluid had come down into the Valles Marineris, and that could mean smoother climbing.

"I wish I had the longest damned rope in the world. I'd shoot it up and rappel out of here," he said in frustration when his efforts revealed nothing but sloping walls.

Hunger was doing its own rappelling up into his brain to gnaw at his reasoning so Fragger quickly decided on a second option--find the best slope available. It didn't take long.

As he looked off to the left, he saw a smaller, side canyon that zigged sideways like a backward 7. At the end, the wall ran upward at an abrupt angle, but it was also studded with rocks and boulders that could act like crude steps to the top.

It's better than just sitting here, the Ranger decided as he rose to his feet and forced his legs into the time honored stride of the grunt--put one foot in front of the other and don't think beyond that. When you get there, you get there.

After he was across the floor of the canyon and half-way up the wall, he realized the grunt's stride on Mars was an entirely different matter than one on Earth.

It fools you, this thin Martian atmosphere, he thought wearily as he paused for breath. *It seems so easy at first, but I've also got to go five times as far to get up to the top of this damnable canyon so it ends up being a wash. Lower gravity, but longer distance.*

The Ranger cut his complaining thoughts short and started up again, trying to find the best method of navigating the rubble-strewn slope. He finally settled on being as light on his feet as possible, giving the rocks minimal opportunity to twist his ankles. It worked until exhaustion caught up with him, and a misstep sent him tumbling face-first into the red-orange dirt. He lay for a while and enjoyed simply not moving. Then, he rose to his knees and looked up the hill. With dust obscuring the atmosphere, it was difficult to judge how far it was to the lip of the canyon.

No, it's not, the Ranger corrected the thought. *It's too damned far, that's exactly how far it is. I haven't had anything to eat for hours, and it's too damned cold, and I'll never make it. It's just not possible.*

Fragger sat down and rubbed at his cold knees, wishing he had something warm to put on. Then a realization shot through the icy fog gathering in his mind.

Cold? I'm not supposed to be cold. The suit's supposed to take care of that.

Hurriedly, he checked his legs for any sign of rips, tears, or holes. There was nothing. Confused, he tried to remember what Lesto had said about the survival suits.

"'As long as you provide energy, you're in good shape,'" Fragger quoted out loud. "Oh, shit! Energy. The one thing I don't have."

Fighting down panic, the Ranger took a deep breath and made his decision--one last all-out effort to reach the top. He'd die trying. Nothing less was expected of a Ranger.

He comforted himself with the thought, *At least, I know I can get a quick death by simply opening up the suit when it's time to check out.*

It was a grim motivator, but it got him moving again. He kept going by summoning up fiendish methods of revenge on every no-neck he'd met in this godawful future. Castration for all the interrogators, a chicken bone stuck in the throat of Chief Mess Cook Bagwell, another scar for the face of Major Shimazu--hell, the list was wonderfully endless! In fact, when he thought about it, there were only two people in this time that he even came close to liking--Watanabe and Red Salinsky, basic grunts like himself. Men you could count on.

"Count. I can do that!" Fragger said, giggling at the thought as he plodded upward. "One, two, three--hell, skip four--I never liked that number anyway--five alive that's me see--see, I told you, I could do it....oh yeah...OW, sonuvabitch!"

The Ranger blinked and came alert, astonished he wasn't on his feet anymore. He'd fallen, apparently slipping on the icy tailings gleaming before his eyes. He had no idea how long he'd lain there, but his visor was half-buried in the cursed Martian dust which refused to be any color but rust red.

I'm delirious, Fragger realized, then tried to say out loud, "No shit, Sherlock", but his lips were too frozen to form the words properly and they came out, "no it, erlock." It sounded ludicrous, like a toddler trying to talk, but Fragger didn't find anything funny about the result. The Martian cold seeped through the suit like icy water, freezing him inch by inch. He tried to get up and could barely feel his hands and feet.

Time to open the suit, Fragger decided and managed to roll onto his back. *Time to let go.*

He knew it was the right decision. There was only one problem.

I can't remember how to open this suit. In fact, I can't even remember IF you can open it.

"Fuck me," his numbed lips said.

You may have won, Mars, but I'm still going out on my own terms.

Somebody had cast his extremities in cold concrete, but Fragger got to his feet, anyway. Staggering upward into the darkening sky, he found that he was near the top of the canyon. A surge of hope churned his legs through gravel heaped by wind below the lip of the rim until he cleared the rise and was greeted with a stunning view.

Of absolutely nothing, the Ranger thought with despair.

A basaltic escarpment stretched toward the horizon, revealing nothing but more rocks, more boulders, and the ever-present reddish dust. Fragger turned away from it and looked back down into Marineris.

I came up a helluvaways, he thought with pride. *Good. It ought to be far enough down for my purposes. Mass can kill me dead.*

"Time to fly and fall," Fragger said.

Stepping to the canyon edge, the Ranger spread his arms wide and prepared to launch his body into Marineris and the gathering Martian night. Instead, he felt his foot slip on the icy gravel, and he sat down hard.

"So much for the grand gesture," Fragger said and tried to rise, but the gravel wouldn't give his hands any purchase. The more he grabbed at it, the looser it became until it gave way completely underneath his body. Fragger slid over the edge, clutching at any close rock, but it was like trying to get up from a bed of slick ball bearings.

The panicked thought--*Avalanche!*--ran though the Ranger's mind as he tumbled down the slope at increasing speed, then just before something slammed his head into blackness, he had a morbidly satisfying image of the message on his tombstone:

Fragger Sparks
Dug His Own Grave
And Filled It In, Too.

CHAPTER 19

Words taunted Fragger from a very long distance away, echoing as if he were in a canyon.

"Duuuummmmb duuuummmmb shiiiiiiiiiiiiit shiiiiiiiiiiiiit!" they said with all the utter conviction of a drill sergeant about a recruit's stupidity.

The same words kept on reverberating until they were replaced by an even more alarming variation.

"Dead deaad shit shiiiit, you you mean mean."

At the mention of death, Fragger panicked at first, then decided he didn't really care if he *was* dead. He just wanted the words to stop. They bounced around inside his head like sharp-edged rocks gouging the bone of his skull. Despite his efforts to make them go away, they insisted on continuing until, to his relief, they eventually stopped echoing in crazy patterns and formed themselves into sentences he could comprehend.

"All the idiot had to do was activate the MPS signal. The satellite would have picked him up, and we could have been out here hours ago," a male voice said with a peculiar accent that sounded like a cross between Aussie and Indian dialects with a bit of Mississippian thrown in.

A female voice answered with the same accent. "Maybe he didn't know how."

The man snorted at the thought. "What kind of a numbskull doesn't know how to turn on an emergency signal?"

"This one, apparently," the woman answered. "Maybe he was too hurt or disoriented to remember to do it. It happens, you know. The MPS probably didn't turn itself on until this avalanche hit him."

"What kind of brainless twit is out here alone?" the man asked, apparently unwilling to cut Fragger any slack. It made the Ranger angry.

"One like you...Quart," the woman said with a snicker in the tone.

"Hey, don't bring that episode up, okay? I was drunk at the time."

"Exactly....Quart."

"Stop calling me that, Kayla! I didn't drink a quart of booze," Quayle complained. "Hell, nobody even uses that old Earth measurement anymore. Liters, that's what everybody uses. Who the hell ever dug up that ancient term, anyway?"

A shrug came in the tone of the answer. "Who knows, but 'Liter' Quayle doesn't have quite the same ring as 'Quart' Quayle, does it?"

"Shit, I'll never live that one down."

"Stop moaning," Kayla advised. "Not many men go running bare-ass naked out of a hooch and make it back in one usable piece on this planet, now, do they? You're just lucky your dick didn't fall off."

"It damned near did," Quart groused.

"You were wearing it out, anyway, visiting all those hookers at the Rocks."

"Hey, Kayla, I don't go to prostitutes!"

"Yeah, and Kayla Quayle is the CPO of Mars."

The bickering finally caused Fragger to open his eyes. It was hard to see through the dust-streaked visor, but two things were immediately obvious. One, he was up to his neck in rocks, gravel, and dirt. Two, he was cold, really cold, so cold he couldn't talk.

"Wonder why he didn't get buried underneath all this crap?" Kayla wondered.

"Who knows?"

"Yeah, but if he was walking along down here, it should have buried him so deep we shouldn't have had a prayer of finding him."

"Maybe he wasn't at the bottom," Quart suggested. "Maybe he was at the top."

"You think he was at the top?" she asked in an incredulous tone.

"Why not?"

"Because, you simpleton, it's a kilometer from the canyon rim down to where we're standing. Are you trying to tell me he survived an avalanche that traveled that far?"

"Stranger things have happened."

"You're a dumb shit, Quart, you know that?"

"I know you've never tired of telling me that during ten years of marriage," was his weary answer.

"That's because you keep proving it to me over and over again."

Christ almighty, Fragger thought. *I'm dying, and they're busy putting each other down.*

The Ranger tried to get their attention away from the bickering by speaking. His mouth was so cold the best he could manage was a grunt. It wasn't much of a sound but it prompted Kayla to ask, "Did you hear something?"

"Nope," her husband answered. "Probably your commlink acting up again.

Kayla slapped a hand against her helmet as if that would fix the communications problem. "If you'd maintain stuff, I wouldn't have trouble with the damned commlink."

"I did the maintenance on that ancient 'link, Kayla. You're just too bloody cheap to spring for a new unit."

Anger flared in Fragger's mind as the couple nagged at each other. He tried to work his rusty jaw free, feeling like the Tin Man in need of oil.

"Unnnnnnhhhhhhh!" he grunted as loudly as he could.

After a short silence, Kayla said, "That was no 'link glitch."

They both turned their helmets down toward Fragger. Two faces registered astonishment.

"He's alive?" Kayla asked.

Quart bent close enough to Fragger so that even in the bizarre Martian light the Ranger could clearly make out two watery brown eyes bracketed by scraggly brown eyebrows. A moustache fled in all directions as if trying to escape the ugly face to which it had been attached.

"I'll be a son of a bitch!" Quart exclaimed. "He *is* alive, and he's trying to tell us something."

"Like maybe, 'Get me out of here', you dumb bastard!" Kayla said. "Come on, start clearing the rocks away while I get the stretcher from the flivver. We might have us a bonus coming if we get him back alive."

Fragger drifted in and out of consciousness as Quart tossed the debris aside. The cold had robbed the Ranger of any feeling beyond his own breathing. It wasn't until the pair slipped the stretcher underneath his body while stabilizing his neck that he realized he was free. They lifted and carried him over the rubble with such ease he assumed they were either natives of Mars or had been living on the planet for some time. It wasn't long before they put him down next to the door of a contraption that looked like a floating pickup with gimbel-mounted lift engines. Whatever the vehicle was, Fragger saw that it had had plenty of use. Even the thick Martian dust couldn't hide the dings, scratches, and dents on the bright yellow surface of the conveyance with the black lettering that read, *EarthCorp.*

Quart slid the door open with a tinny bang, then the pair lifted the Ranger into the flivver. After securing the stretcher, they both clambered into the front of the vehicle, and soon the craft lifted into the sky. Fragger listened to Kayla answer commlink chatter, then drifted off into sleep as he listened to her conversation with the person at the other end of the link.

"...Affirmative, Marsh...He's alive...Yeah, you heard right...No shit...he *is* a survivor."

CHAPTER 20

The shrill, screaming throttle-down of the flivver's engines dragged Fragger out of his sleep. He opened his eyes as the craft banked low over a caldera and saw a complex of buildings set against the extinct volcano's wall. The structures were nearly the same color as the surrounding landscape, but the Ranger had no idea figuring out who the architect was.

Fred Flintstone.

Apparently, people who live on Mars believe in being one with the environment, he thought, amused at the jumbled nature of the complex. As they got closer, it became apparent the builders had used the classic Roman keystone arch design in the construction, and it was also obvious that the environment was probably the last thing on the builders' minds. It was just that all the money had gone into the plant his eyes had missed on their first scan of the ground below. Beyond the crude-looking living quarters stood a sleek maze of pipes, towers and gangways that gleamed with the last rays of the Martian day. On the side of the tallest tower, a large chartreuse number, 24, was illuminated by a spotlight.

Fragger assumed it was one of the oxygen-extraction plants Lesto had mentioned and tried to confirm that fact by asking Kayla and Quart about it, but his jaw still wouldn't work properly. Another grunt was all he managed.

Quart turned back at the sound and shouted, "We're almost there, mate. Hang on."

"As if he could do anything else," Kayla said.

"Hey, I'm just trying to give the bloke some comfort."

"Like you give comfort to those whores down at the Rocks?"

"I told you, Kayla, I don't visit--"

"Please!"

"Well, maybe one," Quart admitted, "but it's all your fault, you know."

"Mine?" Kayla answered, straightening the flivver into level flight with a jerk on the controls. Fragger was glad he was strapped down. The violent turn could have thrown him right out of the craft. "How is it my fault?"

"If you weren't so damned cold to me all the time," Quart replied.

"I wasn't cold to you until my friends got up the courage to tell me you were boffing hookers!"

"I wouldn't have gone to them if you'd been more willing," Quart insisted.

"I work all day, the same as you," Kayla said. "I get tired too. I can't do it every day of the week. I'm not built that way."

"Well, I am," Quart said.

Fragger noted a source of pride in the man's voice and felt a bit of male envy warm his frozen body. *Every day of the week?*

The chill in Kayla's tone matched the Martian temperature outside the flivver. "I want a divorce."

"You got it," Quart answered. "I'm sick of this whole relationship."

Kayla's answer was to power the flivver down into a rough landing. She bounced the machine to a halt in a cloud of dust that slowly dissipated to reveal an airlock with the same number above the door Fragger had seen on the tower.

"That did our passenger a lot of good," Quart said sarcastically as he unbuckled his harness and got out of the flivver.

"Screw him," Kayla said as she helped her husband free the stretcher from its restraints. "He's thrown us off schedule, having to go out and rescue him."

"I suppose you just wanted to leave him out there to die," Quart accused.

"Don't be a dimwit!"

"Well, that's what you said."

"I was just blowing off steam, you imbecile," Kayla replied, then turned her head down to Fragger. "You understand that, don't you, mate?"

The Ranger nodded--there was nothing else he could do--but a groan ran through his head. *I've come six hundred years into the future and survived God knows what only to land in the middle of a marital dispute. If Mars doesn't kill me, these two will.*

"Just get him inside, okay?" Quart said.

To Fragger's relief, Kayla had nothing more to say. She grabbed one end of the stretcher and helped her husband guide it out of the flivver across the short distance to the entrance. Quart hollered a command, and the outer door slid open to let the trio enter the air lock. When the outer door sealed itself, the couple placed Fragger and the stretcher on the floor and waited for the inner hatch to open. As it did, they carried the Ranger inside and put him down again while they unsealed their helmets. Fragger could see their faces clearly for the first time.

Quart was as ugly as he'd seemed before, even uglier when his greasy brown hair flopped down around his shoulders. Kayla was no beauty herself, thin as a rail with a snub nose and a mousy demeanor that belied her nasty temper. Her hair was cut short and stood atop her head like drought-scorched grass in various shades of brown and yellow. She was the kind of woman a man would dismiss upon first sight, but the fierce blue eyes and the intelligence behind them made it obvious she was not a person to be dismissed easily, something Quart apparently found out on a daily basis. As they hauled him out of the lock and into the building's interior, Fragger wondered idly why they'd ever gotten married.

Maybe there's a shortage of men on the planet for some reason or another. War, disease, a frontier environment--who knows? Maybe they've just been married too long.

The Ranger had no more time to think about it as the pair carried him down a corridor into a room hewn out of rock and crammed with all kinds of gear whose purpose he didn't recognize. As Kayla and Quart stripped out of their suits, Kayla made a com call to a name he'd heard mentioned in the flivver--Marsh. The man entered the room soon after their summons. His appearance jolted Fragger at first.

Marsh stood at least seven feet tall with bronzed skin and an enormous chest swelling his overalls. For a moment, the Ranger thought the man had gone in for a grotesque form of body building.

When he looked more closely, he saw the arms and legs were of normal shape and realized he was facing a man who'd been genetically altered to have the lung capacity to breathe an atmosphere non-existent to someone from Earth.

Whatever the case, the man is not pretty, Fragger decided. *He has a face like Abe Lincoln's; that is, if Abe had been unlucky enough to been born with a splayed nose, eyes set so far back into the skull that they look like they're in caves, and a mouth wide as a freeway. He looks like a bad parody of the great president.*

"He *is* alive," Marsh said as he bent over Fragger to examine him. "Amazing. Not many men could survive all that."

"How many do you know who *have* survived, Doc?" Kayla asked.

Fragger noted that there was a faint hint of contempt in her voice for the man.

"None," Marsh admitted. "Charlie Wiggs, back about five years ago, almost made it, but 'almost' doesn't count."

"No argument there," she agreed. "Can you do anything for this guy?"

"Let's get the suit off and put him in a warmer so I can check for injuries. Has he said anything to you?"

"Just a couple of grunts," Quart answered. "I think he's too cold to talk, Doc."

"Maybe. Or perhaps something's broken. You said you found him half-buried in an avalanche?"

"Yeah," Quart answered. "I say he fell a helluva ways. Kayla thinks it caught him at the bottom."

"Doesn't matter," Marsh said, flashing a pen light into Fragger's eyes. "Either way, it's likely rocks tried to squeeze him into a smaller space than a body's designed for. His pupils are responsive, anyway, so that's a good sign. Okay, let's strip him."

Fragger could barely feel their efforts to take the suit off, but was grateful for the limited sensation. The fact that he could feel anything was a sign of progress.

Soon they had the Ranger naked and carried him across the room to a bed bracketed with bright horizontal lights. A gentle warmth swept across his face as they placed him on the mattress. Marsh threw a blanket across Fragger's lower extremities and set to work on the examination, manipulating the Ranger's limbs for any sign of fracture or outright break. The Ranger was as pleased as Marsh that nothing beyond a broken right leg was found amiss until the doctor got to his head. A slight shifting of the jaw by Marsh's fingers made Fragger stunningly aware he was defrosting. Pain shot through his mouth and straight up into his brain.

"Unnnnnnnnnnnnnnowwwwwwwww!" he managed to scream.

"Sorry," Marsh said with a voice as dry and whistling as the Martian wind. "I'll bet that hurt. It should. You've broken it in at least two places from what I can tell. You're going to be doing more writing than talking for a while, I'm afraid, and even the writing will have to wait until your fingers thaw out. The good news, mate, is that the suit did its job pretty well. You've got a touch of frostbite on the fingers and toes, but nothing serious. Nothing has to be cut off. I'll set your leg and your jaw. Sorry, but I don't have a bone knitting machine here so I'll have to wire the jaw shut. But, in a month or two, you'll be as good as new, and a folk hero to boot! "

Fragger's eyes widened at this news. Despite the pain, he shook his head.

"What? You don't want any publicity?" Marsh said.

When Fragger nodded in the affirmative, the doctor narrowed his eyes. "Doing something illegal out there? Water rustling, maybe, or tapping into oxygen lines?"

The Ranger didn't know what Marsh was talking about, but nodded in the affirmative as he thought, *Whatever the penalty is for a felony on Mars, it can't be as bad as Lesto and his men and everybody else catching up with me.*

"EarthCorp takes a dim view of thieves," Marsh lectured. "You may end up doing some time if you can't prove what you were doing out there all by yourself. No sensible person on Mars goes off alone. It's a basic survival strategy or were you so greedy that you ignored the rule?"

Fragger nodded again.

"I thought so," the doctor said. "There were only two choices. Either you had to be after money or were just flat-out stupid."

"I vote for stupid," Kayla said. "He and Quart have a lot in common."

"Ha, ha," Quart responded.

"What do you think?" Marsh asked the pair. "Should we report him to Central?"

"Why not?" Kayla asked. "Take trouble off our hands."

"Give him some time to recover, I say," Quart responded.

"What do you care about this guy?" his wife demanded.

"I'm just not crazy about EarthCorp Security, that's all. Why go to all this work to save him if Security is going to make hash of him in one form or another?"

"All the more reason to hand him over now," Kayla said.

“You’re a soulless bitch, you know that?”

“Who made me that way?”

“Knock it off,” Marsh demanded. “I’m tired of listening to you two cut each other to shreds.”

“Bugger off, yourself!” Kayla responded.

Marsh sighed. “As a medical professional, I’ve made it a point to never get between a husband and wife-”

“That’s a good idea, Marsh” Kayla interrupted. “Why don’t you do it now?”

“Because you people are driving me nuts, that’s why! Either make up or get divorced. Do something, anything, just so I can keep my sanity.”

“It’s none of your business,” Quart said.

“Then, go check the plant output. Check the orbit of Mars and make sure it’s still steady! See if the stars are still in the sky! Just go away!”

“What about this bloke we rescued?” Kayla asked. “What are you going to do? Keep him or report him?”

“I’ll keep him until he recovers,” Marsh answered. “Anybody who survived Mars deserves a little break before Security gets hold of him.”

Quart suggested, "Security might have something to say to you if you *don't* turn him over right away."

"They won't know if nobody tells them, will they?" the doctor responded in a conspiratorial tone and gazed pointedly at Kayla.

"What are you looking at me for?" she asked.

"Because your husband *will* go along with me if we do decide to let this guy stay for a while. However, I'm not so sure about you, Kayla."

"Hey, as long as Security leaves me alone, I don't have any problem with him remaining here."

"Quart, will you vouch for her?" Marsh asked.

"She doesn't do anything I say, anyway, so what's the point in saying I *will* vouch for her?"

"In other words, I can't trust her."

"Not a chance," Quart said.

"Wait a minute!" Kayla protested. "I'm as trustworthy as either one of you."

"Then promise you won't inform the authorities until I say so," Marsh insisted.

"All right, I promise."

"That came out way too easy," Marsh said. "Let me give you another reason for holding off. A reason you'll understand."

"What's that?" Kayla asked.

"Maybe he found something out there that's worthwhile."

The woman laughed at that idea. "I suppose he stumbled over a new source of water."

"Probably not," Marsh admitted. "But you never know, do you? You might be passing up an opportunity to get off this 'rock', as you put it. All it will cost you is a little time."

After a brief silence, Kayla responded, "All right, all right. I'll keep it to myself. It's your responsibility, anyway, so you deal with him. But, remember, any rescue bonus is ours. And make sure we don't have our pay docked for being off the job."

"Will do," Marsh said.

Fragger listened to footsteps fade out of the room. The doctor turned back and looked down at him with a small smile.

"Mate, relax and rest. My patients don't go anywhere until they're healed, and if I can help it, they never go into the hands of Security. I'll put you under and fix those injuries."

Fragger nodded as Marsh prepared a hypo and stuck it into his shoulder. Whatever the drug was, it was fast acting, the Ranger realized, but there was still time for him to hear Marsh's final remark before sleep set in.

"In the interests of fairness, mate, I should tell you one thing. I'm not a doctor. It's just an honorary title."

CHAPTER 21

Fragger shivered into consciousness, opening his eyes to a rocky, rust-colored ceiling that looked as if it had been painted with some sort of clear plastic material. For a moment, he wasn't quite sure where he was. Then he remembered Marsh's last words-"I'm not a doctor"-and sat up in a panic to make sure he was still in one piece.

"Fingers, toes, limbs, they're all there," Marsh said from across the room. He was seated at a desk, peeling a banana with fastidious care.

Fragger tried to talk, found his jaw wouldn't move and glared at the man

"You mad about something?" Marsh asked as he took a bite of the fruit. Standing up, he placed the remainder of the banana on a tray, wiped his hands clean with a towel, and came over to the Ranger. "What's the problem, mate?"

Fragger made a writing gesture.

"Sorry, I forgot about the jaw for a moment," Marsh said. "Let me get you an e-pad so you can write."

Marsh rummaged on his desk, found a stylus and an electronic pad, and brought them over to Fragger.

The Ranger wrote with shaky fingers, You're not a doctor! What did you do to me?

"Oh, that," Marsh said after he'd read the message. "That's right, I'm not a doctor. I'm a company medic who's fully trained to handle simple breaks. Not to worry. I've set many a broken bone in this plant. Maintenance is hazardous duty for the rousters. Always a pipe breaking or an I-beam cracking because of the temperature."

Marsh patted Fragger's shoulder. "Your bones will be okay, mate. It's your body temperature we have to worry about. That's why I've kept you in the warmer. Just want to make sure we get the cold out of your hide, otherwise, you'll probably feel frozen the rest of your life or worse, develop arthritis…Hey, what's your name, anyway? I just can't keep calling you 'mate.' My name is Buurk, B-u-u-r-k."

Fragger realized the confusion about the man's name must have shown in his eyes because the medic said with a bitter smile, "Thought it was Marsh, huh? Don't blame you. No, my real name is Buurk. 'Marsh' is the short, nasty term for 'Martian', a product of a sociopathic genetic engineer. Because I am a product, Quart and Kayla consider me a less than human result. I have to take it from those two because they're EarthCorp, but don't you ever use the term 'marsh', you understand me? Now, what's your name?"

The Ranger nodded, then wrote on the pad, <u>Fragger</u>. It was not quick thinking to give his real name, he realized, but the cold had slowed his thoughts to a crawl.

"Fragger, huh? Well, Mr. Fragger, take it easy. You're going to be with us a while."

On the stylus, Fragger wrote, <u>What about Security?</u>

"They don't know about you yet," the medic answered. "Well, they do know I rescued some poor yabbo who went out beyond the black stump without proper precautions, but they're not all that interested in you at this point. Happens all the time with ignorant Earthers or suiciders. Security's got bigger fish to fry."

Fragger had no idea what a black stump was, but he decided not to pry any further. He assumed he was one of the fish Security wanted to fry, but he was safe for the meantime. It was enough to enjoy the simple luxury of doing nothing. Laying back into the gentle heat of the warmer, the Ranger realized just how lucky he was. He'd survived Lesto and Mars itself, been rescued by Quart and Kayla, and then been attended to by a compassionate Martian medical professional who had no love for the authorities trying to track him down.

In fact, it's all been an incredible streak of luck. Everything bad happens to me, but I keep on surviving. Maybe that's the real reason why they selected me for revival, the fact that I can survive damned near anything.

The Ranger didn't really believe in such extravagant fortune, but it was a thought to keep in mind, he knew. It might lead him to the truth about his revival. Somehow, it seemed important to find out. If he could nail it down, he could use it to his advantage.

And there is the fact that my family has the luck of the Irish without even being Irish. We get--got--in the damnedest fixes, and yet came through. Not always in one piece, but alive, nonetheless.

All his brothers were younger than he was. T.K. had followed him to Nam as a Marine and caught a ricochet in the knee.

Will, he followed me too. Caught a round in Hue. That's what you get, having a Ranger for a father. Everybody in the family wants to be in the military to prove to the old man--and their older brother--they're just as much a man as he was when he survived D-Day and all the other European battles.

Except for Reed, Fragger amended. *He rebelled in his own way. The wrong way, but his own.*

The Ranger shook his head in frustration, both at the fact his youngest brother had become a big doper and at the fact it was all in the past and he couldn't do anything about it, anyway.

It was all six hundred years ago. Six hundred!

Fragger shook his head again to get rid of the useless line of thinking. He was a realist, a pragmatist. He was a Ranger, and a Ranger dealt with things as they are, not as he'd like them to be.

How'd I get off on that self-pitying train of thought? he wondered, then remembered, *Every Sparks survives! Even Reed who'd consumed every drug available on the street and still managed to be rational enough to publish poetry I didn't understand, but that the critics loved.*

The Ranger chuckled as best he could through his broken jaw at the next thought that came into his head. *In its own way, the U.S. back then was as weird as things are now, so it's almost like I'm back home. Well...at least I'm in the same solar system, not hyperspacing around somewhere puking my guts out.*

Fragger dredged a memory up at the thought of hyperspace. Reed had sent a novel to him in Nam even though he knew Fragger wasn't much of a reader except for military history, strategy and tactics. It'd been written by some guy named Bester and was called <u>The Stars My</u>... something or other. The writer had invented a technique called "jaunting", the ability to think yourself to anyplace on Earth or, eventually, in space.

The people I'm with now apparently can't think themselves anywhere, but they sure as hell can pop their vessels up anywhere they want. It's amazing how Bester came so close to the eventual idea. Hell, it's too bad he's not alive to see how much of a prophet he was.

All the thinking tired Fragger out.

I've never been that good at thinking beyond the battlefield, he admitted to himself as drowsiness overcame his brain. One last thought popped into his mind before he slept.

If you want to survive, Sergeant Sparks, maybe you'd better start thinking big.

CHAPTER 22

Fragger's jaw hurt. It felt like somebody had a fish hook in his mouth and was tugging as hard as they could to land him. The muscles ached and flared with pain. The effect was to leave him exhausted and unable to sleep. The future had wonderful painkillers. The trouble was, Buurk had run out of them.

"Sorry," the medic said for the third time as he helped Fragger sit in the therapy chair. "EarthCorp's not good about keeping remote stations supplied. Sometimes, the stuff is interdicted by Ricer forces, sometimes it's pirates or mercs, but most times, it's just plain bureaucratic foul-ups."

Fragger groaned, yet knew there was only one way to take his mind off the pain--concentrate on something else. He took up his e-pad and wrote, Pirates?

"You haven't been up keeping up with the news, have you?" the medic asked after glancing at the pad.

Fragger glared and pointed at his jaw.

"It's a joke, Fragger. You've been on the mend now for four weeks and for about half that time, you were in and out of it with the medications I pumped into your system."

Four weeks! the Ranger thought in astonishment. *Has it really been that long?*

On the one hand, Fragger realized, he felt terrible he'd lost so much time without even knowing it. On the other, it seemed everyone chasing him had lost track of his whereabouts. For once, it was good to be lost and unknown except for the fact that Buurk was a lonely man and talked a blue streak with the Ranger because apparently he was the only one in the complex who would listen to the medic. It was hard to tell because of his limited exposure to the planet, but as far as the Ranger could tell Buurk had been right--Martians like him were like blacks and Native Americans in his time, the objects of racial hatred.

"Anyway," Buurk said as he set the controls on the therapy chair, "the news is that Ricer and EarthCorp forces fought a major battle close to the planet. Apparently, it was a draw because CorpComm isn't claiming victory as loudly as it usually does. I think both fleets are off licking their wounds and while they're doing that, the usual assortment of pirates, freebooters, and mercs are the vultures picking off the carrion floating out there in space. So, that's more than likely why we haven't gotten any more painkillers. We probably won't get any more, either, until EarthCorp forces resume regular patrols."

Interested in finding out the medic's position on the whole matter, Fragger wrote, Who do you want to win?

Buurk read the question, gave him a suspicious glance, then checked his surroundings before answering carefully, "EarthCorp, of course. Why do you even ask such a question?"

No reason, Fragger wrote. Talking keeps mind off pain.

"Of course," the medic responded, then said brightly, "For once, all my blather is doing some good. Quart and Kayla say I talk too much, but they have each other and a way out of this place. I'm stuck here."

Why? Fragger wrote.

Buurk thought the question was bitterly funny. "Where have you been? I'm a Martian, native to this planet. You know what 'native' means in this solar system? It means backwater. It means being poor. It means never getting off the surface and seeing other planets or systems! It means being stuck in a low-paying job, forced to live with the likes of Quart and Kayla…it…oh, hell, don't get me started."

Interesting, Fragger thought. *The future has its disaffected just as much as we did. I wonder if there is some sort of underground opposition on Mars or if EarthCorp has the place locked up tight?*

Now Buurk was glaring at him. Fragger made a "What?" expression at him. The medic said, "You're Terran too. I'll deny anything I just said. You won't be able to prove it."

Fragger wrote quickly, Not Terran.

"Sure you are," Buurk said after reading the message.

No, at least not in way you think.

"What's that supposed to mean?"

Hard to explain. On your side.

Buurk tightened visibly, so Fragger wrote fast again, Escaped.

"You *are* a criminal, then, and not just some blundering prospector," Buurk asked.

Not criminal, Fragger wrote, then tried frantically to think of what to write next. He couldn't afford to antagonize the medic when his care was in the man's hands. Finally, he wrote, Prisoner of war. Underground. Escaped.

"'Underground?'" Buurk asked. "What the hell's that?"

Freedom fighter. Revolutionary.

Buurk raised an eyebrow at this message. "Freedom? For who?"

For me, you dumb shit! Fragger raged silently, but wrote, For all oppressed peoples.

"Sounds like bull excrement to me," the medic said.

Well, it sounds like to me too, Fragger thought, *but there's bound to be some truth in there somewhere.*

He wrote, Not bullshit. My kind wants to be free. Doesn't yours?

"Your kind? What precisely *is* your kind if you're not Terran?"

Think fast! Fragger thought. *Real fast!*

Coloradan, he scrawled as he thought of his home state.

"Coloradan? Never heard of a people called that, but then there's a lot of systems out there that have peoples I don't know. Still, you look Terran to me. What system, what planet are you from?"

Ranger System. Planet, Leadstheway.

"Don't know them. Sounds like a mercenary system though. That what you are, a mercenary?"

No! Fragger scribbled.

"Okay, you're not a mercenary, but what are you really doing on Mars? Hell, this is the outback of our solar system, even I know that. That means there's no reason to try to export freedom to this planet. We haven't got the population to start any kind of revolt."

Have to begin somewhere, Fragger wrote out.

"You know what? I don't believe a word of it. I think you're some sort of agent provocateur."

No! Fragger printed out in big letters.

"What kind of loser would try to foment revolution right smack in the middle of EarthCorp space?"

This one, Fragger answered silently.

Buurk continued, "I'll tell you what kind, either a complete dreamer or some kind of double agent. You don't strike me as the dreamer-type. A double agent who can get himself lost maybe, but not a dreamer."

Not a double agent, Fragger wrote. Escaping!

"Escaping who?"

First, EarthCorp. Then, Ricers. Then, a man called Lesto and his troopers tried to kill me here.

"Lesto? That's a merc name if I ever heard one. There's the House of Lesto. Is that who you're talking about?"

Fragger had no idea, but wrote Yes, hoping that his response would reveal more information about the man who'd tried to kill him.

Buurk gave a low whistle. "You really know how to pick your enemies, don't you? How'd you get free of the Black Hole? That's his nickname, you know, because no one ever escapes Lesto's troopers."

Fragger gave an honest answer on the e-pad, writing Luck.

"That part I believe," the medic said. "What the hell did you do to attract the personal attention of the infamous Lesto and the two greatest powers in the Renowned Systems?"

God, I wish I knew, Fragger thought while he lied and wrote, Tried to free my world from Lesto's grip. Planet is contested by everyone.

"So you didn't really come here to free anyone, Fragger, did you? You just plain got chased onto Mars by luck of the draw."

Lucky, true, Fragger spelled out on the pad, then underlined the words he'd written earlier, Had to escape.

Buurk laughed. "You're not much of a revolutionary, are you? Can't loosen Lesto's grip on your own world, get chased halfway across hyperspace and end up on a planet that could care less about your concerns."

Fragger made another guess, writing, Lesto is EarthCorp's enemy!

"Yes, that's true," the medic agreed, "but I doubt EarthCorp would bankroll any effort on your part. Lesto's deviousness is a byword in our system. They'd probably consider you one of his spies and shoot you on the spot."

"A good thing I've kept you here," Buurk added in a coy tone that hinted his patient owed him something.

And indeed I do, Fragger admitted to himself. *The question is, is he any more trustworthy than Quart or Kayla? Probably not, but what's the alternative?*

He decided to find out where the medic's interests lay, writing on the e-pad, I can be generous.

Buurk's expression was skeptical and asked, "How generous?"

What do you want? Money? Fragger scribbled on the pad.

"Always," Buurk answered. "But I need more than that."

Fragger raised a questioning eyebrow.

The medic bent low and whispered, "I want out of here. Away from Quart and Kayla and any Terran on the surface of Mars."

Where? Fragger wrote.

"Shit, I don't care! Off Mars. Away from EarthCorp. Someplace where I can live life as a free man."

Fragger wrote the lie down on the e-pad, Can be arranged.

"How?" Buurk asked.

The Ranger had no idea, but the hope in the medic's face told him that Buurk was ready to buy any plausible story, so he wrote, First need to hide, then contact my people.

"You want me to hide you?"

Fragger nodded and wrote, You're a native, know places.

"Maybe, maybe not," Buurk said, abruptly becoming coy again.

Kayla's sharp voice slashed through their conversation as she came into the room and asked, "Maybe not what?"

The medic straightened up and turned toward her with the smoothness of a slave deceiving a master, saying, "I was telling him he may be able to get the wires out of his jaw soon, maybe not."

As Kayla removed her helmet and gloves, Fragger saw she was tired from the effort of working outside. Orange-pink dust covered every inch of her suit and had even penetrated inside of it. Reddish streaks dotted her cheeks and forehead. She sat down hard in a chair.

"Well, it doesn't matter that much to us, anyway," she said in an irritable tone, "Security is finally coming down from New Sydney. I know you've been stalling all these weeks, you lazy Martian. There's talk of a big reward for any rescued personnel. A substantial one, much bigger than the usual bonus. If I get the reward, I've finally made enough to get back to Earth and away from Quart. That bastard has been tomcatting around again, but the best part is that you, marsh, can get back to your regular duties. I'm tired of hauling your water."

Kayla's reference struck Fragger as funny although he supposed it was true enough on Mars. There was no surface water as understood on Earth, but they were extracting H^2O from the Martian rocks so, in a way, Kayla *was* carrying Buurk's water. The humor lasted only an instant, cut short by the woman's next remark.

"Tomorrow is Fragger's last day."

"Tomorrow? You never told me that," Buurk exclaimed.

"Since when do I have to tell you anything, marsh?"

"Don't call me that!"

Astonishment showed on the woman's voice at the medic's response. Fragger was equally surprised and dismayed, pleading internally, *This is not the time to get brave, Buurk.*

"What did you just say?" Kayla demanded.

"I said--never mind," Buurk answered.

That's right. Come to your senses if you want to get out of here with me.

The woman stood and stalked across the room to the medic. She was a foot and a half shorter than the Martian, but there was no doubt of who was in command. Her finger jabbed hard into the medic's massive chest.

"No," she said, "I don't think I *will* 'never mind'. You just told me not to call you what you are--a marsh. Marshs do what they're told; they don't tell Corp employees what to do."

Kayla continued to poke Buurk in the chest, driving him across the room and up against the wall. Fragger saw the medic's face get dark and hoped the man didn't reach for the surgical instruments laid neatly in the tray by his side. The Ranger desperately wanted to intervene, but his jaw wouldn't let him say a thing. Fragger stood, preparing to cross the floor and separate the two. At that moment, Quart entered through the door and cut short his attempt.

"What the hell is going on?" Quart said, staring at Kayla and Buurk.

"He told me not to call him a 'marsh'," Kayla said.

"He did?" Quart asked, plainly surprised such a thing could occur.

"Damned right, he did!"

Fragger watched the man digest this information, then compose himself. "Well, shit, we're definitely going to have to punish that kind of behavior. Buurk, you can work the outer plant for a week."

Kayla glared back over her shoulder at her husband. "I had something more appropriate in mind."

"Like what?"

"Like this."

Fragger winced as Quart's wife grabbed a scalpel from the tray and traced a shallow line across the medic's throat. Blood dribbled down the bronzed skin onto Buurk's trembling shirt.

The room went still for a moment before Quart said in a low, soothing voice, "Kayla, use your head. He's the only medic we have. Besides, it's against the law to kill property without Security's consent; you know that as well as I do."

"Ask me if I care!"

To Fragger's relief, Quart took a different direction, saying, "You're leaving me, aren't you, Kayla?"

"Damned straight, I am, you bastard!"

"It's okay, I understand. I-"

"You don't understand a damned thing! I love you."

"I *am* a bastard," Quart admitted, "but don't take it out on Buurk. I can't help myself, but I *can* help you right now."

Kayla gave a ragged laugh. "Yeah, sure. How?"

"Think, damn it! You kill Buurk and what happens?"

"The planet is rid of one worthless--oh."

Kayla lowered the scalpel as her husband said, "That's right, you have to pay EarthCorp for the property you destroyed. Do that, and you're stuck here."

Quivering with rage, Kayla backed away from the medic and turned toward her husband. "You sonuvabitch, you have no right to be right!"

"But I am, aren't I?" Quart said, opening his arms and moving toward her.

A warning instinct ran through Fragger's body at Quart's response. The tone was wrong, simultaneously full of love and condescension as if the man thought he was talking the "little woman" out of yet one more situation.

"No!" he tried to shout through the wires in his jaw, but it came out as "Unnnnnnnnhhh!"

"Oh, be quiet, Fragger! This is between my wife and me," Quart ordered and walked straight into the leveled scalpel. Blood spurted from Quart's stomach as he staggered back and fell at Fragger's feet. A killer's trance held Kayla's face in a rigid mask of joy and horror as Buurk burst past her, shouting, "Let's get him up on the table, so I can stop the bleeding. If none of the vital organs are penetrated, I can save him."

Kayla blinked at him. "You can?"

"Of course, I can," the medic said, kneeling to grab one of Quart's arms. "Fragger, get down here and take the other side. Kayla, you get his feet."

Fragger did as he was ordered and waited for Kayla to act A wan smile crossed her face. Then, she leaped straight onto her husband, slashed his throat hard, and stabbed a tattoo of strokes across his body before Fragger wrestled the instrument away and tossed it aside. Quart gurgled and thrashed on the floor, grasping frantically at his throat, then went still. A pool of red gushed from the body, soaking everyone's knees. Kayla straightened up, blood staining her hands, and said, "Now you know how it feels, husband, except you're lucky. You only had to die once. I died every day you were with one of your bimbos."

A shudder ran through the woman's body.

Realization is sinking in, Fragger thought. *The same thing happened to me the first time I killed a man in combat.*

Kayla shook herself as if trying to get rid of the memory of what she'd just done. Suddenly, her eyes focused into abrupt decision.

"Clean up this mess," she ordered and left the room.

A mixture of emotions clouded the medic's face. Fragger gave him a questioning glance, and Buurk's feelings poured out.

"It's a horrible thing she just did. At the same time, I'm glad, and I'm ashamed of it! I wish it had been the other way around, though. I wish he'd put the blade into her. She's a hateful bitch. But I'm a medic. I'm supposed to care about people. I *do* care about them. But I don't care about her. I-."

Fragger laid a sympathetic hand on the man's shoulder. It was all he could do, but the gesture seemed to help Buurk collect himself as he said, "Go out to the locker next to the airlock. Get your survival suit on, get one for me and help me get Quart outside. There's no way to preserve the body in here."

Fragger hurried off to get the suits. When he returned, he was fully suited and waited while Buurk donned his suit. When Buurk was ready, the Ranger took Quart's feet while the medic hefted the shoulders free of the congealing blood. They carried the body straight to the airlock and cycled out into an evening sun as bloody as the scene inside.

"Where do you want to put him?" Fragger wanted to ask, but had to settle for the medic's head nodding in the desired direction. They lugged Quart past a heavily-dusted, self-propelled auger and were past the maintenance shed when Buurk stumbled.

"Bloody hell," the medic said in frustration over the commlink, then, more softly, "Oh, damn."

Fragger glanced down at the obstacle that had caught Buurk's foot and wanted to retch.

Kayla had torn her suit and mask off. The higher pressure in her body had reacted to the lower pressure of the Martian atmosphere. Her face was a grotesque mask.

"Let's put him next to her," Buurk said. "I guess it's only appropriate."

They laid Quart on the ground, his blood already frozen so hard that parts of it broke off at the impact of the body with the soil.

"Other than kicking me around, I don't think they had any particular religion," Buurk said in his dry voice, "so I suppose there's nothing to say."

A bitter remark, Fragger thought, *yet understandable. I'm glad to see Kayla go, but Quart was an okay guy even if he did cheat on her. Nobody deserves to die that way.*

"Well, Fragger, you wanted to get free from the complex and Security," the medic observed. "Now's the time to do just that."

Fragger glanced at him for an explanation.

Buurk pointed at the two bodies. "You think they're going to believe she murdered him, then killed herself when they've got a Martian and you on their hands? Any theft, any rape, any murder, any violation of the law--I come automatically under suspicion. I'm not staying around here so you'd better come with me. I know some people."

Fragger wished he had the e-pad with him. As a substitute, he knelt and wrote in the dust, Who? Where?

"You'll have to follow me to find out. I'm not about to give you anything they can pull out of your mind."

Fragger nodded.

"Let's get our equipment and food. We've got a long journey ahead of us," Buurk said.

Fragger followed the medic back inside the complex. The Ranger picked up the e-pad and stylus on their way to a storage room where Buurk pointed out several items.

"You take this," he said. "You'll need it."

Fragger checked out the bright green almost fluorescent package that Buurk handed him.

What is it? he wrote.

"Survival tent," Buurk answered.

Easy to find us, Fragger scribbled in dismay.

"Green isn't a usual color on Mars," the medic agreed. "That's the whole idea."

Don't want to be found, Fragger wrote. Isn't THAT the whole idea?

"If you have to use it, I'll probably be dead, and you'll want to be found," the Martian answered in a matter-of-fact tone. "Now, let's get some rations for our packs."

Buurk turned to a drawer and began throwing gray tubes onto a counter. Fragger grabbed one and read the label. It said MMRE.

MMRE? he wrote on the pad.

"Mars Meals Ready to Eat," Buurk answered after a glance at the pad. "Designed for local conditions."

Fragger turned the tube over and read the label on the other side. It said "Hash Flavored".

"Don't worry about the taste," the medic advised him. "There is none no matter what type it is."

Fragger studied the tube carefully before writing, How eat?

"Without freezing your face off, you mean?" Buurk asked. "Just stick it in your cake hole and squeeze."

"Huhhnn?" Fragger managed to say.

The medic pointed out a suit indentation that Fragger had failed to notice before. "That's the cake hole. Stick the tube in there and squeeze the yellow dot hard. That will release the paste into your mouth."

The Ranger wanted to ask why the stuff didn't freeze right in the tube when being used, but couldn't think of a short way to write it down. Besides, he was getting very tired of writing and desperately wanted to talk.

I'm a man of few words, he thought, *but I never appreciated how much I enjoyed those words before.*

Fragger put his longing to speak aside and helped Buurk fill the backpacks with food and water tubes. He had no idea why the water didn't freeze, either, but assumed there must be some sort of self-heating mechanism; otherwise, he'd be trying to drink a tube of ice. Silently, he cursed, *The worst part about being on another world is that you have to re-think just about every damned thing you took for granted on Earth, like eating and breathing. That old cliché--it's the small things that kill you--is like a basic law of survival out here.*

"Finished," Buurk said after the packs were full and set into place on their backs. "That's everything we need."

Not quite, Fragger thought and wrote, Weapons?

The medic laughed. "There's a few PDLs--personal defense lasers--but we might as well throw rocks at any Security forces chasing us, that's how much good they'd do. No, no weapons. They'll be pissed off already so we don't want to add to their aggravation. If they catch us, just give up. At least you'll live a little bit longer."

"Anyway," Buurk added as he adjusted the straps on his pack, "our best defense is hiding. Security is mostly Terrans, and they're lazy when it comes to searching. They'd rather let the machines do it, and machines have their limitations."

Fragger wanted to warn Buurk about the possibility there might be more forces than EarthCorp Security chasing them, but still wasn't certain if he could trust the man with the knowledge of his real identity. The medic hated the Security forces. Yet when it came down to personal survival, Fragger couldn't count on Buurk keeping that knowledge secret. It was better to keep his mouth shut.

Very funny, Fragger thought as he followed the medic out of the complex. *As if I could get it open in the first place.*

CHAPTER 23

Buurk set a long-legged pace away from the complex and across rocky terrain that turned quickly into foot-clogging dunes. To Fragger, it looked like movies he'd seen of the Sahara. On Mars, however, the sand in this region was a cinnamon color, and instead of a light blue sky, the stars overhead showed hard through a dark cobalt atmosphere scoured with perpetual dust kicked up by the winds.

How can a planet with practically no atmosphere have such strong winds? Fragger grumbled as they slogged through the sand. *And why is it that on Mars, just like on Earth, the wind is always in your face?*

The Ranger tried to force the negative thinking from his head. It was hard to do because Buurk didn't seem to find the rapid pace at all tiring. The medic strode across the sand as if he were a camel. At this thought, Fragger checked out the Martian's feet.

They are bigger than normal, he realized. *All this time, I thought it was just oversized boots or something. Maybe they tried to design him like a camel, spread the weight out so it's evenly distributed. He's as ugly as a camel that's for sure. I wonder if a committee planned him.*

A laugh tried to escape through his wired jaw and failed, but the sound caught Buurk's attention over the commlink.

"Something wrong?" the medic asked.

The Ranger shook his head, admitting to himself, *Buurk might be plug-ugly, but he's in his element here which is more than I can say for myself.*

Fragger unlimbered his e-pad and wrote, <u>How far?</u>

Buurk read the message and pointed toward a distant smudge on the horizon. "That's the Wollamaloo Caldera. It's two or three days away."

<u>Volcano?</u> Fragger wrote.

"Right," the Martian answered. 'Extinct, of course. Terran scientists gave the Mars volcanoes Latin names centuries ago, but I don't know what they are. Lots of Australians in mining so they started naming everything around them with familiar names, I guess. It's always been Wollamaloo to me."

Is it big? Fragger wrote.

"No, not really. EarthCorp geologists told me it's an ash shield volcano with a shallow magma chamber. Mostly basalt in composition. That's the scientific explanation. What it means for us once we get there is wading through even more ash and dust?"

Meeting who at caldera? Fragger wrote, hoping to coax some information out of the Martian.

Buurk shook his head. "Good try, Fragger, but I already told you I won't give you anything they can pull out of your mind if you're captured. It's a meeting point and that's all you have to know. No, no more questions. We've got some walking to do."

Resigned to having to wait for answers, Fragger trudged onward behind Buurk and, as promised by the Martian, they were at the base of the caldera wall on the morning of the third day.

The two men unshouldered their packs and dropped into a rust-streaked mound of volcanic ash. Fragger studied the wall as he pulled a food tube from his pack and squeezed a pork-flavored concentrate through the cake hole and into his mouth. He estimated the rim of the caldera rose about 500 feet above their heads. Red dust covered the slope.

Fragger squeezed more food into his mouth and shook his head at the cardboard taste. Buurk's craggy face grinned at him as pressed his own food tube against a helmet streaked with orange dust.

"Don't like this stuff, do you, Fragger?" the Martian asked as he chewed.

The Ranger grunted his assent.

"Well, it's mostly what I've known all my life, so it's okay with me. But Quart and Kayla, they felt the same way you do about MMREs. They called it 'bird food'. They said that on Earth, some birds prechew food for their young, and then regurgitate it into their beaks. They thought the food was as disgusting as that. Didn't really know what they meant since I'd never really seen a bird. I finally saw a holo on the subject on one of the System Wide channels. Threw me off my feed for a while, I'll admit."

"But it keeps you alive, doesn't it?" the Martian added as he finished his tube and tossed it into the dust. "And here's some more good news for you. We're at our rendezvous point right here. All we have to do is sit and wait. We've got time, so let's grab some rest."

Fragger nodded in agreement. The three-day walk had tired him out, and a nap was the perfect cure for exhaustion. He pulled the pack up under his head and stretched out under a dark sky streaked with absurdly pink clouds.

The Ranger woke instantly from a deep sleep when he heard Buurk's voice ask in his ear, "Did you hear that noise?"

Fragger shook his head in the negative.

"Well, I do," Buurk said. "And I'm not sure it's the noise I want to hear. I haven't received any message from our contact. Someone may be conducting an air search for us. Until we find out what we're facing, bury yourself in the sand and keep still."

The Ranger obeyed. It wasn't hard to gain concealment. The wind had piled up plenty of sand at the base of the caldera. He burrowed into the dune next to Buurk and waited until he heard the thin scream of an engine overhead. Against the murky sky, all he could see was the white-hot gases of its exhaust, then the aircraft was gone, a streak of light vanishing over the caldera rim.

I don't know much about their search capabilities but that pass seemed different from what I went through with Lesto and his men, the Ranger reasoned. *The plane was going too damned fast for a search pattern.*

Fragger knew he was right when several other aircraft streaked overhead without engaging in the usual vector pattern he associated with trying to locate an enemy. Turning his head, he threw a questioning glance at Buurk. The medic seemed as puzzled as he did. He rose out of the sand and helped the Ranger up.

"What's going on?" Fragger asked.

"I don't know," Buurk answered. "I was expecting a single ship. Something's up. Something big. They wouldn't be out in such force for just us."

I wouldn't be too sure about that, was Fragger's sour but silent response.

"Come on, let's see what's going on," Buurk said.

Fragger trudged up the slope after the Martian. It wasn't a steep angle, but the volcanic debris scattered across the caldera face made it a chore to pick their way upward and they had to tack their way across and up the wall. As they climbed, Fragger heard increased noise, the shriek of aircraft mixed up with other sounds he didn't recognize. Near the top of the wall, the angle increased precipitously slowing Fragger's ascent to a crawl. He could only watch enviously as Buurk burst ahead and climbed the last few meters with ease. The medic gained the summit and poked his head above the rim. A second later, an expression of awe and astonishment came over the commlink into the Ranger's ears.

"Damn me and all the sands of Mars! Fragger, you got to come here and see this!"

Fragger scrambled up the wall until he was alongside the Martian. He looked in the direction of Buurk's pointing finger in time to see a flash that sent a dazzling bolt of energy into the inner caldera just beneath the two men. Even in the thin air, the blast deafened Fragger.

And what's worse, Fragger cursed as the hot breath of the explosion blew him down the slope, *when I wake up, I'm going to have to climb this frigging wall all over again.*

CHAPTER 24

The blast knocked them all the way back down to the caldera base. Fragger knew this because when he opened his eyes, he found himself looking back up the hill past Buurk's foot which partially obscured his face plate.

"Get off me!" he ordered Buurk.

The medic rolled off into the sand, struggled into a sitting position and groaned, "Damn! Somebody put my brain in a vise."

Fragger understood the feeling. *Anybody's who been on the receiving end of a round knows the effect. Shock, ears ringing, nausea, pissing in your already crapped pants, unable to control your limbs, the whole package that fear delivers in an enemy assault.*

The Ranger got his legs underneath him and stood up. He grabbed for his e-pad and stylus to write a message to the Martian, but found both items gone. He settled for pointing up the hill to signal his intentions to Buurk.

"Go back up there? Are you crazy?" the medic asked. "My God, we're not even fighting, and we could get killed!"

The Ranger made a dismissive gesture and climbed the slope again, not worrying about whether or not the medic would follow him. As a soldier, Fragger just had to see the engagement. He'd fought in Nam, a jungle warfare situation where tanks were, for all practical purposes, useless and in Desert Storm where tanks were supreme so he was eager to what was new and different--if anything--about an engagement several centuries into the future.

When Fragger reached the top and cautiously poked his head up again, he saw the battlefield had not changed all that much since his days. Down in the caldera, a classic tank battle was taking shape. One side was assaulting an enemy defensive position. Wishing the dust and smoke would dissipate so he could sort out the players, the Ranger had to settle for waiting until a troop carrier landed and spilled out a squad of 12 soldiers before he could identify the personal armor. With rising excitement, he realized immediately who the attacking force was--Ricer troops. There was no mistaking the samurai-like armor with the flaring helmets. The squad deployed behind the tanks to support the armor assaulting the dug-in positions against the far end of the caldera.

My God, the tanks are enormous! Fragger marveled. *I'm amazed they need any infantry support at all!*

The Abrams tanks in Desert Storm had weighed around 50 tons, carried 120 mm guns, and had been damned impressive. But the black machines down in the caldera were staggeringly awesome and obviously much more powerful. Through holes in the smoke and dust, Fragger saw huge gouts of soil blown into the air with each blast from the magnetic accelerator cannons as they fired at the hull defilade positions of their enemy. In the minimal atmosphere of Mars, each time a gun fired it sounded like someone was tearing a colossal piece of very thin paper before each detonation.....rrrrrrriiiiiiiiiiiiipppppppppPPPPPP-BLAST!

Jeezus, he thought, *I wouldn't want to be facing one of those monsters. They make the Abrams tanks look like toys.*

Fragger estimated that each tank had to weigh at least 100-150 tons in Earth gravity, and yet their crews maneuvered them as if they were sports cars, firing so rapidly that he knew their gunnery systems were computer-directed. As he watched, a round--or whatever they called a MAC projectile--struck the front of an Imperial Commonwealth tank. The concussion shook the earth with the force of an earthquake. Fragger was amazed when the Ricer tank emerged unscathed from a ball of flame and smoke.

Firepower, mobility and protection are the Holy Grails of armored warfare, he remembered, *and, boy, do these guys have protection!*

For a moment, Fragger wondered how the infantry down in the caldera survived such staggering firepower, then he remembered the quickness of Watanabe, Lesto and the other armored soldiers he'd seen in action. A heavy main battle tank couldn't possibly match an individual trooper's speed, a point that was proved as he watched a Ricer soldier come out of nowhere to slap a charge on the side of a blunt and blocky EarthCorp tank that had foolishly come out of its hull defilade position to engage the Imperial Commonwealth forces.

Fragger recognized the situation instantly. *A gung ho tank commander. Wants honor and glory and ends up leaving common sense and the lives of his crew in the dust.*

As the Ricer trooper raced away from the charge he'd placed, Fragger waited for the blast to destroy the EarthCorp tank. There was a muffled "crummp" from the machine, but not what he expected. Instead, a yellow, luminescent spot appeared, traveling upward like a cancer eating away skin. Holes appeared in the hull, and gases vented out above the red and torn earth. Fragger couldn't figure out what kind of weapon the soldier had placed, but he saw it was effective when a Ricer tank appeared out of the smoke, targeted the yellow spot, and fired at point-blank range before EarthCorp tank commander could traverse his gun into position. Out of a gigantic ball of flame, a turret flew straight up into the Martian sky as another concussion shook the caldera.

The Ranger was impressed by the cooperation between the infantry and the tankers while wondering at the same time, *What the devil did that trooper use? Acid, nanotechs?*

Fragger didn't have time to think about it because an EarthCorp trooper flashed by the destroyed tank and engaged the Ricer soldier who'd planted the charge.

Fragger grew excited and realized, *This is what I really wanted to see because I don't know much about sword play. Hell, in my time, the Japanese were the only ones who still equipped their officers with swords, and, as I told Watanabe, they dishonored their Bushido tradition by using the blades to chop off the heads of helpless prisoners. But this looks like the real thing--man to man combat, where individual skill counts again.*

As the two soldiers closed, the Ranger quickly discovered a soldier had better be damned good with his sword. The Ricer trooper parried a blow from his EarthCorp opponent. The Corpse's blade slid off and struck a knee-high boulder and sliced it cleanly in two, sparks flying up from the hyper-heated rock. The Ricer trooper took advantage of the opening and swung a short, efficient stroke at his enemy's exposed upper arm. The blade cut through the weak spot with ease. The Corpse's limb dropped to the ground along with the sword and the soldier himself. The Ricer trooper finished it quickly with a blow that severed the head.

Shit! Fragger swore in amazement. *Either the Imperial Commonwealth soldier is damned good, or he was fighting a raw soldier new to battle.*

Engaged immediately by another EarthCorp soldier, the Ricer trooper showed he was damned good. He ducked beneath a wild swing, chopped his opponent across the back of the leg which sent the man into a kneeling position. Like a surgeon, the Ricer separated the Corpse's head from his neck.

A melee had developed in the middle of the caldera, but Fragger was still able to pick out the Imperial Commonwealth trooper from the mass of struggling men as the Ricer engaged a third EarthCorp opponent. This time, the two men were obviously equally matched, moving as if they were in a speeded-up film. Fragger could barely follow the blows and counter-blows. The Corpse soldier was taller and seemed stronger, but the Imperial Commonwealth trooper moved with a quickness of a lighter man. The humming buzz and clash of the powered swords rose into the thin Martian air.

"OhmiGod!" Fragger heard a voice say.

Buurk had rejoined him.

"They're slicing each other into pieces," the medic said in disgust, then looked at the Ranger. "How can you watch this? Doesn't it revolt you?"

Fragger signaled the medic to be silent. *There's no point in being noticed, you fool!* he swore silently. *Neither one of us is going to last a second against these guys.*

Buurk grunted, and Fragger was ready to knock the medic on his ass to keep him quiet when he saw that a stray round in the Martian's shoulder had done the job for him.

Fragger shoved his own face into the dirt an instant before a second projectile screamed over his head. The Ranger dropped down to check the medic and saw that the survival suit had sealed itself. There was nothing he could do for Buurk's pain, so he patted the medic on the helmet and risked popping his head up again to catch the action below.

The quicker Ricer trooper and his taller Corpse opponent still fought. The whole scene put Fragger's mind out of joint.

Heavy armor, close air support, weapons that could blast a regiment into pieces, and in the middle of all this, they're fighting with swords! It's bizarre.

But, as he watched, the Ranger admitted he liked the idea of meeting an opponent face to face even if the body was encased in power armor. Somehow, it seemed a truer test of combat.

You're a romantic idiot, that's what you are, Fragger scolded himself as the two soldiers clashed blades. The duel didn't take long to finish. The Corpse trooper, ready to drop a two-handed stroke from over his head, stumbled over rocks littering the Martian surface. It was only a fraction of a second's hesitation, but the Ricer soldier claimed the opening instantly by chopping his opponent's leg off at the knee. The Corpse trooper flailed down into the dirt. Fragger couldn't hear him scream, but could imagine the pain of both the wound and the sudden attack of frigid Martian atmosphere on the man's exposed flesh. The Ricer trooper seemed mindful of this and ended the Corpse's suffering by lopping off his head with a single, quick blow. A mixture of admiration and horror filled Fragger's mind. The Imperial Commonwealth trooper was mercilessly efficient, a fact that became all too apparent as the helmeted figure looked up from his victim and directly at Fragger.

Fragger's first instinct was to grab Buurk and start running, but the Ranger knew they wouldn't get far. With powered armor, the Ricer trooper would catch up with them within seconds. The only alternative was to stay put and fight. Either way was suicide.

I'll stand right here and die like a man, Fragger decided. He pulled Buurk to his feet to give the medic a chance for escape, then put himself between the Martian and the trooper advancing up the slope. Without a weapon, the Ranger stooped, picked up rocks and threw them down at the Ricer. It was a useless gesture, but it made Fragger feel better. At least, he was doing something.

The Imperial Commonwealth trooper ignored the rocks as they bounced off his armor, accelerated, and, before Fragger could blink, was on the ridge with the samurai sword raised high for the killing blow. The blade gleamed with its internal energy as the Ricer swung at the Ranger's neck.

A final prayer went through Fragger's head. He heard the thin, wooshing "snick!" of the passing blade and opened his eyes in astonishment. The Ricer seemed no less startled.

The deadly trooper, who had just killed three fully armed and armored soldiers, had missed Fragger Sparks.

CHAPTER 25

The three men stood rooted at the top of the caldera ridge. Two of them stared at Fragger.

What the hell just happened here? the Ranger wondered, amazed that he was still in one piece.

There was no time for Fragger to figure it out. The Ricer trooper shook himself out of immobility and struck again with his sword—twice.

And missed.

What the devil? The Ranger swore in disbelief while he tried to figure out how the impossible had happened. An expert warrior had missed a point-blank target.

The Ricer trooper lowered his weapon and paused for a moment before asking over the commlink, "Fragger Sparks?"

Fragger shook his head in the affirmative.

"You owe me a life," a somehow familiar voice said.

Fragger gestured openly with his hands, indicating he didn't have a clue as to what the man was talking about.

"You owe me three lives."

Watanabe! the Ranger realized.

"Why don't you speak?" Watanabe asked. "Aren't you glad to see an old enemy?"

Buurk broke into the conversation to explain, "He can't speak. He broke his jaw, and it's wired shut."

Watanabe broke into raucous laughter. "I'd expect nothing less of Sparks!"

Why is he calling me by my name all of a sudden? Fragger asked himself in suspicion. *All he ever called me before was "Rerun".*

"What do you mean?" the medic asked.

"Sparks is a survivor, aren't you, Sparks? He may get bent or broken, but he always survives."

Buurk threw a puzzled glance in Fragger's direction. "How'd he do that? Avoid having you separate his head from his body, I mean."

Yeah, how? Fragger asked silently.

"Sparks is a very special person, Martian."

"I can see that, but nobody survives an armored trooper, especially unarmed opponents. Yet Fragger did!"

"He did, indeed," Watanabe said. "And he doesn't know any more about why he's still standing than you do."

"Explain."

"Damn it, we haven't got time!"

Fragger jabbed a finger repeatedly at the ground to show he wanted an explanation as much as Buurk did and wasn't going anywhere until he got it.

Watanabe cursed them hard for their stupidity, but relented. "All right, all right. Just wait a moment."

The sergeant issued a command over his commlink, nodded when he got confirmation of the order, then turned his attention back to Fragger and said, "All right, I've called for an extraction team. Get down out of the line of fire and while we wait, I'll explain. Sparks, do you remember Leery, the Revival Technician on Khanwat?"

Fragger nodded.

"Our intelligence people broke the encrypted data on the files I retrieved when I hauled your naked ass out of the lab. The spooks said there was a lot of rambling on ad nauseum by Leery about how he wasn't appreciated and so forth, but after they waded through his self-pity, they found he was more than a Revival Technician. He was a scientist, a research scientist and a very eccentric and obnoxious individual, but one with a lot of ideas. He had the misfortune to have a supervisor more than willing to take credit for those ideas. When Leery started making noises about theft, the supervisor labeled him a crackpot and a trouble maker. He demoted Leery to Revival Technician and shipped him off to Khanwat along with a shipload of Reruns simply to get rid of him. This put Leery on an out-of-the way, yet dangerous and contested planet where, I assume, the supervisor hoped his scientist would either rot or get killed. This was bad news for Leery, of course, but it also left him free to pursue his particular passion."

"Which was?" Buurk asked for Fragger.

"Here's the simplest explanation. I know you're a Rerun but see if you can follow it, Sparks. We can move through hyperspace by exploiting gravitic lines of force. It requires complex navigation and a lot of energy. In short, hyperdrive engines and massive ships to house them. Leery was impatient with this 'dinosaur' technology, as he called it. He believed that a human being--the right human being—can detect these electromagnetic lines of force at some level and exploit them. For him, it was simply a matter of isolating, then focusing and amplifying the appropriate mental functions."

"What mental functions?" Buurk asked after a quick read of the Ranger's questioning expression. "That's what Fragger wants to know."

"We don't know any more about it than you do, Sparks," Watanabe answered. "But, two things came together at the same time—Leery's isolation of the mental functions and your revival. Luckily for you, you possess the abilities he was looking for. He'd already gone through over 200 Reruns before he got to you. They ended up vegetables. But you…remember those gravitic lines I mentioned? Leery has amplified your innate ability to detect these lines and given you the "talent" to slide along and between them. He achieved that trick by developing what he called an HSP—hyperspace potential—enhancer. He then incorporated the 'enhancer' into your translator module. You have an ability nobody else has. With you, Leery got his fingers around the ultimate prize of military research. You can move through hyperspace, not for the great distances Leery envisioned, but good enough. You're the most dangerous man alive today."

Fragger frowned and made a "Why?" gesture with his hands.

"You're dangerous because we don't fully understand Leery's achievement. The Corpses don't, either. The irony is, he was conducting research right under their noses, and they didn't have a clue because the supervisor had banished Leery to Khanwat and the Outer Wastes. The only reason they became aware of Leery's research was because, once he'd confirmed his theory and constructed the module, he went over his supervisor's head and squirted a message directly to EarthCorp management. It was one of his habits that did not endear him to the supervisor. A sharp-eyed manager actually read the message and informed his superiors. Nobody believed Leery had actually accomplished anything, but they dispatched a nearby HELOT to Khanwat to investigate. We detected their signature, and that's when we engaged them and I showed up in the lab."

"Remember our conversation with Major Shimazu, Sparks?" Watanabe continued. "We thought then that you might be a MASER, which is a military term for a mentally adapted soldier, experimental. For centuries, military scientists have been trying to create them. Our best guess is that's why the DARPA people of your time hauled you in for testing. It's likely they were looking for ESP, the ability to move objects through mental force, the ability to project terrifying images into the enemy's mind, that kind of thing. They were on a wild goose chase with most of that stuff, but they were on to something with you and probably didn't even know it."

Buurk looked over at the Ranger, awe tinged with fear evident in his eyes, and asked, "You mean Fragger can do all those things in addition to moving through hyperspace?"

"No, you Martian imbecile. He doesn't have those powers--no one does--but when I attacked him a few minutes ago, we saw that he's been given the ability to carry one power to its ultimate conclusion. For lack of a better word, he can "teleport" himself instantly and incrementally out of the way of danger. Not many armored men have escaped Watanabe's blade. No unarmored man ever has. Yet Sparks did it. In him, Leery created the first MASER."

I can teleport? Fragger thought in wonder. *But I don't remember doing anything except trying to get out of the way. Damn, what an advantage, and I don't even know how to exploit it!*

"Come on, Sparks. Enough explanation. We've spent a lot of resources and men tracking you down. We've got a dropship coming to get you and Buurk out of here."

Fragger took a step to follow Watanabe, then stopped dead as he realized, *He knows Buurk's name! How'd he know that?*

The Ranger ran in front of Watanabe and gestured toward Buurk.

"Yes, yes, he's a spy," Watanabe said impatiently. "He's been our mole for years."

Buurk grinned at Fragger. "I told you I hated EarthCorp, didn't I? I've wanted my freedom for years and never had a big enough ticket for the Ricers to get me off the planet. Then, you dropped into my life. Bless you, Fragger Sparks and bless Kayla's murderous heart! The only hard part was listening to you go on with all that nonsense about the 'Ranger' system and being a 'Coloradan' and Planet 'Leadstheway'. Did you really think I wouldn't check EarthCorpNet for that information?"

I'll be damned! Fragger swore.

Watanabe broke the Ranger out of his embarrassed astonishment by snapping, "Help is coming, but we're not out of here yet so I need to communicate with a superior officer."

Fragger and Buurk obeyed while Watanabe turned toward the caldera and the battle still raging below them and barked out a code over the commlink. Soon, an entire company of Ricer tanks, 14 of the monsters, disengaged from the immediate fight, wheeled to the left, and charged toward the enemy's flank at the far end of the caldera, all while still maintaining a steady rate of fire. Gouts of pink-red dust flamed into the air as EarthCorp forces shifted to meet this new thrust.

Feint? Fragger speculated. *Is Watanabe trying to draw their attention away from us?*

The lead Ricer commander accelerated his tank forward toward two EarthCorp vehicles and paid the price for his bravery. The Corpse tankers swiveled their turrets in swift targeting and bracketed the Imperial Commonwealth tank with simultaneous blasts. When the dust cleared, all that was left was the smoldering fragments of the hull. At this result, the rest of the Ricer tankers seemed to panic and threw their vehicles into reverse. Sensing blood, the EarthCorp tankers broke formation and chased wildly after Watanabe's tankers.

Dumb, Fragger realized, *really dumb. They don't see the trap coming.*

Watanabe's men didn't take long to spring it. The fleeing Ricer tanks expertly pivoted about into a V-formation to provide cover for each other, but it was the tanks appearing on the rim above the crater that dropped the hammer on the EarthCorp forces. They poured concentrated fire down onto the disorganized attackers and blew the Corpse tanks high into the Martian air.

Fragger couldn't smell death, but his mind dredged the odor up from combat in his own time. It was the odor of blood and piss and exposed intestines and the indelible pork-like reek of burnt flesh.

A combat death is always messy, the Ranger thought, *but then, dying on the surface of a strange planet, where sound itself is reduced to a tinny, odd tone, seems like a terrible way to go. War is always impersonal. On Mars, though, the very ground on which these men are fighting is just as impersonal and deadly as any human enemy.*

Fragger glanced skyward and saw an aircraft shaped like a mutant and very angry bat streak across the battlefield. It laid a missile straight into the middle of the Ricer tank force that had suckered the EarthCorp tankers into the trap. Metal screamed itself into strange and unnatural shapes. Fragger got nervous as another plane hit the same spot. The Corpses were fighting back, and since this was their territory, it was a foregone conclusion that they had superior numbers in men, weapons and equipment. The Ranger wasn't sure why he was nervous. He'd never been nervous once combat started. Then, he realized, *Of course, I should be nervous. After all, for me, it doesn't matter who wins. Either way, I'll end up in Shit City.*

Fragger decided his preference was that Watanabe would get them off the planet in one piece. The man had saved his life--three times! There was a debt to be paid. Honor demanded it.

The Ranger amended that idea with the bitter thought, *Of course, honor will probably get my head lopped off. Watanabe may still want that single combat.*

Fragger heard Watanabe curse and shout out another code. The sergeant motioned toward the bottom of the hill away from the fighting and ordered, “Come on!”

Another missile streaked over their heads as they scrambled down the slope. Fragger didn’t worry about it until he saw it curve upward and then back toward them. Watanabe swore again, raised his arm and issued a command. A cloud of glittering silver puffed violently up from the Imperial trooper’s forearm and spread rapidly over their heads. The EarthCorp missile, dead on course before Watanabe’s action, wavered in confusion, then exploded harmlessly high in the air.

It’s chaff, Fragger realized with relief, *or whatever the future equivalent of chaff is.*

Watanabe urged them to go faster. When they were down on level ground, he shouted “Get behind that boulder and wait.” As Fragger followed Buurk to cover, he saw the sergeant scan the sky between alert checks of the caldera rim above their position. The wait was not long. High above the setting sun, the Ranger saw spacecraft exhaust mar the sky with incandescent flame. A dropship banked in their direction and then leveled out. To Fragger’s surprise, it shot over them into a hovering position about half a kilometer away and settled slowly toward the Martian surface. EarthCorp forces targeted it immediately. Shell bursts dotted the ground and the sky above it.

“Get ready!” Watanabe ordered.

Fragger stared incredulously at Watanabe, knowing they’d never reach the ship before it was blown apart. He was about to tackle the Ricer non-com and pound this truth into him when Watanabe crouched and pointed.

Impossibly low over the undulating dusty terrain, another spacecraft accelerated toward them, rising and dipping to keep a constant height over the ridges and dunes. Fragger looked back at the first dropship. It was taking heavy punishment from EarthCorp bombardment.

Another deception, he thought in admiration and relief, *but I hope to hell that first ship is automated and doesn't have anybody on board.*

The rescue vessel slowed. As it neared them, it blurred into near invisibility

Damn, that chameleon technology hurts the eyes, the Ranger cursed as he tried to keep the ship in focus and failed. It was like trying to track an insane hummingbird, but, almost before he knew it, the vessel settled to the ground on jets twenty meters away and blinked into a solid shape amidst the smoke and dust raised by the exhausts. As Watanabe hurried them across open ground and through the opened door, Fragger had time to notice the craft looked nothing like a hummingbird, insane or otherwise. Instead, it resembled nothing no much as a warthog with wings.

If it wasn't being used to rescue me at the moment, I'd say it was the ugliest thing I've ever seen.

It bristled with weapon muzzles fore and aft that tracked continuously with the implacable energy of a machine used primarily for defensive purposes. Inside, Fragger erased any doubt about its defensive configuration by tapping his knuckles against the bulkhead. He didn't know if it was metal, plastic or some composite, but the dull knock that sounded in the pressurized cabin told him the wall was damned thick and could take extensive punishment.

My kind of machine! Fragger sighed as he sagged back and fastened himself into a seat.

Despite the heavy armor protection, the pilot lifted the dropship off the ground as if it were as light as a glider. He spun it around like a top and pushed the machine upward into a crazy evasion pattern. The Ranger glanced over at Buurk and saw the medic vomiting down onto his shoes. Across from them, Watanabe sat calmly with his power sword across his knees. Several nearby blasts shook the vessel.

Get this damned thing moving! Fragger urged and, for a moment, thought the pilot had heard him because in an instant he was pinned back against his seat by the force of an enormous acceleration. Risking a glance outside, he saw the sky turn swiftly black, and then they were free of gravity and arcing toward a familiar and menacing shape that blotted out half the stars in the sky--a HELOT ship. Buurk continued ejecting the contents of his stomach until the dry heaves set in.

Apparently, this is the medic's first exposure to zero-gee, Fragger thought with sympathy. *Wait until he goes through hyperspace, the poor bastard. Shit, poor me.*

From the tense chatter in the cockpit, the Ranger guessed the HELOT was under heavy attack. The pilot proved his point by wasting no time in his approach. Within minutes, he had the craft inside the landing bay and locked into grapples. Watanabe didn't waste any time, either. He shoved both men out the hatch into a corridor shaking under the impact of enemy fire. He marched them through the ship and straight to a room whose door was bracketed by two heavily armed guards. Watanabe motioned Fragger and Buurk forward, and then followed them inside.

They were on the bridge of the Tokyo. A familiar figure sat directly ahead of Fragger. The sight turned his spine from bone to jelly.

It was Major Shimazu, her cement-grey eyes pinned on him from the fragmented Picasso face.

CHAPTER 26

"Sparks, this is Captain Ijiro, in command of the Tokyo. He very much wanted to see the source of all the trouble I've brought onto his ship," Shimazu greeted Fragger. The major flicked a contemptuous glance toward the short officer standing next to her chair.

Fragger saw the reason for Shimazu's disdain. Ijiro wasn't imposing. It looked as if someone had stuck a hose in the captain's mouth and inflated his nose and cheeks into three ruddy balloons. The plump cheeks had squeezed his mouth into a permanent childish pout of fleshy lips. A paunch pushed against a spotless white uniform. The Ranger guessed the major's dislike of the captain went beyond the lack of physical fitness. Ijiro had the appearance of a man who'd somehow bought his way into rank or called in favors to achieve it. The thud of heavy weapons fire on the hull wrung sweat from the sallow skin of the officer's forehead and dropped it into blinking eyes.

Ijiro jabbed a finger toward Fragger and, in a shrill voice, asked irrationally, "You? Who the hell do you think you are, Rerun? You've put an entire ship and crew in danger! Do you realize that? Do you? Answer me, damn it!"

"Sir, he can't talk easily," Watanabe interrupted the captain. "He broke his jaw, and it's wired shut."

"What? What?" Ijiro sputtered as his rage ran up against this astonishing piece of news and deflated into the speechless quivering of chubby lips.

"He broke his jaw," Watanabe repeated.

Frustration opened and closed the captain's mouth several times before he decided to direct his anger at Shimazu, "Major, your actions caused my vessel to enter enemy-held space to pick up a man—not even a man, but a Rerun!—pick up a Rerun for interrogation, and he can't even talk! I very much hope you and your superiors know what you're doing on this mission. If my ship is lost, I'll hold you personally responsible. Is that clear?"

"Perfectly clear," Shimazu answered in cold response. "And I'll hold you personally responsible if you don't find a way to break engagement with the EarthCorp forces and deliver the Rerun safely into the Emperor's hands."

"Get off my bridge!" Shimazu ordered.

"I see you are eager for your first taste of battle," Shimazu responded dryly as she stood. "Let's hope your combat skills are as abundant as your perspiration."

"I said, get off my bridge, you insubordinate bitch!"

Shimazu picked up an e-pad and led the group out the door and into an interrogation room a short distance from the bridge. The major dropped the pad onto a table, lowered her wedge of a body into a chair before turning her attention to Fragger. The overhead illumination sputtered and dimmed when another impact shook the hull. It cast Shimazu's face into harsh relief and made the sharp angled cheek bones look as if they were ready to slice their way out of the puckered skin. Shadows transformed the power sword wound into a facial gash so deep there appeared to be no bottom to it. Fragger shuddered at the image and was temporarily grateful when the major twitched ruined lips into a smile and destroyed the illusion.

"A wired jaw, Sparks?" Shimazu said. "I guess it makes sense in a way. A primitive solution for a primitive."

Ijiro was right. She is a bitch! Fragger cursed in his mind. He was almost glad his jaw was wired shut so he couldn't open his mouth and get into more trouble. *But, at least she's using my name now, although I'm not sure whether I like that or not.*

Watanabe jumped in to explain, "If I may, Major. It wasn't a matter of fitting the treatment to a Rerun. The technology wasn't available at the Mars oxygen extraction plant where Sparks ended up. This man--Buurk—was our operative who informed us of the Rerun's presence on the planet. He's also the medic who performed the jaw wiring procedure. As he explained to me, he worked with what materials he had available."

Shimazu nodded at Buurk. "Martian, you've performed a valuable service for the Royal and Imperial Commonwealth. You have our thanks."

"And my freedom and the money?" Buurk asked, still gripping the wounded shoulder with his free hand to keep the pain at bay.

"We will keep our part of the bargain, Martian, assuming we escape the EarthCorp forces. Watanabe, escort him to sick bay and get his wound fixed. Then rejoin the fight. I'm sure our forces could use an extra hand, even that of a *Buraku*."

Watanabe colored at the insulting tone of the major's order but obeyed the command by ushering Buurk out of the room quickly. When they were gone, Shimazu wasted no time in getting to the point. "Sparks, I'll be blunt. We've risked several thousand tons of HELOT and hundreds of troopers to find you, so you know you've been promoted. From a minor irritation to a first-class menace. I didn't like you the first time we met. I like you even less now. Do you know why?"

Fragger shook his head.

"Because you might be my damned Agincourt. Scum though you are, your background is that of a professional soldier. You're well aware of Terran military history. At Earth's Battle of Agincourt, the English long bow demonstrated its superiority over the knight because it proved its lethal, penetrating power against French armor. You might be the modern equivalent of the long bow."

Fragger did his best to grin at her discomfort, but it only hurt his face.

The major continued, "Watanabe informed me that he explained MASER powers to you down on the planet. So, you know that if your ability to 'teleport' in increments is isolated, understood, and exploited by our enemies, the implications could be profoundly disastrous. Assuming EarthCorp is successful in accomplishing this task, it means they'll be able to field entire units of MASERS at minimal cost to them and maximum cost to us. But I'll bet the Corpse fools don't realize there's an even larger ramification. With MASERS common as cockroaches, it's possible any backwater planet unable to afford powered troopers will be capable of mounting a credible threat. Given the right leadership, they might be able to defeat our troopers or those of EarthCorp or any of the other great nation-systems. And that, Sparks, is a direct threat to me, the people of the Royal and Imperial Commonwealth, and my way of life."

Inwardly, Fragger grinned. *Anything you hate, Major, I love.*

The officer heaved her damaged body up out of the chair and continued talking as she walked around the table, "My experts tell me they suspect the Corpse Revival Technician Leery somehow 'wired' you on a neuronic level with that HSP device of his to develop your potential to the fullest extent. In other words, that's expert talk for 'we haven't got a clue'."

Shimazu moved close to Fragger. "And you know what that means, Rerun, don't you?"

Oh,crap! Fragger groaned.

"After we get your jaw fixed, it's interrogation time again. This time we won't fail because we're going to learn Leery's secret even if we have to take you apart cell by cell."

Shimazu leaned into his face until all he could see was the brittle, gray eyes. She went on , "Which, by the way, is a very painful road to death. The ancient Terrans had a ritual called the 'Death of a Thousand Cuts'. A victim slowly bled to death from all the incisions. You'd much prefer that to cellular stripping, Sparks. It's pain at an exquisitely prolonged level. So, if you have any information about your MASER abilities, you'd better spill your guts and be damned quick about it. Do you understand me?"

Fragger nodded vigorously.

Shimazu drew back and ordered, "Wait here for Watanabe. Once we're free of the fight, he'll conduct you to Interrogation."

Fragger watched the major leave the room and lock the door without so much as a glance back at him. When she was gone, he collapsed into a chair and wondered if it was possible to drown in the pool of sweat dripping off his body.

He hoped so.

CHAPTER 27

It was the oldest interrogation trick on the books. Make a man wait a very long time and let him stew in the juices of his own imagination about the tortures planned for him. Fragger knew the tactic well because he'd practiced it on prisoners himself. Still, it seemed to him that Watanabe was taking an unusual amount of time to return and guessed it was due to the fact that the sergeant was still involved in fighting off the *Tokyo's* attackers. The shuddering of the ship's hull under sharp impacts proved the battle was still in progress. Fragger assumed Captain Ijiro would jump to hyperspace as soon as possible, but no nauseating transition had occurred. That meant the ship was either damaged, unable to break contact with the enemy, or in a poor position to make the jump.

Or any or all of the above, Fragger decided as he paced back and forth in the room trying to decide what to do when Watanabe returned. *I damned sure don't want to face Shimazu's cellular stripping torture which means I have only two options—suicide or fight. Make that one option. Fight. A Ranger always fights. Surrender of any kind is not in his vocabulary. I'll take out a few soldiers before they get to me*

Fragger moved to the chair nearest the door and sat down to wait.

A long time passed before Watanabe unlocked and opened the door. The sergeant wasn't wearing his powered armor suit which told Fragger the battle was over and the ship safe for now. He was armed only with a power baton hung on his belt. A stocky, solid trooper, the heavy-jawed Ricer stood three inches shorter than Fragger, but moved as if he was a foot taller, showing the easy arrogance of an elite Ricer Jump Trooper. Only the haggard and drawn face told of fatigue from the battle.

Fragger grabbed the e-pad and stylus Shimazu had left behind. Deciding to put Watanabe off guard before attempting to overpower him, the Ranger wrote, <u>Corpses give you a good fight?</u>

The sergeant read the message and nodded. "They sent a boarding party against us under cover of a barrage, but we met them out on the hull and drove them away. Still, the attack threw the hyperspace drive off line. If we're lucky, the engineers will have it up and running soon. If not, well, we're screwed. We're in EarthCorp space"

Fragger scribbled, <u>Easy fighting in vacuum?</u>

Watanabe gave a flat-out snort at this idea. "It's harder, Rerun. Everything's different in zero-G. Lots of ways to die besides an enemy strike. Lose suit integrity, lose your bearings, lose contact with the hull. Lose any of those, and you lose your life."

Fragger wrote, <u>Lot of trouble just for me</u>.

At this remark, anger clouded Watanabe's eyes. "You got that right, Rerun. We've risked several vessels and many good men against planetary defenses, plus I've saved your life three times, and each life costs me some of my best men. I will mourn long with their families."

Well, fuck you, Fragger fumed internally. *I didn't ask for any of this. It's not my damned fault.*

"Enough talk," Watanabe said. "It's time to get that jaw fixed. So you're ready for your interrogation."

He ordered Fragger to stand and follow him. The Ranger obeyed, then drove a fist straight into the sergeant's belly. Watanabe doubled over, but straightened up quickly and reached for the power baton at his waist. Kicking Watanabe's hand away from the weapon, the Ranger threw two short uppercuts into the Ricer's thick chin. Watanabe sagged and dropped to the deck. Fragger stood indecisively over the unconscious sergeant for a moment, asking himself, *What now, genius?*

He knew what the best solution was.

Kill Watanabe before he comes to and sounds the alarm! But, damn, he's saved my life not once, but three times. I can't do it.

Fragger considered shoving him under the table and out of sight but he couldn't count on the sergeant being unconscious for long. Another solution struck him. He grabbed the e-pad again, wrote on it, then dashed out into the corridor making urgent noises through his wired jaw.

His show of urgency turned several puzzled heads in his direction. He shoved the pad into the face of an armored trooper who had his helmet open. The name *Iyeka* was stenciled on his chest of his armor

Iyeka read his message and asked, “Sergeant Watanabe’s sick? Where is he?”

Fragger pointed back at the room.

“All the medics are too busy to come down here,” the trooper responded. “It’ll be faster to get him to the sick bay on C deck. I’ll carry him.”

Fragger nodded his agreement.

Iyeka looked quizzically at him and asked, “What’s the matter with you? Can’t you talk?”

Fragger gestured at his jaw and made breaking motions with his hands.

“Corpse trooper broke it for you, huh?” the trooper said with a sympathetic grin. “Lucky that’s all you got. Come on. They tell me it’s an easy fix.”

They went back into the room. Iyeka went down on one knee to check Watanabe.

“What happened to him?” he asked Fragger.

The Ranger shrugged and made keeling over motions to indicate Watanabe had collapsed onto the floor.

“I don’t see any obvious wounds,” Iyeka said. “Maybe Watanabe got a wound in battle he didn’t even know about. It’s happened before. Only one way to find out what the problem is.”

Ieyka picked Watanabe up off the floor with the powered ease of his armor and ordered Fragger to accompany him out the door. The Ranger followed in the soldier’s wake as he shouldered his way through the crowded corridors and inward several decks before entering the sick bay door and depositing Watanabe on an empty gurney.

"Corpsman!" Iyeka bellowed. "We got two more wounded over here. One unconscious from undetermined causes. One with a broken jaw who can't talk."

Fragger wrote Thanks! on the e-pad and showed it to the soldier.

"No problem," Iyeka responded as he left. "We take care of our own."

A harried corpsman turned from a trooper with a shoulder injury and told Fragger, "Take a seat over there. I'll be with you in a minute."

Fragger sat and watched the corpsman work without guidance from the grizzled doctor at the far end of the sick bay. The silver-haired physician barked orders at aides to help him hold down a trooper thrashing in agony from the seared flesh on his side. When the aides had the man pinned, the physician aimed a conical device at his patient's head and thumbed a control. Beneath the flickering surgical lights, the trooper's body relaxed immediately and slumped back onto the gurney.

Impressive, Fragger marveled, wishing they'd had such a pain-killing device in his time.

As he checked out the occupants of the sick bay, the Ranger realized the fight on the hull must have been impressive too. He counted at least 50 casualties, ranging from the walking wounded to troopers with sheets over their heads. Then, he heard his name yelled and saw Buurk.

"What are you doing here?" the Martian called.

Fragger frowned and pointed at his jaw, meaning he still couldn't talk, but Buurk mistook his gesture and said, "Oh, they're finally going to fix that, are they?"

Damn! Fragger swore as the corpsman's head popped up at this exchange.

"Finally fix what?" he asked and came toward Fragger with a scowl on his face. The name stenciled above his chest pocket was *Magran.* He put his bald head close to Fragger and examined his jaw with quick, expert motions. Puzzlement entered Magran's eyes until he pried the Ranger's lips open and saw the wires.

"What the hell?" the corpsman said, plainly baffled by what he was seeing. He backed off and studied Fragger as if he were an exotic animal that had somehow shown up in the sick bay. "Nobody broke your jaw in battle. The damned thing is wired shut. I've never seen that outside of ancient texts. Hey, Doctor Gord, come look at this."

Fragger groaned inwardly. *You've got to be shitting me! I don't need this kind of attention right now.*

The doctor gave a curt response. "I'm busy, Magran. Is it important?"

"You want to see something you've never seen before, don't you?"

"Damn it, Corpsman! I haven't got time for games. What is it?"

"It's a broken jaw," Magran said, obviously unwilling to let his surprise be revealed too early.

"So? Then, fix it. The bone-knitter is open at the moment."

"It's a broken jaw that's been *wired* shut," Magran said, a note of triumph in his voice that he'd managed to string the matter out a little longer. He was even happier a moment later when the doctor rewarded with an astonished, "What?"

Dr. Gord strode across the room and pried Fragger's lips apart. He peered into the Ranger's mouth, then repeated the corpsman's earlier statement, "This man didn't get this injury in combat. In fact, nobody on this ship could have done this. Who is he? What's he doing here?"

The corpsman shrugged and answered, "Iyeka dropped him off along with Watanabe. Watanabe is the one who brought the Martian in earlier."

Doctor Gord put his face level with Fragger's and asked in a tone heavy with suspicion, "Who are you? What are you doing here?"

Fragger mumbled and pointed at his jaw.

"Oh damn," the doctor said in frustration. "Right, you can't talk. I forgot about the wires. Look, Magran, you and I have severely wounded patients to attend to. So, you cut the wires out of there, bone-knit that jaw, and get your ass back to assist me. We can find out later what's going on with this man."

Magran jerked Fragger to his feet and pulled him across to a machine. It consisted of two gray pistol-shaped devices pointing inward toward on either side of a chair. The corpsman shoved Fragger into the seat and found a pair of medical snips. Dizziness swooped in and out of the Ranger's head as Magran bent and clipped roughly at the metal holding his jaw in place. At first, Fragger thought the corpsman was doing something to cause the vertigo and was ready to deck the man's butt onto the floor when he realized Magran was doing a professional job. The dizziness didn't come from the medic's actions; it came from elsewhere. Fragger pushed the dizziness away as the corpsman pulled the last bit of wire from his mouth and positioned the bone-knitter pistols against both cheeks and punched a button.

No sound reached the Ranger's ears, but a slight warmth and tingling popped up in his jaw area.

"Sit there and don't move," Magran ordered. "Since some healing has probably already taken place, it should take five minutes max." The corpsman moved off to help Dr. Magran.

Fragger sat impatiently as the machine worked. He hadn't had his voice for so long, he wanted it back *now*.

If I could only scream out loud once more, I'd be more than willing to endure the vertigo sucking at my brain!

The overhead lights flickered again, then went out. "Backup!" he heard Dr. Gord order. Instantly, the room was re-illuminated by harsh emergency lights. The rapid switch into and out of darkness only intensified Fragger's dizziness. While he struggled to remain still and not give into a vomit reflex, the Ranger wondered why no one else seemed to feel as bad as he did. Then, he noticed one of the orderlies reel against a table, knocking instruments into a clattering mess on the deck. Gord raised his head to snap at the man, but the doctor did no better than the orderly. He swayed and went pale a moment before a gut-tearing alarm burst from the ship's commlink system along with Captain Ijiro's panicked voice, "This is the captain speaking. Jumpshift error! I repeat, jumpshift error! Abandon ship! I repeat, abandon ship!"

With admiration, Fragger watched the medical personnel spring efficiently into action. They wheeled patients toward the door in a calm and orderly manner, even though white faces showed the strain felt by everyone. His admiration dimmed when Fragger realized they'd made a de facto decision to evacuate him last from the room.

Well, screw you, you bastards! he cussed at them as a soft chime from behind the chair reached his ears through the din in the room. Realizing the bone knitter must have completed its task, Fragger tested his jaw carefully and found it moved without pain. He tried a few words, found his mouth rusty from the novacaine of inactivity, and cleared his throat to get some lubrication.

"Fuck you!" he tried to yell at a retreating orderly's back as he stood up, but it came out, "Wucck yew!" and didn't strike Fragger as having much effect.

Another wave of dizziness hit, and the Ranger didn't have time to worry about sounding like Elmer Fudd because a strange feeling rolled through his body as if his head had decided to occupy a different spot in the universe from his legs or his arms. He looked over at Buurk to see if he was feeling the same thing, but the Martian's face had decided to become like Major Shimazu's, an imitation of a Picasso. His nose had moved to the side of his head, the eyes were cobbled together close to a distorted ear, and the words coming out of Buurk's mouth were melting his lips like cheese.

Fragger noticed the medic was not the only one capable of this trick. The bulkhead behind Buurk flowed in great lumps of claylike metal toward the deck, and the deck itself was burning its center into a great hole that showed stars beyond the hull.

"Whoa!" Fragger said, impressed by the disaster overtaking the ship. He felt like he was in a child's drawing some one had taken a blowtorch to. When the dizziness shot off the scale, he decided that since no one had taken any action, he'd have to do something about it himself.

The Ranger staggered over to the sick bay commlink which expanded like an accordion on the wall. Irrationally, he called up a sharp picture of the balloon-cheeked Ijiro in his mind at the same time as he slapped at the commlink and shouted, "Captain, you bastard! Do something! Get us out of this mess!"

There was no answer, and Fragger had no more time to shout for help before the hand of God picked him up like a crayon and smeared his color across the face of the universe.

CHAPTER 28

Somebody had strained Fragger through a sieve and then put the pieces back together all wrong. The Ranger was as sure of it as he'd ever been sure of anything in his life. He was afraid to check his body for fear he'd look like a Play-Doh figure shaped by a curious toddler. His elbows felt like eyes, his knees like hands, and his dick....well, he really didn't want to think about that, so he decided to risk opening one eye.

To Fragger's surprise, his body wasn't any different from what it had been before. Although he had a distinct impression of having traveled a long distance, he hadn't even moved from his spot by the commlink. He tried his voice to make sure he still had it as he surveyed the room.

"Like me, the sick bay's decided to return to its usual shape. No walls melting or a hole in the deck. There's only one thing that's changed. I'm conscious, and nobody else here is."

The wounded, the medics, Dr. Gord--they all lay sprawled on the floor as if they'd been decked with a very heavy club. Even though it hurt his head, Fragger grinned at the sight and took the opportunity for some healthy cursing of his captors.

"It's about damned time you people had a taste of your own medicine, you bastards, you slimebags, you maggots, you pukes of the first order!" he yelled at them. "You don't know how good it is to have my voice back so I can tell you what lower life forms you really are!"

Fragger raged on until his anger subsided and transformed itself into a less than satisfying realization. "The trouble is, there's no one awake to hear what I have to say."

Grumbling at the waste of good profanity, Fragger walked among the bodies. He nudged them one by one with his feet. No one responded. For a brief, panicky moment, he thought everyone might be dead and he was alone, but when he bent to Watanabe, he found a strong pulse in the man's wrist. The same was true for Buurk.

"Okay, here's an obvious question," Fragger asked himself, "why am I not out cold on the floor with the rest of them?"

When an answer wouldn't come, he stopped to listen carefully for activity outside the sick bay. The only sounds were non-human--the creaking and groaning of hull plates and decks as if they were relieved to be returning to normal shape.

"My bones know just how you feel," the Ranger said to the ship as he decided to check for signs of conscious crew. He went to the commlink, activated it and said, "Bridge. This is the sick bay. What's our status? Is everyone okay up there?"

When no response came, he repeated the message to the different operational centers listed below the commlink. The result was the same although Fragger thought he could hear some groans over the system. The Ranger stood for a moment weighing his options and made a decision to head for the bridge to see if he could wake Ijiro and his command staff.

After getting briefly lost in the maze of the *Toyko's* corridors, Fragger located the bridge and entered it to find the command staff slumped in their chairs or sprawled on the floor. The Ranger had expected nothing else, but he hadn't expected the sight from the viewscreen. A beautiful spiral galaxy, looking like creation's pinwheel, spun across a wide panorama of space. Mars was not in sight.

"I'm right," Fragger whispered as he drank in the magnificence of the galaxy. "We did move. I don't know where, but we've moved. Even with my limited knowledge of astronomy, I know those stars definitely don't belong in our solar system."

A sudden suspicion entered his mind, causing his heart to double-time around the inside of his chest. For moment, Fragger couldn't catch his breath. Then he was breathing *too* fast as his body couldn't decide what to do with the realization dawning in his brain. The Ranger dumped an officer out of a chair and took her place, sitting down hard as his legs gave way.

"We've moved all right," Fragger murmured. "And I did the moving...I think."

No, that's not right. It's a ridiculous idea. People don't move a giant warship through hyperspace by themselves. It takes tons of machinery and engines with enormous power and hundreds of crew members to make it work.

Fragger tried to think the matter through. *What was the last thing I did after things went wrong? I was standing in the sick bay watching everything melt into psychedelic wax. I was scared enough to beg Captain Ijiro to save us. In fact, I formed a real sharp picture of him in my mind. Was that it? Did I somehow influence Ijiro to do the right thing and jumpshift us out of trouble? Did Leery give me more than the ability to teleport? Can I influence minds as well?*

"An interesting thought," the Ranger said softly as his eyes swept over the unconscious bridge crew. "It's a handy piece of knowledge, maybe one I should keep to myself."

While waiting for everyone to regain their senses, Fragger contented himself with rummaging through the small bridge galley. He found a small compartment labeled "Captain Only" and opened it to find several packages of tea. Fragger made a face at these--he hated tea--and swept them aside to see if there was anything toward the back more to his liking. To his delight, he came up with a glossy bag that read "Jamaican Blue Mountain" in bright red letters. Below that label, Fragger saw the coffee's origin, "Product of EarthCorp."

Even in future wars, commanders somehow have time to confiscate or find the good stuff, he thought in bemusement.

Fragger puzzled out the coffee-making apparatus and turned it on. Studying the bridge layout and controls as he waited for the coffee to brew, he came to the conclusion there was no way he could understand the ship's navigation and propulsion systems.

No surprise there, he concluded, *but hope springs eternal.*

A vague idea of commandeering the HELOT vessel had been running around in his brain, but that kind of action was for Hollywood where taking over a ship or airplane was as easy as making coffee. Fragger knew he would need the crew to operate the ship

It was a depressing situation, one that called for coffee. Fragger poured a cup and sat down to enjoy temporary command of a vessel over which he had no control.

CHAPTER 29

Three hours later, Fragger had a complete and irritating picture of how many sounds the human body could make when unconscious. The crew buzzed, snorted, snawked, grunted, and whimpered in whatever restless dreams hyperspace had planted in their brains. The HELOT ship's captain was the worst, perhaps because he was the oldest. Working his way through more coffee, Fragger glared with aggravation at the seated and sprawled figure of Captain Ijiro, speculating that perhaps due to the small nose, the man was a snorer of epic proportions. It sounded as if gunners were ranging artillery shells in his throat because each explosive series of snores started faintly and worked its way up to a detonation that came close to rattling Fragger's cup.

Tired of the sleepers' noise and of waiting, Fragger decided to move things along. He went to Ijiro and poured a small amount of coffee down the officer's throat. Ijiro choked and spluttered, then opened his eyes and pinned their angry gaze on Fragger.

"What are you doing on the bridge, Rerun?" Ijiro demanded as he sat up in his chair and straightened his uniform.

"Enjoying a cup of coffee. Would you like one? You look like you could use more."

"A stimcap would have been simpler."

"Don't know what that is, Captain, and I don't think you'd want me to be pushing drugs I don't know anything about down your throat."

Ijiro made a noncommittal noise, then checked out the status of the bridge before turning his attention back to the Ranger.

"What happened here, Rerun?"

Fragger shrugged. "This is your future, not mine. You tell me."

Ijiro growled low in his throat, obviously not pleased with the Ranger's answer or his attitude. Another demand came from the Captain, "Why are you awake when everyone else seems to be unconscious?"

"I have no idea. I woke up in the sick bay with everybody unconscious around me. Plus, Captain, I didn't see a single soul awake on my trip up to your bridge."

Ijiro scowled and asked, "Do you mean to tell me that you, a Rerun, are the *only* one awake and functioning?"

"As far as I know."

"And an entire crew of seasoned sailors and troopers are out?"

"Yup. Not up to my standards, I guess."

The captain ignored the jab and said, "Rerun, if I didn't know it was impossible, I'd say you'd somehow managed to incapacitate my people with some sort of agent."

Nettled by lack of response from the officer to the earlier dig, Fragger suggested, "Oh, I used an agent, all right. Me, I'm the agent. I'm mentally and physically superior to your crew, Captain."

Ijiro dismissed this thought with a wave of his hand.

Damn, even though I'm lying through my teeth, if I was speaking the truth, they still wouldn't believe me, they're that certain of the inferiority of Reruns. It pisses me off no end, but...this continual underestimation can work to my advantage.

"Okay, Captain, it was impossible for me work that kind of magic on your crew, but speaking of impossible, have you taken a peek outside your ship lately?"

Ijiro sat bolt upright, exclaiming in sudden realization, "The EarthCorp fleet had my vessel dead in their sights. Did they get us?"

"Look out the window," Fragger suggested again.

The captain looked and swore. "Where the devil is Mars? Navigation, give me our position!"

"Navigation is out cold on the floor," Fragger reminded him.

Ijiro swore and pushed up from his sent to check a console. After a moment's examination, he fell back into the chair, turning a pale color that was entirely satisfying to the Ranger.

"We've come a long way," the captain whispered.

"So? Isn't that what hyperspace is for, taking shortcuts?"

"Yes, yes, Rerun, but I ordered 'Abandon ship'! We should be in escape pods, free of the ship."

"So?"

"You don't understand," Ijiro said. "I'm the only one who can give the order to jumpshift, and I wouldn't have given that command in a million years. It's suicide. There's no way I could have selected a safe path through all the permutations possible in navigation. By all rights, we should be splattered across the cosmos in billions of tiny bits."

Fragger waved the coffee cup around the bridge. "Obviously, we made it."

"You still don't understand," Ijiro replied in frustration. "I'm not in the habit of trying to kill myself and my crew. So, I would never give such an order. And yet...I must have. Rerun, there is no known case of survival in situation like this."

"Really?" Fragger asked, refusing to be impressed. So much had happened to him already he figured one more miracle was all in a day's work. "So, that's the good news. There has to be some bad. What is it?"

"We've escaped the Corpses," Ijiro answered, "but if the instruments are correct, then we've landed in the middle of the Gulag.

"What's that?"

"It's a contested system within the Ursus Combine. It's inhabited by thieves, bandits, thugs, mercenaries, prisoners of Mother Earth, you name it. All the great space-faring nations have dumped their criminals and political refugees there, so, of course, everyone claims it."

"In other words, you exiled people you don't like here. Still, they don't sound like much of a threat to the ship," Fragger suggested.

"Under normal circumstances, no, but we don't know yet what damage has been done to our vessel and with the crew down, we're open to attack."

"Space is a pretty big place, isn't it, Captain? Won't it be hard to find us?"

In a rising voice, Ijiro replied, "Usually, it would be. However, we've taken heavy damage and god knows what kind of leakage signature we're trailing behind us. We may be standing out like a beacon on somebody's surveillance system. The inhabitants of the Gulag are an undisciplined rabble, but every once in a while, a leader manages to emerge and hold them together for assaults. And, let's face it, if we don't have propulsion, then all any enemy has to do is board us."

Fragger frowned at the note of panic in the officer's tone. Ijiro's manner reinforced his earlier impression that Ijiro was a man who didn't like things that fell outside a well-defined military box. Believing that action was always the best remedy for fear, Fragger asked, "Well, there's nothing to be done about that at the moment, is there? Except get your crew up and about and functioning in case we do need to mount a defense."

The captain colored as if embarrassed he hadn't thought of Fragger's suggestion first and replied hastily, "An excellent idea, Rerun. We'll wake the officers first, then organize department by department until we're as battle ready as we can be. After that, we'll start repairs and head home."

Home for you, Captain Ijiro, Fragger thought as he looked out the window into the Ursus Combine. *As for me, I see freedom right here.*

If it ever came to a battle, the Ranger had no trouble deciding which side he would be on. The Gulag sounded like his kind of place. First, it was time to go back to sick bay to give Watanabe a wake-up call with a good dose of coffee.

CHAPTER 30

Watanabe still hadn't forgiven Fragger for punching him out or for trying to execute a half-assed escape plan, but what seemed to bother him the most was the Rerun's pouring of coffee down his throat.

"It's a helluva way to wake up," the sergeant complained as he escorted the Ranger to the brig. "I hate coffee. Tea is the proper drink."

"Tea is for weaklings," Fragger said, delighted with another chance to stick a verbal pin in Watanabe's hide. "Real men drink coffee."

Anger and frustration rippled through the trooper's face. "You'd better be careful, Sparks. I'm beginning to see Major Shimazu's side of the picture, and, believe me, you don't want to face both of us in Interrogation."

Fragger was not intimidated. "I know you better than that, Watanabe. You're a soldier, not a ghoul. If and when we face each other, it'll be man to man. Or, more precisely, man to weakling."

Watanabe growled at the insult, yet said nothing, confirming the Ranger's opinion that the man was at heart an honorable soldier who detested torture techniques. He didn't envy Watanabe's conundrum. Repeatedly, he'd had to deliver a Rerun--an inferior being--into the hands of interrogators who were people who had no honor in his eyes, and yet Fragger Sparks had managed to give them nothing so far.

In other words, Fragger concluded happily, *I've cut the ground out from beneath Watanabe's feet. According to him, I'm inferior, yet I keep beating the odds and the scum interrogators we'd both just as soon wipe out of existence. The poor bastard probably doesn't know if he's coming or going.*

The thought grew a wide smile across the Ranger's face.

"What the hell are you smiling about?" Watanabe asked.

"Just thinking of an old saying."

"What saying is that?"

"Never mind," the Ranger replied. *"Confusion to my enemies" is not a phrase Watanabe would like hear at the moment, I'm sure.*

The sergeant stopped Fragger again and spun him around hard. "Look, Rerun, you don't really realize how serious this situation is, do you? I'm taking you to the brig, then Shimazu is going to personally come to get you so she can interrogate and cell-strip you just like she said. She doesn't fool around."

Shit, don't I know it, you jerk!, the Ranger swore in his head, then decided it was time to add fuel to the fire of the trooper's confusion.

"Watanabe, if she does that, it'll be the dumbest thing she ever did."

"And why is that?"

"Because if she does, I die. And if I die, the secrets go with me."

"Secrets? Are you telling me there's something more to your MASER enhancement that we don't know about?"

"Damned right, I am," Fragger said.

"Like what?"

"You think about it. I'm sure you'll be able to reason it out."

Disbelief registered on Watanabe's face. "You're just trying to avoid the inevitable."

"I'm not trying," Fragger said. "I'm succeeding."

"We'll see about that."

Watanabe hustled him past recovering crew members who, to the Ranger's satisfaction, looked like they were recovering from giant hangovers. He was more than happy to share the suffering imposed by hyperspace transit.

Watanabe clapped him into the brig and keyed the door shut. Fragger sat down on the bed bolted to the wall to examine the brig and discovered quickly it was like military jails everywhere, featureless and dehumanizing. A sink, a toilet and the bed he was sitting on--that was the extent of his surroundings, a design intended to give the occupant time to do nothing but lead to the inescapable conclusion that the only way out was to cooperate with authorities. Fragger lay down to wait for the inevitable visitors and catch some sleep, thinking, *Fat chance of me cooperating. I've got the upper hand now. When Shimazu comes for me, I'll show her just who she's messing with--I hope. The woman scares the hell out of me, and maybe that adrenaline rush will be enough to drive my body into the MASER mode and give me the seconds I need to kill her.*

He settled back and closed his eyes. Hours later, he heard the cell door open and jumped to his feet waiting for the fear to send him into teleportation mode. Shimazu smirked at him as she entered the cell, then raised a hand weapon and fired. Fragger stumbled back from the impact of the projectile, amazed she'd missed killing him from such a close range.

Luck's as big a bitch as you are, Shimazu, he cursed silently and launched himself across the room at the officer.

Only the MASER ability wasn't there, the Ranger realized. In fact, things became very slow as if he had his limbs caught in a thick and hardening glue. Fragger was almost within reach of Shimazu when he fell into that glue and struck the floor and unconsciousness at the same time.

When he woke, he was in a sound-proofed interrogation room. Major Shimazu had hung him naked by his wrists from a chain and pulley system attached to the ceiling. The chain could be adjusted for height to adapt for whatever mayhem she had planned. When she saw he was awake, Shimazu didn't waste any time on preliminaries.

"Rerun, you know what my first thought is?"

"What?"

"My first thought is to start with your manhood and feed it to you piece by small piece," she answered as she paced up and down in front of him, rapping a steel-tipped swagger stick against a table. Looking uncomfortable, Watanabe walked in and sat behind the table beside a small, stern-faced officer who had a black case open on the table. Inside the case were surgical instruments.

Fragger's balls did their best to scream and escape the room, but he put on an outward show of calm. "You aren't going to hurt me, Shimazu. You said yourself that I'm important."

Shimazu slashed him across the thighs with the stick. "Wrong, Rerun, I said that whatever the Corpses put inside you is important."

"You can't have one without the other," Fragger said, gritting his teeth at the sting on his bare flesh.

The major hit him again in the same spot. "Is it possible for one Rerun to be so stupid? You just don't understand, do you, Sparks? If we can't get the information out of you, we're going to make damned sure nobody else gets it. So, you're dead meat sooner or later. Since power is diverted to all necessary systems to facilitate repairs, I can't use standard interrogation devices and techniques such as cell-stripping. That means time-honored methods."

"You beat it out of me."

"Beat, cut, flay, dissect, burn, pull you apart, it doesn't matter to me. What matters are the correct answers."

"I already told you I don't know how I do anything!" Fragger shouted.

This time, Shimazu took aim at his testicles. The Ranger gasped at the blow, then couldn't breathe.

"I think you're lying, Rerun. Even if you're not, you know the truth at some level. Don't you? Well, speak up!"

Hate fought for room in Fragger's head with the desire to get his lungs back. He could feel his testicles swelling.

"Even a MASER with no balls is still no man at all," the major said, then added with a sly smile, "In fact, for all we know, the Corpses somehow tied it all in to testosterone and once I slice those tiny marbles from between your legs, you're going to be nothing more than what you really are, a ball-less piece of revived crap. So, it's your choice, Rerun, you can give us the information we want or lose your manhood. Which is it going to be?"

"I've...I've told you...and told you!" Fragger gasped. "I don't know how the MASER abilities work. I just know that I have one--teleportation--but I have no control over it."

"Liar!" Shimazu said and struck again with the swagger stick.

The Ranger squirmed and tried to jerk away from the blow, but she simply caught him by a foot, spun him toward her, and laid a harder strike into his groin. Fragger howled. Shimazu stood back with a satisfied expression on her scarred face.

"Am I finally getting your attention?" she asked in a mock-sweet voice.

Through gritted teeth, Fragger answered, "You're a whore...a slut...and a disgrace to...the military."

Shimazu rapped him sharply across the shins. "I asked, 'Am I finally getting your attention?'"

"Fuck you!"

The major sighed sorrowfully as if she were dealing with a wayward child and said to the nameless officer. "I guess there's no help for this fool. I'll have to hand him over to you, Lieutenant."

The officer nodded and rose to remove the surgical instruments from the case and arrange them with meticulous care on the surface of the table. Fragger managed to drag his eyes away from the awful sight to flick a contemptuous glance at Watanabe. The sergeant trooper sat motionless except for an expression of revulsion working its way across his face like a worm under the skin.

"Watanabe," Fragger said, "I was wrong about you, wasn't I?"

"Shut up!" Shimazu ordered. "You will speak only when told to."

Managing to ignore the pain of the major's next strike, Fragger continued, "I thought you were a soldier, Watanabe, a man of honor. Instead, I find you in here with sadists and torturers who call themselves soldiers."

"I said, shut up!" Shimazu ordered. She grabbed a scalpel from the table and held it up, the sharp blade gleaming under the harsh interrogation light. "Shut up, or I'll do this myself, and I'm not nearly as neat about it as Lieutenant Hiro is because I haven't had any medical training."

Keeping his eyes off the gleaming blade, Fragger spat at Watanabe. "I may be just a Rerun, but by God, with or without my balls, I'm twice the man you are. The major was right about the *Burakumin* after all, wasn't she? Worthless scum!"

Sweat broke out on Watanabe's forehead. He wiped at it and said, "Military necessity."

"Weak, Watanabe, weak," Fragger said with contempt. "Sadists and cowards are long on justification for their actions. They think it'll save their souls." He jerked his head toward Shimazu and Hiro. "Just think, when you go to whatever hell you believe in, you're going to spend eternity with these two maggots."

Shimazu slashed with the scalpel, and Fragger screamed at the pain.

"Oh, relax, Rerun," she said. "A warning shot, as it were, that's all it was. I merely cut your thigh although I must say the blood is running quite freely so it's possible I may have opened an artery. Of course, I'd be quite happy to staunch the flow if you'd just offer up the information I want. It's really quite simple, you know."

"If I did know what you wanted, you wouldn't get it now! Do you know why, Shimazu?"

"I'm not interested in why, Rerun. I'm only interested in why the Corpses want you back so much."

"Because I can see so clearly now," Fragger continued, ignoring the blood flowing down his leg. "Pain will do that for you, sometimes."

"You'd better see clearly what I want to know," Shimazu warned. "I'm not interested in anything else."

"*That's* what I can see so well," Fragger said, forcing the words out through the pain. "The only thing you're interested in is getting rid of me while inflicting as much agony as possible. You like your job. Only it isn't a job, is it? It's a sick, pathetic love. Better than any man, better than sex, isn't it, Shimazu? It's just pure lust. You're an animal, lower than the Reruns you detest so much."

The major stiffened at this thrust and raised the scalpel above her head into a stabbing position. Fragger closed his eyes, waiting for the final stroke and hoping he'd goaded her into making a true strike. A shriek of rage opened them again, and he saw Watanabe's hand clamped firmly around Shimazu's wrist.

"No, Major!" the sergeant shouted.

"Let go of my hand!" she ordered, struggling to get free of Watanabe's grip.

"No!"

"That's a direct order, *Buraku*! Obey it unless you want to end up in the brig and suffer a court martial. Do you hear me?"

"I hear you perfectly, Major. I will not allow you to kill this prisoner."

"He's a Rerun with delusions of normalcy! We're well rid of him."

Struggling with the scalpel-wielding arm, Watanabe grunted out his next words. "Use your head, Major! Sparks *is* a Rerun, but he's the most valuable Rerun in history."

"Not if he's dead, he's not," Shimazu snapped, her words edged with hate. "If he really is one of a kind, then nothing is lost."

"I don't think so."

The enraged officer struggled harder to break free. When she failed, she summoned Hiro who scrambled over the table and lunged at Watanabe. Without a pause, the sergeant snapped Shimazu's knife arm around. The scalpel buried itself into the onrushing Hiro's eye. Screaming, Hiro collapsed onto the deck, choking and coughing on the blood rushing down his face. The sound-proofed interrogation room swallowed up his shrieks as Watanabe released Shimazu's arm, and it fell dangling by her side.

Fragger was relieved and impressed, all at the same time. *Damn, if I do live, I'm not sure I do want to go one-on-one with Watanabe. The man is lethal.*

Shimazu stared down at her broken arm, then threw a cold stare at Watanabe. "You've assaulted two superior officers, *Buraku*. Your career--and maybe your life--is over."

"Perhaps," Watanabe acknowledged. "I will accept any punishment ordered by my superiors. Of course, I'm sure they'll want to hear how one Rerun managed to get the best of the Imperial Commonwealth's finest in the officer corps."

Shimazu reddened, and demanded, "Call for medical aid, Watanabe."

"Not until you hear me out, Major."

"Damn it, Sergeant Watanabe, I'm not in the habit of taking orders from *Burakumin*!"

"Well, until you take an order from this *Buraku,* Major, I guess I'll just have to stand here and watch everybody bleed around me."

"Fine," the stubborn officer said. "That's exactly what we'll do until you come to your senses."

Without a word, Watanabe threw a jab into the major's injured arm. Shimazu bit back a scream, but her eyes squeezed out tears from the pain.

"I ask you again, Major. Hear me out! Or shall I continue punching?"

Shimazu finally acceded with a nod.

"The Rerun was playing cute with me earlier when he said he had another ability besides the teleporting. He told me I'd have to figure it out for myself, and I think I have."

"Spit it out, man!"

"We did the impossible, Major. We survived a jumpshift error. So far as we know, it can't be done, but here we are."

"So? We were lucky."

"Not a chance. That kind of luck simply doesn't exist, Major. I think Sparks got us here."

"Are you crazy? He moved an entire warship light years across space?"

"In a way. I suspect he somehow influenced Captain Ijiro to make the right jump decision in a nearly impossible situation"

"You *are* insane, Watanabe."

"Where this Rerun is concerned, all bets are off, Major. That's why I stopped you. For the good of the Imperial Commonwealth. Fragger Sparks has the possibility of being the ultimate weapon. There's also one other immediate possibility."

"What is that?"

"If our drive is repaired, the Rerun may be able to assist us in getting us out of here."

Shimazu was not impressed with that possibility. "Repairs are underway, and we're in no immediate danger."

"Not any longer, Major. Before I came in here, the word arrived that ships are approaching at extreme range."

"A few pirates. We can handle them."

"No," Watanabe said. "We must have left a system-wide signature upon our re-entry into normal space because at least four fleets are on intercept course--our own people, EarthCorp, the Spartans, and the Ursus Combine. They've all deployed forces ranging from scout ships to heavy dreadnoughts. The Roller fleet hasn't shown up yet, but the Celestial Warriors of God have always been slow on the battlefield so I'm sure they'll arrive sooner or later. Plus, I know that Gulagers are on the way as well. Vultures that they are, they wouldn't want to miss rich pickings."

Dryly, the non-com added, "I'd say that the word is out on Fragger Sparks."

Shimazu was mute in response to this information.

"Major, get yourself and Hiro to the dispensary," Watanabe suggested.

"I won't forget what happened here," Shimazu threatened. "Your career is over, Watanabe. I *will* bring up charges."

"If we survive, Major. If we survive."

Watanabe helped the groaning Hiro to his feet. After pushing both officers out the door, he turned back to Fragger and said, "I'm going to let you down, dumb ass. Just make sure you don't step in the shit again."

"You owe me another life," Watanabe added as he lowered the Ranger to the floor.

"No," Fragger said, rubbing his raw wrists as the trooper loosened the restraints. "We're still at three."

"What do you mean 'No'?"

Fragger looked the man straight in the eye and said, "Watanabe, you didn't save my life. You just saved your own, and you know it."

Watanabe's eyes shifted away for a second, then locked back on to Fragger's, and the Ranger knew the sergeant agreed with him. Nothing more needed to be said.

"Let's get that cut taken care of," Watanabe said. "You'll want to be in good shape for the next time somebody wants to kill you."

CHAPTER 31

Fragger winced as he climbed wearily up the steps to the enlisted men's quarters, hauling the medkit to treat overflow casualties from the battle. Major Shimazu's scalpel slash hadn't been deep enough to cut muscle, but like all sharp-edged cuts, the wound had a pain all its own and, more annoying, was refusing to heal even two days after the interrogation. For a moment, the Ranger regretted being unable to put the leg under one of the healing machines in the dispensary that knitted skin and bone so easily

Then the smell of torn flesh and intestines washed over him again as he stuck his head through the hatch for the fifth time, and he felt ashamed at such selfishness in the face of the carnage being inflicted on the HELOT troopers, the ship's marines, in particular. Their space suits had lighter armor than the Jump Troopers, and they were obviously more vulnerable to the enemy's weapons. Casualties had mounted so high the dispensary was stacked with the wounded. There were no dead. He'd been told by a clearly desperate marine that they had fitted their fallen comrades with proximity devices and sent the bodies twirling along the hull to act as mines against the assault forces. It seemed that every fleet in the galaxy had caught up with the *Tokyo.*

Fragger limped over to the table he'd set up as his central point for dispensing medications. As he listened to the groans and screams of the wounded troopers, he admitted, *All I'm doing here is killing pain, not really healing anybody. Yet maybe that's not such a bad thing under the circumstances.*

The Ranger loaded the medgun as Doctor Gord had instructed him and moved toward the loudest screamer. All around him, marines lay half in and out of space suits with blast holes in the fabric. Watanabe had told him that the suits were self-sealing-to a point. Apparently, the most effective weapon against an adversary was a "shredder". According to the sergeant, it was simple, easy to operate and repair and devastatingly effective because it threw out thousands of flechettes that overwhelmed a suit's self-sealing capabilities. When hit by a full blast, a marine had two choices of action. He could bleed to death slowly inside his suit or open his visor for a quick death.

Fragger pulled the suit collar away from the screamer, put the medgun up against her neck and injected the painkiller. The woman, dark hair matted with blood, paused long enough in her screams to give him a look that was equal parts gratitude and resentment. It was a look all too familiar to the Ranger. As Fragger treated them, the Imperial Commonwealth soldiers had made it clear they regarded him as the cause of all their troubles.

And so I am, he agreed, moving to the next trooper whose suit had sealed successfully after a clean shot had blown away his right leg. *I didn't ask for any of this, and it's sure as hell not my fault, but try telling that to a soldier who knows he's dying for a Rerun.*

The thought that the Ricer soldiers regarded him as inferior stiffened Fragger's spine, and he pushed aside any thought of guilt in favor of easing the pain of as many of the wounded as he could. When he was finished with the latest round of casualties, he stood back and marveled at the effectiveness of the drug he'd injected. All the screams were gone, replaced by an almost equally unnerving series of giggles and sighs of deep and utter contentment amidst the thumping and clanging emanating from the outer hull of the ship. Once again, Fragger was grateful Watanabe had granted his request to help out.

"There's nothing worse than being in the middle of a battle and being useless," he'd told the Ricer trooper as Watanabe fitted his body into a powered suit, and Watanabe had understood, suggesting Fragger help out with the wounded. Fragger had made a counter suggestion that he be allowed to fight, but Watanabe had laughed that one off, telling him that space combat was no place for a green trooper. "Besides," he added pointedly, "how do I know whose side you'll end up on?"

Fragger re-checked his medkit and found he was already low on the painkiller. The casualties were using it up at a staggering rate. Grabbing the kit, he started on the way back to the dispensary to re-stock supplies. He shouldered his way through corridors against grim marines and troopers who made no secret of their resentment by banging him against the walls as they ran by. Fragger took the bruising without comment until the way cleared to the dispensary.

When the Ranger requested more painkiller, Dr. Gord looked up from working on a shrieking trooper who looked like she'd been torn apart below the waist and answered, "We're out of painkiller, Rerun. I haven't got anything for you or for this soldier.

Without a word, the physician unholstered a laser sidearm and put a pulse through her head. The screaming stopped.

"It's all I could do for her," Gord said as he caught sight of the horrified look on Fragger's face. "In this situation, she was dead already. My equipment is out, my supplies are exhausted. The only thing I can do now is end the pain."

"But, Christ Almighty," Fragger said, "couldn't the enemy do anything for her if they take the ship?"

A pitying smile curved the physician's lips. "Rerun, in deep space, prisoners aren't a high priority. They add weight and mass and affect oxygen, food, and fuel consumption. Warships run high on weaponry and thin on fuel reserves so if it's a choice between getting home safely and taking captives, guess which choice wins out?"

"Man," Fragger responded, "space is a cold place, but you people sure make it colder."

Gord shrugged. "It's a soldier's life. Are you going to tell me you didn't have to make hard choices back in the primitive times?"

The physician had a point that Fragger couldn't answer, so instead he asked, "What now?"

"There's nothing left for me to do but go forward and fight," Gord said. "As for you, I should kill you, but you strike me as a good man, and I'm a physician so I don't take lives needlessly. You're on your own, Rerun. Good luck."

The physician issued a command to his aides, and they filed out of the dispensary toward the sound of battle.

"Wait a minute," Fragger called after him. "What about all the wounded? Aren't you going to help them?"

"Help them do what?" Gord said, sticking his head back inside the door.

"I don't know...anything," Fragger answered, feeling helpless.

"I've issued each functional trooper a deathpill," the physician said. "They'll die painlessly within seconds."

"What about the ones who aren't functional?"

"I've already shot them," Gord said and was gone.

Fragger stood alone among anguished cries and listened helplessly as one by one, the wounded snuffed themselves out by swallowing the pills. In a few minutes, all he could hear was the growing "Whummp" of explosive devices from the forward section of the ship. The battle had all the earmarks of a rear guard action for the *Tokyo's* forces. For a moment, confusion swallowed his brain, and he didn't know what to do. On the one hand, he could hope the enemy forces would recognize him and take him as prisoner--that's what the whole attack was about, anyway. On the other, he'd been in combat long enough to know that mistakes were common. People liked to stay alive so they had a tendency to shoot first and ask questions later.

"And then there's the third hand," the Ranger thought with rueful amusement. "I can just about guarantee Shimazu is looking for me with one purpose in mind. Keep me out of enemy hands at all costs."

The idea of that bitch killing him cleared away the confusion. Stooping by one of the dead marines, he grabbed a shotgun-looking weapon from her side and ran out of the sick bay toward the one place that might give him a fighting chance against both the attacking forces and Shimazu—the armory.

CHAPTER 32

Fragger found the armory and two security guards flanking its door. As he came into sight, they leveled their pulse lasers and fired. Fragger threw himself back around the corner as the white-hot bolts splashed against the bulkheads. He fumbled with the weapon he'd taken off the dead marine, cursing himself for forgetting the first rule of the combat soldier--know your weapon and know it well before using it. With footsteps running toward him, the Ranger quickly figured out the safety mechanism and pulled the trigger as the two guards came into sight and hit the deck in prone positions. Fragger's weapon gave a deceptively soft report, and at first, the Ranger thought he was a dead man because he'd aimed too high, then he heard dozens of flechettes drum against the walls and thud into the flesh of the guards. Fragger stared down at the weapon with respect

Apparently, this is a shredder. I couldn't have missed an elephant. Hell, I'm lucky I didn't end up shooting myself.

Fragger stepped over the bloody, lacerated guards, and ran to the armory entrance, poking the shredder's muzzle in first. One trooper, donning body armor, looked up in panic at the sight of the weapon.

"Get your weapon and get out," Fragger ordered.

"Hey, you're not authorized to be here!" the trooper shouted back at him.

"Tell it to this," the Ranger said, waving the muzzle of the shredder about.

The man paled, grabbed a rifle and ran out the door. Fragger waited for a moment, checking in the direction of the exit in case the soldier had gotten foolish enough to come back to take him on, but footsteps clanged on the deck and faded away.

The Ranger turned his attention back to the armory. His eyes swept across the stacked PPC rifles and other weapons he didn't recognize and didn't want. When he didn't find what he needed, he searched through the rooms until he found one marked "Armor, Power." Stepping through the door, the Ranger saw several rows of powered armor arranged according to their current status. He strode past the backup suits and suits in repair, and found a niche labeled "Ready." He eyeballed the armor, trying to figure out if they were sized to the individual or if they were for general use. Unable to distinguish any difference, he grabbed the nearest one and began pulling it on piece by piece. The legs fit fine, but when he got to the torso, it threatened to squeeze him to death when he ordered it to close. Gasping, he countermanded the order, threw the piece to the floor and tried another suit. Three suits later, he found one that came close to fitting. It pinched his feet, but he didn't have time to worry about it as he sealed himself inside.

"What the hell do I do now?" he asked, trying to figure out the appropriate commands to activate the suit. "It can't be that different from the maintenance suit Red Salinsky had me wear for the refueling of armor."

It wasn't. He ordered "Activate" and grinned as the suit powered up.

The grin vanished a second later as Fragger attempted to move from the niche and banged violently into the wall opposite his position next to a rack of swords connected to power packs. While he attempted to clear the stars orbiting his eyes from the impact, Fragger thought ruefully, *Now I know why Watanabe was so adamant about powered armor being worlds apart from ordinary gear.*

The powered suit was unbelievably quick and responded to his slightest motion. Gingerly, he practiced a slow walk down the aisle, colliding with several suits before he got the hang of it. When he felt reasonably confident, he went back to the sword rack, pulled off a power pack and strapped it to his back, then took a sword and switched it on. The blade hummed into life. Fragger tested it out by slicing at one of the upside down t-bars holding up the power suits. Immediately, the blade cut through the support and the suit clattered to the deck.

"Damn and double damn!" the Ranger said, both pleased with and awed at the sword's lethal potential. *It's one thing to watch a sword in action. It's a whole different world to actually use one.*

Fragger knew no more about sword fighting than he did about hyperspace, but he practiced a few strokes until he got used to the heft and balance of the weapon, then decided he'd just have to hope for the best when he did enter combat. The Ranger guided the suit out the door and listened carefully through the amplified sensors of the armor. There was no doubt about it, he concluded a moment later, the battle was moving steadily in his direction.

His first instinct was to head toward the fight, yet when he thought about it, Fragger realized that if he wanted to stay alive, he'd better avoid combat until he had better command of the suit. He found a ship's layout on the wall and headed hullward, perpendicular to the battle. The suit worked to his advantage as he proceeded "up". Two un-armored security personnel attacked with pulse lasers, apparently assuming he was running from the fight, and he clumsily sliced them in half along with several power cables snaking along the bulkheads. It was unnerving to Fragger how easy it was to kill unprotected humans with the sword. He barely felt the impact when he swung the blade into flesh, and it cut through bodies as if they were paper. Stepping over his latest victim, he looked down the corridor and spotted a surprised, scarred face look back in his direction and then vanish around the corner.

Shimazu! Fragger exulted. *She couldn't have known where I'd end up. Now it's my turn to inflict some pain on her!*

Too quickly, the Ranger set the suit into a run and caromed off both walls several times before he got the armor under control.

"What the hell are you doing, Fragger?" he yelled at himself. "She sure as hell isn't going to outrun you. Slow down and get control of the damned suit."

He forced relaxation into his body and started down the corridor at a deliberate pace. Rounding the corner, the Ranger saw Shimazu peek back from the juncture of main walkways, fire a laser burst with her good arm in his direction, and disappear again.

Fragger slowed again. *Hell, she doesn't know it's me. She thinks I'm just a deserting trooper. I can't play this cat and mouse game all day. Well, hell, if I can't catch her, then I might as well scare her to death.*

"External audio, maximum amplification," he commanded the suit. The response "Compliance" flashed in green on the faceplate.

His amplified voice roared out into the ship. "Shimazu! Shimazu, it's Fragger Sparks, the Rerun. I'm going to add another scar to the one on your face, only this one will run down the middle of your body from head to toe."

There was no response.

"Suit, can you extend listening capability to its greatest range?" Fragger asked.

"Affirmative" flashed up on the faceplate.

"Execute, then."

The suit put up the message "Compliance."

Sound blasted into his ears. Fragger winced and ordered, "Lower volume." The suit obeyed, and the Ranger said, "Target breathing sound of nearest Imperial Commonwealth personnel."

Ragged breathing entered the helmet, disorienting Fragger for a moment because it felt like the person was right inside the suit with him. "How many are there?" he asked. "Answer in voice mode, if possible."

"Two," the suit answered. "One is apparently injured. The other is unhurt, but respiration and pulse are rapid."

"Sounds good to me," Fragger said. "Do you have the ability to identify individual Imperial Commonwealth troopers?"

"In this case, negative. The targets wear no identification markers."

"Distance to targets?" Fragger asked.

"Ten meters."

"Weaponry?"

"Pulse laser hand weapons present. Used for self-defense and no threat to this unit. However, masked weapons are possible."

"So, you don't know for sure what they're armed with?" Fragger asked.

"Affirmative."

The Ranger thought hard. He was aware Shimazu couldn't have known he'd be heading in her direction. However, it was possible that, as part of a rear guard action, she'd laid a trap for the attacking forces and would be more than happy to have him fall into it.

A satisfying thought entered Fragger's head. *Now, she's got me on her tail as well as the enemy. Good, it's about time she tasted real fear.*

The Ranger fought another strong urge to run ahead and strike the woman dead. Instead, he tried to figure out what kind of weapon she could come up with that would disable or destroy a powered soldier. Everything he could think of would end up doing a hell of a lot of damage to the ship as well, so it didn't make any sense that she'd set up heavy weaponry. He searched the corridor carefully and came up with nothing. Then, Fragger mentally slapped a hand up alongside his head and asked the suit, "Examine the corridor for presence of defensive weapons."

After a second, the suit replied, "EMP generators bracket the corridor."

"EMP generators? Explain."

"Electromagnetic pulse generators. They are designed to damage or destroy powered armor and weapon circuitry, rendering suit occupant immobile and vulnerable to attack."

"Level of danger to this suit?" Fragger asked.

"Extremely high" came the answer.

"Means of defeating EMP generators?"

"Explosive devices will achieve success."

"Are we armed with grenades or something like that?" Fragger asked.

"Negative."

"Other means of destruction?"

"Take advantage of EMP generator weakness."

"Okay," Fragger said, "and what's that?"

"After initial EMP burst, generators take time to recycle to full power."

"How much time?"

"Typical time for Imperial Commonwealth model is three seconds."

"So, all I have to do is figure out how to trigger a burst, then slip through?" Fragger asked.

"Affirmative."

"Thanks a lot."

"You're welcome," the suit replied to his sarcasm.

"Idiot," Fragger muttered in frustration, then asked, "Is the EMP device triggered automatically or manually?"

"It has both capabilities," the suit answered.

"Damn. Wait a minute. Can you determine what setting it's on now?"

"Yes."

"Well, what setting is active at this moment?" Fragger asked.

"Manual. Automatic systems have been disrupted."

"Okay, so Shimazu has set a trap for the invaders as part of the defensive action. How do I trigger the trap?"

"The system detects any active or residual EMP-producing device," the suit answered.

"Such as?"

"As stated previously, powered armor or weaponry will emit EMP signals."

"Weaponry?" Fragger said. "Do hand weapons of the Imperial Commonwealth security forces fit into that category?"

"If activated, affirmative."

Fragger backtracked to a dead security man and pulled a pistol from his hand. He turned the weapon on, then returned and took up a position close to the EMP defensive weapon. Instructing the suit to alert him when the EMP generator was de-activated, he yelled, "Shimazu, I'm coming in after you. Kiss your pathetic ass goodbye!", and tossed the pistol into the air. Fragger heard nothing, but when the suit said, "Three second window", he shot forward and down the corridor.

To his surprise, nothing happened.

"Any damage to my armor?" he asked the suit to be sure.

"None."

"Scan the area again," Fragger instructed.

A split second later, the suit replied, "Scan negative other than standard-issue pistols. However, masked weapons are possible as reported before."

"I know. You told me that already, but what the hell is a masked weapon?"

"Electronic and power source signatures are masked from sensors or report false readings. Most commonly used to fool an enemy into thinking that they are facing weaponry of less power than is really present."

"So, for all I know, I could be facing a tank," Fragger said.

"Not feasible in this situation. A tank is too large to occupy space available."

"I was joking," the Ranger said. "What *is* feasible?"

"Short-range, crew-served PPC weapon is most commonly deployed defensive weapon."

Fragger asked, "Danger to suit?"

"Moderate."

"'Moderate?' What does that mean?"

The suit answered, "Under most circumstances, a particle weapon is of little threat to powered armor. However, at close range, a well-placed shot to the visor area can stun, injure and/or kill suit occupant if the PPC is of sufficient power and operator is of sufficient skill and experience."

I can just about count on Shimazu being an expert, Fragger thought, then asked, "Effective range of this weapon?"

"Three meters," the suit replied, then added, "Enemy approaching from rear."

"Hell," Fragger swore. "Can you identify?"

"Signature indicates non-standard suit. Most likely not EarthCorp or other major power."

'Well, who is it most likely then?" Fragger asked, irritated by the suit's inability to get beyond limited responses.

"Probable origin is Gulag region."

"I thought we were being attacked by EarthCorp forces," Fragger said.

"Analysis of situation indicates that several different forces have boarded HELOT vessel and are battling each other as well as Imperial Commonwealth defenders."

"Can you tell who has the upper hand?" Fragger asked.

"Negative. Situation is fluid."

Excellent, the Ranger thought. *Confusion breeds uncertainty, and uncertainty leads to escape. However, first things first.*

"How soon before enemy appears?" he asked the suit.

"At present rate, one minute."

"Armament?"

"Power sword detected. Blunt, hacking type favored by Gulag warriors of Terran Russian origin."

"Typical tactics?"

"Massed frontal assault."

"I mean, typical tactics of individual Gulag soldier," Fragger specified.

"Frontal assault, mirror image of large-unit tactics."

Definitely sounds like Russian influence to me, Fragger thought. *Whatever the situation, apply overwhelming force. Effective, but no finesse.*

The Ranger waited until he heard the metallic pounding of steps from behind and a huge armored figure ran into view looking like a hairless and terrifying bear. When the Gulag warrior caught sight of Fragger, he charged instantly, waving an enormous sword. Fragger stood his ground until the last possible second, then dove backwards onto the deck. Confused for a moment by the action, the Gulag warrior hesitated, then straddled Fragger and raised his sword.

The blast from Shimazu's PPC caught the warrior in the helmet, causing him to stagger back against a bulkhead and drop the sword. Fragger swung his own blade low and sliced off the man's leg at the ankle. The Gulag warrior screamed and dropped to the deck, thrashing in agony. Fragger rolled to his feet and faced in the direction of the blast. The surprised faces of Major Shimazu and the one-eyed Hiro rose from behind the wide-barreled PPC cannon set on a tripod. Fragger kicked the weapon aside and backed the two up against the wall. Hiro began to shiver and plead, but Shimazu straightened and stood waiting for the inevitable. Fragger silenced her partner with a single stroke to the neck. Hiro's head thumped onto the deck while his body sagged into a grotesque sitting position.

"Shimazu, I'm going to do you a favor," Fragger informed her. "Torturers make me puke. They're inhuman scum and deserve the worst that can be served up to them. Yet, I'm going to kill you quick because somewhere in the past you must have had some honor."

Shimazu smoothed out her uniform and responded with contempt, "I take nothing from a Rerun. Do whatever you want. I am a Royal and Imperial Commonwealth officer, and you are insignificant compared to that."

"So be it," Fragger said. "I'll just remind you of the one word you mentioned to me earlier--Agincourt."

The Ranger kept his promise, He raised his sword high and brought it down with full force on Shimazu's head. The blade split her lengthwise as easily as if Fragger had sliced a melon. The two halves tottered for a second, then fell away from each other and crashed onto the deck. Forgetting himself, the Ranger tried to spit on the body and ended up smearing the inside of his visor.

"Crap!" he swore. "The trouble with future warfare is that you can't even get personal with your enemy."

"It is wise to refrain from fouling your faceplate," the suit informed him as it cleaned the mess away with a burst of heated air. "It can affect visibility and, thus, combat effectiveness."

"Tell me about it," Fragger said.

"It is wise-" the suit began again.

"Cease instructions," Fragger ordered.

The suit complied, and the Ranger stood weighing his options.

Revenge tastes good, he thought, *but escape would taste even better.*

"Identify area with least enemy activity and most functional lifepods available," he ordered the suit.

The suit located three areas. Fragger chose the closest and set off at a steady trot, this time without bumping into any walls.

CHAPTER 33

Despite the powered augmentation, Fragger's arms were tired. The suit had guided him in the direction of the fewest number of enemy troopers, but the fewest had turned out to be three scattered along his path. He'd caught the first one, an EarthCorp soldier, by surprise taking off her sword arm as she raised her blade to administer the final blow to a downed Ricer security guard. The second was a massive Ursus soldier whose bulk turned out to be a disadvantage in the confined space of the ship. He'd launched a mighty swing at Fragger only to have his sword catch a massive support girder. Before he'd had time to work the blade free, Fragger had thrust the tip of his weapon into the exposed arm pit and left the man with the his arm dangling by a thread of muscle and tissue from the shoulder area. Now the Ranger was in sight of the lifepod bay, but his last adversary--obviously stationed to prevent escapes--had turned out to be the toughest as well as the best-dressed.

The enemy's armor was white with a red symbol of a cross over the heart, so Fragger assumed it some kind of future equivalent of a religious/military order and couldn't help thinking of the man as a knight.

That short red cape really takes the cake. I can't see any use for it in space. Maybe it indicates a friendly to his side. God knows, it's hard to tell one soldier from the next in this environment.

Fragger shook the opinion on military fashion out of his head and concentrated on the circling opponent. The knight was experienced and, unlike Fragger's last opponent, small and agile, ideally suited for internal warfare on a ship. The Ranger had no doubt the man was equally adept in a zero-g environment as well as the normal gravity they were now in. He'd suckered Fragger into wasting his strength by leaping in with quick feints, then jumping back to avoid the Ranger's awkward thrusts. Fragger fought impatience and concentrated on conserving his energy, trying to work his way around the knight.

His enemy would have none of it. He moved to block Fragger, swinging his sword low to keep the Ranger's feet off balance. Fragger stumbled back, cutting the air wildly to maintain a safe distance from the trooper's weapon.

Shit, I'm losing this one, the Ranger swore as he fended off more thrusts.

Fragger pushed his back up against a bulkhead, grimly determined to make the knight pay dearly for each small advantage he gained. The clash of their weapons rang throughout the lifepod bay, and the odor of mingling ozone and superheated air penetrated the filters of the Ranger's suit. The smell was joined by a ringing in his ears as the knight slipped his parry and landed the flat of his blade along Fragger's helmet. The blow stunned the Ranger, and he was helpless to defend against the enemy's attack. He watched with detached and professional interest as the knight raised the sword shoulder-high and swung.

Fragger closed his eyes as the blade struck.

Damn, death is a real disappointment. The floating part is fun, but, shit, you'd think that God would have gotten rid of nausea. Who wants to spend eternity puking his guts out? Oh, man...of course, I'm in Hell. I always knew I'd end up there.

Fragger opened his eyes to find out what Hell looked like and found it looked exactly like the lifepod bay, only upsidedown. The knight whirled away from him in an awkward flail of arms and legs..

Gravity's gone! Fragger realized. *That knight had me dead to rights so the loss of gravity must have thrown off his aim.*

The Ranger's elation at still being alive was cut short when he saw his enemy expertly recover from the spin. The knight drew up his knees and used his velocity to plant feet against a bulkhead and push off with the sword point aimed directly at Fragger's head. Instinctively, the Ranger twisted his body to avoid the attack. It was a move that saved his life. As the sword flashed an inch away from his helmet, he somersaulted head over heels, bounced off the "ceiling", and tumbled toward the center of the bay. A weak grin lit up Fragger's face as he remembered the truth of an old cliché,

There's nothing more dangerous than an amateur because you never know what he'll do.

Relief was short-lived. Fragger crashed against the wall and spun off in another direction. As his body revolved, the Ranger saw the knight holding patiently to a cable waiting for his victim to come within range.

This really sucks, Fragger cursed as he struggled to get control. *I'm going to deliver myself up to this guy, and he won't even have to break a sweat.*

A voice crackled into his helmet. "Boots, you idiot!"

The Ranger was confused. *Why would this guy want my boots?*

The voice spoke again, ordering, "Damn it, Rerun, activate your boots."

"Watanabe?"

"Yes."

"What am I supposed to do with my boots?"

In less than ten seconds, Watanabe sketched out in profane detail the many sides of a Rerun's stupidity, then said, "The soles are magnetic. Tell the suit 'magnetic mode'."

"Well, hell, why didn't you say that in the first place?" Fragger grumbled, then told the suit, "Magnetic mode."

Nothing happened at first, then as he rotated close to the ceiling, his boots stuck hard enough to the metal to rattle the Ranger's teeth. Upside down, he saw Watanabe tether a space-suited figure to a wall hook so he could be free to battle the knight. Both men had switched on their magnetic soles, and as they clomped toward each other, it looked to Fragger as if the combatants were fighting under water from the waist down while above the belt line their swords clashed freely in a blur of stroke and counter-stroke. The Ranger saw quickly that the knight had made a mistake by abandoning free-fall. With his feet stuck to the deck, the man had sacrificed his quickness and was hard pressed to meet Watanabe's greater strength. The knight seemed to realize this at the same time that Fragger did and cut the magnetic attraction, but Watanabe anticipated the move with a high swing that caught the rising enemy squarely in the helmet. Blood spattered the knight's visor, and

Fragger heard the explosive hiss of escaping air. Cape fluttering, the knight spun away loose-limbed and very dead from Watanabe's blow. His power sword struck the wall in a dazzling flash of light.

Watanabe craned his head to look up at Fragger. "We're back to three lives this time, Rerun. There's no way you can disagree with that."

"Amen, brother," the Ranger said.

Watanabe seemed to puzzle over this remark for a moment, then said, "I assume that means 'Thank you'?"

"Damned right! You can save all the lives I have, as far as I'm concerned."

"You certainly have enough of them," Watanabe said as if irritated and amazed by the thought all at the same time. "And you're going to need every life you can find."

"We're losing the battle?"

"It's lost, Rerun. It's been lost for a long time. Only the incompetence and infighting of the attacking force has prevented complete control of the ship to this point, but somebody has straightened out the lines of command because they're starting to systematically clean us out section by section.

"So, what do we do? Take a lifepod?"

"It's tempting, but I'm betting they've keyed in the *Tokyo's* escape signatures and are just waiting for an attempt."

"We can't stay here, Watanabe."

"You have a genius for overstating the obvious, Rerun."

"Well, excuse me! What's your plan, then?"

"Standing orders are to execute you if capture is inevitable."

For a moment, a chill ran through the Ranger's body, then he realized, "That's not going to happen, is it? You could have let that enemy trooper take me out without much fuss or bother. Instead, you saved me."

Fragger heard the shrug in Watanabe's reply. "My career is over if Shimazu made her report. I struck a superior officer and caused another to be injured."

"Well, I don't know if the report was made or not, but if it's any consolation, you don't have to worry about Shimazu any more," Fragger said.

"You killed her?"

"Yes."

A sigh come over the commlink that was one part relief and one part sorrow. "I won't lie to you, Rerun. She gave me much torment and I'm happy she's dead, but her bravery was beyond question."

"She died with courage," Fragger said. "We'll honor her for that and not for her capacity for hatred."

"Yes, that would be fitting," Watanabe agreed.

"Assuming her report got through, what's the penalty for striking an officer?" Fragger asked.

"In the best case, death."

"Death is the best case? What's the worst case?"

"Shimazu was a member of the aristocracy as well as an officer. In such cases, the offender is denied the honor of *seppuku*. Instead, he and his family are stripped of all identity, lose all property and rights, and are made Reruns. That means my wife, *Yoshiko*, my four children and I will be the same as you."

"What a shame," Fragger said in mocking sympathy.

"Yes, shame is what it's all about," Watanabe said, missing the sarcastic intent of the Ranger's words. "Heaping the ultimate humiliation upon the offender to enforce the system. It's very effective discipline. Even the *Burakumin* do not want to be Reruns."

Despite his anger at Watanabe's attitude of superiority, Fragger felt some sympathy for the sergeant's position. The *Burakumin* had little power and freedom in the Ricer social structure, but a little power and freedom was better than none at all.

"Well, I'm sorry this has happened," Fragger said, "but you have to face reality, Watanabe. You go back, you and your family are Reruns with absolutely no freedom. You stick with me, and you're still a Rerun, but one with the freedom to rescue his family from slavery. I think your choice is obvious."

Watanabe nodded. "It's no choice at all, but freedom in any form is sweeter than slavery. I will renounce my service in the Imperial Commonwealth and lead you to whatever fate awaits us, Rerun."

"Generous of you," Fragger responded.

"You are being sarcastic?" the sergeant asked.

"You bet."

Watanabe's voice showed genuine puzzlement at Fragger's attitude. "You're a Rerun, and you owe me many lives. I would think you'd show me loyalty if not outright gratitude for my offer of leadership."

"Watanabe, I'm about as grateful as one man can get in a time where he doesn't belong, but everybody's idea of loyalty in this century seems to be, 'Stand still, Fragger Sparks, until we can figure out a way to make use of your talents or kill you if we can't.'"

After a brief pause, the sergeant said, "I see your point."

Fragger suggested, "How about we postpone the idea of leadership and settle for I watch your back, and you watch mine? In the end, that's what combat is all about, isn't it? Looking out for the guy next to you?"

"Yes, Rerun, that's it exactly. You've said it well."

"Damned straight, I have. Now that we've agreed to cover for each other, how do we keep our backs alive long enough to protect them?"

"We take our chances outside the ship," Watanabe answered. "That is the only alternative I can think of."

"I've only been in space once, and then I was buck-naked. What do I do?" Fragger asked.

"Follow my lead and whatever you do, do *not* de-magnetize your boots unless I tell you to! I can't emphasize that strongly enough. And your maneuvering jets. You don't know how to use them, so don't turn them on. You go spinning off into space, and you're finished, Rerun. There isn't a chance in hell of finding you. You last only as long as your oxygen does."

Fragger shuddered at the thought and promised, "No way I'll do either one of those things."

"All right then. Grab the cape of that Roller warrior while I power up the lifepods. I'll set the units on time delay and send them and, hopefully, the enemy off on a wild goose chase."

"Why do we need the cape?"

"It indicates a holy warrior with many kills. Roller troopers are big on flaunting their courage. It means they're brave enough to stand out in a battle and take whatever infidels can throw at them."

"Okay, but that doesn't explain why we need the cape," Fragger said.

"Use your head, damn it! Wear it to confuse the enemy. It may buy us some time, and it'll give any enemy pause before he attacks you."

Fragger felt silly but did as he was told, retrieving the cape from the floating Roller warrior and tying it about his neck. He watched as Watanabe worked through a series of protocols at a control panel. When he finished, Watanabe said, "Okay, I've set the pods to launch at staggered intervals. When they launch, we hit the vacuum while the enemy's attention is on the decoys."

"Sounds good to me," Fragger said, "but what do we do once we're out on the hull of the ship?"

"We look for a Gulag vessel."

"How do I know which one is a Gulag ship?"

"Anything that looks like big pile of crap, that's a Gulag vessel."

"I can tell that your opinion of them isn't high, Watanabe, but that's not very damned helpful."

"I'm not joking! And I'm not ridiculing them, either. Inhabitants of the Gulag worlds don't have easy access to technology so they make do with what they can pirate, scavenge or steal, then apply their own ingenuity. That means their vessels aren't pretty. They stand out like a sore thumb when stacked up against standard designs. Now, stop talking and listen. That's Buurk I tethered to the wall. As we fought our way here, he caught a blow on the helmet. It knocked him unconscious. Untether him and follow me."

"Why did you bring the medic along?" Fragger asked as he reached Buurk and untied the restraint.

"Why do you ask such a question?" Watanabe responded.

"Just curious as to why you're willing to put yourself out for the Martian. It's not Ricer style."

"I don't know about the army in your day, Rerun, but in mine, it's always in style to look out for the medic because he just might save your life some day on the battlefield. Now, get moving."

Dragging Buurk behind, Fragger followed Watanabe, having no intention of letting the Ricer out of sight. The prospect of operating outside the ship terrified him. Every advantage was to the enemy, but that bothered him least of all. Soldiers he could fight. To end up falling into infinitely empty space, that was something else again.

CHAPTER 34

Watanabe popped the hatch open and hauled himself out. Following close behind, Fragger stuck his head out cautiously and surveyed a hull crowded with assault troop carriers. To the Ranger, it looked as if vicious barnacles had attacked the giant Ricer ship. Enemy soldiers swarmed over the curving surface. Their helmets turned as one when the lifepods floated free of the vessel and powered up into the avoidance trajectories Watanabe had programmed into their guidance systems. Tracer-like rounds stabbed outward at the pods from the attacking fleets, igniting a fearsome and silent barrage among the escaping vehicles.

"Come on out here while they're busy targeting the pods," Watanabe said over the commlink. "We're in luck. We've got a Gulag dropship close to us and not a Corpse or Imperial Commonwealth vessel. Gulagers are not professional soldiers and their security can be lax. That means we have a chance to commandeer the ship. I'm going to head for it, but I need you to buy me a few seconds of time. Tether Buurk to the hatch and start walking toward the dropship."

"Why?" Fragger asked.

"Have you already forgotten that Roller cape I had you put on? It'll disguise our Imperial Commonwealth armor for a moment. Hopefully, it'll create enough confusion in the guard's head to create the opening I need to drop him and hijack the ship. I'll follow close behind you so he can't see my armor design. All you need to do is keep him occupied. Is that clear?"

"Yeah, it's clear," Fragger answered as he tied Buurk to the hatch. "But how am I supposed to talk to this guy? The Gulagers don't have the same commlink frequency as your people, do they?"

"You're right, they don't, but I'll feed the Gulag frequency to your suit, right…now. Okay, start walking."

Fragger obeyed and had no trouble picking out his destination.

Watanabe's right about the appearance of the Gulag ships, the Ranger decided as he clunked across the hull toward his target.

With all those spikes sticking out at odd angles, it looks like a deranged porcupine. Unfortunately, the guard next to the open hatch seems completely rational—and lethal!

"Identify yourself," the guard ordered, raising a large-bore particle weapon as Fragger approached.

Trying to sound as official as possible, the Ranger said, "Lower your weapon, soldier. I'm Captain Jonathan Sparks of the Celestial Warrior fleet in pursuit of Ricer troopers. Have any come your way?"

The guard snorted at the feeble attempt at deception and kept his weapon trained on the Ranger. "Another Ricer trying to escape. Just because we're from the Gulag, you think we're stupid?"

Fragger broke into a sweat, but stalled more for time by demanding, "What are you talking about?"

"You've got a Roller cape, but you're carrying a Ricer sword and wearing Ricer armor, moron."

"I captured the sword," the Ranger stammered. "Lost my own in the fight and picked up this one."

"And lost your armor and changed that as well? If you're a Roller, then I'm the Lord of All Known Space," the guard replied. "Get rid of the damned sword, or I'll air your suit out for you."

Just keep talking and create more confusion! Fragger thought in desperation. "Hey, I'm not giving up this sword. I won it fair and square. Swords don't grow on trees, you know."

."What the devil are you talking about?" the guard demanded.

"The sword tree," Fragger babbled, "you know, the source of all fine weapons, all great swords-"

"Shut up!" the guard ordered.

"-it's a long, forgotten technology from Terra. The Ricers have--"

The Gulag guard raised his weapon and fired. A bolt of blazing energy shot over the Ranger's helmet. At the same moment, Watanabe jetted silently past Fragger, low to the hull. The guard strove to bring his weapon down to meet the charge. The barrel struck against the onrushing Ricer's shoulder to no effect while Watanabe sliced his blade into the Gulag guard's side. Blood, air and fluid spurted out in a frozen stream. The guard screamed, grabbed at the wound, and then went limp, releasing his particle weapon while he remained stuck near the hull in a haze of red globules. Without pause, Watanabe powered past his victim and into the Gulag vehicle. A few seconds later, the sergeant re-appeared in the door and gave Fragger the all clear sign. The Ranger returned to the hatch, untethered Buurk and hauled him over to the Gulag ship. He stuffed the Martian through the vessel's door and followed him inside.

He asked Watanabe, "Can you pilot this vessel?"

"No, but these two can."

The Ranger saw two suited Gulag pilots with very wide eyes staring through their visors at Watanabe's glowing blade.

"How do we know they haven't already alerted the others?" Fragger asked.

"Because they're Gulag," came the answer. "They don't really want us. They want salvage. Plus, they're sensible, practical tribesmen who know how to live to fight another day--don't you?"

Both pilots nodded their helmets with vigor.

"Okay," Fragger said, "Next question, then. How do we get out of here without getting our heads shot off?"

"We wait, Rerun. We wait for a good opportunity to escape, and then we exploit it. If we tried to break away now, we'd be spread across the stars in seconds."

"Great," Fragger muttered. If there was thing he hated to do, it was wait unless he was setting up an ambush or something that had a direct and practical purpose.

Waiting for an enemy to blow me out of space is just not my style, he complained silently. The kills he'd made in the ship had been satisfying. He'd finally been able to strike back. It was a good feeling, and he wanted more.

Fragger diverted his attention from the frustration by grabbing the floating Martian and strapping him into a chair. Then, there was nothing to do to pass the time but study the interior of the Gulag ship. A quick scan revealed the truth of Watanabe's words about the Gulag's "make-do-with-what-you have" attitude. Mud particles rose from the deck, bumping into dirty utility suits hanging from hooks and floating with flapping arms as if they were trying to get someone's attention. Scraps of food joined the aerial ballet. It was clear that Watanabe, ever the professional soldier, was annoyed by the mess. The Gulag pilots simply batted the debris away when it got into their line of vision.

Definitely not a military ship, Fragger thought. *If it were, those two would be hauled up on charges.*

But he didn't really care about the Gulagers' lack of sanitary habits; he just hoped the damned ship could get them somewhere far away in one piece.

CHAPTER 35

"Damn, it's been six hours," Fragger complained as he batted away a loose food tube that persisted in floating around in the interior of the Gulag dropship and annoying him like a fly.

Watanabe's reply was unsatisfying. "Yeah, and it might be 12."

"What's taking them so long?"

A short burst of laughter greeted the question. "You think EarthCorp or my people are going to let a prize like you get away, Rerun? They're tearing the *Tokyo* apart from bow to stern."

"Eventually they're going to figure out we're not on board," Fragger pointed out.

"True, but I unless I'm badly mistaken, it'll take them some time before they start boarding Gulag ships."

Fragger grumbled, "I'm hungry."

"Why don't you open your visor and eat some of that food tube floating by your head?"

"Very funny."

"Which one of you is the pilot?" Fragger heard Watanabe ask the Gulagers.

"I am," an edgy, high-pitched voice answered him.

"What's your name?"

"Alarcon."

"Well, Alarcon, I don't like the tone of your voice. Rerun, what would you call that insolent attitude in your time?"

"It's a smart-ass attitude."

"That sounds like a good description. You sound like a smart ass to me, Alarcon, and I don't like insolent smart asses. That means you're so low right now, I may have to scrape you off the bottom of my boot if you don't obey orders. Is that clear?"

"Yes."

Watanabe asked the co-pilot, "And you? Are you a smart ass too? What's your name?"

A baritone voice answered over the commlink. "No, I am not a smart ass. I am Bucaram."

"That's good," Watanabe said. "One smart ass is enough. Well, Alarcon and Bucaram, I have a question for you. Don't you two ever clean the garbage out of your ship?"

"What garbage?" Alarcon asked.

"Incredible, Rerun! They don't even know they're living in a dump."

"If they were under my command," Fragger said, "they'd be cleaning out every grease trap in every mess hall I could find."

"I don't know what a grease trap is, but my solution would be to simply separate their heads from their necks," Watanabe said. "I may do it, anyway. If there's one thing I can't stand, it's a sloppy soldier."

Over the commlink, two sets of lungs caught for breath. Fragger grinned, happy to have someone else sweating for a change, but he eased their minds by asking Watanabe, "But they're not soldiers, not real ones anyway, so what would be the point of killing them?"

"You've got something there," Watanabe agreed. "Maybe they can be of some use to us on the surface of a planet. What world are you two from?"

"Jivaro," Alarcon answered.

"Jivaro? The jungle planet? Dr. Shaper's world?"

Interest flared in Fragger. *I don't know who Dr. Shaper is, but jungles I do know! If I can get there, I may find safety.*

"Yes to all three questions," Alarcon answered.

"Who's Dr. Shaper?" the Ranger asked.

"A brilliant sociopath named Tyco Radmüller," Watanabe answered. "He's called 'Dr. Shaper' because of his illegal genmod experimentation."

"That's the second time I've heard that term 'sociopath'," Fragger said. "Back on Mars, Buurk said he was the product of a man like that. Are we talking about the same person?"

"More than likely," Watanabe replied. "Shaper was in an EartthCorp lab on Mars. No one really knows what happened, but the story is that Radmuller was an ordinary researcher when he snapped mentally and became a scientific rogue. If Buurk is one of his creations, then the medic is one of the few good ones. Some are real horrors. He fled to Jivaro when EarthCorp got wind of what he was doing. Apparently, he continued experimentation there. Nobody really knows what's happened to Shaper. The usual rumors—he's alive, he's dead, take your pick. Anyway, Jivaro is a haven-hell for his creatures, making it a very unpleasant place. Which is why the Shuar are the sole inhabitants."

"Shuar?" Fragger asked. "Who are the Shuar?"

"You should have a better command of Terran history, Rerun," Watanabe chided. "Apparently, everybody today knows more about it than you do. They're famous."

"So sue me. Who the devil are the Shuar?"

"Natives of the Terran Amazon regions—Peru and Ecuador. Alarcon and Bucaram are Shuar. Look at their belts."

Fragger squinted at small hairy objects dangling weightless from the belts and asked, "What are those?"

"Shrunken heads," Watanabe answered. "Our two Jivarons are headhunters. Terran authorities forcibly relocated the tribes after deciding they were the best choice to deal with the jungle environment, Shaper, and the proliferation of Shaper's creatures over the planet. And if it didn't work out, they assumed the loss of a people so insignificant was acceptable. Anyway, the headhunters call themselves the Shuar. We call them 'swampers'. But, whatever you call them, they're still headhunters."

"It figures," Fragger said.

"What figures?"

"Everybody in this time is crazy about chopping off heads, so why shouldn't there be headhunters?"

"Actually, back on Terra, they'd dropped headhunting centuries before," Watanabe explained. "Once on Jivaro, they went feral and re-introduced the practice. They say it's a way of honoring their ancestors' traditions, but what it really is, is a means of scaring the hell out of their enemies. Anyway, killing is killing."

"I suppose," Fragger said although the process of shrinking heads somehow made him queasy.

Watanabe turned his attention back to the two headhunters and asked, "Alarcon, did you and your people find Dr. Shaper? Is he still alive or did you kill him and shrink his head? Tell the truth."

"Yes, we killed him," Alarcon answered. "His head adorns a special stake in our village. He's no longer a threat."

"Did you personally kill him or was it someone else in your tribe?" Watanabe asked.

"Bucaram and I killed him," Alarcon replied.

"Must have been a heck of personal challenge," Watanabe suggested. "I mean, Shaper was a big man, close to two meters tall."

"He put up a good fight," Alarcon said. "But even with his great size, we were too good for him."

Watanabe snorted at this response. "Well, Rerun, it looks like we're not only dealing with headhunters but simpletons and liars as well. Radmuller is notorious for being short, barely reaching 1.6 meters."

Fragger did a quick conversion in his head. *About five foot four!*

"So, Alarcon," Watanabe asked, "what's the truth about Shaper? And don't lie to me this time. One person can pilot this ship as well as two, and I'm willing to let Bucaram have that honor after I've deep spaced you."

"I don't know," Alarcon replied quickly.

"You don't know what?" the sergeant demanded.

"I don't know if he's alive or dead. Like you, we hear rumors."

"What's your opinion?"

"We have not seen new creatures for some time," Alarcon responded. "My opinion is that he's dead."

"And you, Bucaram, what's your opinion?" Watanabe asked.

"He's alive," the co-pilot answered.

"Why do you say that?"

"Because, Ricer, we have seen periods before when new creatures have not appeared. It usually means he's busy creating something more vicious."

Fragger interrupted, "Look, you people keep talking about Shaper's experiments and how awful they are, but you never say exactly what they are."

Bucaram laughed harshly. "The Rerun wants a description, Alarcon. Describe one for him."

"All right, Rerun. You want a description, here's one," Alarcon said. "How about the slipsnake? It's Shaper's genetic modification of the green anaconda and a little 'joke' he played to welcome us to the planet. In our Terran rainforest, it's a sluggish, mild snake that hunts along rivers and ponds. It was no threat to us in Ecuador, but it's definitely one on Jivaro. Shaper used implants and manipulation of its genetic structure to include extreme reptilian intelligence, speed, stealth and aggressiveness toward anything within its range."

"Anything?" Fragger asked.

"Anything," Alarcon confirmed. "Including humans. Be careful where you sit on Jivaro, that's my advice. Otherwise, it'll slip up on you and you'll find yourself the object of a nine meter, 225 kilogram appetite."

"I think they're trying to scare us, Watanabe," Fragger said dryly. "Did it work on you?"

"No. I think we've got two snakes right here who are more of a worry than any imaginary monster anaconda. But then the Shuar have a reputation for being liars and dirty savages. They're nothing but a bunch of wild tribes with no discipline or honor or--"

Fragger interrupted and asked, "Can you switch to a private frequency?"

"Sure."

When Watanabe indicated the channel was secure, Fragger suggested, "Look, I knew Alarcon and Bucaram are trying to con us with a line of bullshit, but I think we'd be better off making friends with these guys rather than antagonizing them."

"What? Why?" Watanabe demanded.

"Because we're going to need friends if we make it to their planet. When your fellow troopers discover you've deserted them, they'll be looking for you, my friend, almost as hard as they're searching for me. That means we'll have to hide, and we need somebody who knows how to help us do that, and that means these two headhunters."

Watanabe's tone bristled. "I don't hide from anybody."

"Jesus, focus on the overall picture, will you, Watanabe? In this situation, staying alive is more important than personal honor. Run away to fight another day. Except we're not really running away, are we? We stay low, stay alive, and organize."

"There are times when common sense overrules honor," Watanabe admitted. "And this is probably—wait a minute! Organize? What are you talking about? Organize what?"

"Watanabe, I didn't say I was going to run forever, did I? I'm going to hide first, then organize my own 'tribe' and, for all I know, my own nation and planet or the whole damned universe and God himself--whatever it takes to stay alive and strike back. I plan to make it too painful to capture or waste me. And Jivaro sounds like the perfect place for my base of operations. I'm a jungle fighter. That's what I was trained to do."

Watanabe didn't sound impressed. "The Imperial Commonwealth or anybody else who's halfway serious will kill you before you carry out such grandiose plans."

"They haven't had much luck so far in eliminating me," Fragger pointed out.

"Before this, they weren't fully aware of what your abilities are, Sparks. Now they do. Every system wants you alive to get at those capabilities, but if they can't have you, then no one else will, and that means deploying every weapon in their arsenals--chemical, biological, conventional, you name it."

"Well, shit, Watanabe, the one thing I learned about the jungle is that it's a helluva friend if you know how to live in it. I can hide, and with the Shuar's help, they'll never find us unless they want to defoliate the whole planet."

"Rerun, it's an extreme measure, but it's within the realm of possibility."

Stunned, Fragger asked, "You're serious?"

"Of course, they can do that or blast Jivaro into grains of sand. It calls for considerable planning and firepower, but it definitely can be done."

"Christ...wipe a whole planet out of existence! And I thought nukes were bad," Fragger said, trying to get his mind around the concept of total warfare on a completely different scale. "So, if we land, I'm putting an entire population at risk?"

"Yes, Rerun, if my people and the others want you badly enough, and they certainly seem to."

"But there's nowhere else to go?"

"I don't know. Let's ask." Watanabe said.

Watanabe switched channels and asked the Shuar warriors, "Is Jivaro the only place we can get to?"

"Definitely," Alarcon said.

"What about going through hyperspace?" Fragger asked.

Alarcon laughed. "That would be great. Unfortunately, we don't have the drive. You think we're made of money or something?"

"Is he lying?" Fragger asked Watanabe.

The sergeant did a quick check of the controls and answered, "No, he's not. This antique probably can't even come close to light speed."

"How far is Jivaro at maximum speed?" Fragger asked the Shuar pilot.

"Two standard days. Assuming we can get out of here in the first place."

"You can't outrun pursuit?"

Watanabe made a disgusted noise. "This thing couldn't outrun a glacier."

"Hey!" Alarcon said. "My ship does okay."

"'Okay' isn't good enough in this situation," Watanabe responded. "We need speed or weapons or very heavy armor, preferably all three."

"Defensive particle cannons, that's all we've got," the pilot said.

"Wonderful! Just wonderful. We might just as well be armed with feathers. They'd do more damage."

"What'd you expect from a salvage ship?" Alarcon asked in a snide tone.

"You know what?" Watanabe barked. "I think you'd better start thinking real hard about how to get us out of here before I slice your head off and use it to bombard the enemy. It's fat enough it just might do the job."

"Take it easy," Bucaram put in, a quaver in his voice. "Just take it easy."

"I'll take *your* head off too if that's what you want!" Watanabe warned.

Fragger spoke sharply. "Watanabe, this is no time to lose your temper."

"It seems like a damned good time to me!"

"*You're* the one who said we had time before the enemy located us," Fragger reminded him.

"Yeah, well, that's before I knew we'd come on board a garbage scow whose only defense is a stench strong enough to crack hull armor."

"Can't we do something like that?" Fragger asked.

"Do what? Pretend we're a garbage scow?"

"No, pretend that we're part of the debris of battle and just float away?"

The three men laughed at him.

"Where do you get such ideas?" Watanabe asked.

"I saw it in a submarine movie."

"What's a submarine? Or a movie?" Alarcon asked.

"Forget the submarine," Fragger said. "A movie is a film, a videotape, a television program."

"Never heard of them," the pilot said.

"Damn! It's entertainment, fiction, something that's made up."

"Oh, okay, you're talking about holos," Alarcon said.

Watanabe interrupted with impatience. "It doesn't matter what you call it. Even though this ship looks like garbage, the tactic won't work. It's the oldest trick in the book, and to a good tactical staff, our signature will light up their screens like a beacon."

"And how good are the staffs we're facing?"

"The best, the very best. They'll have us breathing vacuum within minutes."

"Damn!" the Ranger swore. "We can't just give up."

"I think giving up is a hell of a good idea," Alarcon said. "You two may want to be blown to pieces, but *we'd* like to live."

"Oh, shut up!" Fragger ordered and asked Watanabe to switch to a private channel again.

"We've got to make a decision, Watanabe. Alarcon and his buddy know we're in deep trouble and are ready to exploit any opening we give them."

"I agree Rerun. The question is--what to do? We can't outrun the enemy. We can't outfight them. We can't hide from them."

"Let's provoke them, then," the Ranger suggested.

Watanabe responded in a sarcastic tone. "Now there's a brilliant idea,"

"Just listen, will you? When I fought in Vietnam, we had enormous firepower superiority over the NVA--our enemy--when they attacked our firebases. Their solution was to engage us so rapidly and closely that we couldn't bring our artillery to bear without killing our own troops. In effect, they took our firepower advantage right out of the equation, so we had to fight on their terms."

"What are you suggesting?"

"Can we get close enough to one of those warships to blend in without activating the big guns of their defense systems?"

"Sure. We'd be like gnats on an elephant, but that's when they send out marines to commandeer us, so what's the point?"

"The point is to create some havoc and confusion before those marines come out so we can grab an opportunity for escape. Now, of all the attacking forces, who's the most likely to not have good fire discipline?"

"The Shuar, of course. They're probably nervous enough already being under the combined weaponry of the fleets."

Fragger gestured toward the pilot. "Why not put Alarcon to work firing on a few targets?"

"Wouldn't work."

"Why not?"

"We're already targeted, I can guarantee you that," Watanabe answered. "One burst from our cannons, and we're cinders shortly after."

"Shit!" Fragger swore.

Watanabe was silent for a moment, and then said, "But if some other vessels fire, *they'll* be the ones targeted, and that can create the confusion we need."

"What's your idea?" Fragger asked.

"Create the confusion you want. That means you have to keep these two under control while I'm out of dropship. When you see me returning, tell Bucaram to power up, but not to move until I get back. Understood?"

"Understood."

Fragger switched back to the Shuar frequency while Watanabe maneuvered past the still unconscious Buurk and out into the vacuum.

"Where's he going?" Alarcon asked.

"Never mind," Fragger said. "Right now, I want you to keep your hands away from the console until I tell you to power up. Got that?"

The two men raised their hands away from the console, but Alarcon said with a bravado in his voice, "Your buddy's gone, and there's two of us. Think you can handle the situation?"

Fragger activated the sword and laid it close to the pilot's helmet. "I can make it one man to handle if you like. Guess which one of you goes first?"

Silence greeted his warning, and the Ranger settled back to wait for Watanabe's action, keeping his eyes on the curving expanse of the hull outside the Shuar ship. He mentally ticked the minutes off and was at fifteen when he saw Watanabe jetting back low to the hull.

"Power up!" Fragger ordered.

A second later, a red flash snapped first from one Shuar vessel, then another, both shots aimed toward an EarthCorp destroyer. Fragger watched as hits flared on the giant Corpse vessel to no effect. The destroyer didn't return immediate fire as if the officers were stunned by the stupidity of such an attack. The Shuar vessels fired again as Watanabe re-entered the ship and asked, "Powered up?"

"Yes," Fragger answered. "What the heck did you do while you were out there?"

"I killed pilots in two ships and programmed their weapons for delayed fire," Watanabe answered quickly before turning to the Shuar and ordering, "Okay, Alarcon, when I give the command, cut loose from the *Tokyo* and set your attitudinal controls so it looks like we're hit and adrift. Just make sure your momentum is toward that closest Corpse destroyer. Is that understood?"

When the pilot didn't answer fast enough, Watanabe repeated his question with harsher emphasis. "Is that understood or do you want a power sword up your nose?"

"I understand," Alarcon responded in a grudging tone.

"Okay, like I said, wait for my command. The action shouldn't take long to begin."

Impatient, Fragger switched back to the private channel and asked, "I thought you said the Corpses were good. Why are they taking so long to return fire?"

"They're probably trying to stop laughing," Watanabe answered. "Don't worry. The response is coming soon --."

A searing bolt of blue energy punctuated the end of the trooper's sentence. The targeted Shuar ship dissolved into fragments.

"Cut loose!" Watanabe ordered Alarcon.

The Shuar vessel lifted slowly on a burst of jets. It was an agonizing lack of speed as far as Fragger was concerned.

I hate being in situations where you can't do a damned thing about what's going to happen. If those gunners are really good, we'll be ash in a couple of seconds.

Another blast erupted from the Corpse ship, washing the *Tokyo's* hull clean of the second Shuar vessel. Fragger blinked away the dazzle from his eyes and he had vision again but could see no more firing.

"Damn, Watanabe," he burst out. "It's not working. The Shuar aren't foolish enough to return fire on that monster."

"Patience, Rerun. The Shuar won't disappoint me."

When no action occurred, Alarcon said in a smug voice, "Looks like you're wrong, Ricer."

"We'll see."

Fragger marveled at the certainty in Watanabe's voice and wished he felt as sure about the prediction. Their drift toward the Corpse vessel continued and still there was no return fire from the Shuar ships.

"Watanabe, nothing's happening," he said.

The trooper answered with a gesture to be silent.

A second later, to Fragger's relief, multiple Shuar ships rose in ragged formation from the *Tokyo*. As they separated from the hull, the vessels launched a single coordinated barrage on the destroyer.

"I'll be damned," Watanabe said. "They actually can manage some team tactics, not that it'll do them any good. Alarcon, power up your cannons."

The destroyer fired again, targeting the Shuar ships one by one.

Man, their fire control is cool under pressure, Fragger thought with professional admiration. *Even if the Shuar can't do much damage, it takes skill to methodically destroy an enemy like that.*

As the destroyer filled the window of their ship, Watanabe ordered, "Alarcon, target any EarthCorp personnel you see on the hull of the *Tokyo*. Short bursts only."

Fragger heard the eagerness to kill in the pilot's voice as he complained, "Why short bursts? Why not just hose them down?"

"Because, you Shuar cretin, I want the Corpses to think it's return Imperial Commonwealth fire. Any commander who let his men show the lack of discipline you're suggesting would be immediately relieved of duties and reduced to a rank so low that a latrine would look tall to him. So, make it look good."

Alarcon grumbled, but obeyed Watanabe's order. Red bursts of fire lanced out and blew unsuspecting EarthCorp troopers into pieces staining the vacuum of space. The pilot methodically chopped up the ranks of the Corpse soldiers, marching his rounds up and down the hull as if he were scything stalks of wheat instead of human beings.

"Not bad," Watanabe said. "Keep firing until--"

A concussion shook the Shuar ship hard enough to break Fragger's magnetic soles away from the deck. He struck hard against a bulkhead and spun wildly in the cabin before Watanabe caught his foot and hauled him down until the boots slapped onto the floor.

"What was that?" Fragger gasped.

Watanabe laughed with excitement and answered, "Exactly what we've been looking for, and a lot sooner than I expected! The Corpses think Imperial Commonwealth vessels have targeted their troops on the *Tokyo*. The Corpses attacked those vessels, and those ships are returning fire. If we survive the battle, we have a chance of escape. They'll be too busy to worry about us."

"*If* we survive?"

"Of course, Rerun. You know as well as I do that nothing's certain in combat. The ships have unleashed their main batteries. We get in the way, they'll swat us like bugs. Hell, less than bugs."

"That's encouraging."

Watanabe laughed again and Fragger was forced to chuckle in response because he recognized the exhilaration in the Ricer's tone. He'd felt that thrill himself--the addiction of combat, of testing your limits and surviving and then testing them again because you never felt more alive than when the adrenaline pumped full-tilt through your body. It was a small moment, but the Ranger was grateful to Watanabe for unconsciously reminding him of the reason he'd become a soldier in the first place.

Fragger watched the battle outside the Shuar ship increase in intensity, marked by the fireworks of death. Red, green, blue, purple--all the colors he could think of-- indicated detonations as each vessel sought to bracket its opponent and breach a hull.

"God almighty!" he swore as the fire reached such a level that it looked as if space itself had been ripped apart by the ferocity of the bombardment. Actinic glare flooded Fragger's eyes, making him wince despite the helmet's automatic dampening of his visor.

"Now's the time!" he heard Watanabe shout. "Alarcon, take us away from the destroyer and set a direct course for Jivaro, maximum acceleration."

"Are you crazy?" the pilot answered, gesturing toward the light show. "I'm not going to take us out into that. It's suicide."

"Suicide here, suicide there," Watanabe said. "Just follow my orders because if you don't, you'll be dead a lot quicker, and Bucaram can pilot."

Fragger could feel the sizzling temper underneath the tone of Alarcon's grunt of acquiescence to the trooper's command and thought, *If we make it through this, Watanabe will have to watch his back or I'll have to watch it for him because Alarcon has a short fuse. I wish Watanabe would stop yanking his chain.*

Alarcon brought the ship smoothly away from the shadow of the destroyer and accelerated straight into the maelstrom of the barrage. But the pilot's action was not nearly as impressive as the unleashing of energy outside the cockpit window. Concussions rattled the bulkheads so severely Fragger was convinced the hull would split open at any moment, vomit them out into the vacuum, and make them dead fish floating on the surface of space.

Poetic, real poetic, Fragger! he jeered at himself.. *Suck it up! When all your options are taken away, you still have one option left. Face the situation like a man.*

The thought calmed his mind, and the Ranger relaxed until a sun exploded off their port side. A second later, the jaws of the impact locked onto the Shuar ship and tried to shake it spineless. To Fragger's surprise, through the shrieking of tortured metal, he heard Watanabe holler, "Great! Great! It couldn't have happened better if I'd planned it myself."

"What are you talking about?" Fragger shouted as the ship shuddered about him.

"Direct hit! Direct hit on somebody's main fusion engines."

"So?"

"So, we're home free, Rerun. Nobody's sensors will be worth shit for the next couple of minutes. That blast blinded them for sure."

"Yeah, well, it won't do us any good if this damned ship doesn't hold together," Fragger pointed out. "It's shaking itself apart."

Watanabe's response of hooting laughter irritated Fragger who demanded, "What's so damned funny about that?"

"Look out the window, Rerun."

Fragger obeyed and saw nothing but the blackness of quiet space.

"We're out of the battle," Watanabe said. "And the ship isn't shaking any more, but *you* sure are."

Embarrassing as hell, Fragger thought as he realized that Watanabe was right. He ordered his body to stop its shivering.

Like an insolent Ranger, it kept right on shaking.

CHAPTER 36

Jivaro is the only place I've ever been where you can drown without being in water, Fragger complained half-heartedly as he wiped sweat from his brow with an even sweatier forearm and scrutinized their latest camp set-up for its defensive posture. Clearings were few and far between in the midst of the thick Jivaron rainforest, and yesterday they'd been fortunate to find a space devoid of thick junglewood roots, bayonet grass, and slipsnakes. Led by Alarcon and Bucaram, they'd stumbled into the spot on the thirtieth day of their march toward the Shuar villages.

The sun shone high and dimly through the jungle canopy but its heat still had the power to make the swamp boil with its daily farting production of rotting vegetation, humidity, high temperature, and insects hatched in hell. Fragger hated the green and blue swarmbugs the most. The vicious little bastards delivered the instant pain of a hornet's sting along with the never-ending itch of a mosquito's bite. With swollen bumps covering every inch of exposed skin, the three off-worlders looked as if they'd been beaten with tiny clubs. The two Shuar, Alarcon and Bucaram, seemed immune to the swarmbugs and were highly amused at the torment inflicted on their captors.

As he slapped muck on his face to frustrate the pests, the Ranger grumbled, *I thought Vietnam was humid, but this planet makes it seem as dry as the Iraqi desert. Man, I never thought I'd be nostalgic for that hellhole.*

Fragger grunted in amusement at the thought he could actually miss Nam.

"Did you say something?" Watanabe asked.

"Just daydreaming," Fragger answered, watching the Ricer work at maintenance of their powered armor in the middle of the dripping clearing. Buurk sat beside the sergeant, handing him tools in a listless fashion as they were needed. A month after the emergency landing forced by the pursuing enemy, the Martian medic was still not happy being on the same planet as his creator,

Dr. Shaper. Adapted for Mars conditions by Shaper, Buurk was especially uncomfortable in the wet, sticky jungle environment. He complained loudly and often about missing the dry sands of Mars.

Fragger knew how the Martian felt. The Ranger yearned to get back into the climate-controlled interior of the armor. When Fragger had shed his suit, it'd been like stepping into a room full of wet-towel snapping tormentors--the heat and humidity had hit him that hard. But even though they were magnificent fighting machines, the suits had power limitations the same as the weapons in his day. You had to conserve their power and use it only when needed.

"Daydreaming about what?" Watanabe prompted.

"About Vietnam."

"What's that?"

"One of the earth--Terran--countries where I fought."

"It's just like this, you said before?" Watanabe asked, sweeping his hand at the jungle surrounding them.

Fragger laughed. "This place is worse, far worse. I was thinking that Nam was like a beautiful and dangerous woman, but Jivaro...well, hell, it's more like a whore who gives you her body and demands your balls in return."

Watanabe nodded in agreement, wiping sweat from beneath the bandana tied about his bulldog skull. The strips of cloth they all wore only temporarily slowed the flow from the spigot of perspiration opened by the steamy climate of the planet. Although tired by four weeks of the slightly higher gravity of Jivaro, the strain of avoiding search drones while keeping an eye on Alarcon and Bucaram and battling the daily assault of swarmbugs, Fragger realized he'd never been happier in this future life that had been thrust upon him.

I'm free, and that's all a man can ask for! he exulted. *I wish Watanabe and especially Buurk felt the same way.*

Any soldier worth his salt kept his weapons and equipment maintained to the highest peak possible because failure in combat meant injury or worse, but Watanabe had developed an obsessive interest in the duty that kept him occupied every moment when they weren't on the move toward the Shuar village.

He's a front-line soldier in this era's equivalent of a conventional army unit, Fragger thought. *He misses the structure he's used to and the jungle baffles him because there's no well-defined enemy to fight.*

"Good," Fragger said out loud, thinking at the same time, *That means he'll be more willing to accept my leadership when crunch time comes although he's certainly chafing under it now.*

"What's good?" Watanabe asked in irritation as he looked up from oiling a suit joint with a lubricant.

"Nothing," the Ranger answered. "Like I said, daydreaming, that's all."

This answer irked Watanabe even more. "A soldier who daydreams is soon a dead soldier, Rerun."

"A soldier who can't dream is already a dead soldier," Fragger countered and avoided a confrontation by focusing on the direction of his thoughts. He was feeling a little irritable himself. They'd walked most of yesterday to reach the clearing, and he estimated they'd covered less than two klicks in getting to their destination. During the journey, he'd yearned to use his power sword to clear the way, but that would have been a waste of valuable energy. Instead, he'd ordered Alarcon to take the point, and the Shuar slipped through the bayonet grass and over the muddy, rotting floor of the jungle with the ease of a man adapted to the rainforest. His face--cocksure and nasty--had grinned back at Fragger and the others, mocking their clumsiness with sneers of contempt. Only Watanabe's willingness to separate Bucaram's head from his body had kept Alarcon from bolting.

At least that's my assumption, Fragger thought. *He may be simply leading us to an ambush because it'll be a lot easier to get rid of us with superior numbers.*

The Ranger knew it was a distinct possibility. Alarcon and Bucaram had an untamed quality that meant potential for treachery, but which they probably thought of as necessary cunning to survive in a world dominated by tribal cultures. Seeking a comparison from his time, Fragger remembered the Little People in Vietnam, the Montagnards.

Wonderfully fierce people and wonderfully loyal once you gained their trust, and that trust was a hard thing to earn, but definitely worth it. They'd follow you into hell itself.

Fragger guessed that all the Shuar tribes had some of the same traits as the Montagnards, marred by a dismissal of anyone who didn't measure up to tribal standards.

So, it's clear that at some point I'll have to earn their trust one way or another, and if Alarcon and Bucaram's belligerent attitudes are any indication, I'll have do it with a show of force. And, by God, I can provide that show with my speed and armor!

A crashing of branches from the jungle snapped Fragger's enjoyment in the thought of his new found power. He came to his feet and listened intently to the noise before saying, "Can't be troopers unless they're unbelievably incompetent."

"You forget, we're on a world of the Shuar," Watanabe said, aiming his dig at Alarcon and Bucaram who were too focused on the noise to acknowledge the insult.

"What is it?" Fragger asked. "Another tribe?"

Bucaram lifted a finger for silence. The two Shuar exchanged worried glances with each other before Bucaram whispered, "It's a hellhound."

"A hound?" Watanabe asked. "A dog, you mean?"

"Keep your voice down, Ricer!" Bucaram ordered.

"A dog?" Watanabe repeated, refusing to be quiet. "A dog wouldn't make that much noise."

"I'm not talking about a Terran hound, you witless idiot," Bucaram said. "I'm talking about a Jivaron hellhound. It's another one of Dr. Shaper's creations."

"Sounds like a damned elephant to me," Fragger whispered.

"Never seen one other than in a holo," Bucaram said, "but a hellhound is not as big as a Terran elephant."

"That's a relief," Fragger said, "but it must have some size to it to make that much noise."

Alarcon put in, "The hellhound doesn't have any enemies other than human beings, so it doesn't have to worry about detection. When it goes silent, we know we've been scented."

Alarcon added a boast. "We usually hunt them in groups to clear an area around our village for a while, but I defeated one single-handedly."

"You killed the beast like you said you killed Shaper, Alarcon?" Watanabe said.

Alarcon flushed and insisted, "I did kill it!"

"Then it can't be that much of a fearsome beast."

"I killed mine with a knife, Ricer. I didn't need a power sword to do the work for me."

Watanabe snorted at this idea. "You probably got lucky."

Alarcon asked, "Did you ever know a live warrior who didn't get lucky."

That shut you up, didn't it, Watanabe? Fragger thought. He kept the two men from each other's throats by quickly asking, "Just how big is this damned thing?"

"About twice the size of that big Terran species--the Great Dane?" Alarcon responded. "Very much faster, I'm told."

"It has claws then?"

Alarcon laughed. "If we're lucky, they're only four inches long, about the length of its incisors."

"How did it get to be called a plain hound?" Fragger asked.

Alarcon explained. "The story is that Dr. Shaper started with bloodhound stock, enhanced it with his usual gene-mix and implants, and came up with a nasty predator."

Fragger asked, "You said they were enhanced by Shaper. What does that mean?"

Alarcon grinned. "It means you have a predator that can outthink you if you're not careful."

"You mean he increased its intelligence?"

"Smarter than a Ricer warrior, that's for sure."

"Watanabe, lower the sword!" Fragger ordered as the trooper flushed and raised his weapon. "Christ, isn't it enough that we have to fight the whole damned universe without you two busting each other's chops?"

"'Chops?'" Watanabe asked as he failed to identify the word's meaning.

"Never mind. You get my drift. Just stay away from each other."

"Alarcon's smell alone will do that," the trooper grumbled, but his sword relaxed from the ready position.

Alarcon cocked an ear toward the jungle, and then announced, "The hound's gone quiet. We're in trouble. Let's hope it comes after us."

Fragger wasn't sure he'd heard the Shuar right, but he knew his ears were okay when Alarcon clarified, "Hellhounds travel in loose packs. If this one is a scout, he's gone back for the others. If we're lucky, he's a hungry sort and will want to make the kill first so he gets the choicest parts of a Ricer's stringy carcass."

Watanabe shot back, "There isn't an animal on this world or any other that can bite or claw through powered armor."

Contempt laced the words of Alarcon's response. "I would have expected as much from a Ricer. You hide behind your armor as a woman hides behind her skirts."

Watanabe's skin grew blood-red at the insult as he spat out a response to the Shuar's challenge. "Care to find out how an Imperial Commonwealth trooper handles garbage in human form?"

Oh, shit! Fragger groaned inwardly, *Will I ever get Watanabe to consider the big picture instead of playing macho games? The man's temper is more dangerous than his sword.*

Not backing down, Alarcon snapped, "I care to find out how a Ricer faces a hellhound as a Shuar warrior would."

Before Watanabe could respond, Fragger shouted, "Okay, you two. That's enough! I'm going to end this right here and now!"

The Ranger powered his sword on residual charge and sliced Alarcon's head from his shoulders. Forming the base of a bloody fountain, the Shuar's body collapsed into the muck of the jungle floor.

While Watanabe stared stupefied at the Ranger, a peculiar confusion came into Bucaram's eyes as they flicked nervously between his dead comrade and the jungle. To Fragger, it looked as if the Shuar couldn't decide whether to drop to his knees to mourn his friend or flee in terror.

What the hell? Fragger wondered. *I expected Bucaram to come right after me to avenge Alarcon. This hellhound must be something to reckon with.*

Watanabe shouted at the Ranger, "What did you do that for?"

"I did it, you imbecile, because we've got a mission here, and all you can think about is avenging an insult to personal honor. You've got the brains of a rock, you know that?"

Watanabe's face purpled to the point where Fragger thought the man's head would detonate into fragments like a grenade. The Ricer raised his sword, and Fragger matched the move, but neither soldier had time to engage because a snarling blur exploded into their midst, knocking both of them to the ground while Bucaram fled screaming from the clearing.

The Ranger rolled to his feet, sword at the ready, and got his first clear look at the animal tearing apart Alarcon's corpse while maintaining a nearly subsonic rumble of a growl at anyone who might try to share in its prize.

"Damn!" he swore as he took in a blood-matted head twice the size of a mastiff's. The hellhound was definitely canine in origin, but it looked like an insane breeder had crossed a hyena with an insane human mind and thrown in a bit of tiger just to spice up the mix to create a living definition of instant, slavering death.

Fragger glanced over at Watanabe who was also at the ready and repeated, "Damn!" He hoped his eyes weren't as wide as sergeant's which showed more white than Fragger thought possible.

In a low, strained voice, Watanabe said, "Alarcon never killed that thing with a knife."

"Not a chance," Fragger agreed as he watched the predator tear out the organs from Alarcon's stomach and gulp them down. "He was a bullshit artist, that's for sure, and got what he deserved."

Watanabe beat the Ranger to the obvious question. "What do we do now, Rerun?"

"Don't take your eyes off him and back away."

"Think it'll work?"

"If we were back on Earth, I'd say 'Yes'. Here, I don't know. May depend on how hungry he is. Buurk, goddamn it, snap out of it unless you want to end up as lunch meat. Back away so we're between you and this beast."

His command startled Buurk out of a wide-eyed stare at the predator facing them. The Martian retreated slowly toward the edge of the clearing.

Watching the hellhound rip Alarcon's flesh from the bone while it kept intelligent and calculating eyes shifting among its three potential victims, Fragger had the uncomfortable feeling the dead Shuar was merely serving as an appetizer to the main course. A second later, the feeling became a certainty as the hound sniffed at Alarcon's head, bit off the nose, then with unbelievable speed, launched itself at Watanabe in a shrewd feint that caused the sergeant to swing wildly and miss while stumbling backward and windmilling his arms to keep his balance. The beast swiveled about instantly and launched another attack at the fallen Ricer.

Fear drove Fragger into action and, for the first time, he felt his mind consciously drive him into the teleportation mode. He met the hound in mid-leap with his sword. The blade cut through one paw and gouged deep into the predator's muscled chest. Momentum drove both of them to the ground. Fragger leaped to his feet, wishing he could clap his hands over his ears to block out the terrible sound of the hound's agony.

But what I really wish is that the power sword had killed the damned beast! he thought as he took in the amazing fact that the predator was up and attacking despite the bloody gash and missing forepaw. Fragger accelerated again, relishing the power, and this time aimed a stroke at the dog's intact front leg. The leg tumbled to the ground along with the hound who howled out his pain. The Ranger ended its torment with a straight thrust to the heart and felt a moment's pity as the dog's body quivered spasmodically into death.

An ashen-faced Watanabe grinned weakly at Fragger. "Rerun, I'm sure as hell glad you've got that MASER ability."

"Me too," the Ranger answered, his body twitching almost as badly as the hellhound's as he relaxed out of his accelerated state. To keep his mind off the trembling, he looked about the clearing and asked, "Where's Bucaram?"

Watanabe shook his head, then shouted the Shuar's name several times. Lunatic bird calls from the jungle were the only answer.

"Gone." Fragger said.

"Yeah, off to alert his tribe, I suppose."

"Fanfuckingtastic! Now we not only have to dodge the drones and hounds but take on the natives as well."

"Things couldn't get much worse, could they, Rerun?" Watanabe said.

"I know one thing that would make the situation better."

"What's that?"

"Stop calling me 'Rerun'. That's not my name."

"But you *are* a Rerun."

"No, I'm not! I'm sick and tired of that insult! I am *not* a frigging Rerun, Watanabe. I'm Sergeant First Class Fragger Sparks, a Ranger and a non-commissioned officer of the U. S. Army."

"Not any more, you're not!" Watanabe retorted. "There is no U.S. Army and you were revived so that makes you a Rerun."

Fragger glowered at the Ricer, frustrated by his inability to penetrate the man's prejudice. He decided to try a frontal assault on Watanabe's attitude with an example from the past. "You know, my countrymen had racial terms for your ancestors during our Second World War on Terra. Nips. Slant Eyes. Little Yellow Bastards. We thought you were inferior little monkeys."

Watanabe snorted in disbelief. "You're making that up."

"Not a chance. We also kicked Japan's ass, and I'm willing to kick your ass right here and now unless you stop calling me 'Rerun'. I'll gut you like I did this deranged dog."

Watanabe bristled, but looked down at the eviscerated hound and nodded his reluctant agreement. "All right then, what do you want me to call you?"

"Sparks. Fragger. Ranger. Anything but 'Rerun'."

"Sparks it is, then. Now what do we--."

"One more thing," Fragger interrupted. "Do not--I repeat--do not ever go off half-cocked again like you did with Alarcon. We need each other alive if we're going to survive, you silly bastard. I need somebody with a cool head who can't be tricked into a stupid duel to prove who's the best man. I need a right-hand man I can count on."

Watanabe raised an eyebrow. "Right-hand man? Who made you leader?"

"I did. If I can't count on you, we part ways right here and now."

"That'd be stupid, Sparks. This place is bad enough facing it together. Going it alone would be suicide."

"Exactly," Fragger confirmed. "But if you stick with me and lose your temper again, I'll kill you myself, is that clear? You know I can do it. I'll never be the swordsman you are, but, with my special ability, I don't have to be, do I?"

Watanabe didn't flinch, but acceptance came into his eyes as Fragger held his gaze and let the sergeant see the certainty in a Ranger's mind. In that quick exchange of glances, everything that needed to be said was said.

"All right, then," Fragger said to get Watanabe focused on the job at hand, "what do you think our next move should be?"

"Back into the suits, definitely. If another hellhound or a pack of them sets upon us and we're not armored, we're dead meat."

"Agreed, but have we got enough power to find the Shuar without Bucaram's help?"

"Reru--Sparks, how the hell do I know?"

"Can we track him?"

"I doubt it. On the ground, the jungle is just as confusing to our sensors as it is to those recon drones trying to find us."

"We know the general direction they were heading," Fragger said.

"But do we want to meet up with Bucaram's people at all?" Watanabe asked. "They'll be just as willing to kill us as our off-world enemies."

"True," Fragger admitted, "however, if Bucaram and Alarcon's attitudes are any indication, then the headhunters will respect a display of power. I think we have a couple tokens of that power here."

Watanabe followed the direction of Fragger's gaze toward the ground where the bodies of Alarcon and the hellhound lay, then chuckled.

"Which head do you want?" the Ranger asked.

Watanabe flashed a wicked, satisfied smile and answered, "Alarcon's, of course."

CHAPTER 37

Nauseated by the bloody heads carried by Watanabe and Fragger, Buurk irrationally insisted on leading the group into the jungle so he wouldn't have to look at the sight. Recognizing shock when he saw it, the Ranger let the medic stumble through the mucky vegetation for half an hour. When the Martian finally sank to the ground in exhaustion, Fragger played his trump card.

"Buurk, you can sit there and wait for the hellhounds to come eat you or you can hop on my back and survive another day to give Watanabe and me shit about our savage ways. It's your choice."

Buurk didn't answer, but made a weak gesture of assent with a muddy and leech-covered hand. Fragger reached out with the glove of his powered armor and lifted the medic easily onto his back.

"Hang on," Fragger advised, "and keep your head low. We're going to try to make some speed."

The Ranger strode forward again into the jungle of Jivaro, scanning the bush for signs of the hellhounds and the canopy above for signs of the tireless recon drones. Every time Fragger or Watanabe powered up their swords to cut through particularly thick foliage, one of the drones would pop up, forcing them to switch back into standby mode until the machine got confused by the endlessly conflicting signals generated by millions of acres of jungle eating at its innards to produce more jungle. Fragger was simultaneously grateful to the wild landscape and tired of the constant obstacles it placed in their way. Even in the power suit, he found it as bad as walking through mud simply because it took so much time. When they did run into actual mud, it became like treading through molasses. Buurk's complaints about the severed heads thumping against the suit belts added to the fatigue. Fragger resisted the temptation to fling the medic straight out into the jungle and let him take his chances with the hellhounds, but contented himself with a light poke to the Martian's chin to let him know that the bitching wasn't appreciated.

It wasn't until two days later that Fragger realized that he *did* appreciate Buurk's whining. It had kept him focused on the trek through the jungle simply so he wouldn't have to listen to the medic anymore.

It was either forge ahead or kill the Martian on the spot, Fragger thought, doing some grumbling of his own as he lifted his head to a familiar scent that the suit filtered into the helmet.

"Smoke?" he asked. "Do you smell smoke, Watanabe?"

"Yeah, we're near Shuar for sure, Sparks. How should we approach them?"

"Directly, I guess. They probably already know we're here," Fragger answered. "We haven't exactly been quiet in these suits. They'd have to be deaf not to have heard us."

"I'm sure Bucaram made them aware of our presence," Watanabe suggested.

"No doubt about that. What kind of weapons can they bring to bear, do you think?"

"Nothing I can think of that could dent a power suit."

"Well, if you were one of the tribe, what would you do?" Fragger asked.

"Run like hell and hide or try to get us out of the suits so I could deal with us on an equal footing."

"Right," Fragger agreed, "which means we stay inside the suits at all costs."

"Yes, definitely."

"Well, man, let's find the village and raise a little hell to get their attention."

Half a klick into the jungle, attention came to them.

Fragger heard something clink against his armored leg and knew instantly, *Mine!*

A muffled "whummp!" sounded underfoot, but did nothing more than lift his foot off the ground.

"You okay?" he asked Buurk.

"Yeah, yeah!" the medic shouted from the back of suit where he still clung tightly about the neck of the armor. "Don't put me down, though! Just don't put me down on the ground!"

Damn, but these armored suits are good! Fragger thought. *Wish we'd had them back in my time. It would have saved the amputation of a lot of legs.*

Before the Ranger had any more time to lose in admiration of the technology he was wearing, shots pelted against his armor as if someone had fired a shotgun. Checking his sensors, he saw that again no damage had been done.

"What are they firing?" he asked Watanabe.

"Anything they've got, I suppose," the Ricer answered. "Flechette weapons, pulse weapons. Nothing that can penetrate armor. Doing the best they can with what they've got."

Fronds rustled ahead, and Fragger squared himself to give Buurk maximum protection. This time, several weapons fired and a hail of rounds struck against the suit. Fragger leaped forward, swinging his sword. Figures came out of hiding and ran the other way. The Ranger pursued for a short distance along a mucky trail, then stopped to listen. Immediately, another fusillade broke out.

"This is getting tedious," Watanabe said from behind him. "Let me take a few of them out, and we'll be rid of the problem."

The sergeant sped by Fragger without further word. Afraid to expose Buurk to further fire, the Ranger kept his position. Watanabe's sword hummed to life as he disappeared into the bush in pursuit of the attackers. A thought nagged at Fragger's mind until it burst into full realization.

This is too easy!

"Watanabe! It's a trap! Break contact with the enemy now!"

"Oh shit!" answered him over the commlink.

"What's your situation?" Fragger asked.

"Oh, shit!" came again.

"Damn it, Watanabe! Give me an answer. Are you hurt?"

"No, Sparks, but I'm not going anywhere, either. Clever bastards. Come ahead, but do it carefully. I'm about 20 meters in front of you."

Fragger followed the instructions, keeping an eye out for the headhunters until he pushed through vines and saw Watanabe up to his neck in mud.

The Ranger laughed. "You dumb Ricer! And here I thought you were in real trouble."

"Sparks, I *am* in trouble."

"What do you mean?"

"I'm sinking into this muck."

"So?"

"So, Bucaram and his people have probably dug one hell of a deep hole, and that means I'm sinking in over my head."

"Well, when you hit bottom, walk on out of there," Fragger said.

"Sparks, even a power suit has its limitations. This stuff is like glue. It's working its way into the joints. When I hit bottom, I will be able to move for a while. But, it's going to take all the power I have, and I guarantee you I'm going to end up dead down there. In fact, I'd already be down at the bottom if I didn't have something to stand on."

"Stand on?" Fragger responded. "If you can stand on something, why not just work your way to dry land?"

"Because whatever it is, it keeps moving. I can't keep my footing for very long."

The snickering voice of Bucaram shouted from the bush, "You're standing on the head of one of our enemies, Watanabe, and you're going to join him soon! But, you'll be glad to know that I'll rescue your head from the mud so it can adorn my belt in payment for Alarcon's death."

"Damn!" Fragger swore. "Okay, Watanabe, just hang on. I'll get you out."

"Get down," he ordered Buurk, who refused in a panic, shouting, "Fragger, I can't! There might be more mines!"

"I'll take care of it," the Ranger said and stomped a good area of vegetation flat. When there were no explosions, he ordered Buurk down again, and the Martian obeyed, dropping to a prone position to avoid enemy fire. Fragger searched the surroundings until he found a small tree. He toppled it with a single stroke of his sword, then carried it to the mud hole and dropped it across close to Watanabe. The sergeant was quick in locking his arms about the trunk.

"Can you pull yourself out now?" Fragger asked. Shots rang against his suit again, but he ignored them as he waited for an answer.

"I can, Sparks, but this stuff is so thick I'm afraid I'll lose all power and the armor will be useless."

"I'll drop some more trees," Fragger said. "That'll give you more leverage. Work your way up onto them a little at a time, okay?"

Watanabe nodded his muddy helmet, and the Ranger set to work again slicing down trees while rounds hit his suit and whined off into the jungle, complaining of their inability to penetrate the armor.

"Won't they ever stop?" he heard the medic moan.

"What are you complaining about, Buurk? They're shooting at me, not you."

"Fragger, you sonuvabitch! I'm not wearing armor!"

"Sorry, Buurk. In my day, there was no armor so I keep thinking that I'm in the same danger as you. Just keep your head low, and I'll get us all out of here."

Fragger appreciated the medic's position. All it would take was one stray round, and Buurk would be hellhound food. But there was nothing he could do about the Martian's situation so he continued to drop the tree trunks across the mud trap. Watanabe grabbed at each log, gaining purchase an inch at a time only to lose two. It was clear the trooper would need more help, but when Fragger heard Buurk scream from behind, he realized that the tribe was directing its fire away from him and at the medic. As he hesitated, Bucaram's voice shouted out again from the jungle, "Give up, Sparks! You can't cover Buurk forever and even if you try, then the Ricer goes down!"

"Bucaram, you bastard!" Watanabe yelled in a panting curse. "Kill the sonuvabitch, Sparks, and I'll gladly sink to the bottom of this trap."

"Oh, shut up!" Fragger ordered, quickly sorting out his options.

'Surrender, Sparks!" Bucaram shouted again. "Or I'll give the order to take out Buurk. You can't be two places at once."

The Shuar's last remark gave the Ranger the opening he was looking for. *He didn't see me kill the hellhound in MASER mode!*

Fragger realized. *He was too busy running. For all practical purposes, I can be two places at once.*

Fragger detached the hellhound's head from his belt and held it high. "See this, Bucaram? Call off your attack, or I'll add your head to my collection!"

Come on, Bucaram, open your big mouth again so I can locate your position.

Laughter erupted from the jungle, and a burst of automatic weapon fire pinged off Fragger's armor.

"You think I'm shitting you?" the Ranger shouted.

"You think *I'm* not serious?" Bucaram responded. "You killed my friend!"

"Your friend deserved to die."

"He was Alarcon, a brave man and a Shuar!" Bucaram bellowed. "He didn't deserve to die the way you kill him. He killed a hellhound by himself!"

Putting as much sneer into his voice as he could muster, Fragger shouted back, "Alarcon? Are we talking about the same man? Bucaram, there's no way he could have killed a hellhound with a knife, and you know it. Hell, he couldn't have killed one if he had a whole army behind him."

Taking a stab in the dark, the Ranger added, "You never saw him kill that hound, did you, Bucaram? I'll bet he just walked back into the village one day and told you that he'd done it, and you decided to believe him, you gullible fool."

Gotcha! Fragger thought as the jungle grew quiet for a moment before Bucaram's head popped into sight with a PPC rifle aimed straight at Buurk. The Ranger accelerated into the line of fire. The suit took the full blast of the weapon without effect. The Ranger grabbed the astonished Shuar by the throat and was back to his original spot before Bucaram had time to start choking. Fragger dropped the man to the ground, lifted him again by the seat of his pants and held him squawking and sputtering over the mud-choked hole.

"If Watanabe dies, Bucaram joins him!" Fragger yelled at the attackers. "Then I come after the rest of you and hunt you down so I can stake you out for the hellhounds to find. Is that clear?"

When no response came, he shouted again, "Is that clear?"

Slowly, figures rose out of the bush.

Fragger pointed at the base of a tree. "Drop your weapons over there and get to work. Pull my buddy out of that trap."

When they hesitated, Fragger dropped Bucaram into the mud hole. "Now you have two people to rescue. I'll add more if you don't get your hind ends in gear."

Headhunters rushed from the jungle, dropped their weapons by the tree, and hurried to the mud trap. When a rope appeared in the hands of one of the Shuar, Fragger said, "Get Watanabe out of there first. Better hurry or Bucaram will be breathing nothing but mud."

The rope was tossed quickly out to Watanabe. The Ricer grabbed it with an armored hand, then hung on as several grunting tribe members pulled him slowly from the trap. Near the edge, Watanabe found footing and stumbled free.

"You're a sloppy disgrace to soldiering," Fragger said with a grin, unable to resist a jab at the mud-caked trooper.

"Shut your mouth!" Watanabe replied in an irritable growl.

A moment later, a sputtering Bucaram was hauled out of the hole. Watanabe pulled Alarcon's head from his belt and tossed it down next to the Shuar.

"Alarcon sends you his greetings from the afterworld," the Ricer said. "Care to join him, Bucaram?"

"No!"

"Care to join *us*?" Fragger asked.

At this invitation, Bucaram's face grew impassive, blocking clues to his emotional reaction to the unexpected turn of events. Both he and Fragger knew there could be only one answer, but the Shuar needed to retain the respect of his men, and the Ranger was happy to grant him the opportunity to save face.

I need his help, and I'm certainly not going to jeopardize the chance to bring good jungle fighters over to my side, Fragger thought. *Unless I miss my guess, I simply have to play out a short game of negotiation, and Bucaram will bring his men under my command*

While the Ranger waited patiently for Bucaram to speak, he studied the warrior. The man had the brown skin and high cheekbones of all Shuar. The jet black hair was cut straight so that it hung just below the cheekbones. Bangs hung down over the forehead close to bushy black eyebrows. Thick eyelashes covered slitted eyelids, giving the impression that Bucaram peered at the world from a thicket of hair. The nose flared like the blade of a plow. Beneath the nose, a full mouth curled upward to the right. It gave the Shuar a permanent sneer above a strong chin.

I suspect the sneer would be there anyway if it hadn't occurred naturally, Fragger thought. *He may have earned the right to sneer. It takes courage for an unarmored man to take on the likes of Watanabe and me. Plus, I never paid much attention to that necklace he's wearing, assuming it was some sort of tribal decoration. But it's made of croc teeth and hellhound fangs!*

Bucaram broke his silence, saying, "I am an *uwishin.* That could be of help to you."

"A what?" Fragger asked when his translator failed to provide a definition.

"A wise elder," the Shuar explained. "A shaman. A shapeshifter."

"That means you have influence among all your tribes?"

"Yes," Bucaram said.

"Enough influence to convince them to join us to fight the Corpse and Ricer forces and whoever else there is circling this planet?"

As Bucaram wiped mud from his face, he shook his head and admitted, "Perhaps not that much influence. We don't challenge the great nation-systems. It's suicide."

"Probably," Fragger agreed. "Of course, your options are kind of limited. Either I kill you right now or you fight with me. Seems to me, the first option doesn't offer you much. But, if you fight alongside me, you just might live through it all."

Bucaram shrugged. "If I choose to fight with you, what difference will it make? The Shuar tribes are few compared to the forces of the enemy. How can we fight thousands of armored soldiers and vehicles and have any hope of surviving?"

"You'll just have to leave that up to Watanabe and me. Right now, we want food and a safe place to hide from the drones."

"Food we have," Bucaram said, then continued bitterly, "but no village to go to. After I escaped, my comrades found me and told me their news. Your enemies burned our homes. They said they would be back to kill every tenth person if we did not locate you for them. That's why we attacked."

"Bucaram, I'm sorry you and your people are suffering, but, here's the important point to remember--Watanabe and I aren't going to give ourselves up. So you're going to lose those people anyway when the enemy comes looking for us unless you bring the tribal members out into the jungle to join our force."

Watanabe jumped in, "Personally, I think Sparks is crazy. But, there's no love lost between your people and the Corpses and the Imperial Commonwealth and all the other powers, is there? At least, we're giving you a chance to fight back."

Bucaram gave a derisive laugh. "Some chance."

"It's a better chance than you think," Fragger said. "There's nothing more difficult to fight than a guerrilla war, especially on tough ground, and this is definitely tough ground--take it from an old jungle fighter. My country fought a group called the Viet Cong. With all our military might, we couldn't really defeat them."

Of course, I won't mention that the VC believed in what they were fighting for, unlike this situation. We'll be lucky if the Shuar don't end up shooting us in the back.

Bucaram finally shrugged in acquiescence. "What choice do we have?"

"None," Fragger said. "Look at it this way, though. Stick with us and there's always the chance of gaining wealth like you never dreamed of."

Interest gleamed in Bucaram's eyes as he looked the Ranger full in the face for the first time. "What kind of wealth?"

"Armored suits, vehicles, weapons, ships with all their contents," Fragger answered. "Who knows how much is out there? But all the spoils of war are available for your taking if you've got the balls to fight."

"These spoils of war—what percentage of it goes to me and my people?"

Fragger was tempted to say the tribe could have it all, but sensed Bucaram wouldn't have any respect for a man who didn't claim a healthy share of confiscated goods. "Sixty percent for Watanabe, Buurk and me; the rest to your tribe."

"Forty percent?" Bucaram cried. "That's all? Forty percent when we would be doing all the work? Where's the justice?"

Fragger suppressed a smile at the false indignation and answered, "All right, sixty-five percent for us; thirty-five percent for the tribe."

"What? That's even worse!"

"Okay, then seventy percent for us and--."

Bucaram held up his hands. "All right, all right. Forty percent for us and sixty percent for the greedy. This is all a fantasy, anyway. How do we fight the Ricers and Corpses and God and everyone else? We haven't got the arms to stand up to the kind of weaponry they can muster against us."

Fragger replied, "First, we disappear. Second, we harass, steal arms and disappear. Third, we reappear and defeat them on our terms."

"Easily said," Bucaram responded. "Not easily done."

I don't feel all that confident about success myself, the Ranger admitted. *But I have no intention of letting my doubts show.*

"No, it won't be easily done," he told Bucaram. "But our war will succeed."

"How do you know that?" the Shuar demanded. "How do you know it will be successful?"

"It's simple. It will succeed because our enemies haven't faced Fragger Sparks before."

CHAPTER 38

"They're coming!" Watanabe announced as he plopped down into the muddy water next to Fragger. "It took them six months, but they finally caught up with us."

"Good," the Ranger answered as he checked the positions of his troops via hand signals. He'd ordered complete commlink silence to avoid detection by the efficient combined Ricer and Corpse forces. The hand signaling was a crude system and the day's strong winds whipping the tropical vegetation about made the process more difficult than usual. Thrown down in bucketsful by low clouds, the afternoon rain didn't help signaling, either. Fragger blessed the elements, anyway. The use of chemical and biological weapons was an impossibility in this weather.

Of course, the weather isn't all good. B*eing in Jivaro's thickest swamp is like living inside a giant fart with all the methane rolling off the rotting vegetation. The smell is awful.*

Watanabe picked a six-inch leech off his muck-smeared arm and complained, "I still don't like being out of my suit."

"Me, neither. But you'll stay alive longer without it in this particular battle."

"Was all this mud smearing really necessary?" Watanabe complained again. "I smell as bad as this swamp."

"Keeps the swarmbugs off and confuses the sensors, doesn't it?" Fragger answered, realizing the sergeant's bitching was just nerves before the battle. "Put on another layer of muck, and maybe you'll live forever."

"Funny, Sparks, funny. These damned leeches will have all my blood before the enemy does."

"You know, it's a wonder you've survived this long as a soldier, Watanabe. What'd you do to your enemies before Jivaro? Talk them all to death?"

Watanabe chuckled at Fragger's thrust and settled into a position to scan the swamp area ahead of them. "This is a good spot. I couldn't have chosen better myself."

Fragger replied with a dry "Thank you" that amused Watanabe further, then returned to his check of the ambush site. After quizzing Bucaram and other knowledgeable Shuar, the Ranger had found they all agreed that the Yacuambi Triangle was the absolutely worst area on the planet. It was swampy, mucky, and accessible only by hand-paddled pirogue or powered fan-floater. Now that they'd fought through skirmishes with the enemy, proto-crocs, and hellhound packs and settled into position, Fragger knew only too well that the Shuar hadn't been exaggerating about the difficulty of the terrain. Nobody but him was too happy about it.

They're all tired, hungry, and scared out of their wits about going up against veteran troops, but one taste of victory will go a long way toward taking care of that.

It had taken some scouting to find the perfect place--a boggy V-shaped channel off the Lon River with the narrow end pointed inland. Fragger had stationed his troops along each leg of the V with strict orders not to fire until the signal was given. At the point farthest away from the river where there was a slight hook to the left, he'd lashed his power armor to a junglewood tree, and Watanabe had programmed it to emit intermittent signals as might be given by a faulty suit or a trooper trying not to give away his position. The sergeant had placed his own armor farther back with the same programming in order to create the illusion that he and Fragger were communicating with each other.

A frantic hand signal from Bucaram jerked Fragger out of his thoughts and back to the present. He looked in the direction of the Shuar's pointing hand, saw nothing, but heard the faint hiss of enemy floaters as they skimmed along the yellow-brown surface of the Lon. Sternly, he signaled back to the excited Bucaram to stay quiet. He'd impressed upon all the tribal members that to attack prematurely was to invite instant death, but since he'd never been in combat with any one of them before, he had minimal confidence in their ability to follow orders.

It's the best way to enter into a fight, he assured himself. *That way, you won't be relying on support you might not get.*

The hissing grew into the breathy buzz of drive fans carrying heavy loads. Fragger kept his eyes fixed on the point around which the enemy had to come. In a couple of minutes, a scout floater buzzed into sight. The Ranger asked Watanabe for an assessment of its capabilities and troop-carrying capacity.

"A 20-troop floater," the sergeant answered. "PPC cannons fore and aft, medium armor. Standard Corpse model but with mixed Corpse and Imperial Commonwealth armored troops, some equipped with jump packs. Interesting. They're working together even more closely than I thought. Likely have two light mortars and one crew-served weapon per unit."

"How many floaters total, do you think?" Fragger asked.

"Hard to tell. If they think we're important enough--and they obviously do--they might have dispatched several floater platoons."

"Good," Fragger said. "I hope they sent as many as possible."

Watanabe raised a questioning eyebrow at this remark. "I like honor as much as the next man, but aren't you being a little over-enthusiastic about facing too many of the enemy?"

"Agincourt," Fragger replied.

"What?"

"Never mind. Wait and see, Watanabe, wait and see. Just get busy and make sure Bucaram and the others stay down until I give the order to attack. Execute the plan *exactly* as I say. If you don't, we could end up as carrion."

Watanabe rose and slopped off into the mud without further questions.

Fragger nodded his head in approval of the sergeant as he turned his attention back to the enemy. *The man's a good soldier, and I'm glad to have him at my side.*

As more floaters came into view, the Ranger could see that their V-formation matched the shape of the channel and provided maximum firepower coverage. Beneath the floater skirts, powerful fans churned the water into a nervous frenzy. A gimbel-mounted PPC cannon flared as a gunner spat red fire toward signals emanating from Fragger's and Watanabe's suits. The burst chewed up jungle in a vicious, shredding sound.

When the gunner let up on the trigger, Fragger held his breath for a moment. *Don't panic,* he urged his troops silently, *it's only a probe!*

A second burst rang out, chattering across the water.

Silence came from the bush, and Fragger relaxed as the firing ceased and his men remained in position. When he heard the revving up of fans from beyond the point, he realized a signal had been passed to the enemy's rear elements. A second later, the rest of the floaters roared into sight.

Fragger's spirits rose as his count of the vessels topped forty, crowding in on each other in a scramble to put the troops onto shore and into the chase. The Ranger never let the landings occur. He rose, stationed himself behind a tree and then drew his hand across his throat several times in both directions to make sure the "Execute" command was understood. Shuar warriors on either side of him repeated the gesture back to him to confirm that the order was understood, then turned and passed the order down the line. A few seconds later, light weapons fire erupted from the jungle aimed at the rearmost floaters.

Watanabe had told him there wasn't much damage they could do to the Imperial Commonwealth or Corpse vessels, and the first results of the fusillade proved him right. PPC rounds bounced off the powered troopers and pinged harmlessly off the floaters' armored skirts.

Thank god, there's more than one way to defeat a powerful enemy, Fragger thought as he raised his hand and gave a second command. The results came almost immediately and undramatically. From the jungle, Fragger heard the muffled explosions of the crude, rock-filled claymores he'd jerry-rigged just below the surface of the river, aiming their faces upward. Beneath the skirts of the floaters, water roiled, then the scream of shattered fan blades shrieked across the water.

Well, it isn't exactly the shit hitting the fan, but the results are pretty good, Fragger decided with satisfaction as some of the floaters skittered across the surface, lost power and dumped the occupants into the water. Unbalanced and out of control, other machines got away from their drivers and slammed into other floaters crowding the channel. Everywhere Fragger looked, powered troopers dropped into the river and floundered in the sucking mud of the bottom. Some disappeared instantly; others kept their heads above water and tried to force their way toward shore.

"Now, aren't you glad I had you test it out, Watanabe?" Fragger said to the absent trooper. Watanabe had not been at all happy about being "volunteered" for another dunk in the Lon's mud to see if it would hamper powered armor as effectively as the mud in the Shuar trap had done. To the Ranger's delight--and Watanabe's irritation--the river's mud proved to be even more potent. It clogged the suits like glue and had taken the sergeant hours to clean it out.

Fragger set his sights on accomplishing the third objective of his ambush. His forces were still no match for powered armor if any number of the troops got to shore, so he had to make sure few of them reached solid ground. Not having the luxury of the English archers at Agincourt of standing off and launching arrows at a foe mired in mud, the Ranger had settled on the next best course. He gave another signal, and his forces shifted from a concentrated volley to sustained fire designed to keep the trapped enemy forces too busy to notice the pirogues launched from shore with Shuar volunteers. They'd thought he was crazy when he armed them with buckets of a mud-sand mixture he'd concocted, but he'd pointed out that an enemy trooper who couldn't see anything through his visor was a useless trooper.

Bending low, the Shuar paddlers raced their dug-out canoes into the midst of the Ricer and Corpse forces. A PPC blast tore the lead pirogue apart, but the recoil of the weapon dunked the trooper under water and when he came up, the next pirogue threw the cement-like mixture straight into his helmet visor. Unable to see, the disoriented trooper fired wildly, then went under water again.

"It's the little things that kill you," Fragger murmured into the noise. "Always the little things." Then the Ranger added a reminder he intended to keep permanently branded into his thinking,

"That, plus the overconfidence that superior weaponry can give you."

Proto-crocs surfaced in the middle of the melee, snapping up bloody Shuar body parts from around the capsized first pirogue. They were no danger to the mired troopers, but Fragger worried that the spreading blood might provoke the crocs into attacking his own men.

Those reptiles are damned near as big as one of the pirogues. If one of them gets a tail into a canoe, the crew will go into the drink for sure.

Looking like a cross between a Komodo dragon and the biggest crocodile the Ranger had ever seen, the proto-crocs possessed the speed of a torpedo and, like that weapon, detonated on contact with prey.

Fragger relaxed momentarily when he saw the Shuar warriors paddle quickly away from the proto-crocs to wait for the predators to settle down. From the number of missing toes and fingers he'd seen on tribe members, the Ranger knew the Shuar had developed a healthy respect for the beasts. He was glad to see that common sense attitude take effect in the middle of the battle confusion

It bodes well for their future. Ninety percent of survivability on the battlefield is staying calm. Maybe I do have the makings of an army here.

The Ranger hadn't been so sure in his short travels with the Shuar. They tended to prize individuality above all else and, other than in hunting and in initially trying to kill him and Watanabe, teamwork was a nearly foreign concept to them.

I'll kill them credit for persistence, though, Fragger thought. *They certainly made enough attempts to kill me and Watanabe.*

Recognizing that Buurk was both harmless and valuable as a medic, the Shuar had left the Martian alone and come after Fragger and Watanabe. It'd been up to the two soldiers to demonstrate that they possessed the first of two qualities the headhunters respected--strength. After ten heads had adorned the ends of power swords, the Shuar warriors had realized that the two off-worlders had the will to decimate the entire tribe without breaking much of a sweat, and they had settled down into a sullen acceptance of foreign leadership.

Today, Fragger was demonstrating the second thing they respected--success. Showing a patience he didn't think they had, the Shuar held off until the proto-crocs disappeared, then paddled back to the floundering and sunken armored troopers and did exactly as the Ranger had asked them to do--slap mud on the visors of their enemies and attach small orange-flagged poles to the armor by any means possible to mark the spot where each blinded trooper was immobilized. Fragger had no intention of losing any of the powered armor to the river because the suits would give them a semblance of equal footing in conflicts to come.

A gleeful whoop broke though Fragger's thoughts. He turned to see Bucaram burst out of the jungle jabbing his arms into the air in triumph. A more subdued Watanabe followed behind, but the grin creasing his muddy features said everything that needed to be said about his mood.

"Good work!" Fragger shouted.

"'Good work'?" Bucaram said in mock anger. "'Good work? That's the best you can say? It was better than good! It was damned fine work, that's what it was. Tell him, Watanabe!"

Watanabe laughed at Bucaram as the headhunter danced in the clearing, jabbing an imaginary sword at the trees as if they were the enemy. "I don't agree with this savage much, but he's right this time, Fragger. It was good work. And you know what?"

"What?" Fragger asked.

"It was the result of fine planning on your part."

Fragger acknowledged the compliment with a nod and asked, "Willing to admit now that Reruns know how to fight?"

"Well, maybe one Rerun does," the sergeant answered with a wink. "That's all I'm willing to concede at this point."

"Stick with me. You haven't seen half of what a Ranger can do."

"Keep it up, and you just might measure up to an Imperial Commonwealth trooper," Watanabe retorted.

Fragger chuckled. "Well, Ricer, do you want to stand here all day in a pissing contest as to which of us is the better man or shall we finish the job we began?"

"Finish the job, of course. What needs to be done?"

"First, I want you to program some of those floaters to broadcast a 'hot pursuit' message, then send them on their way to give the enemy a false trail and buy us some time. When you're done with that, have Bucaram find a couple of pirogues and lash them together. I want you to get your armor on and have him take you out on the river to those trapped soldiers."

"Why?" Watanabe asked.

"Use your commlink to find their suit frequencies and give those men a choice. They can either die in their suits, or they can get out of them and have two options--brave the jungle alone or join us."

Watanabe nodded and slopped off through the mud to pull Bucaram away from his celebration. The two men headed toward the river. Minutes later, Fragger saw a double-pirogue glide out from shore. The armored Watanabe stood atop the craft, distributing his weight across the bows of the two lashed-together boats. Following the Ranger's instructions, the sergeant first located several floaters and programmed them for random movement. After they'd been sent on their way, Watanabe worked his way from one trapped soldier to another. When he had agreement to Fragger's terms, Watanabe took the sword from the trooper and tied a rope about the armor. At his signal, Shuar warriors pulled the suit free of the muck and dragged the soldier to shore behind their pirogues. It was long and tedious work, but by sundown, Fragger's men had a large group of EarthCorp and Imperial Commonwealth troops huddled on shore, intimidated by their loss of armor and threats of throwing them to the proto-crocs by their Shuar captors.

Fragger cupped his hands and hollered out to Watanabe whose pirogue floated close to shore underneath the branch of a junglewood tree, "How many left?"

"Three," Watanabe answered. "We'll have two up in no time."

"What's the problem with the third man?"

"You want his exact words?"

Fragger's first impulse was to say "Not really" and tell Watanabe to leave the stupid bastard stuck in the mud, but the suit was too important to lose, so he shrugged and answered, "Yeah, sure."

"The words are in Old Terran, but he insists that you'll understand them."

"Oh, for Christ's sake, just tell me!"

Watanabe answered, "His exact words are, 'Go fuck yourself, Rerun!' What does that mean?"

Fragger broke into laughter and answered, "It means you've got only one man in this godforsaken time who would know that phrase."

"Who?"

"Watanabe, he's your EarthCorp counterpart--a hairy-assed non-com who's stubborn as two Terran mules. You've got only one advantage over him."

"What's that?"

"Your breath is better."

"Huh?"

"Never mind. Just give Red Salinsky *my* exact words. Tell him that he'd better get out of that suit before the *gark* fumes kill him."

After a moment, Watanabe relayed Salinsky's reply. "He says he's not surrendering to anybody, much less a Rerun."

"How much power does he have left?"

"I'd say he's good for another 12-14 hours."

"Post a couple of guards just in case and let him stew about it overnight. When morning comes, he'll see things in a different light."

Despite the success of the battle, Fragger shook as the adrenaline rush finally left him. He sat down hard and remained silent for a long time until the celebrating Bucaram brought him a skin flask of the vile local brew with a name that translated as "crocshit." Fragger eyed the flask warily. To keep his mind clear, he'd avoided alcohol up until this point. He started to hand it back to Bucaram, but thought better of it.

After all I've gone through, I'm due for some R&R even it's only out of a Shuar flask, Fragger rationalized. *I've survived being naked in space, being shot at...tortured...Lesto and Mars...and a jungle that stinks worse than Salinsky's breath. But, still, there's still work to be done. Now's no time to have a shot of the local liquor kill me.*

Fragger drank deeply anyway.

CHAPTER 39

A shudder woke Fragger into the clammy jungle sunrise. It started at his toes and worked its way up his body until it exploded out the top of his head. Then, a thousand hangover shock troops jumped into the hole in his skull and started beating his brain into jelly with rifle butts. The Ranger groaned and puked into the swamp. It didn't make him feel any better because the smell of vomit mixed with the rotten-egg stench of the puddle at his feet created an odor that made him heave again and again until his stomach finally gave up in exhaustion. Weak from the effort, Fragger sat up and squinted into the dim light filtering through thick fronds. Watanabe and Bucaram, seated side by side on a rotted junglewood stump, grinned at him.

Watanabe shook a gurgling skin of crocshit at him and asked, "Want a drink?"

Fragger tried to puke and came up dry. The two men laughed.

How the mighty have fallen down drunk, Fragger moaned as he held his head up with his hands to prevent it from rolling off into the swamp where it would never be found again.

"You'll never make a Shuar warrior," Bucaram said.

Fragger snarled, "Leave me alone."

"Can't do that," Watanabe said. "It's a new day, and we need to be in a different location before the enemy figures out we chopped up their forces."

The Ranger groaned but forced himself to his feet. His brain reeled at the effort. "All right, then, let's get the troops on the move."

"Aren't you forgetting something?" Watanabe asked.

"Man, this is no time for games. Just tell me what I forgot, get it done, and move out."

Watanabe pointed out toward the water and said, "Salinsky."

"Oh, yeah. Shit! You mean, he's still down there?"

"Yeah, I talked to him a few minutes ago."

"What did he say?"

Watanabe shrugged. "Same thing as yesterday."

"Obstinate idiot," Fragger swore.

"Just leave him," Bucaram suggested. "It's okay to die an honorable death, but anybody who's stupid enough to die that way deserves to be left in the mud. Me, I prefer to die in combat."

Despite the throbbing in his skull, Fragger managed to say, "That's not a bad idea. Offer Salinsky a chance at single combat, I mean."

Both Watanabe and Bucaram showed interest in the idea. "Is he any good?" Watanabe asked.

"I don't have a clue," the Ranger answered. "I wouldn't let a duel take place anyway."

"But you just said--"

"I said we'll offer him a chance. I didn't say we'd carry through with that offer."

"That's not very honorable," Watanabe said.

"In this case, screw honor," Fragger said. "I need all the good men I can get. I'm not going to take the chance of losing one and maybe two to serious wounds. I'd be a fool to let anybody fight. You want honor, fight the people chasing after us."

"Sensible," Bucaram said while Watanabe swallowed the idea as if he had tasted something bad and asked, "What if he won't fall for this trick?"

Fragger rubbed at his aching temples. "Then, we'll try something different. Watanabe, make the offer to Salinsky. I'll be down shortly for his answer."

As Watanabe headed off, Fragger hollered after him, "And find Buurk and take him with you in case Salinsky needs medical attention."

The Ranger turned his attention back to the Shuar and pleaded, "Bucaram, for God's sake, find somebody to get me some coffee."

The Shuar warrior looked blank. "Kaw-fee?"

"Oh, damn...I keep forgetting...you people don't have coffee here! Crap! Find me whatever it is you drink in the morning to get awake."

"We drink water," Bucaram said, looking with concern at the Ranger. "Just like always. Are you all right, Sparks?"

"I'm just fucking fine! I've got the worst hangover in the history of civilization, and I don't have any coffee."

"This kaw-fee, it cures the effects of drink?" the Shuar asked.

"No, it doesn't cure a thing, but it sure helps. Not talking helps too!" he snapped.

"Drink makes you mean, Sparks," Bucaram observed.

"No shit."

"I have something that will help."

"Just take me out and shoot me. That'll do the trick."

"Don't tempt me," the Shuar said.

Bucaram beckoned a warrior over and gave him a command. The man nodded, ran off, and returned quickly with a small pouch covered with proto-croc hide. Bucaram dug two small roots out of the pouch and handed them to the Ranger with the instructions, "Chew on these for a while, then take some water. That will ease your head."

"What are they?" Fragger asked as he took the roots in his hand and rubbed dirt from their wrinkled and spongy surfaces. They looked like off-color carrots left too long in the refrigerator.

"Headroots. Our women gather them for a drink cure."

The Ranger bit off one of the roots and chewed. The flesh had a bitter, aspirin-like taste. "Cure?" he complained. "There is nothing that cures a night of heavy drinking, except not drinking."

"Just keep chewing until it's all gone," the Shuar advised.

Fragger chewed while he grumbled, "You better not be poisoning me, Bucaram. On the other hand, I hope maybe you are."

The Shuar warrior laughed. "Poisoning is a woman's way, Sparks. If a Shuar wife wanted to kill you, that's how she would do it."

"Your First Wife wouldn't need poison, Bucaram. She could twist my head off with her bare hands."

"Don't I know it?" the Shuar said, rubbing at his neck. "She has given me many children and an equal amount of pain."

"Reduce the number of wives," Fragger suggested, continuing an argument they'd had all to the Yacuambi Triangle to pass time. "That should make her more pleasant."

"Never! A leader of a Shuar tribe is measured by the number of wives he has. To do otherwise would be suicide. He would be challenged all the time for being less than a man."

"Your First Wife calls you less than a man now. What's the difference?"

Bucaram burst into laughter again and conceded, "Good point, Sparks, very good point! But I miss her, I admit. It's been a long time since I've been in her arms."

Try not being in a woman's arms for several hundred years, Fragger thought, wishing the hangover would disappear. Then realization struck him. "Hey, my headache's going away!"

The Shuar warrior nodded. "I told you."

Fragger studied the remaining root and asked, "What's in this stuff?"

Bucaram offered a shrug.

"Good god, man, I'd be rich in my time if I had this root. Don't you sell it off-planet?"

Bitterness etched the Shuar's frowning mouth. "Yes, but we can only do it through EarthCorp or Imperial Commonwealth trading companies. They control the spaceways and the profit."

"You and your people would like to be free of them, then?" Fragger asked.

"That's a stupid question, Sparks. Of course, we'd like to be rid of them"

"What's stopped you so far?"

Bucaram sighed and explained, "We are too many different tribes with too many different ways. The Ashuar, the Aguaruna, the Huambisa--we have united in the past and have been successful on the battlefield, but once honor is satisfied, our alliances do not hold together. EarthCorp, the Imperial Commonwealth, they exploit this."

"Then as my old drill sergeant, Ed Wompner, used to tell me, 'It's time to get your shit together' because opportunity is staring you in the face."

"What does that mean?" Bucaram asked.

"It means we'll have to unite the tribes."

"They won't die for you, Sparks. You are not a tribal member."

"You're right, I'm not. I'm better than that."

Bucaram bristled at the remark.

"Relax," Fragger soothed. "What I meant was my MASER ability makes me tough to beat in single combat, so that's what we'll do--challenge the leaders to single combat one by one until they all fall in to line."

"Ambitious," the Shuar warrior said, "however, we are not out of the Yacuambi Triangle yet, and our off-world enemies have not given up the chase. In fact, there are soul-less Shuar on Jivaro who may have made alliance with the off-worlders."

"Bucaram, it'll be hard, I admit that, but we're the only ones here with the muscle, brains and cunning to accomplish a union. You like a challenge, don't you?"

"I like credits and profit," Bucaram groused, but Fragger saw the interest in the warrior's eyes.

"It'll be profit on a scale you never dreamed of," the Ranger promised.

"It could be death on a scale I never dreamed of, Sparks."

It was Fragger's turn to laugh. "And that's the idea you love best of all, isn't it, Bucaram?"

The warrior gave him a sly smile.

"I promise you this," Fragger said. "Follow me and I promise you either a glorious death or a fat, happy and rich old age with your wife, which is probably the same thing as death."

Bucaram cackled at this remark. He held up his hands and said, "I surrender, Sparks, to whatever you have planned. You are a man to follow if nothing more than the fact that you make my miserable life easier to bear."

The two sat talking until Watanabe returned.

"Well?" Fragger asked.

"Same answer. Salinsky says he's not going anywhere. Told both me and Buurk to 'fuck off'."

"Does he have enough power left to do anybody any damage?"

"Not likely. He's barely got enough for life support in that suit."

"Okay, then," Fragger said as he stood. "We'll do it the hard way. Find some rope."

"What are you going to do?"

"Haul his ass out of there, what else? Now get the rope and meet me where Salinsky is."

Watanabe obeyed and shortly they were at the river bank. A junglewood tree flared out over the water where Salinsky remained stuck under the surface. Fragger and a group of Shuar stood under the tree and watched Watanabe climb into the lashed-together pirogues. The sergeant worked his way out to the end until he reached the spot where an orange flag poked through the water, marking Salinsky's position.

Fragger ordered, "Secure that rope around Salinsky, then throw the other end up over that big branch above your head so we can grab it and haul him up."

Watanabe nodded and dove under the surface. He came up a minute later, clambered up onto the pirogues and tossed the line up over the junglewood branch.

"Grab the rope and put your backs into it," Fragger ordered the Shuar. They obeyed, grunting with the effort. Buurk arrived and watched along with Fragger as first Salinsky's muddy helmet appeared, then the shoulders and a jump pack. When the entire suit cleared the surface, streaming water from the joints, Fragger noted with worry that Red's arms and legs were limp.

"Pull him to shore quickly," Fragger commanded. "We need to get him out of that—"

Red's jump pack ignited in a fury of steam and heat. Salinsky shot up into the air on the column of thrust.

Fragger swore and shouted at the Shuar to loop the slack around the trunk of the tree and hold tight. The suit powered its way up above the leaf canopy, then like a hooked fish, jerked as it hit the end of the line and fell flailing back down until the rope caught in one of the branches. Above their heads, Salinsky swung helplessly back and forth.

"Watanabe," Fragger shouted. "I thought you told me he had barely enough power for life support!"

Scrambling out of the pirogue, Watanabe explained, "but he diverted it all to the jump pack in an idiotic attempt to escape. If we don't get him out of the suit, he's definitely going to suffocate."

"Somebody lower the idiot down from there," Fragger directed. "And even though he deserves it, don't let him fall on his head. We want him in one piece."

As Shuar warriors jumped up into the tree to untangle Salinsky's suit from the rope, the Ranger asked Watanabe, "You can you get him out of the armor, can't you?"

"Sure. It's standard Corpse issue."

"I'll take your word for it, but no more surprises, okay, Watanabe? Get in your suit just so he knows he's outmanned."

Watanabe flushed at the criticism, but acknowledged Fragger with a nod and left to retrieve his armor.

As a precaution, the Ranger had most of the Shuar stay back and wait for Watanabe as Salinsky was lowered onto the swampy ground into a circle of warriors. The armored Watanabe pushed his way through the men to the downed soldier. He leaned over and gave a probing punch to the corporal's chest and waited for reaction. When none came, he knelt down and tapped at Red's helmet.

"No response," Watanabe reported. "None on commlink, either."

"All right," Fragger said. "Crack the suit open and see if we've still got a breather."

The circle was quiet as Watanabe fumbled with the powered armor until Fragger heard the distinct "snick" of safety catches being released. The suit opened like a clam shell. Inside was the familiar bullet head with a red brush of hair atop the point.

"Damn!" a Shuar cursed. "He stinks. What is that smell?"

"Is he dead?" Fragger asked anxiously, thinking Red might have killed himself in the escape attempt and his body was already voiding itself.

"I don't know," Watanabe said. "Buurk, take a look at him."

The tall Martian strode forward and squatted by the opened suit. He checked Red's eyes, breathing and pulse, then turned back to Fragger and reported, "He's unconscious, but looks okay. I'll have to examine him more closely one he's out of the armor...What *does* this man eat?"

"*Gark*," Fragger said.

"What's that?"

"It's a mildly narcotic plant. Kills hunger."

"Well, it's killed any appetite I might have had, that's for sure!" Buurk said.

"Forget the smell," Fragger ordered. "Get Salinsky out of that suit and make sure he stays healthy. Watanabe, secure the armor."

"Secure it?" the sergeant said. "Hell, it's as safe as it can be. Nobody's going to go near it until it's aired out."

Once several of the Shuar had been assigned to dragging the unconscious Salinsky out of the suit so the medic could check his condition more closely, Fragger said, "Watanabe, give me the report on our other prisoners."

Watanabe responded, "Still surly. They don't appreciate being captured by Shuar headhunters led by a Rerun."

"I don't care what they think of me or the Shuar. Just tell me what their attitude is toward joining us."

"About what you'd expect. Like you or me, they're looking for the first opportunity to escape and are willing to wait for it."

Fragger asked, "Have you separated the soldiers from their officers yet?"

"No, why?"

"Do it, then, and assign the officers to all the dirtiest grunt work you can find without injuring or killing any of them. Give the non-coms lighter duty and better rations."

An uncertain grin twisted Watanabe's mouth.

"You have a problem with that, Watanabe?"

"No, I don't think so, Sparks...it's just that...."

"You don't expect officers to be treated that way?"

"Well, that...and the fact that I wish *I* had thought of that one before."

Fragger chuckled. "What non-com doesn't love to see an officer share the shitload? Besides, without officers, they'll be leaderless, and that makes it our first step in breaking their loyalty to the Imperial Commonwealth and EarthCorp and transferring it to us."

The Ranger watched Watanabe stride off to carry out his orders, and then swung his gaze to the river. It was still strewn with wreckage from yesterday's battle. Smoke and steam drifted up from those floaters that were un-salvageable, filling the air with the stench of detonated munitions and blown engines. One of the machines capsized suddenly, painting the dark green of the jungle with an explosion of orange and black. The Shuar working near the stricken floater didn't flinch, Fragger noted with satisfaction. Instead, they cheered briefly and turned back to their salvage work, obeying his instructions to complete salvage operations quickly so they could get on the march before the enemy detected the activity and sent more troops. Beneath the Shuar's rough exteriors and boasting speech lay the hearts of warriors, and they'd been delivered into his hands through a combination of luck, circumstance and his own hard work.

You make the most of what you've got, Fragger thought as he broke his reverie to continue organizing details of future strategies against his enemies. *And you always--always!--give the enemy more shit than he gives you.*

CHAPTER 40

Fragger squatted in the open-sided hut watching the afternoon rain beat down from clouds as sullen as the prisoners he'd taken six weeks ago in the Yacuambi Triangle. He had underestimated their discipline. His separation of the officers from the enlisted men hadn't worked. Instead of losing unit cohesion, they'd become royal pains in the posterior, disrupting his plans to use their talents to expand and train his Shuar army.

Watanabe squatted beside him, chewing on a piece of headroot. During their march through the jungle, the Ranger had discovered what the Shuar already knew. Headroot was an amazing plant. It not only took care of headaches and hangovers, but dulled the appetite as well, a blessing for perpetually hungry soldiers.

And perpetually complaining, Fragger thought, doing some griping of his own. The only good news lately had come from Watanabe's monitoring of commlink traffic. It had become clear that the heads of the combined fleets--nervous to be in proximity with each other in the first place--had started bickering among themselves. But, the infighting hadn't slowed down the pace of dropship landings. A seemingly inexhaustible supply of troops had chased them deep into the jungle and there was no sign of the pressure letting up.

As if that wasn't bad enough, Dr. Shaper seemed as determined to get rid of them as their off-world enemies were. Fragger's forces had been harassed by the hellhounds and a predator the Ranger particularly detested—the giant slipsnake. Liar though he was about many other things, the Shuar, Alarcon, had told the truth about the reptile. It was Shaper's adaptation of the Terran green anaconda. Somehow, he'd made the snake extremely aggressive, extremely irritable and then topped off the genetic modification by providing the beast with the ability to improvise ambush tactics. More than a few of his men had ended up as lumps in a 20-foot long digestive tract.

It was glum path Fragger's mind was traveling so he shook the negativity out of his head and asked Watanabe, "Well, my plan for the prisoners certainly hasn't worked, so what can we do to get them on our side?"

Watanabe's answer was as gloomy as the day. "I don't know. I just don't know. A few of them have come over, but not enough to make any difference."

"Hell," Fragger said, "we set some of them free with rations, and they got lost just like we knew they would. So, we tail them, bail them out, and what's the result? Not a damned thing."

Watanabe nodded, but shifted anxiously as he stirred the grass with an aimless finger.

"Problem?" Fragger asked.

"Yeah."

"Spit it out, then."

Watanabe looked the Ranger straight in the eye. "We both know where the source of resistance comes from."

"Where?"

The sergeant simply kept an unwavering gaze until Fragger admitted, "Okay, okay, so it's Red."

"The man's got a will of iron, Sparks. He's not the brightest Corpse I've ever met, but he carries all of them with his stubborn leadership. It's amazing he never rose above the rank of corporal. But rank doesn't make the man, does it? The man makes the rank or rises above it in special circumstances. I can't think of much more special circumstances than these."

It was Fragger's turn to nod. "You think I've been avoiding the obvious?"

"Yes," Watanabe said in unflinching reply.

"Damn it, I don't want to lose Red!"

"He's a damned fine soldier, Sparks, and we can hardly afford to lose his talents. But, we also can't afford the resistance he's putting up. It's costing us valuable time. I say we execute him."

"I can't do that," Fragger replied.

"It's not a pretty thought," the sergeant agreed. "If we turn him loose, though, he's just tough enough to survive the proto-crocs, the slipsnakes, and anything else that's thrown at him. If he does survive, he'll provide the enemy with detailed intelligence, and that will get us all killed. In the end, survival of our so-called army is your first responsibility."

"I know, I know," Fragger agreed.

Watanabe continued to trace the grass with his finger before saying, "I'll do it for you, if you want. I promise it will be swift and painless as befits a warrior."

"No," Fragger sighed. "I owe it to him to do it myself. A man can't do otherwise. It's just a waste, that's all, and I can't seem to make the bullheaded sonuvabitch realize that."

The two men fell silent under the onslaught of jungle noise. High in the trees, hipmonks chattered and scratched at the outrageously large haunches that enabled the ur-primates to leap astonishing distances from tree to tree. The rising "shoop-shoop-SHOOP" of the tinybirds punctuated their conversation along with the chittering buzz of swarmbugs. Fragger had come to hate the bugs even more since he'd discovered that they had the ability to inflict Jivaron malaria on his troops. Half of them shivered and shook through the night and sweated themselves into exhaustion during the day. Bucaram had them all chew headroot, but, for all its powers, the best it seemed to be able to do was suppress the symptoms. The enemy forces had cut off the supply of all vaccine supplies, hoping the disease would do their work for them.

And it will if I don't decide upon a course of action soon, Fragger knew.

Watanabe diverted the Ranger's attention from this thought by asking, "When?"

"When what?"

"'Don't shit me, man.' Isn't that phrase you use from your time? When will you execute Salinsky?"

"Now. I'll give him one last chance. If he says no again, he gets the duel I promised, and I take his head off. It's as simple as that."

"Do you want me to go along, Sparks? I can still do the job for you."

"No."

"Are you sure?"

With a snarl, Fragger answered, "It'll get done. Don't worry about it. Go check the commlink chatter to see what the enemy is up to. That damned 'surrender or else' repeater message is getting old. Maybe they've come up with something new and exciting."

"All right," Watanabe said as he stood and left the hut. Fragger picked up his sword and did the same, getting soaked by the downpour the minute he was out in the open. He found the trail and walked down to the encampment where he paused to study the prisoners before entering their ranks. Despite their confinement, they remained divided into groups of Imperial Commonwealth and EarthCorp troopers.

Loyalties so strong it prevents them from working together to organize truly effective escapes. A soldier values loyalty above all, and yet it's his Achilles heel.

The Ranger had used the division to his advantage as much as possible, but the man in the middle of the clearing had kept resistance going through sheer strength of will. The other troopers, officers included, heard Fragger's approach, and their eyes turned immediately toward Red Salinsky. Beneath the brush of red hair, Salinsky's eyes were already on Fragger, calculating as he flicked a drop rain away from the wrecked cartilage of his nose. The Ranger stepped into the middle of the prisoners. Red's glance flicked toward the sword and back up to Fragger's face.

Quietly, he asked, "You gonna cut my head off, Rerun?"

"Unless you change your mind, Red."

"Never happen," was Salinsky's response, then he added contemptuously, "I didn't think you were low enough to execute a helpless man."

"I'm not going to execute you, Red. I'm going to give you a sword, and you can fight me man to man, but you know you'll lose. There's no doubt about it. Join me, instead. Think about it, man, think about it hard. EarthCorp owns you lock, stock and barrel. You're doing to die for a society that doesn't give a rat's ass about you unless you're not paying your debts. I can give you better than that. Money of your own. More rank. The opportunity to fight with some of the best soldiers around."

Red made a dismissive "Tsssuh!" sound, then said, "Best soldiers? Headhunters and Ricers, led by you?"

"Yes."

"I'll die before I accept orders from a Rerun."

"Why not? You're already a Rerun and don't know it. You've just got a fancier uniform, that's all."

"Hey, I'm not here to handle crap insults from the likes of you. Come on, give me a sword!" Red demanded. "I'll teach you a lesson with the blade that you'll never forget."

Fragger smiled sadly at the braggadocio. "Red, I've improved with a little help from Watanabe, and you already know one important fact. With my MASER abilities, I can slice you into croc food with little effort."

"So you say, Rerun. I haven't seen any evidence of it."

"Give him a charged blade," Fragger ordered one of the guards. The sword was handed to Salinsky, and the corporal cut the thick jungle air with practice strokes. Its power hummed up into the trees, disturbing tinybirds into flight.

"Are you ready?" Fragger asked, powering up his own weapon.

Red's answer was a full-bore charge across the clearing. Fragger accelerated and sidestepped the point of the blade and watched the trooper stumble over a root and go down hard. Red sprang to his feet quickly and switched to the more cautious tactic of circling his opponent. Prisoners and guards scrambled back to stay out of range of his wildly swinging sword.

Fragger kept his attention fully on Red's eyes. It was no time to get overconfident and make a stupid mistake that would get him killed in spite of his considerable advantage. He didn't want to humiliate Red, either. He needed the respect the prisoners had for Salinsky if the corporal somehow came around to his way of thinking.

Red's aggressive cutting and slashing told Fragger that a change of mind was not going to happen. The Ranger parried thrust and cut with ease, dancing in and out of hyperspace with the ease that seemed to come only with constant practice. Out of the corner of his vision, he could see the prisoners' eyes grow big and envious at his actions. Watanabe had told him it was like watching a sword at the end of a blur as if the weapon were directing the action rather than Fragger himself. Opportunities to cut off Salinsky's head came with each second of the duel, but Fragger held back, reluctant to deliver the final stroke. Instead, he let Red exhaust his strength, hoping the futility of his efforts would sink in, yet Salinsky fought on with berserker madness, grunting with each miss until the muddy ground betrayed his feet and he fell onto his back. Fragger put the sword to his throat and said quietly, "Give up, Red."

Salinsky glared up at him. "Kill me, Rerun. Do it now or let me do it myself."

Fragger withdrew his sword and saluted the corporal with it. "Do it yourself then, Red. I owe you that much. It's a waste, though. A damned shame."

Red flopped over in the mud and got into a kneeling position, digging the hilt of his sword into the ground and placing the point near his gut. Looking up at Fragger, he grinned and gave him the finger, then took a deep breath and arched his body back so he could put his full weight onto the sword.

Shit! Shit, shit, shit! Fragger swore.

A foot lashed out and kicked Red's sword clattering against a tree before Salinsky could impale his stomach on it. A snarl of anger erupted from deep in the corporal's throat. Fragger's head swiveled along with Red's to discover the source of the kick.

It was Watanabe.

"What the hell are you doing?" Red demanded.

"My question as well," Fragger said.

Watanabe held up a commlink screen. "I know you're in a hurry to die, Salinsky, but I thought you should see something before you spit yourself like the smelly pig that you are."

"Go to hell," Red said.

Watanabe got hold of a short scruff of red hair and jerked Salinsky's head back, then shoved the screen in his face.

"What does that say?" he demanded.

"Let go!" Red hollered.

"What does it say?" Watanabe insisted. "Read it, then I'll let you go."

Salinsky's watering eyes scanned the screen, and he sank back onto his knees, stunned by what he'd read.

"What is it?" Fragger asked.

"Tell him, Red," Watanabe ordered as he released his hold on Salinsky's hair.

"It's a General Order. When you boil down all the fancy language, it states that the Rerun, the Shuar and anyone under his command...or...or under his control are to be shot on sight," Salinsky said as if he were swallowing a large and very bitter pill. "They've given up on trying to capture Sparks."

Fragger gave Salinsky a pointed look. "Red, you still want to fall on your sword for an EarthCorp that's willing to kill you and your men to get at me? Seems like a hell of a waste, dying out of loyalty to people who show you none."

"Shut up, damn you!" the corporal shouted at the muttering that had arisen among the prisoners. Red checked the screen again as if trying to find a different meaning to the words he'd read, then said to Watanabe, "You swear this isn't some trick you dreamed up?"

"I swear it. Check the commlink traffic for yourself if you don't believe me."

"All right, then I will check--," Salinsky began, then stopped. His shoulders sagged as he lowered the screen. "No, I don't need to check. This is real."

Red struggled to his feet, saying simply, "I'm yours. The others can do as they like, but, as for me, EarthCorp has just ended my allegiance to them."

Several of the prisoners stepped forward to join Red, but from amidst a knot of EarthCorp troopers a voice called out, "Why don't you just give yourself up, Rerun? You'll save a lot of lives!"

"Who said that?" Red roared. "Step forward."

When no one did, Fragger held Red back from plowing into the group to haul out the offender. "It's okay, Red. Every man has a right to speak. Besides, it's a good question. Why don't I just give up and save everybody a lot of trouble?"

The prisoners stood silent in the rain, waiting for his answer. Fragger paused because he had no idea of what he was going to say. He damned himself for hesitating and simply started talking.

"I'm a Rerun, right? Before I had MASER abilities, I could whip damned near everybody's ass here. Now that I have those abilities, I can beat your butts twice over without breaking much of a sweat. But, at heart, there isn't one of you here who thinks of me as Fragger Sparks, a fellow soldier, an equal. To you, I'm trash from the past. And you know what? That pisses me off! I was a member of the finest unit in the U.S. Army on ancient Earth--the Rangers--and you people still treat me lower than the rankest recruit. That pisses me off even more! So, do you want to take a guess as to how I feel about EarthCorp, the Imperial Commonwealth, or any of the other warring nations in this shit future? Do you?"

Some of the troopers shuffled their feet in the mud and refused to meet Fragger's eyes; others glared at him.

"I don't give a flying fuck, that's how I feel," he said, all the fear and anger bottled up inside his head since he'd been awakened by Leery on Khanwat pouring out in his words. "Maybe you think that's cold-hearted, and you'd be right. It *is* cold-hearted. Your nations have been first-rate teachers of heartlessness. Ever since I arrived here--not by my choice--somebody's been trying either to torture information out of me or kill me because they don't want anybody else to get that information. It's hard to care about people like that, wouldn't you agree?"

Fragger didn't wait for an answer to the question. Instead, he plowed on, saying, "Well, even in this time, I'm still a Ranger, and, unlike you pussies, Rangers don't give up. They never give up. They lead the way."

"Lead the way to where?" one of the prisoners demanded. "Where the hell are we going to go?"

Fragger spat at the ground to emphasize his low opinion of the men facing him. "You people just don't have much imagination, do you?"

"Cut the crap. What are you talking about?" Red asked.

"In my day," Fragger answered, "in my day, we had a saying. 'There are worlds to conquer,' that was the saying. Of course, there was only Earth at the time. However, in this time from what I understand, there are thousands of worlds for the taking. Isn't that right?"

"It's right," Red answered, "but we haven't got a ship. Hell, we haven't even got a simple launch to get up into orbit."

"They've been landing dropships all over the place, haven't they, and they'll keep on landing them. Correct?" Fragger asked.

"Sure," Salinsky answered. "They'll keep up the pressure any way they can."

"So, we find a dropship and take it."

Watanabe responded this time, saying, "Hell, even if we get hold of a dropship and get into orbit, we'd be blown into pieces before we could set a course for anywhere."

"That'd be suicide, I agree," Fragger said. "But I'm not talking about going into space."

"But you said there were worlds to conquer," Salinsky protested.

"There are, Red. We're just going to start with this one, that's all. One step at a time."

"So, why take a dropship, then?"

"They want to kill us all? Then, I plan to make it an expensive proposition," Fragger answered. "They've been chasing us around this planet. Now, it's our turn to chase them. We go on the offensive with everything we can throw at them."

"This is all easier said than done," Watanabe pointed out. "It would be great to have our own dropship, but commandeering one is close to impossible."

"But *not* impossible!" Fragger argued. "What's the worst can happen if we attack a ship—we die. But we die on our own terms.

It's a glorious death. You can have the glory, though. Me, I plan to survive."

"Talk is cheap, Rerun," Salinsky interjected.

"It is! No argument there, Red, so why are we standing here talking about it when we could be laying plans for our campaign?"

Salinsky looked at Watanabe and snorted. "'Campaign' he says. Now there's a grand term for a raggedy-ass bunch of bug-bitten, malaria-ridden misfits."

Watanabe offered a fatalistic grin. "Think big, Salinsky, think big."

"You're with the Rerun, then?"

Watanabe nodded. "My bridges are burned. I'm with Sparks all the way. Of course, Imperial Commonwealth troopers always did have bigger balls than Corpses so that's no surprise, is it?"

Red snorted at the insult, but said, "Okay, what choice do we have? I'm in. We succeed or go down together."

Fragger hollered at the other prisoners, "How about the rest of you? You want to wait for the enemy to hunt you down or do you want to teach them not to betray good soldiers?"

A chorus of angry agreement rose from the men.

"Good," Fragger said. "It's time to plan then, but I want to establish one rule before we begin."

"What's that?" Red asked.

"Nobody calls me 'Rerun' anymore. Understood?"

"Well, shit, that's going to be hard to do," Salinsky complained. "I mean, that's what you are."

"No," Fragger said. "I never was one, and I'm not one now."

"What should we call you then?" Red asked.

Watanabe said, "I think we should pay him the ultimate insult."

"Wha--?" Salinsky started, then caught the Imperial Commonwealth trooper's meaning. "Oh, you mean make him an officer?"

"Yeah, I think a promotion is in order," Watanabe said with a sly smile.

"What rank shall we give him, Ricer?"

"I don't know, Corpse. Sparks, what was the most worthless officer's rank in your army?"

Fragger answered, "A Second Lieutenant fresh out of Officers' Candidate School."

Watanabe asked Salinsky, "I don't think he's really that worthless, do you?"

"He's close, but not quite that bad."

"How about Captain, then?" Watanabe suggested. "As I recall, that was the next rank up in the ancient armies. True?"

"Yeah," Fragger said.

"But it's not very impressive to our enemies," Salinsky objected. "How about Colonel?"

"Colonel it is, then," Watanabe agreed.

"Thanks for asking me," the Ranger said.

"Hell, don't be so sarcastic. If we'd left it up to you, you would have promoted yourself to general or something equally uppity," Watanabe said, slapping Fragger on the shoulder. "It's a good thing we're here to keep your head out of the clouds and your feet on the ground."

Salinsky drew himself to attention and saluted. "Colonel Sparks! What's your first order as the very first Rerun to ever achieve the rank of officer?"

Fragger glared at Red. "My first order is to stop calling me 'Rerun', damn it."

CHAPTER 41

The beetle-shaped dropship had powered down from Jivaro's humid sky in a bone-shaking roar. With grudging approval of the landing site the pilot had selected, Fragger re-scanned the dry area into which the ship was now settled. Surrounded by croc-infested water, the perimeter bristled with weapons manned by troopers in powered armor. PPCs, MACs, energy weapons he didn't even recognize--the place was a temporary fortress with the swamp as its moat.

"They aren't taking any chances with this one, are they?" he asked Watanabe and Salinsky.

"No doubt that. They've actually set up two large-bore assault cannons," Watanabe responded. "They could blow a good-sized hole in a HELOT with those weapons. I guess, they don't appreciate losing two ships. The price you pay for being popular, Colonel."

"Well, I don't appreciate the fact that we had to destroy them. Dead ships don't do us any good," Fragger said as he studied the bluntly curved vessel. Even several minutes after the landing, the heavy smell of scorched earth still rolled over the patch of grass in which the three men were hiding.

"That's not an Imperial Commonwealth or EarthCorp dropship this time, is it?" Fragger asked. "The lines aren't the same as either one of those."

"No, it's not," Watanabe confirmed. "Looks Gulag to me."

"The others were all vessels of the great nation-systems. Why the change?"

"I don't know, Colonel. Heavy commlink traffic indicates something is going on with those orbiting fleets. Maybe we've gotten lucky, and they ended up at each other's throats. Confusion like that would allow a Gulag ship to slip through."

"Or maybe it's some kind of trick to draw us out," Fragger suggested.

Watanabe shrugged. "Perhaps, but there's not much we can do about it, is there?"

"Damnit! Tell me some good news, will you?"

"Actually, I do have some."

"What?"

"Either they've got some troopers just out of training or troopers they can't trust."

"How can you tell that?" Fragger asked.

"Some of those armor suits are slaved to an officer's suit."

"What's the purpose of that?"

"If an officer has green troopers or ones he can't trust, he can install an AI module in the wearer's suit and order it to follow his commands. The software is sealed into the chest so no self-styled 'tech' trooper can get at it. It blocks independent control of suit function."

"So, slave a suit and the wearer is just along for the ride then?"

"Yes," Watanabe answered. "It prevents the problem of panic or retreat. Or it can be used for discipline. Cut it to minimum power and march a soldier around all day in heavy armor, and he comes around real fast."

Fragger turned and slid down the hummock on which they'd been sprawled. He pulled a piece of rotting cloth away from his body and tossed it into the swamp.

"Well, gentlemen, looks like we haven't got any choice but to attack this ship and commandeer it, not destroy it. We're coming apart faster than my uniform."

His gallows humor had served him well during their trek though the jungle, but this time it brought a sharp rebuke from Salinsky.

"Give the lame jokes a rest, will you?" Red snapped.

Fragger gave a mild reply to the Corpse trooper's short-tempered remark. "That fever isn't doing you much good, Red."

"Damned right, it isn't! Jokes aren't getting us anywhere. What's the point of assaulting this dropship, anyway? We'll never commandeer it. Green troops or not, they've got way too much firepower for us. They'll cut us down like so much grass."

Watanabe's eyes swept along with Red's toward Fragger. In the sergeant's gaze, the Ranger saw doubt about their mission for the first time.

They're both close to exhaustion, Fragger realized. *And if these two have reached their limits, the rest of the troops are in worse shape. We've got enough left for one last try, that's all.*

Summoning all the command presence he could muster under the circumstances, he said, "As usual, you two are looking at things the wrong way."

"Wrong way?" Red cried. "What wrong way?"

Fragger jerked a thumb back toward the dropship. "This is the last one. It has to be. There've been no other landings since we destroyed those other ships. Take this one out, and we're safe—safe from our off-world enemies and safe from Shaper's damnable hellhounds and slipsnakes."

Red dismissed the idea with a snort. "We'll never be safe, Colonel. You know that."

"Then, we'll be safe for a while, Red. Take what you can get, okay?"

While Salinsky muttered under his breath, Watanabe said, "The question is, how do we get inside this particular dropship? As you predicted, Colonel, the others were overconfident and made stupid mistakes. Whoever commands this vessel is smart."

"I don't know how we do it," Fragger admitted as he began searching his mind for quick answers.

Think, Fragger, think. You don't have many advantages in this situation, but every defense has its weaknesses. It's not overconfidence this time so that means you have to look for something different...Shit, the only edge I can think of in this situation is me Yes, me, and a whole lot of deception....

He was following this train of thought when Salinsky broke his concentration.

"We could surrender and avoid a lot of bloodshed, that's definitely another choice," Red blurted out.

The statement shocked Fragger. *Shit, has it gone that far downhill? I need to act now! I can't give my troops time to think, only to fight.*

"Don't be an idiot, Red!" the Ranger snapped. "They have orders to kill us on sight, you know that. It's just the fever talking. Pull your act together."

"I'm too bloody tired to plan, Reru–Colonel." Red slumped back, rubbing at the welts on his face inflicted by insects and the razor-sharp grasses of the swamp as he slipped into the half-conscious daze being experienced by all of the men.

Fragger flicked his gaze to Watanabe to see if he still had the sergeant's support. Watanabe confirmed it with his response. "I'm game, Colonel. What are your orders?"

The Ranger issued orders quickly to keep his two non-coms from dwelling on their situation. "First, feed the men. Find them fresh meat anywhere you can. Use your sword on crocs or hellhounds or whatever you can find, but be sure to get some crocs and save me the heads and skins."

"What for?"

Fragger glared at Watanabe. "Just save the stuff, okay? Tell the men to fill their stomachs and order them to rest. Once they're rested, set up a perimeter and put them into attack position."

"Then what?"

"Then, Watanabe, tell them to maintain silence and to keep their eyes fixed on the enemy camp."

"What are they going to see?"

"Something special. I'll have more orders for you and Bucaram soon."

"All right," Watanabe answered, then nodded toward Salinsky with a questioning look.

"Corporal Salinsky!" Fragger ordered. "Up off your sorry ass and get back to our position. I want you in decent shape tonight."

"Hunh? In shape for what?"

"To find that out, my smelly friend, you're going to have to stay awake."

CHAPTER 42

A moonless night. In the old days, it would have been just what the doctor ordered for a night raid, Fragger thought as he slipped into the pirogue covered crudely with croc skin by soldiers under Watanabe's direction. *Now, with the powered armor's array of sensors, it doesn't make a bit of difference whether there's a moon or not, so deception is my best bet to surprise the enemy.*

Watanabe had displayed unexpected wit by nailing a proto-croc's head with wide-open jaws to each end of the boat, making the craft look like the future's nasty equivalent of a Pushmepullyou.

"You sure you don't want your armor?" Watanabe asked as he steadied the pirogue while Fragger stepped in, found the pole and got squared away.

"My assault wouldn't be half as impressive that way, now, would it?" the Ranger answered.

"No, still…"

"Hey, I'll carry out my mission. You carry out yours, okay?" Fragger said, touched by Watanabe's rare show of concern.

"It'll be a good show, I promise."

"Make sure the lines for the other two pirogues are secured to this boat, then shove me off," Fragger ordered.

After checking the lines, Watanabe gave a quick push to the Ranger's pirogue. The sergeant's form disappeared into the darkness as Fragger grabbed the pole and maneuvered his craft out past a small spit of the vegetation the Shuar called "bloodgrass" because its sharp-edged leaves drew blood from skin with the ease of a scalpel. The nasty plant had plagued them every step of the way across Jivaro, and Fragger was glad to be free of it, for however brief a time. Towing the dugouts, he propelled the pirogue out into the swampy open water until he was halfway across to the dropship, then quietly shipped the pole and lay down in the boat to wait.

The jungle is an incredibly noisy place, Fragger mused as he stared up into the low and occasionally dripping clouds that hung over the trees like a trooper's wet laundry. Giant roarfrogs bellowed for mates while ur-primates chattered like excited women high in the branches and, far away, the growling baying of the hellhounds signaled a hunt. The lack of wind made the sounds from the dropship camp seem like they were occurring right next to the pirogue, but the Ranger kept his nerves calm by blanking his mind as he'd always done before going into combat.

Fragger started at a sudden flare-up of flickering light across the water and raised his head to check the area where his men lay in wait. He was pleased to see that Watanabe had carried out his orders with the usual embellishment. Flames rose from stacked piles of junglewood trees with the smoky hiss of swamp vegetation, but the blaze was bright enough to illuminate the dozens of shrunken human heads impaled on stakes or hung from branches. Pulled by invisible strings, hellhound skulls and slipsnake jaws danced a grotesque eyeless jig among the headhunter trophies.

Helluva a psyops operation, Watanabe and Bucaram, he saluted his men.

Fragger couldn't decide which was the better effect--the illusion that the heads were floating free above the fires or the shrieking of the Shuar as they imitated the terror of the dead. Shifting his attention to the enemy perimeter, he was happy to see the armored guards rushing toward the direction of the deception to fire wild shots. Checking an eagerness to get inside their perimeter, Fragger analyzed the soldiers' actions carefully. When an officer kicked a few backsides and restored order, he knew he had the man he was looking for.

Keeping an eye on the officer as the man walked along the perimeter checking positions, Fragger untied the other pirogues and pushed them toward the shore as a diversion. The movement brought a quick burst of PPC fire. A dull "thock-thock-thock" of rounds stitched a line in the water along the Ranger's pirogue, but failed to penetrate the boat. When the firing stopped, he stuck his hands in the water and paddled the boat with slow and silent strokes until it slid through rushes and bumped against the shore. Fragger froze as the armored legs of a guard appeared close to the pirogue. The trooper cut loose with his assault weapon before the Ranger could react. The burst tore away the proto-croc head at the bow of the boat and left Fragger untouched.

"Stupid crocs!" the guard said to Fragger's target as he approached. "Lieutenant Haygar, I don't know what's worse, them or those idiot primitives jumping around in the jungle."

The officer answered with a nasty chuckle. "Nervous, Ladert? Afraid the Shuar boogeyman is going to find you and shrink your head?"

"Yeah, right," Ladert answered, but Fragger noted a shaky rise in his voice.

Nervous. Good!

"Well, don't worry about it," Haygar advised. "If anybody's going to hand you your head, it'll be me, Ladert."

"What for, Lieutenant? I haven't done anything."

"Exactly," Haygar replied. "You're too busy keeping your eyes on the crocs or on those stupid heads hanging over the fires. Keep them glued on this side of the perimeter or didn't it occur to you that the Swampers might be throwing us a feint?"

"Sorry, sir," Ladert answered.

"Carry on," the lieutenant ordered and headed across a large gap between Ladert's position and the guard next in line.

Fragger recognized his opportunity. He slipped into the water with his sword to follow the officer. At the same time, he pushed the pirogues toward Ladert. The guard opened up on the boats immediately.

Lieutenant Haygar swung about to swear at him. "Damn it, Ladert! It's just crocs. You think the swampers are going to swim through all those reptiles to get at us?"

"Sorry, sir," Ladert said again.

"Idiot!" Haygar muttered and turned as Fragger accelerated onto land and laid his blade straight across the vulnerable neck area of the lieutenant's armor.

"Not a word!" the Ranger warned.

"Where the hell did you--?"

"I said, 'not a word" or I'll slice your head off before you take your next breath. I'm the Rerun you're looking for so you know I can do it. Understand?"

The answer was a strangled, "Yes!"

"Slave Ladert's suit to your own," Fragger ordered.

"What--?"

"Just do it!"

A second later, a yelp came from Ladert's position. "Hey, Lieutenant, what the hell are you doing? I don't need to be slaved."

"March him over here.

In a moment, Ladert was beside Haygar, complaining about the officer's action. With a single stroke, Fragger cut his complaint and head off.

"Order the suit to pick up Ladert's head and tuck it under an arm," Fragger commanded.

Lieutenant Haygar obeyed, and, despite himself, Fragger shuddered at the eerie sight of the battle armor picking up Ladert's head and tucking it under an arm.

"Order the suit to turn about and circle the perimeter, Haygar."

"You're a sick-"

"Do it!"

The headless suit turned about and marched toward the dropship and the main defensive force.

"Thanks," the Ranger said. "Your turn now. Sorry."

Lieutenant Haygar attempted to raise his sword, but Fragger cut through the officer's neck in a clean stroke. He caught the body before it fell and dragged it down to the edge of the shore. He retrieved Haygar's head and waded into the water with both body parts. Finding his pirogue lodged among the other dugouts, he pulled it free and jammed the lieutenant's head sideways into the open jaws of the undamaged croc head Watanabe had fastened to the boat. Manhandling Haygar's body into the pirogue, Fragger propped it upright by placing the pole across the boat and leaning the armored chest against it. Once he had everything arranged to his satisfaction, he waited until he heard the yelps of shock at the sight of Ladert's head-carrying armor then shoved the boat toward the growing commotion.

Fragger waited until a new round of screams broke out at the sight of Ladert's head in the croc's jaws. Instantly, he accelerated out of the water and caught the first guard to panic and run. He sliced a leg from under the man. When the soldier fell, Fragger quickly quartered him and threw the body parts high over the heads of the milling guards and out amidst the pirogues he'd directed toward the opposite end of the island. In a few seconds, the swamp exploded with proto-crocs thrashing among the boats. The sight of the reptiles wolfing down human flesh had the effect Fragger had intended. The ranks broke in terror and fled mindlessly toward the safety of the dropship. The Ranger sped up again and cut the troopers down one by one until there was one bewildered but calm officer left. The man stood his ground, waving a sword back and forth in anticipation of an attack by an enemy he had not been able to spot. Fragger decelerated and stepped into the glare of a dropship light so the officer could see him.

"You're looking for Fragger Sparks, aren't you?" he asked. "I'm right here."

"What the hell?" the trooper swore, swinging his blade in the Ranger's direction.

"Do you want to live?" Fragger asked. "You're the only one left, you know."

There was a second's hesitation before the officer replied defiantly, "I'm not afraid to die."

"Good for you! You've seen what I can do, right?"

"Yeah. So? You're still just a Rerun."

"I took your buddies out quick. I think I'll arrange it so I feed you to the crocs piece by piece. Of course, there's another option. I can have the Shuar shrink your head while you're still alive. I don't know if it can be done, but it'd be interesting to find out. I understand they start by cutting up from the back of the neck and then removing the skull and brain before dipping it in hot water and eventually filling it with sand and rocks.

Fragger paused, then added, "I don't know. Which option do you like better?"

An audible gulp came over the commlink.

"Don't like either one, huh? How about this? You get me inside that buttoned-up dropship, and I might let you live. What do you say?"

"I.....yes, okay...I can get you inside."

"Good," Fragger said. "What's your name and rank?"

"Captain Rallard."

"Time to carry out my orders, Rallard. How do you gain entry to the ship?"

"It's keyed to my suit plus a password."

"You're going to march over there with me right behind you and do everything by the book, you understand, Rallard?"

"Yes."

"Get going then."

Fragger fell in step behind the officer. When Rallard hesitated at the dropship entrance, the Ranger whispered, "Remember the options, Captain. Is a slow and very painful death to your liking?"

"No!"

"Then give the password."

The officer pronounced slowly and clearly, "Entrance requested by Major Rallard. Password 'Operation Rerun'."

"I'm flattered," Fragger said as the hatch hissed open and a ramp extended down to the ground. A plume of mist gusted out as the colder air of the interior met the humid, warm air of Jivaro. The Ranger quick-marched the officer through the fog and up the ramp. As the air cleared, Fragger shoved Rallard hard to the deck and held his sword ready for whatever came. For a moment, there was no sound except for the whining of motors as the hatch closed behind him. Then someone spoke from high in the shadows at the back of the room in a harsh voice.

"Rerun, I told you I'd greet you at the gates of hell, didn't I? Well, here I am."

It's a familiar voice, Fragger realized, *but who the devil is it?"*

"Don't remember me?" the voice asked. "Well, you must remember the *Lethal* and Mars."

The owner of the voice moved out of the shadows. He wore armor, but the helmet was off and beneath an arm. Fragger saw black hair, ice-pale blue eyes, an axe of a nose, and a long, thick black beard.

"Lesto!" the Ranger exclaimed. "You should be--"

"Dead? We damned near were. Our suits were immobilized, and we were going nowhere fast until one of my extraction teams found us."

Lesto delivered his speech from a safe distance, Fragger noticed. He stood behind and above a solid line of troopers on a platform that couldn't be seen. Rallard raised himself from the deck and joined their ranks. All swords were powered and ready.

When he'd recovered from the shock, Fragger simply said, "Well, Lesto, it seems we're both survivors."

"That's *Lord* Lesto, Rerun," Rallard informed him.

"Lord, huh?" Fragger said. "Can't say it surprises me. I thought I detected an aristocratic tone back on your ship, Lesto. You'll be happy to know I have a title now as well"

"Not a noble one, I trust," Lesto said

"Nope, a military title. Colonel."

"That's good. It would indeed not be worth being of noble birth if swampers and their ilk were to start granting titles of aristocracy."

"Well," Fragger responded, "the Shuar and my men are a little more particular about such things. They grant titles only to people who have actually earned them."

Lesto twitched a smile through the beard in response to the insult. "I see that arrogance has grown along with your MASER capabilities, Rerun."

"It's only arrogance if you don't back up what you say with actions, Lesto. Proof of my actions lies on the ground outside your ship."

"Impressive, indeed," Lord Lesto acknowledged. "I expected no less of you."

"I fed your men to the crocs. I can do the same with you."

"Oh, no doubt, you would take many of us with you," Lesto said. "But you're in a confined space with at least 30 troopers. Sheer numbers will overwhelm you."

"But I'll die happy, won't I?" Fragger said. "Tell me, why are you here?"

"To find you. What else? We slipped through the blockade for the same reason we came after you on Mars--to discover and use your MASER abilities for my own world of *Aifor*. Soldiers with your capabilities, well, just let's say they would be a valuable--and inexpensive--tool for me to use in uniting the noble families under one banner and gain ascendancy among the worlds of the Ursus Combine."

Fragger gestured toward the ship's surroundings and asked, "You slipped through a blockade in this thing? I don't believe it."

"Rerun, you have such little faith in me," Lesto responded in mock dismay. "I captured this vessel years ago and modified it for raids. Unlike most dropships, it has hyperspace capabilities. As you might remember, stealth, speed, and deception are among my specialties."

"All right, all right, Lesto. I'll accept what you say for now. Just knock off the self-congratulation and cut to the chase. What do you want?"

"You're coming with me--now! I'll pry the secrets of your amazing abilities out of your hide anyway I can. Or, if you want to make it easy, give me the information, and I'll extend my protection and give your life back to you."

"And my freedom?"

"Of course."

"What a lying sack of noble shit you are, Lesto. I can see you're a qualified member of the aristocracy. The upper ranks have always been a home with a fancy name for thieves and murderers. Once I gave you the secret, you'd kill me on the spot. In fact, you never broke through the blockade, did you? You've been with them all the time. The truth is, the Corpses, the Ricers and everybody else circling this planet have you by the short and curlies."

"The what?"

"Your balls, Lesto. They have you by the testicles, and they're not letting go. If I give you the secret of my abilities, you'll give it to them, and I can kiss my ass goodbye that much sooner."

Lesto offered a twitch of a smile. "Sorry to disappoint you, Rerun, but none of my enemies know I'm here--at least not right now."

"I don't believe a word of anything you say, Lesto. But you can believe this: I don't know how the damned ability works. I haven't got a clue. But I do know one thing--the more I use it, the better I get. And I plan to use it in here!"

Fragger accelerated straight for Lesto, but the troopers had anticipated this action and massed into a wedge that allowed them to cover each other while under attack. The Ranger cut the legs from under the point trooper and squared up against the next two in line. He sliced through the one on the right, adjusted the blade angle and sliced upward into the ribs of the trooper on the left. The blade buzzed with its energy output, then sputtered into a squeal as it caught in the armpit of another soldier. Lesto's men immediately piled onto Fragger and knocked him to the deck underneath crushing weight. A second later, a pistol barrel poked itself in between his eyes.

Lesto squatted by Fragger and asked, "Are you faster than a pulse laser, Rerun?"

The Ranger shook his head.

"No, you're not, are you? We're going to slap some cuffs on you, and you're going to behave like a good, docile Rerun."

Lesto paused, then added, "You're turning very red under all that weight, Rerun. Oxygen must be getting very low. Did you understand all of what I just said?"

Fragger nodded.

"You're sure?"

"Screw you, Lesto!" the Ranger cursed, managing to squeeze the words out with the remaining air in his lungs.

Lesto instructed his troopers, "Pull his arms out of there and put the cuffs on."

Fragger winced as the soldiers grabbed his hands and jerked his arms straight out over the deck. In a second, the cuffs clicked and whirred themselves tight on his wrists.

"All right," Lesto ordered, "get off him."

Fragger rolled onto his back and gasped in precious air as the troopers unpiled.

"On your feet, Rerun," Lesto ordered.

When Fragger didn't obey immediately, one of the troopers laid an armored boot into his head.

"Stop it, you idiot!" Lesto shouted. "Even if he is a Rerun, this is no ordinary prisoner. The next trooper who hurts him I'll feed to the crocs myself. Is that clear?"

A chorus of "Yessirs" sounded immediately.

"Get up, Rerun!" Lesto ordered again.

Fragger rolled onto his stomach, worked onto his knees, vomited, then fought the dizziness to rise to his feet.

"Summon the doctor to take a look at him," Lesto commanded.

"Lord, why not take him to the sick bay? It'd be faster." The question was asked by the trooper who'd put his boot into Fragger, obviously anxious to get back on good terms with Lesto.

"Halfwit, do you want him loose in the middle of the ship?"

"He's in cuffs now," the trooper answered weakly.

"I know that," Lesto responded in an acid tone. "What I don't know is what the Rerun's true capabilities are. He has a nasty habit of surprising us with something new. I know he doesn't appear to be much, but you're looking at a relic from the past who can resist the best interrogation techniques, pop in and out of MASER mode at will, and, in the process, has managed to set the great nation-systems at each other's throats throughout known space."

Lesto paused to let that information sink in, then continued, "I made that little speech to make it absolutely clear to you how important this Rerun is. He's more important than your individual lives, is that understood?"

"'Yessir!' rang out again.

"You will die to keep him safe. *Or*, if he is in danger of being captured by unfriendlies, you will kill him. Why? Because anyone who figures out his secrets wins the battle, wins the war, wins entire systems, and I want us to be with those winners!"

Lesto stretched a hand toward Fragger. "This Rerun is our key to eventual dominance of our enemies even though they have us by the throat today. With him, we not only survive. We prevail!"

Cheers erupted and echoed off the bulkheads. Lesto waited until the noise died down, then continued, "The Rerun stays here, and you stay here with him while pre-flight checkout is completed. The only person permitted to enter or leave this room is me."

The troopers watched Lesto exit. When he was gone, Major Rallard turned back to Fragger and said, "Don't move, Rerun. Don't talk. Don't say a thing. I lost some good troopers out there, and I'm not real happy about it."

The Ranger tried to comply. He was still dizzy and had to concentrate to stay on his feet, but no matter how hard he tried the swaying wouldn't stop. Then, he couldn't help himself. There was a thumping in his ears, and the deck swung up hard to meet him.

Shit, Rallard knocked me down, anyway, Fragger thought as sparkling lights danced around in his vision, *I'm going to get a beating now!*

He curled his body into a tight ball, waiting for the first blow, then noticed all the troopers sprawled on the floor with him, shouting in confusion.

"What the hell?" the Ranger said as everything went into slow motion. The hatch blew itself inward in a shower of molten pieces. Through the choking smoke, shrunken heads danced into the room. Fragger realized they were atop poles attached to the backs of the Shuar who boiled into the dropship with screaming, painted faces and flaring energy weapons. Lesto's troopers staggered and dropped around Fragger, but the Ranger saw Major Rallard head-butt a Shuar, turn around and start purposefully toward his prisoner. Fragger scrambled away, trying to put bodies between him and the officer. Rallard hacked them out of the way and kept coming.

I just need to buy some time! Fragger thought in desperation. He tried to accelerate and went nowhere. He tried again and failed again.

Oh, Christ, I cant concentrate! My ability isn't there! That kick to the head must have done something. God, I hope it's temporary, or I'm screwed now.

The Ranger darted through the melee, avoiding the wild swings of other combatants while keeping an eye on the stalking Rallard. The smell of burned flesh and boiled blood did nothing to help his dizziness, and finally he tripped over a dead Shuar and fell to the deck. Rallard was over him in a second, raising his sword, and slashing downward. Fragger twisted away and screamed as the blade seared across his face. Rallard raised the sword again. Before he could strike, the officer separated into three parts. His head flew off into a struggling mass of men. His torso thumped onto the bloody Shuar. His legs stood quivering in the same spot, then toppled over.

Fragger shook away the vertigo long enough to realize that Watanabe had taken Rallard high and Salinsky had taken him low with their swords. Through the blood obscuring his vision, he saw both men grin down at him.

"Get him!" Fragger shouted.

"Who?" Watanabe asked.

"Lesto. Lord Lesto. A big man with a black beard, mean blue eyes, and a nose like a hatchet. He's the commander."

Watanabe nodded his understanding, and both men disappeared from Fragger's sight. He rolled over onto his stomach and crawled to the headhunter he'd tripped over. Ignoring the gushing blood, he pulled the Shuar's body on top of his own for protection from the fight, then passed out.

CHAPTER 43

Fragger dragged his aching mind out of a comfortable darkness and into the glare of the Jivaron sun. He was flat on his back outside the dropship. He winced at the sun's brightness and shaded his eyes with a bloody hand. One eye didn't seem to function properly. His nose worked perfectly fine. It was filled with the stench of emptied bowels and scorched flesh. A shadow moved to blot out the sun, and Fragger squinted at the source kneeling over him. It was Buurk. A look of concern lay in the Martian's eyes set deep into the unsettling burlesque of an Abe Lincoln face. Behind him, Watanabe, Red, and Bucaram stood, anxiety written on their features.

"Are you okay?" the medic asked, then didn't wait for an answer. "Your left eye is damaged, Fragger, I'm sorry. I can't help you with that, but we've captured a ship's doctor along with the rest of the crew. Maybe she can fix it. How do you feel?"

Despite the pain rippling from his jaw to the top of his head and back down again, Fragger was happy to see Buurk firing on all cylinders once more. *In his element again,* the Ranger thought wryly. *Nothing like blood and guts to restore a medic to normal functioning.*

Fragger answered the medic's question with difficulty. It felt as if an angler had a hook in his mouth and was tugging hard, trying to land him as a trophy fish. "I fee- -ike -it."

"What?" Buurk asked.

Fragger worked his jaw, trying to get his mouth around the words he wanted to say. "I said, I feel like shit, damn it! What's wrong with my mout-?"

"The blade damaged some muscles, most likely."

"Great," Fragger muttered. "What's -appening with the dropship and Lesto?"

"We've got control of the ship. Lesto is another matter."

"Where is -e?"

Watanabe answered the question in a grudging tone of admiration. “Colonel, Lesto and several of his soldiers fought their way out the ship after we gained control of the bridge. The man can handle a sword.”

“Damn!” Fragger swore.

“I don’t understand one thing,” Watanabe said. “What’s a Gulag lord doing here?”

“ -e’s the one who spirited me down onto Mars.”

“And he wants the same thing everybody else wants--your abilities?”

Fragger nodded. “What else? Claims -e slipped through the combined forces in secret.”

“Well, he’s probably right about that,” Watanabe confirmed. “We’ve been able to monitor commlink traffic more accurately with this ship’s system. The Imperial Commonwealth, EarthCorp, the Rollers, everybody, they’re all at each other’s throats out there. Apparently, they’ve got another melee going on. For now, I’d say we’re of secondary interest.”

“I’ll be damned,” Fragger swore. “For -nce, he was telling me the truth. -e *wasn’t* with them.”

“You up to making some decisions?” Watanabe asked.

“Yeah...abou- what?”

“About this ship. It’s ours now. What do we do with it?”

“What’s its status?”

“We could lift off right now if we wanted to, Colonel. We probably wouldn’t last very long, though, once we hit space. The combined firepower we’d face would be too much, and I don’t fancy our chances of repeating our last escape from enemy ships.”

Fragger pointed out, “Lesto got through, didn’t -e? We should be able to as well, -specially with the fleets in confusion,”

Watanabe shook his head in the negative. “Last time, we had Bucaram and Alarcon to pilot us. Unfortunately, the dropship pilot was killed when we secured the bridge. His co-pilot is badly wounded and in no shape for flight. He said Lesto is the only other person who could do it.”

Fragger mulled the situation over until Watanabe interrupted in a concerned tone. "Are you all right, Colonel? You're still bleeding pretty bad."

"-ead wounds always bleed that way. I'm fine," Fragger assured him. "-ere's my decision: We don't -ave to go anywhere right now, anyway. For the short term, Jivaro looks to be the safest spot. Set the men to work camouflaging the ship while you get the crew to do whatever the -ell it is you do to -ide a ship's power signature. Learn their weapons systems at the same time. We seem to -ave bought some breathing room. We'll use it to rest and refit and learn everything we can from our prisoners."

"What should we do about Lesto?" Watanabe asked.

"Nothing for now."

"He's obviously dangerous. Red and I took him on, Colonel, and we couldn't handle him."

Fragger fixed his good eye on Red to judge his condition. The corporal's armor was streaked with strike marks and a good-sized dent marred the helmet he was carrying under his arm. Bruising colored his nose and jaw and the side of his head.

"Are you okay?" Fragger asked Salinsky.

Red rubbed at a purple spot on his bullet-shaped skull and replied, "I'm good. The only thing hurt is my pride. Lesto knocked me on my ass. Watanabe got in the way before the death stroke could be delivered. "

"Watanabe got in the way?" Fragger asked. "He saved you, is that what you're saying?"

"Well, yeah, that's what I'm saying," Red admitted. "I hate to say it, but I'd be croc food if it wasn't for this little Ricer puke."

"Another life? You've saved another life, Isoruku Watanabe?" Fragger shook his head in amazement, wincing at the pain it shot through his face. "Just -ow many can you save in one lifetime?"

Embarrassed pleasure rippled muscles in Watanabe's massive jaw.

Fragger chuckled at the Ricer's discomfort. "A simple compliment can disarm you, Iso? Now I know the secret to defeating you in combat. I'll praise you to death!"

Watanabe answered the Ranger's jab with a dismissive snort.

"That's the best you can do? Blow snot at me? Nothing to say, Iso?" Fragger ribbed him.

"Yes, damn it! I have something to say!" the Ricer barked in his rough voice.

"Which is?"

"Stop fooling around and tell me--what are your orders about Lesto and Shaper?"

Fragger thought Watanabe's question over, then decided, "I don't think Lesto is the immediate problem. -e'll have to deal with the crocs, snakes and hounds, the same as we did."

Watanabe responded, "If he *does* survive Shaper's creatures, you will have a worthy--and dangerous--opponent still on your hands."

"No doubt about that," Fragger agreed. "But if our off-world enemies are off our backs for the moment and Lesto is occupied, I think Shaper is our immediate problem."

"Shaper?" Red asked. "Why him? He's just a puny little psychopath, ain't he?"

"e's a psychopath all right, Red, but a very smart one. Very smart, apparently. -e's first on my list because those damned creatures -e creates seem to get more cunning all the time. On our march here, we lost more soldiers to his animals than we have to our human enemies. If we don't get him, -e'll eliminate us piecemeal."

"Besides," he added, "I think we owe Buurk a little payback, don't you?"

Fragger swung the gaze of his good eye onto the medic and said, "Shaper basically made your life and then made that life miserable, or so you've been telling me halfway across space. Are you ready for justice?"

Buurk started at the question. "I don't know…I mean I'd love to have him dead, but I don't really want to face him. He *was* my father, in a sense and, well,…I don't really know. That's all I can say."

"Civilization crosses galaxies, and Oedipus goes with it," Fragger remarked.

"Who?" Buurk asked.

"Never mind," the Ranger said. "Look, I'll make the decision for you. We can't afford to dither about this man. We -ave to make sure we kill -im before -is creatures kill all of us. Iso, Red, once the men are rested, we'll go after -im, then Lesto. Are those orders clear?"

"Yes, sir," both Watanabe and Salinsky responded.

"Good, then---ow, sonuvabitch!" Pain seared through Fragger's jaw so hard he forgot what he was going to say and simply shouted, "Damn it, where is that doctor!"

"I'll check right away," Buurk said and hurried off.

A few minutes later, the Martian thrust a woman carrying a medical kit into Fragger's line of vision. Her black hair was cut short in a professional, military manner, but it couldn't hide the fact that she was very beautiful—thin and golden-skinned with a small, yet elegant nose. She was the kind of delicate woman a man automatically wanted to protect.

Until the man sees those eyes! Fragger amended as the doctor's gaze swept over him in contempt. *They're as blue and ice-hard as Lesto's. She's definitely a member of his family.*

"What's your name?" he asked.

The woman issued a defiant attitude in her answer, "My rank is major. Since you're a Rerun, that's all you need to know."

"You're now my chief medical officer, Major. I like to know the names of my officers."

"I'm *not* your officer! I am not an officer for any Rerun! I am an officer of the--"

"Cut the bullshit," Fragger ordered. "You're my prisoner! Fulfill your medical oath, and you will be treated with the -espect due your rank. Fail to meet your obligations, and, well, Bucaram -ere always -as a need for another wife. No doubt you would add greatly to -is prestige as a *uwishin*, a shaman."

"This little monkey?" the major said after a sneering appraisal of the Shuar. "He doesn't look man enough for any woman."

"Oh, -e's man enough for several women" Fragger corrected. "But after -e's taken you to bed, Bucaram would be the least of your problems. You would have to deal with -is First Wife. She's –ell on wheels."

"'Hell on wheels?'" the major asked. "I don't understand the term."

"Your life would be very unpleasant. She's meaner than swarmbugs, -ellhounds, and slipsnakes put together."

"I tell you, I will not be anybody's wife!" the major shouted. "I am a Lesto, of the House of Lesto. I--."

"Have already slipped and said too much?" Fragger suggested. "So, we -ave a Lesto in our hands. The question is, what is your relationship to Lesto? -is wife?"

When the major remained stubbornly silent, Fragger asked, "No? -is sister?"

"It's none of your business, Rerun!"

"If not a sister, then the resemblance is so close it could only mean one thing—you're -is daughter."

The major's eyes shifted away for a fraction of a second, and Fragger knew he'd scored the truth.

"Yes, that's it, isn't it?" he said. "-is daughter. Let me congratulate you on your good fortune."

"My good fortune?"

"Yes, you are nowhere as ugly as your father," Fragger said. "In fact, you are quite beautiful. Except in the eyes. You -ave that same look as your father. You're an arrogant predator like -im."

"My father is an honorable and great man!"

"Well, since -e keeps trying to kill or capture me, we have a slight difference of opinion on that matter," Fragger remarked. "So, now that we know your family relationship, what is your name?"

"Andriana to my friends and equals," came the curt reply. "To you, it's major or milady."

Amused at her haughtiness in the face of a precarious situation, Fragger asked, "Those are my only choices, then?"

"Definitely!"

"Afraid not. I'll call you by your medical title—doctor. You *are* a real doctor, aren't you?"

Andriana Lesto arched an eyebrow at this impertinence. “Of course! Why would you think otherwise?”

Fragger shrugged as best he could in his prone position. “You look too young to be a doctor.”

“My father and mother married young. It’s the custom on *Aifor* where life is made hard and short by the Corpses and the Ricers.”

“I see,” the Ranger said. “Well, Doctor, in my day, physicians followed something called the -ippocratic Oath. I don’t remember it all since I’m not a doctor, but, as I recall, it said physicians -ad special obligations to all fellow -uman beings. Does that principle still hold?”

“It does.”

“Fix me, then.”

“No.”

“Why not?”

“The oath says we have special obligations to all fellow human beings. You are not a human being. You are a Rerun and property at best.”

“This property -as your life in his hands,” Fragger reminded her.

“You wouldn’t dare kill me,” she retorted.

Several snorts of laughter burst from Fragger’s men at this remark.

“Doctor, the colonel has a special hatred for aristocrats,” Watanabe clarified. “He’s already killed one member of the High Family of the Imperial Commonwealth who tormented him, Major Shimazu.”

The doctor blanched at this information and whispered half to herself, “I know—knew her. We met at a treaty negotiation.”

“I split her in two with a sword,” Fragger said. “Vertically.”

The Ranger added, “There’s another reason for you to treat me, doctor.”

“Which is?”

“I’ll spare your father’s life if you do so.”

“You lie.”

"No, doctor, I'm not lying. I did plan to kill him before I knew of your identity but your services can be invaluable to me so I'm willing to make a deal."

"I don't make deals with Reruns!"

It was Fragger's turn to raise a brow. "Really? Isn't that what you're doing right now? Dealing with me?"

"Be still!"

"Or are you going to tell me your father's life is worth nothing to you?" Fragger pressed.

Lesto's daughter shook with fury as indecision warred with outrage across her face. Finally, she acceded.

"All right, Rerun, I'll do as you say. Now, let me--"

Watanabe interrupted. "There's one more rule you'll have to obey, doctor. No one calls the colonel 'Rerun'. Is that understood?"

"But he *is* a Rerun!"

Watanabe chuckled. "I remember saying that myself. But you'll soon discover that Fragger Sparks is more than a mere Rerun. He may be more than a mere human."

"He'll have to prove it to me," she said with an audible sniff as she knelt to examine Fragger's face with cool fingers. She opened the medical kit, withdrew an instrument that hummed quietly as she moved it near his jaw.

"Well?" Fragger demanded.

Her response was blunt. "I can fix the jaw in the ship, but not the eye. I don't have the proper instruments. We left *Aifor* in such a hurry that our dropship wasn't fully outfitted. The best I can do is eliminate any infection."

"Do what you can, then. Buurk will monitor your actions to make sure you don't get any ideas of killing me through medical means."

The doctor nodded, but, in her lovely face, Fragger saw a deep revulsion toward Reruns surface. Unable to resist the temptation to humble the woman, he pulled her head down and kissed her firmly on the lips.

The doctor jerked away, spitting and wiping at the blood he'd smeared on her face. She turned and vomited into the grass.

"I always bring out the best in women," Fragger said to his men with as much of a grin as he could manage with his injured mouth.

Raucous laughter erupted. It died as quickly as it had begun when the doctor pulled a curved surgical scissors out of her medical bag and struck straight at the Ranger's face. Fragger's body accelerated automatically to the threat.

Thank God, I still have my abilities despite that kick to the head! he thought in relief

At the same moment as the thought, his hand caught her wrist in a blur of speed. He stopped the scissors tip an inch away from his good eye. The physician stared at the Ranger in astonishment.

"I wouldn't try that again, Doctor," Fragger warned as he took the instrument from her struggling hand. "If you do, I'll use it to cut your father's balls off before I kill -im and hand -is head to Bucaram to be shrunk. Are we clear on that point?"

Andriana Lesto blanched at the threat, sagged and nodded.

"Then get me into the ship and fix me up," Fragger ordered.

A stretcher was found. Two Shuar lifted Fragger onto it, picked the stretcher up and started toward the dropship main hatch. The Ranger's men formed two lines, one on each side of the entrance. Watanabe stood at the head of one line, Red at the head of the other. Watanabe shouted out a command. The Shuar warriors saluted raggedly but enthusiastically. The ranks of Ricer and Corpse soldiers snapped out crisp salutes. All except for one soldier. Red gave Fragger the finger.

The Ranger laughed, returning the salute of the main body of his soldiers and matching Red's finger with one of his own before resting his head back on the stretcher. Pain and fatigue washed through his body as he truly let down his guard for the first time since being awakened in the future. Drowsy melancholy seized him as he thought, *Things haven't changed a whole hell of a lot despite my efforts. EarthCorp and the Imperial Commonwealth and all the other space-faring nations are still after me. Lesto is back, ready more than ever to kill me because now I have his daughter. Plus,*

I've added a new enemy—Shaper. And I still miss my family—Amanda, John, Libby. Centuries dead, all of them, but not to me.

Tears threatened to start. So his men wouldn't think him weak, Fragger held them back by first concentrating on one fact--*I'm alive, by God. I'm alive again!*

Then another.

In life or death, I'm a Ranger, and Rangers always lead the way!

End of the First Misadventure

Printed in the United States
17582LVS00002B/149

9 781591 133957